SECRET OF THE REAPER SEAL

A LOST ORIGINS NOVEL

A. D. DAVIES

CRATER OF THE NORTH PUBLISHING

NOVELS BY A. D. DAVIES

Lost Origins Novels:

Tomb of the First Priest

Secret of the Reaper Seal

Curse of the Eagle Plague

Co-Authored:

Project Return Fire – with Joe Dinicola

Adam Park Thrillers:

The Dead and the Missing

A Desperate Paradise

The Shadows of Empty men

Night at the George Washington Diner

Master the Flame

Under the Long White Cloud

Alicia Friend Investigations:

His First His Second

In Black In White

With Courage With Fear

A Friend in Spirit

To Hide To Seek

A Flood of Bones

To Begin The End

Moses and Rock Novels:

Fractured Shadows

For my friend Bernard who will be sorely missed

PROLOGUE
MAY 11TH, 1473, AD

MONTROSE, SCOTLAND

Habib Masouli was a priest in name only. A benevolent imposter, but an imposter nonetheless. He abided by the church's teachings, believed in the principles espoused by the Pope and others if not the stories themselves, and wore the garbs handed to him by James IV, king of Scotland. He now stood before the parish of Lish on the outskirts of Montrose, a coastal hamlet that suffered greatly during the sacking by the Lairds of Dun.

They'd arrived on horseback in the middle of the night. Men in black with no banner. They swept the region, razing property and seizing livestock to shepherd back to their lands west of here. The burghesses sent an appeal to the Duke of Montrose for help, but the messenger never appeared, believed to have been intercepted and murdered.

It took several more days for word of the incursion to reach the palace of King James IV.

By that time, much farmland in and around Montrose had fallen. A scout was dispatched swiftly to assess the conflict, and more specifically the small church overlooking the village of Lish.

Thankfully, the young man reported that the building remained intact.

Still, it demanded attention.

Habib Masouli was not a warrior, though. He lingered at the back of the armed forces rallied by the king, ordered to end the violence plaguing this region. Combined with news filtering out from Portugal of an explorer's return and then the announcement from Rome regarding who now owned the lands making up the New World, Habib had little choice but to leave behind his life of luxury and fulfill his oath to a higher purpose.

While the fighting played out in mud and rain, he dined with the commanders and bathed in private. His dark skin made him a figure of suspicion at first, but when his name was uttered, all knew him to be a member of the king's inner circle, one of a pool of advisors on matters of state and of morality. Dressing as a priest helped. A convert from savage lands was somehow viewed more favorably than someone of his hue born here.

Habib first studied the Jewish religion, then the Catholics and others branching off that original group who worshiped the son of God, and the followers of Muhammed, too. He knew of other religions from the far east—the Buddhists, the Hindus, and more. But it was the Abrahamic texts with which Habib busied himself. So much so that he could minister at any religious house in the world.

Why his interest?

These people wanted to wipe out any history that didn't fall into their preconceptions. All three groups, willing and able to deny facts if it meant holding onto their followers. And the Lairds of Dun had come so close to uncovering a trove that would cast doubt upon many beliefs of the modern world.

After driving the invaders from the king's lands and securing the people's properties, Habib led missions to deliver food and water, to allocate the hands of men in an effort to rebuild. He waited a respectful two weeks before begging his leave and taking a unit of six men to Lish.

The delay was not a problem. Via the scout dispatched at the outset, Habib had received news from the true priest here, Father Eric Goswelt, a scholar and local resident whom Habib first met in London. The priest confirmed that the Lairds laid siege to the church for hoarding food and feeding the injured and bereaved. But once the priest gave up everything in his stores, they left him —and the building—in one piece. It was a necessary capitulation to protect what the church was built to conceal.

Habib led his men up the path from Lish where they stowed their horses, and around a cliff under constant and brutal assault from the wind. The gray ocean churned, and drizzle bloomed all around as they carried items in a chest braced by poles on the shoulders of four men, soaked in minutes on the steps hewn from the natural rock.

But they did not falter.

Once they reached the entrance, the elements gifted them a degree of respite. The wind lessened, and the rain fell more gently. Father Goswelt greeted them at the doors.

When one man mentioned the climb's difficulty, Father Goswelt answered in his guttural Scottish brogue, "True believers prove their strength of faith by journeying like this. It affirms their belief when they feel the hand of God could flick them into the sea anytime he fancies."

Habib shook the man's hand and asked to see the vault.

They passed through the doors, despite one wall having been ripped out as punishment by the angry Lairds' men, through the vestibule into the church's main body. Habib and Father Goswelt led the entourage down one aisle and paused at the altar, now stripped of all gold and finery, where they bowed their heads in a brief prayer to the figure hanging from a cross. At least, Habib assumed Father Goswelt was praying while Habib just wanted to leave the statue to its solitude and get to his business at the wall off to one side.

Much work lay ahead.

When finished, Father Goswelt rose and eased himself away

from the altar, crossing the floor to where he counted the bricks until he identified a specific one. He had to reach up, where he pressed it firmly.

Some lever behind the brick activated the hidden cogs. A clunk signaled that he picked the right one.

A satisfying amount of dust sifted out of a crack as a vertical line of bricks slid farther inside, proving Father Goswelt kept his word and stayed out of this part of his church. The doorway formed, allowing Habib to push the repositioned wall inward and then to the right on a rail designed by persons unknown to him.

He accepted a torch from the resident minister and lit those on the walls as he progressed through the darkness. The passage coiled to the left, taking them down in a circuit.

"You see now why this place is built so high?" Habib said, without turning to the men. He'd assimilated a Scottish accent, but never rid himself of his own Persian roots.

"Aye," one of the men carrying Habib's case on his shoulder replied. "Will ye be telling us where we're headed soon?"

"We are almost there."

The trek down ended in a hexagonal room, thirty steps in each direction. It reminded Habib of an arena in miniature where doors would rise on each side. But here, only one door was required.

The six men filtered in and at Habib's signal, they lay the box down and removed the carrying poles. Habib placed his hand over the seal atop the plain rock lid and pressed. The lock clicked open.

The soldier in charge bore the name William and had not been briefed about the true nature of this mission. Habib would only say what he had to. He would also feel no guilt about lying on holy ground.

Habib gestured to the two smooth doors ahead, darker than the surrounding rock and barred by a stone slab hung across it as a buttress. "Please, open this vault."

"Me?" William asked.

"The key was lost long ago, but I am told you and your men are strong and cunning."

"That's right."

"Then take off the braces, remove the bar, and open the vault."

Not used to being ordered around by non-officers, William bristled but obeyed, his standing orders to follow the man in the priest's clothing.

The stone bar was four times the thickness of a man's arm and braced against the walls on either side of the vault entrance, holding shut a pair of doors worn as smooth as glass. A brute force solution. At the brace-points, metal had been embedded in the rock, locked in using a key long-since lost, and the mechanism inside the slab would have been fused by the sea air, anyway.

All this happened decades before Habib's birth, and so proved difficult to dislodge. Still, the men went at it valiantly, employing the tools from within Habib's chest: picks of hardened metal, axes shaped from iron with handles of wood imbued with stones unlike any the men had seen before.

But the brackets holding the stone bar were secured deep in the bedrock, and after two hours, the men needed feeding and supplying with ale.

They returned topside, where Father Goswelt was more than happy to oblige. After what felt like long enough, Habib ordered them back to work.

The first bracket securing the bar gave way after another three hours, allowing them to pull free its opposite end.

Habib ran his hand over the smooth double doors, locating the crack that denoted the split between the two. "You see why we need to secure this? If the Lairds could have easily accessed it..."

William sounded exhausted alongside his men. "Easy?"

"Clean up the mess." Habib indicated the chunks of smashed stone, the former bar to the vault, the metal braces.

"We're not bloody cleaners."

Habib rounded on him. "You are in service to me, and through me you serve our Lord Jesus Christ. This is God's work. Do not leave this holy site unfit even for pigs."

William would not break his orders, Habib knew, but he would attempt to save face. He stood tall before Habib. "A little water before we start?"

Habib nodded ascent, and the men who had breached what was considered unbreachable a century ago grumbled back up the spiral passage to where Father Goswelt would furnish them with water and more food.

Once alone, Habib found himself surrounded by silence. A pleasant moment to center himself, to absorb the significance of what he was charged with doing.

From his case, he removed a seal, much like the one he pressed to open the lock, only slightly larger. He laid it over the crack between the doors, where it sunk into the stone with ease.

Father Goswelt coughed from the doorway. "Are you ready for me?"

Habib nodded and stepped aside. "The men?"

"It is better they do not witness this."

Father Goswelt touched both hands to the seal which now lit up in a soft, green glow, the pattern a left-turning spiral. The light was muted from years of handling, the dirt of the world adhering to it, bleeding out from behind the black of time. He removed his hands and clasped them together in prayer.

Habib could never explain fully to his friend what just took place, allowing him to believe the power of God secured the vault now the holy seals had been located and shipped over from Portugal. He offered Father Goswelt a scroll within a casement, locked in using another mostly black but green tinted seal, this one no longer than his finger.

"Only someone worthy can open the scroll." Habib calmed as Father Goswelt accepted it. "Like the vault. This is the reason you cannot stay here."

"But my flock..."

"I will minister to them." Habib gave him a kindly smile, one he hoped conveyed honesty, for Father Goswelt would never willingly allow a non-believer to take over his church, even if it meant defying the king. "Take this to Rome. It explains everything. It will dictate the future of our church and secure you a comfortable parish as a reward. Pack now, ask no more questions. This is where we part ways."

They said goodbye with handshakes and shoulder slaps, as men do, and when he was alone again, Habib did not regret his decision. No one could open this seal, unless they proved worthy, proof through a simple touch.

Yes, he was now committed to preach the word of the Christian prophet, the son of God, and give these simple people meaning in their lives. It was a good word, too, one he could live with.

Life as a benevolent imposter, bringing peace to the peasants of his friend's parish, while guarding the one thing that might threaten the enlightenment which men of his ilk hoped would herald a wider peace.

Eventually, if the return voyage this September from Portugal to the New World proved successful, perhaps a greater knowledge of the Earth would descend. Perhaps it would inspire more men like Habib to throw off the shackles of superstition, and humanity could rise once again.

Sadly, he did not believe he would live to see that day. All he could do was play his part and hope someone worthy continued his work.

And with that final resignation, he ascended the stairs, where he would acquaint himself with his new home and introduce himself to his flock.

PART ONE

"The river flows at its own sweet will, but the flood is bound in the two banks. If it were not thus bound, its freedom would be wasted."

- Vinoba Bhave

CHAPTER
ONE
MODERN DAY

LOSNESH, CAPITAL OF STRIOVIA

A woman sat on the throne, her chin tilted upward, eyes roving. She wore her pantsuit with an elegance usually reserved for royalty, and from her elevated position, she gazed across the castle's reconstructed throne room where people hung genuine artwork from the recent Striovian past alongside fake armor and weapons and flags of various nations.

The catering staff equipped a table that stretched as long as a school bus, adorned with steel plates and goblets. The dozens of workers could have been prepping for anything, from a state visit by the Prime Minister of Great Britain to a wealthy couple's wedding. They barely glanced at the overseer, instead concentrating on their tasks without tripping over Toby Smith at the foot of the throne's pedestal.

The woman extended a hand toward Toby. "What do you think?"

Toby bowed as he had done before several monarchs in his life, although this was more in jest. "It suits you, General Yanovna. Like Queen Ana-Maria Otvos herself. Might I compliment you on the new statue in the courtyard? It's very... noble."

"It's vulgar. No one in Losnesh needs a thirty-foot statue, no matter how much the locals love the woman." When he straightened, Yanovna laughed and stood. "Oh, Toby. You are lovely." She spoke with the hybrid Russian-Ukrainian accent that most English-speakers had in Striovia, a softer lilt than either of those countries. "And do not call me General."

"Oh, I thought you retained your highest military rank upon leaving the service."

"I still technically hold the title, but I only use it during official occasions, or… when I need to flex my muscles." She gave a little giggle and posed like a bodybuilder. "Call me Zimina."

"Zimina." Toby spread his hands. "Thank you for seeing me."

The woman stepped down from the replica of a five-hundred-year-old throne and stopped beside Toby, her elbow crooked to take in his. She stood a foot taller than him, which made it awkward, but he accepted the gesture with one arm, his weighty briefcase in the other hand.

She led him from the room, explaining, "This place is pantomime, of course, but we like to set these things where our citizens can see them. Our little museum up top is our gift to the people."

"These tunnels…" Toby had been fascinated by them as soon as the meeter-greeters escorted him down there.

Having made this appointment only the day before, it was pleasing to gain access to what was once the seat of power in Striovia. A former castle, now a more modern installation on the capital's edge, it served as a museum. It retained little of the original stonework, amounting to a few feet stretching from the foundations, and was even titled *Tarasivna Castle*. Beneath the facade, though, the tunnels formed a rabbit warren of wonders.

In a cavern converted into an art gallery, Zimina Yanovna turned slowly as she crossed the floor. "These are works retrieved from all over the world, originally plundered by the Nazis and the Russians during their war in the 1940s. We rotate them out with others in the public spaces."

Portraits, landscapes, impressionist works. No organization, no theme to them. Toby would have loved to volunteer to arrange the pieces, but that wasn't his purpose here.

"You've been recovering a lot of Striovia's relics and artwork since independence," Toby said.

"Indeed, indeed."

"Including your language, I believe."

Zimina smiled wide and proud. "Yes, we had our own language throughout modern history, but most of us speak Russian or English now. Many, especially the young who do not remember life under the Soviets, are learning of their heritage. One day, perhaps we shall reinstall it as an official language."

"Like the Welsh." Toby returned her smile. "Ensuring your language doesn't die keeps something alive that no one can take."

"I knew I would like you when we finally met in person. You understand."

"Ease up on the arse licking," came an *actual* Welsh voice through the subvocal comms unit in Toby's ear. It was Charlie Locke, a woman of Welsh descent, now manning a series of computer terminals. She was feeding information to Toby's team currently stationed off site, awaiting their instructions. "They'll get suspicious."

"Indeed," Toby said in answer to both Zimina and Charlie. "These tunnels, they're around five hundred years old?"

"We think so, yes." Zimina waved a hand up and down one roughly hewn wall. "The deepest ones were sealed when Striovia fell in the 1800s and only rediscovered when we took back our country in the early 2000s."

Falling behind, Toby murmured under his breath so Zimina would not hear, "Minimal security cameras so far. Plenty of motion sensors, though. And I came through some rather intense scanners."

"Copy," Charlie said.

They wandered inside the bowels of the place where the average history buff could not venture. Cleaned and smoothed out, the tunnels were now modern corridors, with labs and storage units branching off, only minimal areas of bedrock apparent. Up-to-date tech helped maintain an agreeable climate for the archaeologists and other scientists there, and the empty room, which Zimina accessed via handprint, was no different. Tiled in white, it held six long bench desks resembling those from a university's lab. Bare cupboards, blank monitors, boxed equipment.

"Our latest laboratory." Zimina disengaged from Toby, strode to a desk, and hopped up onto it, her legs crossed at the ankles. "Ready to show me my gift?"

A gift.

Yes, that was how Toby described it in accessing the person in charge of Striovia's Historical Preservation Ministry, a subsection of their Interior Ministry.

Although they enjoyed a convivial relationship online throughout Toby's time working for the British royals, Zimina was less willing to meet in person, citing her reluctance to involve herself with a nation that plundered other cultures' remnants as if they were their own. Even after leaving to set up his own institute, previous attempts to meet up on Striovian soil had failed; these had ranged from misrepresenting himself as an ambassador from a renowned British institute to simple bribery.

Donations, though, usually unlocked plenty of doors. Not in this case.

Toby laid his briefcase on the desktop beside Zimina, who smiled as he clicked open the clasps. He opened the lid and slipped on a pair of cotton gloves. Zimina did the same, producing gloves from her pocket as she sat straighter. Toby lifted a book from the case, its dimensions almost the same as the case, and held it flat on his palms. "An Eastern Orthodox Church Bible once owned by Emperor Justinian I, looted, I understand, in 1452."

Zimina stared at the black leather-bound tome, its gold piping still partially intact down the spine. Gray cracks in the hide spider-webbed the surface. Zimina leaned sideways to view the pages, impeccably preserved. "You know of its history?"

"Just what was on Wikipedia." It was also getting heavy in this position, so he wanted her to take it.

"In the 630s, the castle above us now was a church, based on the Church of the Holy Wisdom in Constantinople." She ran her hand over the bible in Toby's hands. "After the sacking of Constantinople by the Fourth Crusade in 1204, this place was burned by separatists seeking a split from Rome and replaced by a castle capable of withstanding a siege should the crusade reach our door. They hollowed out these tunnels in preparation for a war that never came, as somewhere to store food, to hide, and to flee if necessary." She paused, head tilted as if amused, enjoying story time. "The decisive break hit in the 1450s, a separation between the Roman Catholics and the Eastern Byzantine Churches. This bible is among the final batch approved by the Pope before the split. Where did you find it?"

Toby's arms ached. Not only was he aging badly, but he had the muscle mass of a pre-teen girl. "Zimina, would you care to hold it?"

She accepted the book, first weighing it in her hands, then turning it over, beaming with delight. "Answer the question, please, Toby."

"Question?"

"Where you found it." She hadn't taken her eyes off the bible since receiving it.

"Oh, in Brittany. It was part of a collection that hadn't identified it as being significantly important. At least, not until *yours truly* examined it. My institute procured it on your behalf."

She lowered the tome back into the briefcase, leveling her gaze his way, all traces of her smile gone. "So, this is not a gift? You want something in exchange?"

Toby spread his arms. "Zimina, the book is yours, regardless of how the remainder of our meeting goes. A goodwill gesture. I can only ask you to hear me out and maybe you'll return the favor."

Her smile returned, but less enthusiastic than before. "Then thank you. Perhaps you could say what you are interested in."

"Seals." Toby stuffed his hands in his pockets and let his shoulders drop. "Sumerian agricultural seals that went missing from the National Museum of Iraq. I would like to repatriate them. If you are amenable, of course."

Toby followed Zimina as requested. She told him she knew the cache to which he referred and was happy to talk about it.

"We keep the seals together because they appear to share a history with those discovered on Striovian land." Zimina led him to the lower level and entered a long, cavernous storeroom at least the square footage of an Olympic pool, its ceiling a couple of feet over Zimina's head. "We believe they may have been carved by the *same* hands. Within *our* borders, not Persia. Perhaps even on this very spot."

"During the fall of Baghdad in the last Gulf War," Toby said, "many treasures were lost. Some through extremists destroying heretical items, others stolen for sale on the black markets. They're some of the oldest hand-carved pieces ever discovered. Between 4.000 and 5,000 years. The ones I'm interested in were dug up by a farmer, of all things. Five-centimeter cylinders made of ivory, jade, a few others. Some were used to seal wax over messages, others to secure scrolls or other communications between villages. Others still may have been simple art to be rolled over wet clay."

"Yes, yes, I know these items." She sounded impatient. "But we have a legitimate claim to them."

Toby doubted that. It was a common refrain when a collector did not want to give up property they deemed themselves to have bought in good faith. "And you have them to hand?"

"I'll happily show them to you. But first, let me present you with something that may explain our position a little better."

The lab was laid out identically to the previous one, except this lacked the white tiles and sterile milieu. Where the ceilings met the walls, uneven rock joined the sections, so it felt akin to a hastily refurbished cave. Two people in lab coats looked up from cleaning tiny carvings over bowls of various liquids. Their tools ranged from scalpels to brushes, to handheld tubes with nozzles that Toby knew would shoot a pressurized jet of saline solution to clear away tougher dirt.

"No doubt it is this discovery which allowed you to connect the Sumerian seals to us." Zimina signaled the men should carry on. "Each of these items was located in one of our old salt mines during our Dragon Quest project."

"Dragon Quest?"

"A comical name for a serious investment. Geologists believe deep under the salt mines, the ground is fertile for fossils, and since it dates back to the upper-Cretaceous period, they are hopeful of discovering dinosaur bones. We have never dug up a dinosaur within our borders, so it feels like uncharted territory. The boys are very excited."

"Quite." Toby would have been excited too, but refocused his attention on the matter at hand, unhindered as he inspected the technicians' work.

The items being washed were cylindrical. Those yet to be cleaned bore a crust of white.

Most people will have seen TV and films where an envelope gets a blob of wax and someone presses a ring or stamp into it. This was the same principle, except the objects would have been rolled across the wax or, more likely, wet clay, the larger ones used to shape over a chest or box before being transported to an important person or celebration.

Each cylinder on display measured less than two inches and appeared intricately carved. They may have been wooden to the untrained eye, but Toby had seen plenty of similar carvings; many were like the Sumerian ones—jade or ivory—but rarer items were made of limestone, blackened by time, originally carved over several weeks. The figures depicted a story of harvest, the central figure a woman, most likely a goddess.

"We do not know her name." Zimina maintained her gaze on the object. "But this was part of over a hundred discovered in a chest, secreted in an area untouched since the period in which our new bible was stolen. The Roman Empire valued our salt reserves greatly, so it was a well-guarded facility."

"This goddess features on the Iraqi seals too." Toby produced a magnifying glass to examine the detail. "So revered, it is said she had a throne made of men. This one of yours shows her on a hill, accepting livestock, with women and babies leading away."

"Indeed." Yanovna was smiling when Toby glanced up at her. "Fertility of the land allows fertility of the womb. Without one, you cannot have the other."

Toby returned to the seal. "Circle of life."

"As they saw it, yes." She stood close to him, her hip touching above his own. "And this symbol, we do not understand it, but it appears to represent either the sun or, as you say, the circle of life."

She indicated a circle in the sky of one rendering. Only it wasn't a complete circle; it was interrupted by a zigzag.

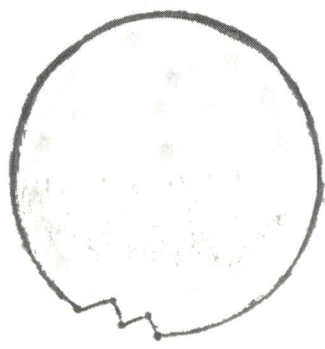

"Possibly lightning," Toby suggested.

"Or the sea, or danger, or many other possibilities. But it is here *and* on the Sumerian seals. It provides a link between ours and theirs."

Toby nodded. "Just because you found your own seals here does not mean they are not Sumerian. They could have been taken by the Romans and secreted here—"

"Buried. In an old salt mine. Not accessed for centuries."

"I don't doubt your honesty." Toby held up a placating hand, lowering it when her features softened again. "In fact, the Striovian government has done little to conceal their existence. I know you are not attempting some deception."

"If these seals are Striovian, then perhaps the Sumerian ones are too."

"May I… may I see them?"

She stared for a moment.

Toby held his arms to the side in a half-shrug. "This is a government facility and I'm an old man who struggles to run for a train. What harm can I do?"

Zimina dismissed the technicians with a terse order in Striovian. When they were gone, she crossed to a cabinet, which she opened with her thumbprint, and removed a tube as long as a drumstick and two inches thick. She presented it to Toby.

It appeared to be made of a smooth, dark stone inlaid with green flecks, a visual cue that caused his heart to clench in recognition. He concealed his surprise by directing his gaping mouth and eyes to an inscription in Latin:

TATUM NE ACIDUM MANDUCANDUM COGNITION DIGNIS APERIAT

Toby translated the text. "Only the worthy may open lest acid eats the knowledge."

There was also a wax blob on the end featuring the pictograph from the Roman seal Zimina showed him.

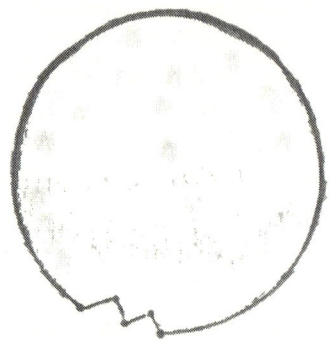

Zimina withdrew the pipe-like container and turned it over, admiring it as if for the first time. "A common security measure pioneered in the Far East, I believe. If you decipher the puzzle, you get the message. Get the puzzle wrong and attempt to open it, and the message is dissolved by a release of acid."

"I've never seen one like this. I've studied bamboo and wooden scroll cases, but never stone."

"It is hollow, with channels containing a liquid, but X-rays and MRIs give no clues to the puzzle. I do have one theory on how to open this, but until I can be one hundred percent certain, well... it has remained a mystery for decades here, centuries elsewhere. It can wait a little longer."

Toby considered sharing his theory about the stone, and even what he knew about a certain artifact made of an incredibly similar-looking substance, but held his tongue for now.

"This scroll, and the Roman era seals in here, were found recently," Toby said. "You mentioned others? From an older find?"

Zimina locked the scroll tube away and advanced farther into the lab, where she stood before a riveted door with a dark window no bigger than a man's hand. She flicked a switch, and the glass lit up alongside a six-foot panel in the wall that also turned out to be a window.

Inside, on shelves running ten lines high and dozens more going back into the structure, hundreds of intricately carved cylinders sat on tiny plinths. They varied in clarity, some caked in dirt, others fully cleansed. All appeared to be arranged by both style and size, from the smaller three-centimeter ones through to the handful of drum-like rolls approximately twenty centimeters long and wide enough to fit around Toby's head. Those latter items must have been used for artistic purposes. Or sealing something huge.

Zimina sighed, hands on her hips. "You know why so much international effort has gone into recovering artifacts looted during the Iraq war?"

"Identity." Toby had seen this zeal so often, it was not a difficult concept. "Iraq is a twentieth-century design, so they hang onto their older heritage fiercely."

"And you appreciate the troubles my country faces today."

"Indeed. With Russian forces barracked a few miles east of your border, it must be worrisome. The nationalists and the pro-Russians make things… *tense*, from what I can gather."

"Tense. A wonderful understatement. But you understand what this represents? The seals? The history?"

Toby considered it, and considered the other countries in Eastern Europe, their recent histories in relation to the former Soviet Union. "The nationalists will see you giving up the seals as a betrayal. The pro-Russians will view it as weakness, which will give them strength."

Zimina returned to the viewing glass. "This was not always a nice room. As recently as the Cold War, the Soviets kept political prisoners here. Starved. Tortured. When the original Tarasivna Castle stood over our heads, many hundreds of years ago, it was a dungeon for the King's most wretched enemies. Now, we house our history here."

She input a six-digit combination on an electronic pad, then removed the cotton glove and pressed her hand to a sensor. The door clicked open, and she replaced the glove before leading Toby inside.

It smelled of dirt. The good kind. It reminded him of the aftermath of an archaeological dig where the backbreaking labor was done with, and the business of trying to understand the finds could begin.

Ten rows of shelves stretched back along what was once a cellblock, divided down the middle by an aisle easily wide enough for Toby and Zimina to walk side by side. They moved too quickly for Toby to examine the seals near the front, the new finds from the salt mine. Nor could he check the pre-cleaned middle section made up of those the Iraq-based purchases. Zimina remained silent until they reached a glass wall at the far end where a collection of gray, near-white objects occupied the storage space.

Like the darker stone items that Toby was interested in, they curved into cylindrical shapes, some hollow, most solid, all carved in stunning detail, their figures defined as dark lines in the off-white tone.

"Many seals were found during a prospecting expedition in the late 1800s," Zimina said, "but no one understood them. After we won our independence in 1998, after the people took back control, we rediscovered them. Once just a curiosity in the nineteenth century, we dated them using modern techniques. And realized they should not exist."

"You studied them, even as a general?" Toby asked.

"Actually, the study came later. I was a warrior, and nothing else. A commander. These seals..." She took a five-centimeter-long totem from the shelf, its soft cushion remaining in place, and held it in both hands as a wine merchant might present a miniature but highly valuable bottle of Bordeaux. "These seals piqued my curiosity. The more I learned, the more I needed to know. They are what prompted me to study archaeology, history, the science behind such endeavors. It took me to London and America. And I brought that knowledge home, to analyze what should not be here."

Toby accepted the seal, holding it close to his eyes to see it depicted a seafaring picture. "In what way? Why should it not be here?"

"These seals were not found in a chest on a Middle Eastern farm or a stash of Roman merchandise. Those are the more recent identifications. These, the originals, were dug up by prospectors, pulled from the ground wrapped in cloth. Buried in a site that housed this fine gentleman."

She activated a room behind the darkened glass, fluorescent tubes flickering to life to illuminate a final section: a large cell housing a figure on a slab. Swathed in gray cloth, it held a human form, a man or a woman, approximately seven feet long.

"Sealed in a plain stone sarcophagus." Zimina's tone softened. "The only mummy ever found here. Pulled from the bedrock of our country. Please do not try to tell me we have no claim to him."

Toby closed his mouth, having only just sensed it was gaping wide. "Of course not. I wouldn't—"

"And the items inside his sarcophagus, you agree they also belong to us?"

"Yes, yes, but—"

"Look closer at the seal, Toby."

He did so.

"And this one." She swapped it out for a larger example, one twice as thick as Toby's forearm and almost as long as his elbow to his wrist. "The engraving is more intricate. What do you think it represents?"

Toby turned it over in his hands, reading the pictorial representations etched in relief: the people, the diagrams, the wavy lines, the circle interrupted by the zigzag overlooking it all. "Precision-tooled. These markings suggest a map, but the figures in it... humans in a field. The same goddess as the Sumerian seals taken from Iraq. The symbol. And this character here..." He tapped a cloaked anthropomorphic rendering whose face was hidden beneath a hood, holding a scythe aloft, while two women stood shoulder to shoulder with it. As Toby rotated the seal, it revealed men and women bowing before the trio. "Death. The Grim Reaper."

"And here is the mystery, Toby." She accepted the seal back and replaced it on its shelf. "We found our mummy preserved in rocks formed over 50,000 years ago."

Toby frowned. "But the depiction of death as a cloaked figure didn't appear until Christian artists began their interpretation of the Four Horsemen of the Apocalypse. That must be an incorrect estimate. Like the *ooparts* people often talk about."

"Ooparts, Toby?"

"Yes, yes. Out-of-Place Artifacts. Things like a brass bell located hundreds of feet down in a coal seam. Conspiracy theorists say it proves either ancient people had advanced technology, or that coal forms much faster than science states. It never crosses their mind that the earth opens and closes regularly and can consume objects found on the surface, only to close around them again. Nor does it enter their thinking that maybe, just maybe, it is a hoax. Zimina, do you not think—"

"The cloth in which the seals were preserved was also dated back approximately 50,000 years. We had to date it with radon."

"No." Toby shook his head. "The cloth would disintegrate. The elements—"

"Treated with something. An oil or liquid that we have not identified. But more importantly, the coffin was sealed, Toby. Airtight. The joins were held together by what looked like rubber, but we could not conclude its origin. A cement of sorts which turns to powder under examination."

"May I?"

"What? See some of it? I'm afraid not. It is locked away for preservation. Until we can develop a technique that will not damage it."

Toby handed the seal back and placed a flat gloved palm on the glass. "In here?"

"Yes. Our mysterious guest has remained in state since 1889. Not always in optimum condition, of course, but here… here, he is safe. No further deterioration."

She walked back down the aisle to where the exhibits Toby originally came to see were laid out. He was dizzy from what Zimina had revealed, trying to equate it to anything he'd seen before and came up with only one incident: the stone bangles they'd liberated from an obsessive, psychotic billionaire five months ago, and the tomb to which they'd led. There, they'd discovered many items that defied explanation. They were still examining those they'd retrieved, but like the substance Zimina described, so far, they had been unsuccessful in offering a conclusion. He saw no way to explain how books could have been written tens of thousands of years before writing was known to have developed, nor how they'd been preserved for so long. All their analysis proved was that the books did, indeed, exist, and that they were definitely older than made any sense.

"50,000 years ago." Toby pondered the cloth's age. "If this person was interred fifty millennia ago, this part of Europe would have been covered in ice. Sheets thousands of feet thick..." He literally felt out of breath, his lungs struggling to keep up with the energy required to power his brain.

They progressed to the exit, but Zimina paused beside a desk and slid out a drawer from which she removed a laptop computer. It booted up fast as she said, "We sourced the seals looted from Iraq for two reasons. First, because of their similarity to those located recently; we wanted to compare them to the older ones we found with our mummy friend and to see if they shared any history. Second… well, second, we needed to be sure no one kept them for their own ends." She turned to him with soft eyes. "We always intended to return them to Iraq. *When we were ready to do so*. Once we proved they were not Striovian. Here."

She nudged the laptop toward Toby.

Photographs. A number near the bottom right—1/1,120—suggested a trove of pictures. The current one was a print of the seal he'd first handled. Rolled across wet clay or something similar, it had generated an illustration of the goddess taking offerings and, in return, bestowing the people with food and fertility. Toby clicked to the next to find the picture had been enhanced with more defined lines, and a digital artist had colored the third.

Zimina pointed at the screen. "Go to sixty-four."

Toby obeyed and found another image in clay, already augmented, this one featuring Death holding his scythe aloft, accompanied by the two naked women. Not apparent in the original etchings was the object in Death's free hand: a circle. An orb, to be precise, emanating lines indicating a glow, like a sun.

"As you say," Zimina continued, standing close behind Toby, her breath on his ear, "images like this, the Angel of Death, the Grim Reaper, whatever its name, they did not appear until artists captured the apocalypse in paint. Even so, Death, one of the Four Horsemen, did not take on his own legends until at least the eleventh century."

"And the scythe was only a regular adornment in the 1400s." Toby clicked to the next, a close-up of the character. A skull's jaw protruded from the hood. "The carving is… marvelous."

"And impossible in the age they date from."

"Couldn't… couldn't someone have planted them? I mean, taken 50,000-year-old cloth, and wrapped the seals, then replaced them?" He felt odd making excuses like this when he'd seen with his own eyes the possibilities of time. "A hoax?"

"Like your ooparts? No, Toby. This was removed from rock still ingrained in permafrost. It is the real thing."

"And the other seals?"

"The ones we found in the Roman salt mine also show the reaper figure, and the goddess character, that odd circle, and several others. The five hundred and eighteen recovered from the Baghdad Museum looting match the goddess, with smaller ones showing the Angel of Death. But they were not in a good state. Some chipped, others unreadable."

"The Sumerian seals from Iraq alone date back to 4,500 BC. Pre-dating the reaper image."

"You see our interest now?"

"Yes." Toby clicked more photographs, racing through until he came to a close-up of the Reaper Seal's opposite side. "This looks like a map."

It was a wide, jagged rhombus shape, with what appeared to be waves near the bottom. To the right, approaching the ocean section, they'd drawn a circle within a circle. An eye?

"Corresponding to nothing on record," Zimina said. "We suspect it was an attempt to show the southern Mediterranean region. A different shape than what we know now. Perhaps because they had no power of flight, no satellites."

Toby had his own theory as to the shape of that land mass but kept it to himself. He'd been blinded by Zimina's intellect and familiarity with him, indulging in the inconsistencies and how they might link back to his own research. Despite that, despite his fascination and Zimina's friendly demeanor, something was not right here.

An ancient mummy buried millennia before the first writing.

Seals carved with true precision, 50,000 years old.

Similar seals discovered recently, dating to the 1400s.

A scroll in a deadly puzzle box from that same era.

And Sumerian seals purchased on the black market.

All connected somehow: copied, mimicked, or related.

The finds of a lifetime.

Toby straightened, pulled his suit jacket straight, and faced his host. "Why are you showing me all of this? You have no intention of releasing the Sumerian seals. The mystery surrounding your mummy in there appears impenetrable at this stage. I doubt you'll let me have a crack at that scroll puzzle. And clearly, there is some etymology between the original seals from the fifty-millennia-old permafrost and the Sumerian ones found in Iraq. Not to mention those hoarded by the Romans. I'm not sure what this... *tour* accomplishes."

Zimina placed both hands on Toby's shoulders, her eyes boring into his. "It is called a distraction, Mr. Smith."

Toby frowned, his stomach falling away, weightless as he fought against weakening knees. "Zimina, I am unsure I—"

"Save your denials. Did you not notice your earpiece died some time ago? After your friend told you to *ease up on the arse licking*?"

"Wait. Zimina, it's not what it looks like—"

"What it looks like is a foreign national penetrated a government facility under false pretenses. It looks like a team in place nearby is preparing a theft of state property. And it appears a skilled computer hacker has illegally accessed our systems, following your progress on our own security cameras. Or they were until about ten minutes ago."

"Zimina, please let me explain."

"No." She shoved Toby, so he had to brace himself against the desk on which the laptop sat. "We have neutralized the hack and cut off your satellite phone signals. We have located your team, and we are moving in to arrest them."

"Zimina—"

"Don't you dare address me that way, Mr. Smith. My name is *General Yanovna*. Now watch the skill and ingenuity of the Striovian security services, as your team is captured, and you all face life imprisonment for espionage."

CHAPTER
TWO

Captain Denis Igoravich was born and raised a Soviet, under constant threat of the secret police. Now, as he prepared to lead his unit's breach on a house two miles north of Losnesh's central district, he had to chase away a brief notion that their paramilitary approach mirrored the tactics of old.

According to his superiors, the people he was about to arrest were spies, threats to the state—and they should be taken alive if possible.

If possible.

No escape could be permitted; whatever force Igoravich deemed necessary was sanctioned, and this gave the dutiful soldier pause.

Denis's parents had been deeply conservative, his father loyal to the Communist Party. He'd hated the West, hated outsiders, and hated women. He'd loved Denis's mother, but only in the way one loved a pet. She was his property, as was Denis, a son he'd called names whenever Denis acted in a less-than-manly way. "Girl," his father would say. "You are *girl*. You grow up to be a girl. Useless girl."

Nationalists were the only life forms lower than girls. Ungrateful scum, unable to fathom the kindness handed down to them by their overlords in Moscow. Yes, times were hard in those days. Queues were long, disease was rife, violence was a daily hazard, and—back in the 1970s—openly carrying a loaf of bread in the wrong neighborhood would get you knifed in the back.

The Igoravich family had not lived in the wrong neighborhood. They resided in a gated community reserved for high-ranking members of the Communist Party's elite, where wine and vodka flowed like blood in a war-ravaged street. Food was airlifted in, and the residents were shuttled around in armored cars.

As the Cold War thawed and the Berlin Wall crumbled, things got marginally better. Denis's father had appeared proud that the citizens of what was once known as Striovia no longer starved to death in their homes or froze in the winter. He attributed their change in fortune to the strength of his own commitments, to the willpower of great men, all of them garrulous blowhards soaked in vodka, red of face and round of belly. And when the young Denis announced his intention to join the military, his father finally expressed pride in his only son.

Although the training was hard and three of his friends perished in it, Denis Igoravich had excelled in every field, from fitness to marksmanship to hand-to-hand combat. What he told none of his assessors or his father was that his determination was born of a desire not to serve their Soviet benefactors or make his parents proud, but to prove himself worthy of a place in Zimina Yanovna's revolution.

It had started as teenage rebellion, cemented by his father's treatment of his mother. His gut ached whenever he could not protect her from a slap or a fist, or if he could not block out the muted squeals of pain that accompanied the heaving springs through his bedroom wall.

A girl was his way in, naturally. A girl he'd met in the police cadet program, an initiative designed to induct the next generation of eavesdroppers and informants to weed out those disloyal to the authorities. It wasn't the first time he'd tried vodka, but at fifteen, a pretty seventeen-year-old girl plying him with alcohol meant only one thing to Denis.

She'd led him by the nose to what the local council believed was a youth club for the party faithful's children, hiding within its walls a back room swept regularly for bugs and unwelcome ears. When it turned out Denis's new friend did not wish to ravish away his virginity, he'd held his frustration in check, such was his anger at his father and his vow to never treat a woman as badly as that fat, glowering monster had done.

The girl—Nelya Dmytrivna Honchar—offered no apologies as she explained how she'd watched Denis's eyes glaze over at the propaganda spewed by the police cadet instructor, the disgust he'd demonstrated initially but hidden at the idea people should be assumed seditious if they did not immediately conform or pledge loyalty to the State. Questioning the State, according to the ruling party, was a betrayal of the people. Because the State *was* the people.

Others had joined them that night, adults and kids alike. Over the next two hours, he learned the truth about Striovia's history, about the covert education programs funded by Western governments intended to counter Soviet lies and sow the seeds in a future generation who'd take over when communism finally fell.

He listened.

He learned.

He fell in love with Nelya Dmytrivna Honchar—not just for her looks or her passion, but for the guidance and brilliance she offered. And he was heartbroken when she was arrested.

They'd put her on trial immediately and hanged her the next day alongside eleven others from his group. He never found out who betrayed them, but he suspected himself. One sloppy moment may have tipped off his father, but he could not investigate without revealing his hand.

So, he'd remained heartbroken, but never scared; there were others who lurked in the shadows, those who preached a new way, who promised events were progressing, and they needed soldiers. At a secret memorial for Nelya and the others, the maturing seventeen-year-old Denis Igoravich met Zimina Yanovna for the first time. There, she revealed Nelya was her cousin, and she had spoken proudly of Denis. And Yanovna told Denis what she needed him to do.

The revolution, when it came, was as swift as it was brutal. The first domino had been the Berlin Wall's demise, an event that shook Striovia to its foundations, which people like Denis's father denied was a defeat but an intentional step toward greatness.

Denis knew differently.

And as he'd ascended through the army's ranks, he kept occasional contact with Yanovna and recruited dozens from within his own units. After a while, those would-be rebels also enlisted, creating a spider's web of hardened military grunts who—when Yanovna signaled a government-in-waiting had formed behind the curtain of secrecy—rose up and seized control of the installations in which the communists had trained them.

The west had called it a bloodless coup, but in reality, much blood spilled. Not at the military's hands, but the freshly emboldened citizens smashing the party residences' gates and government buildings. It was *the people* who burned Tarasivna Castle to the ground, a symbol not of their own history but of the party faithful who occupied it.

Yes, fittingly, *the people* spilled almost all the blood. Angry people, dragging officials from their homes, went smashing the opulence hoarded and denied to those the leaders claimed to protect; dozens were beaten to death in the streets, their bodies roped to lampposts and signs hanging from them, reading "traitor" and "murderer."

Denis's father was a lucky one. He'd survived what became known as "The Night of the People's Revolution," but was picked up at the border trying to smuggle his wife to safety—heading west, of all places. They held him captive, and when Denis Igoravich heard of this, he drove three hours to make the arrest himself.

The man's ruddy face had turned even redder. He spat at his son, and called him a *girl*, as he'd done so many times in the past. But Denis was no child now. He was a soldier, one of the best his country had ever produced, and there he was, alone in the back of a van with his parents. What else could he have done?

Denis asked his mother to step outside.

His father had glanced at the woman as if expecting her to support him, to claw at her husband's arm and refuse to leave his side, or maybe lobby her son to grant mercy. Instead, she leveled her hooded eyes at the fat man, one still bruised from some mishap or another, and slapped him. Then she spoke to Denis words that chilled him even now.

"Do not make it quick."

Actually, Denis resorted to a single bullet to the man's head. This was not about revenge, or making people suffer. It was about the future and always had been. Striovia's future, as a strong, independent nation.

So, in that future, when a foreign entity threatened his country, and an order came down from the department run by General Zimina Yanovna, Denis Igoravich was apt to obey without question.

And right now was no different.

The basement apartment was accessible from both outside and inside the run-down townhouse, so he posted men at both ingress points. Taking the external breach point, Igoravich led four men down the tight stairs behind black railings that marked the start of the street.

It didn't strike him as an ideal staging area for a raid on Tarasivna Castle, as one dispatcher suggested. Constitutionally, they were on dicey ground, and any exploit of this could have consequences at a trial. It was only a direct attack on the government that permitted an army unit to deploy on Striovian soil, but Yanovna requested him personally.

They used fiber-optic lines to scout for traps, and when the outer door was called clear and the inner team radioed the same, Igoravich gave the command to blow the hinges.

Wood splintered.

Metal cracked.

They smashed the doors in, flashbangs deployed, and eight combat-trained special forces soldiers stalked in, guns raised. In gruff, simple English, Igoravich ordered the spies to surrender.

No reply.

Through gas masks, they searched the rooms and passage-ways, finding nothing but pristinely made beds, unused coffee cups, and empty wardrobes. No people, no cell phones, no sign of habitation. On a second sweep, a younger recruit, one who would not remember the revolution personally, located a loose floor-board which Igoravich raised with a knife blade. Inside, a tiny laptop hummed, attached to a phone line running under their feet.

Igoravich peeled off his gas mask and stepped outside past the sentry and called HQ. "They are gone, General."

"They escaped?" Yanovna replied.

"No. They rigged a computer to make it look like they trans-mitted from this point. But I do not think they were ever here."

Silence.

Then, "How? Where are they?"

"We will find out."

CHAPTER
THREE

Dan Vincent had schlepped through plenty of sewers in his time, but rarely one so wet. Usually, there were walls, or walkways, or the streams were navigable with knee-high gaiters or a decent pair of gumboots. This one forced them to wade waist-deep. Compared to some pipes and tunnels, though, he found himself grateful for the weak stench and fluid route.

If waste disposal came color-coded in terms of vileness—say, a chart ranging from white for empty to a rotten brown for the worst humanity could produce—the Losnesh facility hovered somewhere in the yellowy-orange hue. Still, his colleagues were not too happy about it.

"You never mentioned this little bonus," Harpal said.

"It wasn't this deep two days ago."

Bridget pinched the material near her shoulders. "I'm burning these clothes."

"Quit whining and move," Charlie ordered in their earpieces.

"Easy for you to say." Harpal sloshed onward. "You're not even in the country."

"The police handed jurisdiction over to the army, so they'll be sweeping every building nearby. It's only a matter of time."

They'd been stationed in a basement apartment, burrowed

under the floorboards and through the adjacent building's wall to secure a decoy computer that acted as a relay. Once the ruse was up, it would not take long to locate their safe house next door, or the emergency escape route.

It felt good to be back in the field after several months off. Running errands such as securing scientific equipment, or using his brawn for building and the like, wasn't Dan's idea of excitement. And excitement really was one reason he'd joined the Lost Origins Recovery Institute in the first place. Sure, the money was good too, but it wasn't a bottomless pit. And it was running lower than it had in years, meaning Charlie broke out her rainy-day cache of intel.

Obtained through hacks and sweeps of media and the dark web, her reserves of data consisted of clues and hints at who may be selling items of interest on the black market, breadcrumbs that agencies like Interpol lacked the manpower required to follow through—bread and butter to the Lost Origins Recovery Institute. *Easy money.*

Usually.

Here, it appeared, a hoard of Sumerian seals, stolen from Baghdad during the US-led invasion, had surfaced in the tiny country of Striovia. It was Dan who petitioned for this mission over the half dozen others they could have picked, primarily because he'd been stationed in Baghdad at the time the seals went missing, along with thousands of other items.

He still recalled how the museum's workers barricaded themselves in and called for help, and to this day he harbored real anger at the orders to secure only his sector of the city—no one had given facilities like the museum much thought. A museum was low priority; the airports, palaces, key roads, and oilfields required greater attention. When the military brass and politicians eventually recognized the value of protecting Persia's ancient heritage, American and British troops wrangled the area back under control, and Dan's Rangers unit was one of those ordered to help clear out any armed stragglers. Afterward, protecting the museum perimeter proved a truly dull assignment. But the staff's determination to protect their few remaining exhibits, their passion in rooting out the trespassers so not one single item more went missing, inspired Dan to delve into that country's history.

If it hadn't been for the looting, Dan would never have developed an interest in ancient things, never would have sought assignments in the private sector associated with protecting digs and exploratory missions, and never would have met Toby Smith or agreed to join the man's institute full time.

And he wouldn't be there, waist-deep in water transporting feces to whatever treatment plant the Striovians employed.

Charlie advised them to run as soon as Toby's comms unit went dark, but no one wanted to leave their boss, Bridget least of all. Even when the troops jogged past, their boots clear through the basement room's window, Bridget insisted they stay.

"He'd do it for us," she said.

"We are not a paramilitary unit." It was Charlie's frequent refrain, her constant caution whenever danger loomed. "*I'm* in London watching out for you," she began. "*Bridget*, your expertise is *language* and *codes*, not fighting.

"*Harpal*, you think you can talk your way out of anything, but you can't.

"And *Dan*, you are good with your fists and guns, but not taking out ten well-trained soldiers.

"And last, your standing order from Toby is to retreat if he's caught in a lie. Now do it! All of you!"

Although firmly outvoted, Bridget had still disagreed. They packed everything away in dry bags—the computers, cell phones, travel documents—and heard charges go off next door as they slipped through the hole cut into a closet floor. Dan shut the door behind them, and Charlie guided them via GPS through the filth.

They couldn't know how long they had until the Striovians discovered them.

The group emerged into daylight, a ten-foot-wide concrete channel that served as a storm drain. It sluiced rainwater from the capital to the river and the unoccupied floodplains six miles south of the city.

The trio walked for ten minutes north through there, then climbed a ladder to a former inspection unit at the base of a trail leading from a busy retail park.

They were now behind the main shopping area, a spot of gravel-covered land large enough for three vans, and a sealed pipe into the sewer they trekked through.

This was where Dan had stashed a car days earlier and where they now changed their soiled clothes for the spares in the trunk. They permitted Bridget to use the interior while the men dressed outside.

Dumping the wet garments, they took their positions in the vehicle with Harpal at the wheel, Bridget the passenger, and Dan in back arming himself in case of pursuit. He hoped he would not have to fire the AK-47 he was now assembling, or the two pistols he stashed under the seat.

They swept from the inspection trail and maneuvered into the retail park's sluggish parking lot. Shoppers' cars crawled to the exit, then onto the main road, which led to a freeway dotted with light traffic. This would, in turn, deliver them to the border.

Charlie kept them up to date with developments as best she could, but informed Dan and the others that the government was onto her Trojan horse inside their network, and could not remain in place as their eyes.

"What about Toby?" Bridget asked.

"No word," Charlie said. "Best thing you can do is follow through. All of you. Get out now."

That's when Dan spotted the first helicopter. "Can't be good."

"Okay, so pucker up." Harpal squared his shoulders. Game face on. "This is the squeaky-bum part."

Bridget was certain she still stank of sewer. Or the boys did. One whiff and they were done for.

Harpal's passports got them *into* the country, all entering via different routes, but would they get *out*? The border guards would undoubtedly have been briefed to be extra vigilant in their document checks.

A half-mile from the border, three police helicopters circled, waiting for runners.

Oh yes, this was definitely going to be touch and go.

Toby and Charlie were certain only the British, Mongolian, and Indian authorities flagged their faces for monitoring, and none of those countries had trade or quid pro quo agreements with Striovia.

The fledgling country had dropped visa requirements from a handful of nations, which included England and the rest of the UK but not the US. This forced Bridget and Dan to carry EU passports and effect what Toby called *strangled* English accents to grant them simple tourist entry. English was widely spoken, so an alert customs agent might spot an American twang, but not a dreadful British one.

The border guards were taking their time, carefully filtering traffic through their checkpoint.

The helicopters circled.

"No matter what happens," Harpal warned, now only three cars from the booth reminding Bridget of the US-Mexico border in southern California, "don't run. They'll have sharpshooters in place."

Dan had returned the machine gun and pistols to the custom compartment beneath the rear seat, a lead-lined construction he'd pulled together with Harpal following Charlie's instructions. He now relaxed, pretending to be asleep, per Harpal's suggestion at the planning stage. While Dan acted as the group's sergeant major, the *man-at-arms* as Toby labeled him, Harpal was their logistics expert, and when maneuvering safely through unfamiliar countries, Dan deferred to him each time.

Usually.

They pulled up to the checkpoint.

On the way in, Bridget flew commercial from Kiev, and customs waved her through with barely a second glance. She didn't even have to strangle the Queen's English to get the stamp on her fake passport and fend off exactly seven offers from men who wanted to help carry her luggage, which was odd.

Bridget never considered herself a beauty of any extreme, although she attracted her fair share of attention when socializing in the bars and cafes around their Brittany base. Seven chivalrous offers was a bit much though. And she did not trust strangers with her luggage. It was all non-essential stuff, of course. She'd been tempted to bring one of the less delicate books with her to work on during their downtime, but she could not be sure they wouldn't have to run at short notice, like now.

Now, the only question was if the authorities knew who they were looking for. If they only *suspected* Toby had accomplices, they'd make it. If they had identified LORI specifically... well, Bridget didn't want to contemplate *that* "if."

The guard wore a stiff green uniform with red epaulets and, like ninety-seven percent of Striovia's population, he was Caucasian. Aged about twenty-five, Bridget's age, his shorn head bore a peaked hat that only covered the crown. He spoke Striovian first, which Bridget had spent the past week studying. "Passports."

Bridget handed hers and Dan's over, while Harpal passed his own. The young guard opened Bridget's, then Dan's, and peered at the "sleeping" hulk in back.

"What is wrong with him?" the guard asked.

Bridget attempted Striovian. "Drunk." She hoped she said it right. If she got the enunciation wrong, she would convey Dan was happy.

The guard nodded with a smile. His English was serviceable. "Enjoy your stay?"

Bridget returned the smile. Tried Striovian again. "You have a lovely country."

"Thank you."

He handed back Bridget's passport, checked Harpal's, and returned that, too. But then he walked around the side to place Dan's photo beside the sleeping man's face. Angling it strangely, he frowned. He called to a colleague.

An older guard waved through a single, suited man who was driving a BMW before joining the young man next to Dan's window.

Bridget swallowed, frozen to her seat, eyes front. But did that appear suspicious? If she concentrated on staring ahead, would she seem scared? Hiding something? What if they searched the car?

Why the hell did Dan insist on firepower?

The older border guard rapped on the window. Dan pretended to wake, looking around bewildered, and wiping his mouth as if worried he may have dribbled.

The older guard opened the rear door. "Out."

Dan gave the universal groggy reply for when a freshly woken person can't grasp what's going on: "Wha...?"

"Out," the younger guard said. "Border check."

"Serves you right, mate," Harpal called from the front. "Lunchtime drinking doesn't agree with you."

Dan gave a tired chuckle, and Bridget imagined his eyes still looked droopy as he shuffled along the seat and heaved himself out. She risked a glance and saw he stood taller than either guard.

They took their time comparing the passport photo to the man himself.

To Bridget, it seemed all three helicopters now hovered, pointing directly at them, hornets preparing to strike at the most innocuous provocation.

"Your vodka." Dan's British accent came out as a Monty Python-esque upper class twit. "It is much better than Russia's."

The younger man smiled. Looked to the older man, who also nodded happily. Actually, their vodka sucked, but they were immensely proud of anything that set them above their overbearing uncle that once ruled them with an iron fist.

The older guard placed Dan's passport onto the big American's chest and patted it. "Have good journey."

Dan nodded. "Have a nice day."

He ducked to climb back into the car when the older guard gripped Dan's upper arm.

Have a nice day, Bridget thought. Could you be more American?

Dan returned to the pair.

The guard spoke slowly, deliberately. "Have... nice day?"

"Sure." Dan's mouth pulled into a cold smile.

Harpal adjusted his grip, his head shifting minutely, and he murmured so only Bridget could hear. "British passport. Terrible accent."

No one moved.

Bridget sensed Dan adjusting his stance, his hips now fractionally lower than they were five seconds ago.

"Take it easy with vodka." The guard slapped Dan's shoulder and gave a big laugh.

Dan joined the hilarity with a strained smirk and a nod so enthusiastic his head must've been close to dropping off. The younger guy laughed too, and the pair strode aside, waving the car forward.

As soon as Dan was inside with the door closed, Harpal pulled away and everyone made their own noise of relief as they finally exhaled.

The helicopters continued to circle the snarled-up traffic as three-fifths of LORI entered Russia, used visas organized by one of Toby's diplomatic connections to access the country, and shuttled onward to the small airport that offered flights to Kiev, Budapest, Moscow, and ten other Russian cities.

Once they recovered their backup luggage and genuine passports and papers from the lockers, Harpal departed for Kiev where he would spend two days on a sleeper train to Geneva, Dan headed for Budapest to catch a connecting flight to Paris, and Bridget flew to Moscow. No point in risking all of them being picked up at once if their covers failed. They were all on their own until reaching the agreed rendezvous.

Except, Bridget couldn't let go of the fact Toby was a prisoner in one of Europe's less human-rights-oriented nations. Their original plan had failed. It was time to try something different. She hoped the team would forgive her going rogue for a few days.

CHAPTER
FOUR
AUGUST 14, 6:30 A.M

NEW YORK CITY

Bathed in the intense orange glow of sunrise, Jules Sibeko ran through Central Park alongside fellow fitness aficionados and flabby, red-faced folk who'd be back at the burger bar before the month was out. It was too early to wait on the yoga group he'd joined last month, so figured another circuit would take him to 6:50 a.m.—enough time to hydrate before an hour of stretching and strengthening his core.

As he passed over the field and rejoined the tree-lined path, bladelike sunbeams cut across his route, dappling the asphalt for everyone to enjoy. Even the white cop he passed barely glanced at him twice over his coffee.

It was mornings like this that gave him hope for his city. At least for his place in it.

With his share of the money awarded to himself and LORI earlier in the year, he picked up a loft apartment on the Upper West Side, dirt cheap because the artist who formerly owned it got murdered within its walls. The place was also trashed by the perpetrators, so any buyer had to clean it and fix it up, which was cool with Jules; he didn't have much else to do anyhow.

Plus, he learned a new skill: home improvements.

Saws, drills, hammers, measuring stuff just right. He'd started out with the intention of a minimalist living area, then expanded his ambition, ending up with a mezzanine bedroom, a tiled floor, and a kitchen suitable for a Michelin-starred chef.

So far.

Choosing Manhattan over his native Brooklyn was tough. For a while, it was as if he'd defected to a foreign nation, but as he pushed harder that morning, he did not regret the decision. Old memories closed in on him every time he crossed the Verrazano–Narrows Bridge, and although logic taught him those bad feelings would fade eventually, a clean break appealed even more.

Jules finished his final leg at 6:47 a.m. and drank from the tiny bottle in his belt before taking his place on the grass to wait for Belinda to arrive. He hoped she would give out some spare mats that she usually carried; he hadn't brought his own.

It was a great start to the day. And all he had planned was to try out a new juice bar half a block from his apartment, sand a slab of wood he intended to convert into a table and complete an application form that he'd put off for the past month.

It wasn't quite the hipster paradise Jules expected, and it wasn't only a juice bar. The former Irish pub also served twelve different types of coffee from a choice of four beans—a total of forty-eight options to ingest caffeine. Furnished with the usual array of flea market chairs and couches, polished wood, and breakfast bar stools, it was far larger than most of these places, likely due to the previous business needing the space.

He queued for five and a half minutes before he was tempted to reveal his angry face to a guy in a $1,000 suit and $100 haircut, as the customer *hummed* and *ahh*ed over which bean to grind into his morning cappuccino.

"Which is the strongest?" the master-of-the-universe type asked.

The female barista's patience outshone even her smile, and Jules couldn't help but wonder if macho men now indulged in potent coffee to impress prospective hook-ups instead of chugging beer or downing shots. The guy's tone suggested he'd expected her to swoon or something.

"The Guatemalan is great," Jules said.

"Huh?" The guy in front turned to Jules with a squint.

"The Guatemalan Blue Jasmine bean." Jules pointed at the board. "Earthy, slightly bitter, just a hint of chocolate. If you're into your full flavors."

The guy nodded, still frowning, a little nervous maybe. "Sure. Sure, I'll have that."

"Coming right up." The barista flashed her smile at Jules and turned to fulfill the order.

The guy eyed Jules. Still nervous? Whyever would he be nervous?

Jules recalled dressing in a non-threatening way after his run. The cop had been a pleasant surprise, not hassling or even giving him a second glance, but since he'd been little, his mom always taught him never to conform to the stereotypes white people sometimes held over their black brothers and sisters. Cops, especially.

Always cooperate with cops. Try not to draw attention.

So, his dress sense was sedate. Today, he'd gone for a light brown leather jacket over a black tee-shirt and blue jeans with Caterpillar boots. Still, the guy being served acted as if Jules was in a basketball hoodie and low-slung jeans, waving a snub-nosed .38 while trying to sell him crack.

Maybe it was the fourteen-year-old boy inside Jules's twenty-four-year-old body, or maybe the smarmy asshole deserved it, but Jules opted simply to stare at him until the barista delivered the Guatemalan bean cappuccino. The customer accepted his beverage, squared his shoulders, left a hefty tip, and nodded firmly at Jules as he exited.

The short server beamed Jules's way. "Wow, you know more about coffee beans than I do."

Jules shrugged. "I don't know jack about beans. I heard other people say that stuff. How about you whip me up a carrot, apple and ginger juice?"

She flashed a different smile, one Jules couldn't quite read, and hopped off to make his order.

He bought it to drink on the premises as he enjoyed relaxing in places like this, listening to an audiobook on 1.5x speed as the world passed by outside and early morning graduated into mid-morning. Today, he claimed a soft chair with a low table by the window and continued a schlocky but satisfying crime thriller, all while surfing on his phone for a reclaimed wood store that might stock lengths suitable to serve as legs on a dining table. After coming up short, he finished his juice and gave his situation a little more consideration.

He had tried pizza for the first time recently and didn't like it, sensing the fat and salt as it dropped into his stomach, but that didn't mean he was absent *all* junk food.

Having gained four pounds, he still looked like an Olympic gymnast or runner to most, but he could see that morsel of additional weight in the mirror. That he kept up only light exercise compared to his previous regime hadn't helped, but nor had his newfound taste for fresh pastries. He tried not to eat one daily, but so far this week he'd failed. Hence the extra run before his yoga.

On the pastry front, he would fail again.

He bought a chocolate-filled croissant and a Guatemalan double espresso at the counter—strong fragrant coffee being another new vice—and resumed his seat. The audiobook's plot had reached an important if violent turning point, and he expected he'd be able to listen to this section completely before confronting the tail he hoped he was being paranoid about.

Only, he wasn't being paranoid.

His sojourn to the counter *was* mainly to furnish his butter-soaked pastry addiction, but it also allowed him to scan the other patrons. There was no mistake.

Yet, he sat there, thinking. Thinking about his options. About his choices for the rest of the day. Allow his tail to keep its distance or nip it off right now?

No, not right now.

After his croissant.

This one was filled with hazelnut chocolate spread rather than the hard tubes you sometimes get in cheaper places, so he ate it slowly, tearing the food into eight pieces and sipping the coffee ever so slowly. When he was done, the chapter had come to an end, so he paused the reading and dialed a number.

A phone chimed behind him, exactly where he expected. The warbling ringtone cut out as a woman answered in Jules's ear. "Hello?"

"Hey," Jules said. "Come join me." He hung up.

CHAPTER
FIVE

Then she was standing beside him. "Funny," she said.

"How's the leg?"

"Sometimes it's tender. It'll need sunblock forever."

Bridget Carson placed her coffee down and shook off her coat.

"You're a terrible spy." Jules indicated the chair opposite. "You should leave that to Harpal. Is he here? Hiding in the bathroom? Or across the street with Charlie hijacking a satellite?"

"I'm alone." Bridget sat. "And Charlie hasn't quite progressed to piggybacking government space junk." Bridget's Alabama accent had fascinated Jules from the moment they'd first met. Somehow, it came across as languid and unhurried, yet her quick-fire mind kept it going at a regular pace. "How you been?"

"Okay, thanks." He stared into his empty cup, wishing he hadn't drunk it so fast. "Learning tai-chi. Bit slow for real defense, but it's good. Centers me. And I got Netflix now. Do you have Netflix?"

"Sure." She frowned. Leaned forward. "Wait. *You* have *Netflix*?"

"Oh yeah. That, and a bunch of other channels besides. Shame *The Wire* ended when it did. And how great is *Breaking Bad*? But I'm slowing down on the binging. Trying to alternate, y'know?

Some comedy too, but I'm not sure I get all of it. *Modern Family* is cool. And I cannot *wait* to see how *Lost* ends."

"Yeah, alternating is good." Bridget sat back in her chair. "Don't put all your eggs in one basket, and all that."

"Why? Do they get bad? 'Cause The Wire and Breaking Bad were great all the way thr—"

"You sound bored."

Jules's turn to frown. Bridget's interruption deflated something inside him; chatting about these TV shows with someone he knew generated excitement. He had found people to converse with in Manhattan, but they were always *doing* things. Yoga, tai-chi, the gym, running, the organic food store where he shopped for groceries... "I'm not *bored*. I just watched the British show, *Sherlock*."

"How's the money holding out?"

"It's okay. I don't need to work yet, but a bit of variety can't hurt. Figured I'd apply for a job."

"What job?"

Jules looked out the window. "Doesn't matter."

"Y'know," Bridget said, "you *could* always go back to recovering stolen artifacts for reward money."

He turned to face her again. "Or?"

"Or..." She swallowed. Hands in her lap. Eyes on the table.

Uh-oh. Something ain't right. "Tell me."

She wet her lips and hooked a strand of long copper-colored hair behind her ear. "Toby's missing."

"Toby? Where'd you lose him?"

"Striovia."

Jules leaned forward, elbows on his knees. "Okay, what happened?"

"He's not actually *missing*, as such. He's in prison. Awaiting trial."

"Charges?"

"Espionage. Conspiracy to commit theft from the government."

"Is he guilty?"

Her mouth pinched for a second, but a second was enough to show she didn't want to answer. "Only technically."

"Technically?"

"The two-way subvocal bud in his ear is evidence of espionage, and he made it clear he wanted to relieve them of a collection of antiquities. Agricultural seals. Looted from Baghdad."

Jules ran through what he knew about the country. "Striovia ain't the most advanced place, but it's strict. Tough."

"Paranoid." Bridget sounded worried at that. "Do you know much about that country?"

"Only what I read. And I ain't read much."

"The British Foreign Office is negotiating for Toby, trying to get the charges reduced from espionage to, maybe, trespass or something less. But Striovia was part of the *Soviet Union*. Russia would love to bring it back into the fold like it did with Crimea, and last year, they stationed a battalion less than fifty miles from its eastern border. So, you got two factions now in the country." She held up one finger. "The nationalists who love that they're independent and want to defend it. They say looking west is the answer, go more international, maybe consider EU membership. This is the only reason we're hopeful. Problem is, number two." She held up a second finger. "The ethnic Russians. About forty-five percent of the population. Many of 'em believe the Striovian ministry is corrupt."

"Is it?"

"Of course. But no more so than America. The ethnic Russians value *strength*, and they think strength lies in unity. Unity with their homeland."

Jules saw the problem. "So, with both sides, the people holding Toby can't show weakness."

"The person in charge of Toby's case is Zimina Yanovna. Her official title is 'Curator of Striovian Antiquities and Historical Heritage.' Still holds the rank of general, just like retired military vets do here. She *is* trying to affect change. Through her work. But that's an internal problem."

Jules waved her on. "Okay, that's enough background. You wanna talk about the seals?"

Bridget outlined the Museum of Baghdad's looting, of which Jules was already familiar having earned a few thousand dollars for items he'd recovered over the years, but she added a little detail. "Toby's theory is that these, along with others that may still be out there, together make up a codex, part of a wider map. A story leading somewhere."

"Like a Sumerian treasure map." Jules tried to keep the mocking tone to a minimum, but from her slow blinks, he guessed he didn't hide it well.

"You can't pass down that sort of thing as an *oral* history. The Striovians are claiming they found a bunch of seals in an old Roman-run salt mine a couple of years ago. What we know for sure is, they purchased hundreds of seals from Iraq on the black market shortly after."

Jules scanned his memory for more detail on the seals—both Striovian and Iraqi—but came up empty. "So, did Toby plan to steal them?"

"We rarely steal. We prefer to trade. In this case, we'd obtained a bible they were interested in and returned it to them as a good-will gesture. That was the last we heard from Toby."

"You were gonna steal the seals if Toby didn't get 'em through charm, though, right?"

"I guess. But it isn't stealing if you steal from someone who shouldn't have it, right?"

Jules considered his own moral outlook on theft. It had always been more fluid than Bridget's, aimed as much at the assholeness of the person holding the object as the asshole's right to own it. No longer hunting down a specific artifact, he was unsure how he felt about that now. "Big reward money?"

"We're low on funds, yes. But… the more we looked at the

Striovian situation, the more we figured they must be hiding. A rumor. Conspiracy theory, as some might say."

"The oopart?"

"Correct. Look deeper at that daft story. Think about the pieces supposedly recovered."

In his former life, Jules researched all his target items thoroughly, through books and the internet which often led to outlandish YouTube videos. He watched as many as he had time for, these idiotic theories of old-world technology serving mostly as amusement.

But, occasionally, he found some factual background intelligence. Sources. The conclusions were usually utter nonsense, little more than a starting point, but could not be dismissed out of hand.

The Striovian Mummy was one of those.

He said, "Mummified remains dating back 40,000 or 50,000 years. Pulled outta permafrost. And the coffin was full of stuff that shouldn't have been around for another 30,000 or 40,000 years. That the one?"

"Correct."

"You think the Sumerian seals are older than 6,000 years?" Again, he failed to keep his tone entirely condescension-free.

"You're writing this off? After what we saw in India? The books? The sculptures? The..." She obviously wanted to say *magic*, but Jules had explained much of it away.

"Through the possible *physics* we witnessed," Jules finished for her. "Some of it quantum, some of it molecular."

"Right, right." Bridget nodded rapidly, eager to move on. "We still don't understand it, and until we work out a viable *provable* conclusion that'll survive peer review, we can't go public."

"You really got a taste for it now. This advanced ancient civilization..." He wafted his hand, searching for the word. "Business."

"The Striovian seals, if connected to their permafrost mummy, could be like the Aradia bangle. Possibly the same *origin*. We aren't sure. But we do know they shouldn't languish in a Striovian government facility... no matter how much they want to hold out on a Russian takeover."

This wasn't how Jules operated. "I ain't equipped for that. Harpal's better. Charlie too. Hell, get old Colin Waterston from the Brits. He owes you after India."

"*No.*" Bridget's demeanor changed. Teeth together. Eyes narrow. Like an animal. "I can't leave it to chance. Toby is stuck, and the seals belong in Iraq."

"And they might lead you to something. More books?"

"Who knows? And it might... yeah. They could help us understand more."

"Isn't that more knowledge for the sake of knowledge?"

Bridget again focused on the table before flicking her attention back to Jules. "Is there a better reason?"

Jules made a decision: he needed another coffee. "Reason? For living? Well, first I'm gonna drink an espresso. Then I'm gonna take a walk. Then I'm gonna fake my resumé and start season five of *Lost*. You wanna join me? Rest up before heading home? I got a spare bed and a new shower head."

"I don't believe you."

"Don't believe me? About the bed or the shower head?"

"That you'd let Toby rot."

Jules smiled. "If you tell me the truth, maybe I'll help."

Bridget again evaded his stare. "I did. The seals, they... they don't belong there any more than Toby does."

"You didn't. Your plans for the seals. Tell me."

She sighed and crossed her arms. "Fine. I want to take them all, examine them, and return the stolen ones to Iraq. The Sumerian ones. Which we believe were copied from older versions, like those found more recently in the Striovian mine. The seals in the permafrost are the real mystery, though. Anything we can't conclude is definitely stolen... we'll return them to Striovia. But they're all part of a bigger puzzle. Part of something... *more.*"

Jules was sometimes pleased to spot deception indicators.

Sometimes not. He was glad today he knew the truth, but less so that Bridget thought she had to lie.

"So, just to be clear." He placed his hands flat on the table. "You need my help to rescue Toby, recover a bunch of objects that might lead to something more interesting—but you don't know where they lead yet—and return 'em to the rightful owner. All while hoping I don't end up in the same place as Toby."

"More fun than padding your resumé. What sorta place hires a guy whose skills are basically extreme burglary and running real fast?"

Jules shifted his hands to his lap. "And you can promise the Iraqi seals don't belong to the Striovians?"

Bridget gathered her things, happy now. "Oh, and one last thing. The rest of the team doesn't know I'm here asking for help. So, make out like it's your idea, okay?"

CHAPTER
SIX
AUGUST 15, 7:00 A.M

LOSNESH, CAPITAL OF STRIOVIA

Toby Smith had few regrets in life. He never looked back and yearned for an alternate timeline to open up and show him what could have been, nor did he grow broody around children or happy couples. He didn't even feel hard done by whenever he landed in a jail cell.

He'd occupied one or two in his time, after all. Some deserved. Some not.

Today, he deserved his frightfully basic accommodation: four unpainted brick walls, a seatless commode, no window, and a bench for a bed with a mattress so thin it justified quotes around the term.

A "mattress."

Food was, like the room, basic. Lots of bread, overcooked meat, overboiled vegetables, all floating in gravies of varying degrees of thickness. He had eaten enough to keep him going, and since this was a holding cell in the same building as the seals he came to liberate, his only exercise was between his "mattress" and the various interrogation rooms and supposedly private offices. In these, he conferred with a lawyer who seemed more interested in cutting a deal than getting him out.

Or, a "lawyer."

As far as Toby could tell, he was the only occupant in the former dungeons of Tarasivna Castle, an indulgence by Zimina Yanovna, no doubt. She loved her symbolism; keeping a spy in a cell used by the Soviets would be a neat irony to her.

Toby learned from his lawyer that they were close to the city's main court building, and under a deadline of two days to submit a guilty confession—a confession that would reduce the prospective death sentence for espionage and sedition to a mere twenty-five years in prison. He planned on holding out until the last minute before signing any such thing. Either his government would arrange his release, or he'd win his freedom by other means.

Today, he'd been given two sets of clothes to replace the garments he was wearing when he took up residence: one, a suit for court and formal sessions, the other a set of sweatpants and a long tee-shirt to wear around the cell.

He had to admit, the gray slumming clothes were mighty comfortable. But at that moment in time, as the door swung open and Zimina Yanovna entered, he wished he was wearing his court suit.

Zimina looked fabulous in a pinstripe pantsuit, hair loose and shining, her makeup sparse except for a deep red lipstick which caught the light. She stood there for a second, just staring, with a tall, broad-shouldered man in a blue camo uniform and beret at her left shoulder. His face was scarred, an old wound running into a thick, brown beard, and his name tag read *Igoravich*.

"Hello, General." Toby inspected his hands first, then met her eye. "Thank you for seeing me at last. I hope to explain myself—"

"Let's not do this." Zimina glanced at Igoravich, who backed away but did not close the door or lose sight of her. "I do not make a habit of visiting prisoners who are awaiting trial for capital crimes, but the British Ambassador asked personally. He's such a darling. Thinks being married hides how gay he is."

"Zimina." Toby placed his hands together in an approximation of prayer and stepped toward her.

The soldier advanced, but Zimina held up a hand to halt him. "Toby, this is Denis Igoravich. I have known him for many, *many* years." She wet her dark red lips. "If I were to ask him to beat you to within an inch of your life, he would do so without hesitation. Is that not right, Captain?"

"Is correct," Igoravich answered, his accent much stronger than Zimina's, his voice deep and rocky.

"So why, Toby, should I listen to you again?"

"There is more at stake here than national pride." Toby quelled his restless arms; exaggerated movements would do him no good. "I can't go too far into what these seals might be, or why I would love to take a closer look at them. And that fascinating scroll case, of course."

The tube's appearance was what surprised him the most, but now he thought about it, the ghost of a fact whispered in one corner of his mind.

Why did that item, that date, that Latin inscription ring a bell? A faint bell, but it was definitely there.

"I won't elaborate," Toby continued, "partly because you won't believe me, but mostly because I don't even know why. Genuinely, all I wanted when I arrived was to return the Sumerian ones to Baghdad. But the more you showed me... we have so much to learn. And I can help you."

"How?"

Toby closed his eyes and inhaled. He held the breath. He didn't want to talk about that, but nor did he wish to die. So, he exhaled, willpower keeping that upper lip as stiff as he'd been trained. "Because I know a lot about out-of-place objects, things found out of time, in the wrong place. You have the expertise, the equipment, the seals themselves! Perhaps we can do it... together?"

Zimina observed Toby with what he took to be care and consideration. She held herself extremely still. "I have listened, as requested. Now it is your turn."

"Of course. I'm all ears."

"You will appear in court the day after tomorrow, where you will have your lawyer present. We swapped out the one hired by some foreign holding company. A company that appears to be funded by money from a tax haven, which is forbidden. Your government has provided new counsel."

"Zimina, please..."

She blanked him. "At this hearing, the judge decides if you have a case to answer, and brings whatever charges are suitable. Then, in the afternoon, you will face the trial—"

"Wait, the afternoon?"

"Yes. Justice is swift here. You must meet your replacement lawyer. Now."

Zimina stood aside and Igoravich stepped back from the door, allowing Toby to exit. He did so with a thick head, fuzzy, a confused man woken from a deep sleep.

The afternoon?

"Zimina, we were friends."

"*Were*, Toby." She retreated from the room and pulled the door shut. "That ended when you tried to deceive me into giving up priceless heirlooms belonging to the Striovian people. Goodbye, Toby."

Captain Igoravich escorted Toby out of the cellblock, which was smooth and clean, and more modern-looking than the interior of Toby's cell. They passed the interrogation rooms in which, a day earlier, a stranger placed papers Toby couldn't read before him and demanded he sign them. This next room was new. More like an office.

Inside waited a man with stubble over his head, a goatee beard, and a cheap gray suit with a yellow tie. The man stood, extended his hand, and with a plummy British accent said, "Hello, I'm Arthur Fitzpatrick. I'll be representing you."

Toby shook the man's hand and Igoravich shut them both in the room.

The lawyer bowed his head and leaned back. "Mr. Smith, you are in a lot of trouble."

"I know, but are you versed in Striovian law? We don't have long to prepare—"

"By the way, Colin Waterston sends his regards."

Toby sat heavily in the chair opposite the lawyer. He was in more trouble than he thought.

CHAPTER
SEVEN
AUGUST 15, NOON

CHÂTEAU CACHÉ, BRITTANY, FRANCE

Stationed in the drawing room full of olde-worlde mahogany paneling and overstuffed green leather chairs, Charlie Locke wasn't sure what surprised her most: the fact Colin Waterston seemed adept at using FaceTime or that he treated her with a modicum of sympathy as he delivered the verdict she'd been dreading through the screen of her MacBook Pro.

"Sadly, Deirdre at the Foreign Office tells me old Toby is in very deep trouble. I made subtle inquiries after your little archaeology club too, and they are in the clear. Luckily, Striovia doesn't have a great deal of facial recognition technology. Otherwise, *if* Toby's friends had been in Losnesh with him, they might also have been flagged."

Officially the Head Curator to the British Royal Family, Colin's tendrils crept into the higher echelons of UK politics, affording him the access and freedom of movement normally associated with superspies like James Bond. Colin was nothing approaching suave, though.

Charlie thought of him as creepy. The way he made a sneer sound like a physical manifestation of his cynicism, the leering manner whereby he observed people down the length of his hawk-like nose, and the precision with which he held himself and changed his overpriced watches twice a day, it all added up to a pretentious idiot unaware of how ridiculous he seemed in others' eyes. His only saving grace was that he was talented at what he did, making him bearable to the powers that be.

If Charlie ever met the Queen, though, she swore the subject of this man would surface. "So, we can visit if we choose?"

Colin scratched his cheek and checked his watch. "If you think it will do him any good. But please don't make things worse. I know you can't always behave in a way that engenders diplomatic goodwill."

"I don't know what you mean." Charlie was about to bid him goodbye, but he stared off-camera, a sad grimace etched on his face. She couldn't cut him off yet. "What is it?"

He sighed. "There's no love lost between myself and the old bugger, but I have no wish to see Toby boy flung into a Striovian gulag. However, he *was* engaged in an activity he knew to be illegal. It's slow. But you *must* allow diplomacy to take its course."

Charlie flinched. "I'm fairly sure they don't have gulags in Striovia anymore."

"Let's hope."

They bade a polite goodbye and Charlie closed the lid on her MacBook. She stared at it a moment, having completely forgotten Dan and Harpal were sitting across the coffee table opposite her.

"Well?" Dan asked. "You think he's lying?"

Charlie frowned. "What about?"

"About us not being flagged by Striovia. Could we be arrested if we head back?"

"I don't know. I doubt it, but who can say?" She sat back. The plate of meat, cheese, and bread that Margarete had brought for them thirty minutes earlier lay almost untouched. Charlie picked at it, trying to eat, but the past three days had been hard. She closed her eyes, fighting sleep. "I just don't know."

"I think he's genuine," Harpal said. "Toby was his mentor in the royal antiquities field, and their history goes back even further. To wherever Toby won't talk about."

The team had long suspected Toby formerly worked as some variety of spy. Not a skilled intelligence operative like Harpal, but a proper old-school *spy* and that his archaeologist persona was a cover in which he immersed himself, allowing him to travel unmolested. His biography before the collapse of communism was a closed book and, having adopted his former cover as his new reality, he dismissed any questions as *ancient history* and *irrelevant*.

Harpal once explained to them how the Official Secrets Act covered far less in the modern age of transparency. Whatever Toby—and any students he mentored—got up to during that time would remain concealed via the threat of imprisonment.

Harpal went on, "We know Striovia's got hardly anything in the way of advanced surveillance. We once asked them for intel on Chechens supporting a terrorist group, and they didn't have a record of the bad guys entering the country, let alone their addresses or faces on file."

Dan crossed his arms. "So it's unlikely they've got any deep intel on us."

"Unlikely but not impossible." Charlie shook her head. "We *have* to go. We can't let him face this alone."

"Alfonse sorted a lawyer for him." Harpal edged forward. "They won't torture him. He'll have visitors from the British Embassy, and he's... he's *Toby*. He'll do okay."

"If it was you, Harps, what would you do? If it was your decision?"

Before Harpal could reply, a woman's voice answered from the doorway. "We go in."

Charlie jolted at the accent from America's southern states and spun to see Bridget striding in. Both Harpal and Dan stood from the couch and wandered around the sides to greet her. She gave each a peck on the cheek.

Harpal resumed his seat. "Told you she'd be okay."

Dan leaned on the wall. "Yeah, she's a big girl now. We've trained her well."

Bridget gave a playful, "Pfft."

Charlie couldn't help a grin either, showing her relief at Bridget turning up alive and well. But nor could she help her maternal instinct kicking in. "Where the *hell* have you *been*?"

"Seriously, Charlie?" Bridget plopped herself into a chair at the end of the coffee table. "You expect me to believe you didn't check up on me?"

While Charlie's own kids were all under ten, she was biologically old enough to be a mother to Bridget, although not necessarily legally. And she hated when Bridget saw through her. "Well, don't keep us in suspense, lass. How is Jules?"

It was Jules Sibeko's turn for an entrance, sauntering rather than striding. "I'm getting annoyed with the makers of *Lost*. Season Five ain't really up to it. Just answer some damn questions from Season Four already."

Harpal winked. "Nice outdated pop culture reference."

"She thought we needed your help?" Dan asked, more seriously than Harpal.

Bridget picked at Charlie's discarded food.

"Leave no man behind and all that." Jules offered Dan a mock salute, which Charlie hoped Dan would not react to. Dan remained silent, and Jules halted but didn't sit. "Yeah, so, I kinda saw on the news some British guy got arrested. Toby's name came up, and I figured I'd call Bridget, see if there's anything I can do."

Charlie arched an eyebrow. "And?"

"And, y'know, Bridget came over personally to fill me in. I insisted on coming. I mean, Bridget said I wasn't needed... like, you guys have got this handled. Clearly. But I've been meaning to say 'hey,' so I loaded up a few TV episodes and Bridget's folks paid my airfare. We cool?"

Dan scoffed and stepped away from the wall. "You had a ten-hour flight, and that's the best lie you can come up with?"

Bridget rolled her eyes at Jules. "You told me you had this."

"They'd have guessed," Jules said. "They're fairly smart."

Charlie's eyebrow-raising tough-girl stare returned. "Fairly?"

"Compared to me." Jules grinned. "Sorry, arrogance mode still keeps kicking in."

"I thought it was a perpetual state," Harpal said.

"Good one. So, what's the plan?"

"We wait." Charlie glanced at the guys, challenging them to override her.

Neither did.

Harpal nodded.

Dan's face hardened. "Leave no man behind." He shifted his gaze from Charlie to land sternly on Jules. "That's a *code*. It *means* something real to people. Please don't use it casually." That was enough for him. He headed for the exit. Without turning, he added, "Waiting seems like the best way of getting Toby home right now. So we wait. I'm going for a run."

"Waiting?" Jules shrugged, looked around as if missing something. "You didn't think about exploiting their obvious security flaw?"

Dan paused again in the doorway. "What obvious security flaw?"

Bridget grew animated, in a way Charlie hadn't seen in a while. "The security flaw that lets us get Toby *and* the seals out. A flaw that'll help us locate… wherever the seals send us."

"More books?"

"Does it matter? Books, cave paintings, half-rotted wooden beads…" It was times like this when Bridget's eyes widened so much, they caught the light and almost literally shone. Like when she decoded even a single word of the ancient text, despite it having no context. "Don't you just have to *know*? We can do it. And Toby'll be *so* happy."

Harpal leaned in, interested. "So, what exactly is this *security flaw*?"

Charlie didn't like the sound of this but was too slow in shutting it down.

"Lack of manpower." Jules blinked a couple of times. "And an arrogance about their superiority."

"You'd know all about that." Harpal pointed a finger and depressed his thumb like a gun's hammer.

"One." Jules used his thumb to start the count. "They got a lotta low-rise buildings making up their town center. Two..." His first finger extended. "There's a thousand years of tunnels under that city. Half the country's built on a series of mines. They even used a ton of those tunnels for sewage, air vents, all that jazz. Plus the museum they got under their main government building. That castle thing they rebuilt on the old foundations."

Charlie detected a charge from Dan and Harpal, both motionless but fully alert. She'd already researched the things Jules spoke about and considered a number of approaches, but they'd been too dangerous. "And you just happen to have the blueprints?"

"Sure." Jules opened his jacket and tapped an iPad stashed in a wide pocket there. "I got 'em from their historical society, cross-reffed with the government's own maintenance website, which ain't quite as complete, but it looks legit. Just need Charlie to check they're current against the utility companies and fire department."

"Fire department?" Bridget said.

"Instead of coming up with a white lie like Bridget told me to..." He winked at the blushing young woman. "Between smoke monsters and polar bears on the TV shows, I looked at all the intel she gave me instead. This is workable. As long as Alfonse has some extra cash. And if you're up for it, we can get Toby, *and* the stolen seals."

All turned from Jules to Charlie. She wanted to call her husband, ask his advice, but she knew what he'd say.

Don't go.

Don't put yourself in danger.

Her abdomen still ached from the bullet wound that missed major organs but caused significant tissue damage. She was two months out of the wheelchair and only three weeks walking unassisted. She'd promised—again—to stay away from activity that could place her in a similar situation.

"Okay," she said. "Let's try. But if we're doing it, we're doing it right. We get the seals, we get Toby. We get him pardoned retroactively."

"Go big or go home," Dan said.

"Go big or go home. So macho. But I'm serious. We have to justify this. We're not just breaking a criminal out. We're taking looted artifacts back to where they belong. And, at the same time, rescuing a man who attempted to right a wrong, and is being unjustly punished. Clear?"

"Clear," Harpal said.

Bridget almost glowed, her voice bubbly. "We're really doing it?"

Charlie confirmed she was on board, but this was unlike anything they'd attempted before. And it might just be the stupidest thing they'd ever tried, too.

PART TWO

"Civilization begins with order, grows with liberty and dies with chaos."

- Will Durant

CHAPTER
EIGHT
AUGUST 17, 9:00 A.M

LOSNESH, CAPITAL OF STRIOVIA

In many ways, Dan saw Striovia as a modern, thriving country, full of coffee shops and fashion chains. There were larger capitalist symbols springing up too, such as Apple's first Striovian outlet opening next month and the impending arrival of an Amazon distribution center, although its own country suffix was some way off. An area in which they lagged behind, though, was one Dan did not mind: automobiles.

Import taxes were high, so stealing a motor vehicle was as simple as breaking the lock, cracking the steering column, and yanking out the ignition wires to spark them together, as they do in old movies. Like in Cuba, Striovians looked after their cars, such was the cost and difficulty in replacing them.

The Ford Sierra Cosworth—circa 1984—was a breeze to steal, and when Dan drove it, he could feel the raw power under the hood; it'd do well. He hoped to return it to the owner with no damage.

Officially, they were in Striovia to offer support to their friend, but having arrived in town the day before and applied to meet Toby Smith, they were denied on grounds of security.

Dan had observed from afar as Charlie spoke with Zimina Yanovna in person, meeting her in the public art gallery of Tarasivna Castle. He saw little progress other than the sympathy emanating from Yanovna deepening somewhat. Charlie didn't smile once. She simply watched Yanovna leave her before exiting the building to meet with Dan and the others.

"After," Charlie said.

Hustling away from the grand stairs, Dan had glowered back at the building, a modernist take on a classic castle shape. "What does that mean, *after*?"

"That we can see him after his acquittal or in jail following his conviction."

Bridget had pulled her coat tighter. Although it was summer, most of Striovia and all of its capital were situated at a higher and therefore colder elevation than Western Europe. Bridget shook her head, shivering a little. "I still don't get why we don't just find the leverage."

"Because Toby needs to be part of it," Harpal said. "He needs to be the wronged party. To be seen as the guy helping Striovia in order to make the pardon more palatable. Otherwise, both the nationalists *and* the separatists will use it as a stick to beat the government with."

Secretly, Dan had preferred his backup plan from the outset. Without voicing it to the group, due to their preference for simplicity and aversion to risk, he expected it to become the only thing that would work. "Plus, if it goes bad, the UK and US got no extradition treaty with Striovia, so he's peachy."

Charlie's warning stare confirmed she didn't like the idea of even one minor mishap.

"As long as we make it outta the country," Dan had added.

That was why Dan was now riding down a spacious road in a sporty hatchback toward the center of Losnesh, with Harpal driving a garbage truck in his rearview.

When the time came to abandon this plan and go scorched earth, Dan hoped the others wouldn't hesitate.

BOBBY'S PREMIER HOTEL, LOSNESH - 09:05 A.M.

Charlie *literally* didn't have to be there. She could have flown her new drone—her "unmanned aerial vehicle," or UVA— stationed in France or even London, listening out while Phil readied the kids for nursery and school. She could've shouted through for a coffee if she needed one, or even sat with him as she worked.

But no.

In Toby's absence, despite there being no official chain of command, the Lost Origins Recovery Institute had turned to her as his deputy. It was a duty she did not relish, but accepted the burden, since—objectively—she was the one best suited to the role.

Dan was too focused on allocating labels like "them" and "us" which meant he defaulted to a conflict situation and his tactics always reflected that. Harpal had similar shortcomings, but with added ambition that LORI just couldn't match in terms of exper- tise, numbers, or financing, ideas like flying in using wing suits or undercover ops that involved bribing officials and security personnel. Jules wasn't even a part of the team, but it was his plan they now followed.

Charlie wasn't sure if it was some attempt to impress Bridget or if he genuinely cared for Toby, or even some adrenaline rush akin to Harpal's preferred methods. Jules also acted more relaxed than he'd been throughout their last encounter, no longer utterly obsessed with a single object.

Bridget concerned Charlie the most, though. After retrieving a tiny fraction of the ancient books sequestered inside a burning structure, she'd made it her mission to understand those works. Five of them. All in different languages, all differing in age, the oldest dating back to when conventional wisdom suggested all human brains were capable of was slapping colors onto a cave wall and calling it *art*.

But that had no bearing on what they were doing.

Toby was their focus. The seals were a new mission. Their secrets were a separate question to answer.

Alfonse Luca served as their benefactor in this, financing a more expensive drone than they were used to. Instead of a $300 toy store model, Charlie now piloted one of a pair of $2,000 units utilized by the movie industry. She'd set up the double joystick control panel in a seedy hotel room—unpleasant, but her tests, in its lobby when weighed against the four others they tried, proved Bobby's gave the best Wi-Fi signal. This fed a 4G receiver jerry-rigged to the drone itself, which allowed her to break the law in flying it without maintaining a line of sight. It was a risk, but she could not be found in the vicinity.

Currently, it cut through the air a half mile from Tarasivna Castle, close to a rooftop, buzzing around behind a water tank's struts. Its camera pointed directly at the roads surrounding the Interior Ministry's building.

Down below, police cleared the throng of press and members of the public to one side, and a small convoy edged out of an underground structure: a 4x4 police vehicle, followed by two motorcycles, then a converted van with grilles on the windscreen —a prisoner transport—followed by two more bikes and a standard cop car.

Once clear, Charlie landed the observation unit, planning to retrieve it later, and switched joysticks to activate the UVA stashed closer to the expected route. This was an identical model, but she could not chance hovering it nearby. It rose from behind a row of shops, the laptop image a vertiginous high-definition cityscape, the prison convoy like scale miniatures in the distance.

Most of the security was for show, but still too much for LORI. They were no special forces unit, after all.

The drone's camera switched to a tighter zoom, now a hundred feet off the ground without lingering directly over the route. Charlie checked ahead and found a straight thoroughfare, cleared earlier. She angled down to the van that she assumed held

Toby, and accelerated the UVA toward it, as if on an intercept course.

Closer, Charlie hit a sequence of keys and a target appeared on the screen. When the crosshair was almost directly over the line of vehicles, she fired.

A black dot shot out from the bottom of the screen and arched down to the van.

Charlie allowed herself a fist pump. "Backup tracker secured."

She pulled the drone away, following from a distance that would not get it shot down, and as it pursued the beacon on autopilot for a few seconds, she opened a second laptop and entered a password.

A grid of the city popped up. Four signals activated: the prison transport, Dan in one car, Harpal in the truck, and the third party in position.

"Bridget, Jules," Charlie said. "Copy?"

"Loud and clear," Bridget answered.

"Toby's out. Proceed."

CHAPTER
NINE

KRASIVAYA DRYA MINE, OUTSKIRTS OF LOSNESH

Jules's research revealed *Krasivaya Drya* was intended to be a premier tourist attraction aimed at couples on city breaks. Unfortunately, the city break market never made it to Losnesh; bachelor and bachelorette parties from Western Europe were its biggest tourism draw, attracted by cheap booze and cheaper strippers of both genders.

The excursions were limited to two square miles, largely because of the conservative nature of the people. Prostitution was illegal and strippers were licensed, and the city leaders who hoped for a higher class of visitor would have to wait a while longer to utilize the classier aspects of their home.

In terms of Striovia's classic industries, coal and tin had replaced salt centuries earlier, but it was a long-sealed salt mine that Jules had discovered during his research.

Krasivaya Drya literally translated as "The Beautiful Hole," which had made for a lot more giggling than Jules expected from a team of adults around Château Caché. He put it down to nerves, as sometimes witnessed at a funeral.

Observing it in person, he and Bridget attempted to paint

themselves impressed amid the scattering of hung-over party-goers killing time before the bars reopened, regular Striovians with their children, and other scant tourists carrying maps and flyers. Essentially a preserved village, the attraction pressed narrow homes together, the walls bowed inward through age. The guidebook assured them everything there was original, dating back to when salt was a valuable commodity amid a landlocked region.

Jules didn't go too much into it. He didn't care; extraneous details were a distraction.

"You sure about this?" Bridget asked for the seventh time that day.

"Yes," he replied. For the seventh time!

"And we can get in this way?"

"I went through this seven times. Eight if you include back in France. Do I really need to make it nine?"

She stepped away from him, a stern expression aimed his way. "Okay, Mr. Grumpy Pants. What's got you riled?"

In truth, he didn't know. Normally, when all the variables were mapped, his pulse would barely rise as the starting point approached. Burgling a government institution was about as exciting as opening a car door if he did it right.

Today was an elaborate setup, though, where too many of those pesky variables needed to come right. LORI had proved themselves capable on plenty of occasions, but Jules still couldn't command them from on high, couldn't watch their every move. Something as innocuous as a thorough bag search could derail things.

The little town gave way to a path where a Japanese family of four kids and a mom posed glumly for a photo taken by, presumably, the father of the kids.

Jules offered his hand, which remained empty as Bridget held hers by her side. "Come on, we're supposed to be a couple, right?"

Bridget reluctantly slipped her hand into his. They pulled

close and wandered the path between boulders overgrown with moss and thick clumps of grass. She didn't speak as they rounded a corner to be confronted with Tarasivna Castle a mile away and a hundred feet higher than their current position.

"You sure—" Bridget started but cut herself off.

Jules took pity on her as they walked, understanding that sometimes inane chatter helped calm people. "The passages from the original fort used to lead to the mine. An emergency escape route for the kings and whatever they had in the original castle. They found the salt reserves during the construction and used the digging as cover. The tunnels to the new structure'll be cut off and sealed up now, but the route's still there."

"If it's publicly available, won't it be well-guarded?"

"Hell, yeah. But remember why it's important?"

She smiled up at him with cold-rubbed rosy cheeks. "You told me eight times."

"You got it?"

"I got it."

The mouth to the mine itself was secured only by two skinny youths in uniforms akin to those of mall cops. No guns. Jules and Bridget flashed the paper wristbands allocated on arrival, and the kids on duty asked to look inside both Bridget's bag and Jules's oversized daypack. They didn't grow even passingly suspicious of Bridget's thermos and candy bars, nor Jules's sandwiches at the bottom of the near-empty rucksack.

Not thorough by any stretch. Thankfully.

Jules and Bridget passed into the initially dark entrance.

Shored up with bricks and mortar, the wooden beams were shaped like a lower-case *n*, just for show. Once around the first corner, artificial light took over, dim fluorescence to keep the vague impression of darkness, built into plastic reproductions of flame torches on the ends of sticks. Jules had no trouble walking upright, another amendment to the original construction.

Every hundred yards or so, an information board invited visitors to read up on another interesting fact or statistic. There were so few people in this section that Jules and Bridget didn't have to feign interest.

Within minutes, they'd lost Charlie's signal and were on their own until they surfaced. She'd suggested using an invention of hers, what she dubbed "comms relay pods" that worked like Wi-Fi signal boosters for phones, but if things didn't go quite right, they'd make damning evidence against the Institute. All Jules had was his plus-sized cell phone.

Operating offline via GPS, he'd mapped the mine and overlaid it with the old escape routes from the fort. What he hadn't mentioned to anyone was that the linking tunnels were his own invention, digital artwork created when melding the two sets of plans together. It was the sort of guesswork that he'd have called stupid a few months prior, but his home improvement project taught him the value of improvisation.

In this case, the deepest part of the publicly accessible tunnel would require some form of drainage, and none showed on any official document. Perhaps it was the irony that made him so uncomfortable—that he worried about relying on other people when his own slice of the pie was a gamble.

They'd built the mine experience as a loop to prevent low-speed head-on collisions between visitors, and this section sloped downward. When something sloped downward, there had to be a low point.

Jules was not disappointed to find the drain cover at the exact spot he predicted, but was *deeply* disappointed to find a family of at least eight, including one elderly man, staring at an information plaque housed in a display unit directly opposite the drain. It also concerned him that the cover was only a couple of feet square—enough for both of them to squeeze in, but if it was a long pipe, there was no guarantee they'd be able to use it.

"Let's read," he said.

Bridget stood behind the family, rising to her tiptoes to glimpse the words describing what lay farther inside and how it was too dangerous for modern people to venture there. Jules speed-read it and flicked his eyes from side to side, hoping to locate another access point.

None.

He scanned the floor as far as the wan light allowed, but it was flat, if somewhat rocky.

The ceiling.

Yes.

He almost missed the grille screwed flush to the roof, but now he saw it, the size was encouraging.

Ventilation systems were rarely spacious enough to infiltrate secure facilities the way those super spies did on TV, but occasionally, an access point started wide and led to other areas. The reason for this was inspections. Vent tubes didn't need to be large enough for a man to crawl through uniformly, but certain points demanded access for short lengths.

As the family shuffled on, Jules asked Bridget to maintain the ruse while he checked on something. She did not object, and Jules scaled the display unit to get a closer look at the metal covering above and to the side. He used his phone's flashlight to peer through the grille and saw a three-way T-junction.

The part that passed lengthways stretched over his head along the corridor while the stem of the T branched off toward the same wall as the drain. "Listen out."

Bridget nodded without a word and trotted away to the point where she'd spot any others arriving.

Jules put his phone away and removed his multi-tool, a contraption he valued above almost everything else he carried. In his belt, he'd prepped the mini flashbangs that occasionally came in useful, and up one sleeve he carried an extendible baton that doubled as a crowbar. But it was the multi-tool's flat head screwdriver that made fast work of the vent's grille, and he needed to inch it out from its housing, stretching his arms to reach.

Before he could lower the cover, Bridget hurried toward him. "Someone's coming."

Jules hopped back down. He hadn't had time to press the

grille back into its molded place, so it hung there at the mercy of gravity. One corner was completely displaced, the other three jammed into the rock.

Bridget clocked the situation. "What do we do?"

Jules turned her around to stare at the plaque, removed the backpack to lay it at his feet, and pulled her close.

His chest rested against her back, his arms wrapped around her. His chin nestled on her shoulder, and by the time four sullen-looking women trudged into view, Bridget had leaned her soft cheek against Jules's.

He felt her smile. Her hands covered his.

The girls spoke with harsh British accents, wore scruffy jeans and unsuitably high-heeled shoes for a grim day out like this. Jules pegged the accent as a northern one from the Liverpool area. *Scouse*, as it'd be termed in the UK.

"Ehh, Patty, here's another one."

"Right, what's it say?"

Of the four, three were overweight in varying degrees, with the other wearing a wedding veil and still slightly overweight. Jules noted this because, in his experience, it was unusual for an entire group to appear so unhealthy.

A scrape drew his attention to the ventilation grille. A second corner came loose.

Each woman bore the droopy eyes and wobbly demeanor of deeply hungover human beings.

Although Jules had never experienced a hangover, he'd suffered a concussion twice and imagined it to be fairly similar.

The foursome spent twenty-seven seconds reading about a disaster from two hundred and sixteen years ago, then moved on, the bride-to-be glancing at Jules and Bridget as she passed. She wobbled on her heels and twisted her foot, her shoe coming off. Amid a flurry of mild swearing, the woman fumbled to get it back on.

Jules stared at the cover right over the party. It shifted minutely, a drizzle of dust floating down. He broke out of the embrace and eased Bridget gently aside, readying himself in case the grille fell.

The bride-to-be squeezed her foot back in the shoe and all four went on their way.

Bridget resumed her post. Jules rushed to the vent, reached up, and it fell easily into his hands. He leaned it on the wall to the side and sprang to grip the edge.

Finding it marginally more difficult than he would have before meeting Bridget and the others, he nevertheless heaved himself up and braced using his knees and one elbow. With his free hand, he again shone his flashlight inside.

As expected, the pipe running over the tourist attraction was hollowed out for airflow only—too small for a human—while the section ahead was wider. It extended beyond the wall with the drain in it.

Jules switched direction and leaned into that larger branch and crawled in on his belly. It was tight, but plenty to pass tools and equipment through, or to reach into for basic maintenance or set rodent traps.

Three feet beyond where Jules calculated the wall stood, a second grille presented itself over a dark tunnel, one his light couldn't penetrate. He made out just enough to confirm he'd be able to stand upright once he got down there. A faint trickle of water appeared to confirm his drainage theory.

Carefully reversing, Jules folded himself into a sitting position and called to Bridget. She tossed her bag up. He placed it aside and reached for her, pulled her up, and told her what he saw.

"Another sewer?" she said.

"Drainage," he assured her. "Probably."

"Do we need to replace the cover?"

Jules had already considered that. "By the time they notice something's wrong, it'll all be over."

Jules led Bridget to the sealed section of tunnel where he donned gloves and used a squeezy bottle with a narrow nozzle to seep a corrosive liquid into the fittings.

It ate through the screws and, like the other, the grille held itself in place against the edges. Jules simply pressed it out. One side first, which he caught, then dislodged the other and pulled it up to rest safely inside.

He climbed down, then helped Bridget out—help she initially rejected, but then realized she was fractionally too short to do it herself. Once down, she removed a larger flashlight from her bag, hidden beneath the thermos, and lit up the scene.

It resembled the tourist tunnels, only filthy, unattended to in years. Evidence of rodents was everywhere, from the smell to the droppings to the scurrying noises far ahead. Spiderwebs hung. The wooden beams were not supported by modern brickwork.

"The air needs to circulate." Jules whisked his finger to highlight the process. "Even in the olden days, this was active. It needed to come out somewhere."

"I thought you already knew it came out here."

"I did. Of course I did."

Jules couldn't see her expression, but the lack of a reply suggested suspicion.

They pushed on, not speaking, wafting dust out of their way. The former mine closed in the deeper they went, and Jules's phone took them to the left, in the opposite direction from the passage he'd guessed would link to the fort's old escape route. Then a tributary passageway arrived, and he turned right.

They broke through a phalanx of wooden planks bearing a sign reading *Danger - Keep Out* in Russian script, Striovian dialect, English, and Cantonese.

Another fifteen minutes of trekking followed, where they found an opening through which water trickled. It came from the lower road that curled back on itself in its approach to Tarasivna Castle.

Bridget aimed her flashlight ahead. "Are you sure about—"

"I *got* this."

Jules led her on at a jog, rounding the next corner, then pausing to check a ladder set into the wall. He pinpointed his location on the phone one last time and reactivated his subvocal bud. "Charlie, you read?"

"I hear you," Charlie answered. "Where've you been? You're ten minutes behind schedule."

"The map wasn't to scale. Where's Toby now?"

"You have about three minutes."

"Sure, no problem."

Jules said no more before climbing the ladder.

It took him into a tube intended for human use, and he heard Bridget bringing up the rear. They switched off their flashlights and climbed higher, a different light source leeching through ahead.

Jules slowed his pace, so he ascended in silence until he found a horizontally slatted grate, looking out onto a tiled corridor along which men and women walked by.

"We're ready." Jules held his hand out below.

Bridget passed up the thermos and Jules lifted it to his level, unscrewing the outer cap.

"Okay, Charlie, just say the word."

ST. AGNUS'S HOSPITAL, LOSNESH - 09:42 A.M.

With their vehicles in position, Harpal and Dan skimmed through a corridor in the sprawling building, wearing scrubs liberated from a supply cupboard scoped out earlier. The facilities were as clean and efficient-looking as any hospital Harpal had seen in Europe or America. But there was a tired feel to the place, of staff stretched to accommodate the tightening budgets demanded in all countries. It was only the security angle he would recommend for serious upgrades.

Harpal blended in well to most places; a change of clothes, a haircut, a sculpting of facial hair, but his most important camouflage was looking like he belonged.

If he *felt* as if he fit in, he *did* fit in.

And even though Harpal's brown skin would probably stand

out in any other setting across Striovia, their medical staff was approximately sixty-five percent immigrants. Which meant it wasn't difficult for the pair to negotiate their way to the roof.

Losnesh had no air ambulance, but they were due to acquire one by the end of the year, and the helipad atop St. Agnus's was a testament to this. Occasionally, helicopters touched down, sometimes carrying an injured soldier or dignitary, although it would be the standard, basic machine. Usually several years old, like the cars.

The Robinson R-44's owner had landed as previously arranged, thanks to a Charlie-orchestrated hack to add an entry to the hospital's calendar. Harpal had answered the for-sale ad and spoken to the guy on the phone in Russian, arranging to meet right there for a test drive.

Harpal felt bad about the deception, but they would compensate the man. Not the full $200,000 he wanted for the four-seater machine, but a little thank you for his time and the loan of his property. In fact, as Dan gently lowered the guy to the floor for a nap and withdrew the needle from the man's neck, Harpal slipped a bulky envelope into the pilot's belt. The pair then moved him inside the building where he would come around shortly.

It didn't take them more than two minutes to familiarize themselves with the controls. Dan rode the stick, Harpal beside him, which was as they usually flew, and Harpal prepared himself mentally for the next phase.

"We're in the air," Dan said. "Everything else in place?"

BOBBY'S PREMIER HOTEL, LOSNESH - 09:55 A.M.

At Dan's hail, Charlie scanned the three screens before her, dots and data representing the operation: Toby's convoy en route to the courthouse, a split screen between the drone's long-distance view and the GPS tracker going through the streets; Jules and Bridget ready to move on the storage vaults; Dan and Harpal flying low across the city.

"Stand by." Her fingers tabbed to the screen tracking Toby's progress, which pulled up a box requiring a ten-digit, alphanumeric code. She typed it in, then tabbed back to Toby's GPS.

A final dot up a side road represented one of the two vehicles stolen earlier.

All Charlie needed to do was hit the "submit" button. It would blow the brakes and send the refuse truck into the convoy's path. She just had to time it correctly.

"Charlie?" came Dan's voice.

He'd be close to the ambush point now.

Toby's dot rolled smoothly along. Less than fifty yards.

She struck the button.

"Okay, it's a go. Everyone. Go, go, go."

CHAPTER
TEN

09:58 A.M.

PRISONER TRANSPORT VEHICLE, LOSNESH

Although Zimina Yanovna no longer wore a uniform, she still held what was technically a high rank, so volunteering for prisoner duty felt like something of a step down. It was an indulgence, arranging to sit in back with Toby Smith, who was shackled to the floor, wearing the neat suit she'd picked out personally. Procedure required her to don a flak jacket and appropriate pants and boots, plus a helmet akin to a combat grunt's, while either side of Toby, Rasamov and Dimitev were fully equipped with body armor and weapons. They knew who she was, of course, and did not object when she removed her helmet and let her hair fall free.

"You still haven't told me why, Toby."

Her old colleague looked up sharply.

They had briefed Toby about the no-talking rule, and back at the castle he'd received a punch in the back from a transport officer when he asked to clarify a point.

He was understandably wary of opening his mouth. "No. I have not."

"Do not play the wounded puppy. You knew what would happen if you got caught."

"I thought you would understand..." He swallowed, averting his gaze.

"Is that shame I see, Toby? Shame for your actions or for your miscalculation?"

He faced her. "Honestly? A little of both. An additional soupçon of disappointment. In someone I considered a friend."

"Friends don't deceive one another. I think you know this."

Toby nodded.

Yanovna's heart thumped slower. Slower, but a fraction harder. "You can still be helped. I have influence."

He let out a tiny laugh. Just one breath, then it was gone. "You wouldn't believe me. And to prove it, I would have to sacrifice much more than my freedom."

Yanovna folded her arms and crossed her legs, satisfied at the sliver of progress.

To prove it...

That meant he *had* proof. "Do you know what hard labor is?"

"Yes," Toby answered. "It's against the Geneva Convention."

"Of which Striovia is not a signatory."

"There are no gulags in Striovia, Zimina. Please don't pretend you'll open one especially for little old me."

"No, but our prisons require a certain amount of participation. Striovia is expanding. Its population, its international reach. Our prisoners make bricks, shape wood, pound metal. A small payment is issued upon release."

"Control of people and resources. Like the old guard?"

His words spiked in her gut, and she jumped to her feet. "We are *nothing* like the old guard."

She composed herself, annoyed he'd got to her, and sat.

The road rumbled beneath them. A helicopter sounded far away.

Yanovna crossed her legs without looking at him. "Your labor could serve the State in another way."

He did not reply immediately.

She said nothing more. She would not beg.

"How?" he asked.

"The artifacts. More like the ones you saw. And others. Some are only 1,000 years old, but still, we have no record of what they might signify for this region's history." She now resumed her open posture, hands together, his insult pushed aside for now. This was business. "You will spend your nights in a prison, of course, but six days per week, you will be shuttled to a facility where you will work with great minds. With me, sometimes. Studying. New knowledge. First, we must understand what our salt mine seals mean, if they are crafted by the same hands as the Sumerian ones, and how they relate to the permafrost finds. All you need to do is cooperate. *Before* we get to the courthouse."

"And my sentence?" His eyes were small but round, his cheeks hanging like a faithful dog awaiting affirmation from its master.

"I can recommend the minimum sentence for espionage of twenty years. But it will not be twenty years like a murderer or a traitor. It will not be life inside, and death is absolutely off the table."

Toby inhaled. Held it. Then said, "You can drop the espionage charge, Zimina. You have that authority. Burglary. Lying to an official. Espionage is too… too *much*."

Sadness swept through Yanovna. It was true. Espionage was overkill and charging him with such a crime was an emotional response to his betrayal. "If there is enough evidence to imprison, we always convict. Reduced charges is not an option." She kept steel in her voice for the benefit of the two officers. "You must cooperate. You will lose your freedom, but it will be bearable." She checked her watch. "This is your final chance."

Toby clasped his shackled hands together, leaning as far forward as the chains allowed. "Fine. I'll tell you all I know. And I'll help you learn more. About the seals, and about the scroll puzzle box."

"You believe you are one of the worthy?"

"Merely a scholar with insight." Toby's mouth pulled at the corner. Not quite a smile, but... okay, maybe it was a smile. From the rest of his life in prison to most of his life in servitude. "I will help, Zimina."

"Starting now. Talk, Toby."

"The artifacts you found *could* be over 20,000 or even 50,000 years old. No mistake in testing. We have identified advanced items of a similar age, and—"

The transport van screeched to a halt, throwing Yanovna sideways. She adjusted and righted herself. The chains held Toby in place. Rasamov and Dimitev gripped the bench seat to avoid crushing Toby.

In Yanovna's ear, the driver barked, "The road is blocked. Go back, go back!"

Yanovna glared at Toby. "This is you, is it not?"

Toby shook his head. "I know nothing about it."

Something in the shake of his chin, the widening of his eyes, his very demeanor shrinking, suggested he was being truthful.

She lingered on him a moment longer to see if he wavered, but he did not. This was not a plan of his making.

"Could be a jailbreak," she told the two officers, "or it could be vigilantes. Separatists will kill us all to get to him."

The pair stared back, stoic nods preceding a check of their weapons.

To Toby, she said, "Prepare yourself. This may be rough."

ELEVEN

BOBBY'S PREMIER HOTEL, LOSNESH

Charlie's screen zoomed in, the elevated drone camera losing a little definition as the sabotaged refuse truck rammed into a parked van.

The convoy halted.

An incendiary device planted amid the waste sparked to life, creating an impressive pyrotechnic display. Both the lead and rear bikes performed one-eighty turns and waited for the prisoner transport to perform a hasty three-point turn. The new point-bike shot off to the left, taking the vehicles away from the original route to a wide boulevard.

"They're taking backup route alpha."

"On it," came Dan's reply.

"Stay back. Let's see how it plays out."

Dan made a frustrated *tut*. "We've dealt with tougher people than this."

"They were *bad* guys." Charlie's fingers tensed. "People willing to kill us for profit. Do I need to remind you these folks are police?"

"I'm not gonna kill anyone." Dan sounded like a chastised teen.

"But they're well within their rights to kill *you*, boyo. If there's any doubt, any doubt at all that you can extract Toby, you back off. Understand?"

A pause. It extended into a silent non-response.

Charlie added, "You know it's what he'd order himself."

Another pause, this one ending in, "Copy that."

Charlie closed her eyes and rubbed them before resuming her monitoring of the three-pronged mission.

This was not how they operated. At least it shouldn't be. The bad guys they'd "dealt with" in the past had been small terrorist cells occupying areas in which they were working, and several mercenaries hired by a competitor. One terror cell rendered her lover—now husband—paralyzed from the waist down, and the competitor's mercs had shot Charlie in the gut. Had LORI been better prepared or allowed their egos to deflate, it might have been different.

Charlie's phone sneezed. The tone for an incoming message. It was Phil. She had to squint to read it.

Can you FaceTime?

Before replying, Charlie wondered if it was high time for an optician's appointment. She'd been getting worse in almost undetectable increments. But now, when turning from a screen to a darker place, it took longer to adjust. She was post-forty, so the fact she'd gone this long with no need of assistance was a positive.

Her vision clear, she replied to the text:

Sorry, hon, I'll call back shortly.

He replied:

Just two mins. Kids want to say hi before school.

Charlie glanced between the phone and the screen. The convoy hit a wide route, the only one sufficient to take a swooping chopper between its buildings. The lead vehicle halted, likely scouting for danger.

The transponder in the stolen chopper flagged Dan and Harpal as media, but that ruse would soon expire. They had only minutes before the police launched a bird of their own.

She typed:

Sorry. I'll try soon.

Then:

Kiss them all for me.

She placed the phone face down, heard the sneeze of a final message, but resisted reading it.

HELICOPTER, AIRBORNE OVER LOSNESH

Harpal was not as skillful a pilot as Dan, but he'd argued successfully to take the stick at this stage. Dan was also more accurate with firearms and explosives, and since they were using live ordnance yet planned to avoid a single casualty—not even a wound—it would require the man-at-arms to operate the more dangerous equipment.

Normally, what they termed a "scorched earth" rescue involved flying in, launching flashbangs disguised as explosives, then descending in a helicopter with one or the other manning a flamethrower that belched flame like an oversized Bunsen burner; that is, flashy but lacking the sticky fuel. They designed it to make the enemy scatter, to inject fear without collateral damage. The non-lethal weaponry was backed up with very-much-lethal handguns and a rifle ordinarily employed in army operations—for precision where the bad guy didn't take the fiery hint.

As they commenced their approach, Charlie confirmed the prisoner transport had resumed its trail to the courthouse's second entrance.

The boulevard reminded Harpal a little of one of the lesser Vegas streets. It boasted a mall, several modern office buildings, and a strip of green down the middle. Normally, this would be dotted with a mix of high-end cars, old bangers, and public buses and trams. The tracks for the latter gleamed as the morning sun brightened.

"Ready?" Harpal asked.

"Ready." Dan slapped a flashbang into a snub RPG launcher.

"Damn useful having a guy like Alfonse bankrolling things, eh?"

Dan didn't sound enthusiastic, even as he instinctively glanced at the flamethrower setup and the pistols. "We'll see how that works out soon enough."

"Ten seconds," Charlie said.

They had almost completed the crescent-shaped run and were about to execute a sharp banking maneuver to swoop into the boulevard when another voice came on the comms—Jules.

"Hold off on that, guys. We got a big problem here."

CHAPTER
TWELVE

TUNNELS BENEATH TARASIVNA CASTLE

The thermos Jules took from Bridget contained a benign-seeming liquid that could be drunk without dying, although anyone dumb enough to do so would waste most of the afternoon on the can. When not drinking the concoction, it reacted with potassium carbonate in a way that didn't quite explode in the quantities he and Bridget used, but the fumes expanded exponentially in an oxygen- and nitrogen-rich atmosphere and put people to sleep for a good hour.

With his and Bridget's mouths and noses protected by scarves laced with a neutralizing agent, Jules aimed the receptacle out through the grille.

The space beyond was soon filled with invisible gas, its occupants collapsing slowly to the floor, spreading too fast for anyone to react to the fumes.

Unlike what filmmakers in old Bond movies would have folks believe, people don't simply flop over when drugged. As expected, those visible to Jules saw instinct kick in as the cloud of drowsiness hit them. They lowered themselves to the ground or leaned on a wall. Then, instead of falling like a tree, which would crack most of their heads open, they slid slowly into a safe slumbering position on the floor.

No, it was a steady but swift process.

Jules knew the labs formed their own structure within the larger building, so the new A/C system in the government facility above remained separate from the climate control down there. They wouldn't suddenly find an entire building of people dropping off for a nap. The subterranean space meant an exponential deployment through the corridor and, if all went to plan, beyond; a hangover for several people, which would last two or three hours at most.

Jules jimmied the mesh from the wall, and he and Bridget clambered through. They kept their scarves on while Bridget checked her printed building schematic.

"That way."

"Good luck," Jules said.

Bridget headed for the exit leading to the main part of the castle, swiping an RFID security pass from a prone worker's white lab coat. Seemed she was more assured these days.

Jules put the thought aside and likewise grabbed a chipped badge, taking the opposite direction with an empty rucksack over one shoulder.

He used his stolen pass to access a janitorial cupboard where he ducked inside to acquire a cap and dark blue vest.

If the gas didn't spread as far as he calculated, he'd need to blend in before the alarm got raised.

With the cap pulled low, his scarf remained in place as he mentally checked off his progress, his near-eidetic memory feeding him the building schematics. He kept his pace slow, peeking through each alcove as if he might be assaulted at any moment.

Through one doorway, he stepped over a security guard. The space opened into a wider passage, beyond which laboratory windows shone with people clad head to toe in white suits hard at work. They were shut off, escaping the knockout fumes.

Isolated, though, so no one had noticed their colleagues dropping.

Within minutes, Jules found himself in the "dark" areas, those places Toby had ventured without Charlie tracking him and for which he had no plans in his head.

Following the flow of the corridor, the next two smaller, well-lit rooms held labs with no people inside. The third was an anteroom leading to a storage space, currently in darkness. Outside, a pair of men in lab coats slept peacefully in a heap. But this had more security than the other rooms.

He'd found what they were looking for.

Bridget thought she'd done a good job concealing how scared she'd been back there, and now she calmed for real, milling around the public areas of Tarasivna Castle like any other tourist. And there were dozens of tourists.

Although it was essentially a government building, they granted access in the same way people could visit Windsor Castle, the Capitol Building, or the Washington Mall. They gave a quarter of the ground floor over to a winding display of art, antiques, and educational material, organized into themes by time period. She spotted the bible Toby had donated.

She hadn't risked coming in the front way, since security was actually tighter there than down below. The team was worried she might be found suspicious if caught with the items in her backpack's concealed pocket.

Her main job was to watch the escape route. If security acted oddly or if stern-looking men turned up to wander the crowds, examining faces, she had to inform the others. If anyone spotted her talking to herself, she possessed the academic chops to fake that she was composing her thoughts on whatever painting or sculpture presented itself. Such as the statuette before her now—a miniature reproduction of Queen Ana-Maria Otvos, whose oversized statue dominated the exterior.

Even as the plan's rescue phase commenced outside, she browsed the displays' edges, near the bathrooms where Jules was due to emerge. There was little she could do to help him except reassure him it was all clear.

For now, anyway.

Jules had bypassed fingerprint, palm print, and retinal scanners before, plus the occasional combination pad, breath monitor, and voice recognition lock. The idea was the same in all these: convince the computer it read a legitimate positive. When receiving a command such as "unlock," it requires specific conditions to be met.

It was all about ones and zeroes.

The hand scanner, for example, created the condition that needed a palm print shown to the computer to be repeated, which it took as a command to unlock.

Condition met = 1.

Condition not met = 0.

If input = 1, unlock.

If input = 0, remain locked.

Once a person understood the gist of it, circumventing the systems was nothing more than a matter of time. In this case, unscrewing the casing, rigging it to a custom smartphone, and delivering a command string that swapped the condition met/not met conclusions, took all of ninety seconds. When Jules added his palm to the screen, the light pinged green, and he worked immediately on the combination code. Another two minutes, and he had the door open.

Jules removed his scarf and scanned the shelves stretching farther into the room as the lights flickered on. He took in the sight, a matter of seconds to absorb what most people needed minutes for.

Suddenly, things weren't as simple as breaking in.

There was far more to it than he'd expected. Yes, the Sumerian seals he'd studied beforehand were present, but so too were additional items, ones resembling his target, but... different.

No.

Concentrate on the task.

Don't get sidetracked.

No mission creep.

He put those other objects out of his mind, yet could not resist picking up the first Sumerian artefact with his gloved hand. It was no longer than his palm and twice as thick as his thumb. Squinting to make out the patterns, he processed them and reversed their images, presenting a clear picture in his mind's eye of the scene as if it'd been painted: a sun, a harvest, animals, and humans with arms raised to the sky in thanks, then back to the sun again.

These had been stolen so long ago, taken most likely by people who did not understand their significance—just like his mom's bangle as she'd lain dying in a New York pizzeria.

He placed the artifact into his backpack, and made his way along, unable to forget the other shelves he'd seen.

Did Bridget know? Did she send him there to view the other things?

Did she lie?

Hundreds of the smallest seals, his target, lined up ten-deep on the metal storage units. He would have preferred to encase each one in tissue or bubble wrap, but there was no time. Instead, he gathered handfuls and lowered them gently into the bag. He packed them tightly to prevent them knocking and potentially chipping, lying the larger ones on top to weigh them down and slot them together more snugly.

A phone rang. It came from a lab assistant sleeping outside.

Jules was almost done as the ringing ended.

The other guy's phone rang. Then the first one joined in. A digital melody filled the air, then died after a few seconds.

Jules added the final seal and hefted the rucksack. It was essentially a bag of stones, so it took a serious effort on his part, having to crouch before strapping it on and rising under the power of his legs.

Boy, I'm out of shape.

Not compared to most people. Compared to most, his fitness levels approached professional athlete status, but back when he'd been performing tasks like this as a matter of life or death, he surpassed many such professionals.

Obsession will do that.

And while Jules was relieved to be free of that burden, what had he replaced it with?

TV.

Cinema.

Home improvements.

He tightened the straps and headed for the door. Mission accomplished. No reason to hang around, especially with all hell about to break loose.

And yet.

Those other items, deeper inside the storage room.

He set a timer in his head for thirty seconds and jogged toward the back.

The cell phones burst into life again, near-simultaneously.

But Jules needed to check, to *know* if what he saw was accurate.

Split into two delineated sections, the first presented a collection of white cylinders. Some were clean, others crusted with dirt and more white crystals. Like the Sumerian ones in his possession, the smallest samples depicted scenes of harvest, but larger ones appeared to tell a story. While it was possible those the size of his thumb would leave an impression in wax to seal a document or offering, the ones as wide as coffee cans were more intricate—depictions of battles, of seafaring feats, of specific characters.

Goddesses. Warriors. Demons.

Jules's internal timer hit fifteen seconds, so with the merry ringing from the lab assistants' phones in the background, he progressed to the rear. There, he found an array of items that appeared crafted with the same intricacy as the salt-tainted ones. Only, these were clean. They'd been there a while.

Jules picked up the biggest one. Thicker than his arm, nine inches tall, he turned it in his gloved hands.

A Grim Reaper image.

Two women beside him.

A mass of bodies before them.

Trees and crops behind.

Most people would not see the full image without enhancement, but Jules blocked out all other thoughts, all other stimuli, and concentrated on what it must look like laid out—every detail, even its damaged sections, its imperfections.

The Death character, in addition to his scythe, held a sphere radiating light, while the women accompanying him were naked with fleshy hips and small breasts; the perfect woman in days gone by, ripe for childbearing. The people bowing before them were plainly mortals while the vegetation that followed looked lush and healthy. Then he came back to the Reaper again.

But what gave Jules the most pause, what set his internal alarm to snooze for fifteen additional seconds, were the green flecks that caught the light as he turned it.

A coincidence, possibly.

But unlikely.

He replaced the item and selected the one beside it. This was not as ornate but depicted lines akin to the world's continents. Except, much of it was wrong, drawn not to scale but with approximate dimensions. Northern Europe was larger with no British Isles, and the two American continents looked squashed, while Africa was askew, closer to Asia. Australasia was nowhere to be seen. Oddly, a mass that appeared to be Antarctica lay at the bottom.

Again, the green just beneath the gray surface shimmered in the fluorescent light.

Jules kept the seal in his right hand and removed his left glove, holding it in his teeth. He trembled, recalling the effects his touch had on his mother's bangle, so similar in appearance, and which his mother had tried to keep safe all those years. He did not for one second believe it was a coincidence.

Bridget knew these were here.

This wasn't about returning Sumerian artifacts to Iraq. It was about *her*. About her quest for knowledge, for figuring out where this might lead. All to satisfy her own thirst.

She expected him to find these items and take them.

The phones' ringing intensified, triggering his own overdue alarm.

Jules withdrew his fingers without touching the seal.

A whole minute had passed, and as he tuned back into the real world, the phones grew louder and more convoluted. More than two trilled through the complex. More than four, more than five.

"Ready," came Dan's voice in the subvocal.

Jules rushed out through the anteroom, the bag dragging so hard on his shoulders that he expected bruising later. Not that it mattered. Because now, every phone along the route was ringing.

Every single one.

Harpal mentioned something about Alfonse being great, then Charlie said, "Ten seconds."

Jules scouted the corridor, aiming to return to the tunnel entrance, but Striovian voices emanated from that direction.

"Hold off on that, guys." Jules pulled his scarf back up over his mouth and nose. "We got a big problem here."

CHAPTER
THIRTEEN

PRISONER TRANSPORT VEHICLE, LOSNESH

Yanovna had almost made it back to base. Once she suspected foul play, she tried to raise the people in the catacombs.

Receiving no reply from her deputy in the museum, she immediately demanded the Historical Preservation Ministry instigate the protocol for times of crisis. When the simultaneous ringing of every phone only elicited responses from those not located beneath the castle, she raised the alarm.

Whoever was in charge of security that day would be *severely* punished…

Wait. That wasn't her job anymore. No, she'd left that behind long ago. She was a curator, nothing more. She'd done her part for her country, and the aftermath of this breach would be up to someone else to sanction.

Now the motorcade had abandoned its original destination, Yanovna believed they should return to the holding cells adjacent to Tarasivna Castle, and the captain of the guard agreed.

But there was still the question of *purpose*.

Why the garbage truck?

Why the…?

A shiver spread through her.

If the police and ministry concentrated all forces on preventing the assault on Toby's transport, pursuing someone wrenching him from their custody, that meant a distraction.

It meant they were not in danger from separatists.

She thumbed the radio. "There is no jailbreak. Take the most direct route back to base."

BOBBY'S PREMIER HOTEL, LOSNESH

Charlie was furious. The comms from Jules gave Harpal and Dan pause. Instead of initiating the rescue, they requested more intel. Charlie, too, waited. Jules explained he was now stuck, hiding in the janitorial closet, and when asked how that affected the scorched earth part of the operation, he said, "It doesn't. Except, they know we're here. So, they probably know we're after Toby too."

By then, the motorcade had U-turned again, this time snaking off the boulevard into another narrow run of buildings dating to the latter half of the nineteenth century. Too sheltered for a helicopter to penetrate.

Charlie realigned the drone, so it soared higher, keeping Toby in sight. "If they're heading back to the castle, you'll get another chance. Come around from the blindside."

Bridget joined the conversation. Quietly, almost a whisper. "All's quiet up here. But I'm ready. Jules, did you get them?"

"Sure." Jules sounded short, presumably to remain concealed. How long until they commenced searching places like closets?

"Ignore the secondary for now," Charlie said. "Jules, if you have to ditch the seals, that's fine. Priority is Toby."

"What about the trail?" Bridget asked. "If we abandon the seals, we'll never—"

"*Toby* is more important. Dan, where are you?"

HELICOPTER, AIRBORNE OVER LOSNESH

Dan still wasn't convinced this was the best approach, and if at any point the odds switched against them, he would not hesitate to abort. Toby was only the priority if his escape was possible. If not, remaining invisible to the Striovian authorities came first.

Dan had even taken back control of the helicopter, much to Harpal's annoyance.

"Just peachy," he replied to Charlie. "Taking a wide arc to come up on the blindside of Tarasivna."

"Good," Charlie said. "Jules, can you get out?"

Jules responded quietly. "As long as Bridget's in place and the two supermen did their bit."

Dan rankled but kept his tone professional. "Confirmed. You just need to get there."

"Thanks."

Harpal pointed. "What's that?"

Dan focused as directed. Squinted. Couldn't make it out. A fleck in the sky. "That dot?"

"Yeah, the dot."

"The one getting bigger?"

"Yeah, the one getting bigger."

Dan discerned what it was. "You mean the dot getting bigger and looking a bit like the Apache AH-64 US Army attack helicopters? The ones we sold to Striovia when sanctions were lifted a few years back?"

"That's the one."

"Huh." Dan swung the stick left, taking their own civilian chopper away from what could be interpreted as a threatening approach to either Tarasivna Castle or Toby's transport. "Guess I should lose it."

Harpal nodded. "Would you mind?"

"If you're about to do something dangerous," Charlie said, "let me know if you need rescuing."

"Gotcha." Dan dropped their altitude, dipping into the original boulevard—above the phone wires but beneath the larger buildings to conceal them from the Apache—and prepared for the worst.

CHAPTER
FOURTEEN

TARASIVNA CASTLE

Jules hadn't flexed his brain this much for several months. It used to be second nature, often annoying himself how no situation, be it social or business, could pass without calculating every variable. But the brain was a muscle; when in constant use as it had been for the preceding nine years, and when it came with a natural ability to retain knowledge and experience, those instincts were all but impossible to switch off. With great effort, Jules had done so, and now he was struggling to access the muscle memory needed to figure a way out of this closet.

Their voices were low.

Footfalls soft.

Either well trained or scared.

At least two lingered outside the supply cupboard. They spoke with one another in Striovian. Waited. Then spoke again. Careful, deliberate footsteps. Slow. Coming closer.

Jules loosened the straps on his rucksack, ready to release himself.

His Aikido and Krav Maga training had waned of late, but he was confident it would come back to him if needed. While he didn't *want* to hurt anyone, the seals he carried belonged elsewhere, and when he weighed things up against doing temporary harm to people signed up to accept such risks, the ethics fell easily on his side. If he'd stolen the other seals, though, his choice would have been far harder.

The footfalls receded. Jules counted to ten, tightened the straps, and cracked the door.

Out in the corridor, Jules hurried silently away, counting in his head how far he traveled to ensure he didn't spread out farther than the structure above. He found the fire exit in an alcove, almost hidden beside a goods elevator that required keycard access, and noted a more robust crash bar than a standard door. He squatted to check he was right and, sure enough, there were additional contacts between door and frame.

Alarmed.

If he'd had enough kit, he'd have been able to open the double doors, activating nothing, but he didn't have the time. "Okay, Bridget, I'm gonna be coming at you from the north side."

"Hang on," she answered.

Jules waited, assuming she was checking which way was north.

"Okay. North," she said.

He depressed the bar and ran through.

The klaxon blared from nearby in a *bwoop-bwoop-bwoop*—just one speaker, not a whole raft of them.

Jules clanged up the steel steps two at a time, the bag on his back ridiculously heavy, pulling on his shoulders and chest, rubbing welts into the skin. His thighs protested under the strain, like carrying a man up the switchback staircase. After one floor, he broke a sweat. After two, he was short of breath. After three, he halted. Listened.

People were following.

One floor to go.

He pressed on, reaching the middle of the staircase with an exit door. He pushed through this and waited in a passage that lit up automatically. It, too, was alarmed and set off a muted *bwoop-bwoop-bwoop* ahead of him.

Meaning there could be someone coming to investigate.

Jules didn't wait. This two-step exit was his only choice. Before going out the last door, he pulled his pack off, found what he needed inside, and heaved it back on. Then he dropped his scarf so it looked like a neckerchief, opened the final door, and emerged into a bright channel with men's and women's washrooms, plus a baby changing room. As soon as Jules stepped out, a mustachioed security guard approached.

He was around fifty and armed, but the gun remained holstered. As he neared, his hand reached slowly for the piece.

"I found these." Jules offered a handful of cylindrical seals, six fitting into his cupped hands. "Some guy dropped them."

The guard came closer, hand on the butt of his gun, unclasping it, angling that hip away from Jules. "On knees."

Jules pointed behind him. "The guy! The guy who lost these, he went that way!"

The guard shifted his attention to the door, open on its jamb. He looked back at Jules. "Guy?"

Jules figured the man spoke a smattering of English, but not enough to hold a conversation. Added to the unusual figure of Jules, there was more than likely an alert out for anything suspicious.

"On knees," the guard said again, now curling his fingers around the gun, ready to draw.

A pair of women in their sixties rounded the corner, gasped at the scene, and the guard spoke to them in Striovian without taking his eyes off Jules. They backed away.

Jules now had little choice. He would have to hurt this guy. This guy, just doing his job, who'd go home and have to explain to his wife why he'd been fired—

"Oh, my, there you are!" Bridget trotted into view, her best *gosh-darn* Alabama twang in full swing.

The guard stood aside so she could pass, his eyes darting, assessing if this newcomer was a threat.

In Striovian, Bridget said, "I am Dr. Carson. I was hoping to have time to study some of your rarer finds."

No one was good enough to learn a new tongue fluently in a matter of days, but she'd rehearsed thirty-four phrases on the way over, with Jules replying phonetically to help her understand possible responses. Even with his higher-than-average capacity for learning, Bridget far surpassed him in languages.

As she pretended to notice Jules for the first time, she added another practiced phrase. "These shouldn't be out in the open like this. They're kept locked away in the vaults." She addressed the rent-a-cop directly. "Is this what the alert is about? If you can take these to your boss, he will be extremely happy."

This was always one of their backup plans. If Jules couldn't sneak out the way they came in, he'd have to escape via the public domain. And that meant "bamboozling" anyone they came across, as Charlie had put it.

The guard responded to Bridget, words Jules didn't catch, but Bridget nodded sagely. She replied, and whatever she said worked, as the guard now accepted the seals from Jules's outstretched hands and adopted a sense of urgency as he turned from them.

Bridget offered Jules her smaller backpack and in Striovian asked, "Would you mind my things, James?"

Jules replied with one of the very few Striovian phrases he'd learned. "Yes, ma'am."

Bridget accompanied the nervous guard away while Jules slipped into the men's lavatory.

In the bathroom, Jules accessed the hidden pocket in Bridget's bag and switched his clothes for ones that didn't look like he'd crawled through a sewer. He fitted the extendible baton up one sleeve of his new sweatshirt, the grappling hook with elastic bungee cord up the other and strapped on his belt containing a series of miniature flashbangs. Usually, the belt also contained six throwing knives too, which he'd left at home.

Knocking someone out with gas, anesthetic, or even a choke-hold was nothing compared to stabbing an innocent cop or security guy. He'd rather serve the time.

Next, able to move freely among the tourists, he needed to exit via an unconventional route.

The pair who'd chased him up from the catacombs had already rushed by, their footsteps and urgent whispers loud past the porcelain-laden bathroom. Jules now slipped out and mingled with people exploring the nation's physical history.

Security was searching bags and no doubt they would cover the exits.

It was a shame someone sounded the alert. The original plan to depart as tourists would have been far simpler.

Never mind. At least the fresh outfit gave him time.

The bag weighed just as heavily as before, but he glided along, acting as if it was clothing. He'd dried his sweat in the bathroom, but that wouldn't prevent more from forming if he had to exert himself. In fact, the pinpricks waiting to leak out burdened him all along the museum's track, which behaved like an Ikea store's layout; they were long, winding, and ushering people past every item of interest in an elongated series of S-shapes.

At the apex of one of these curving channels, a frosted window allowed natural light to filter through, but no actual view of the outside world. Even without the visual cues, Jules assessed he was in position.

He paid great attention to the two-foot statue beside this window: a woman wielding a sword against a demon, carved from a block of dark rock and polished to a high shine so it seemed black against the cream wall.

Officially, this was the ground floor, Striovia using the UK-style numbering for the stories—ground, then first, second, third, et cetera. However, the way the castle was constructed now meant there was the equivalent of a three-story drop to the road bordering the building.

A family of Russian-speakers made *hmm* noises that suggested Jules was hogging this exhibit. Not wishing to cause a fuss, he shifted aside with a placating smile. The family moved in, reading the plaque.

A woman's scream echoed across the floor.

It appeared Bridget was right; escorting the guard to the restricted area meant she was ordered not to enter, so she could leave, feigning offense at being excluded.

As all attention flew in that direction, Jules mounted the windowsill and plucked his multi-tool from one pocket and a suction cup from another. He stuck the sucker to the pane, flipped out the glass cutter from its housing, and drew a vertical rectangle large enough for him to climb through. With a wiggle and a tug, the glass came loose and the cold breeze swirled in.

He checked all was well with Bridget as she hopped about near the exit, insisting a huge goddamn rat just scurried over her feet. A guard, dressed and armed like the one she'd furnished with information about the seals, offered calming body language, which Bridget followed, then strode outside in a huff.

In a flash, Jules hopped up onto the windowsill and calculated the length of bungee cord he would need to reach the ground. When he added the backpack's weight, he realized he'd made a serious error.

The cord's tensile strength would not take the combination of Jules and the bag. At least, not the way he normally used it— namely dropping straight down, allowing the elastic to slow him to land safely. It would either snap or the claws on the secure end would bow and slip from the housing.

Commotion resolved, the Russian family turned back to the female demon slayer and chatted among themselves until the little girl noticed Jules, stuck on the windowsill, working out one final possibility. It had taken twice as long as usual.

"Hey." He waved at the girl.

The girl's family all looked around as Jules pulled the scarf up over his lower face, then leaped from the window, out into the morning chill.

Having fed out and tied off a length, with the bungee cord already in his hand, Jules threw the grappling claw end like a javelin. The line trailed behind as he dropped, the rucksack's added heft spinning him like a tortoise so he faced the sky.

Clouds gathered, gray ones, preparing for rain.

The claw shot through the bent arm of the thirty-foot-high statue of Queen Ana-Maria Otvos, pinged off her face and pulled taut against the crook of her elbow. Jules jerked at first, but the elasticity allowed his shoulder to remain in place. He brought his other hand to the cord for balance and stability. Gravity dragged him downward. The rope slowed his descent and yanked him away at an angle and his stomach loop-de-looped as the swing sped up.

Although the courtyard around this side was deserted, the entrance out front attracted dozens of visitors every hour. Therefore, Jules needed to time the next part just right.

Twisting against the bulk on his back, he used his hips first, as if whipping them around for a martial arts turn, and the rucksack full of stone followed.

Unchecked, the turn would spin him through three-hundred-and-sixty degrees. But since the asphalt rushed up at him, he could run in mid-air. As the tightening cord stopped him hurtling at full speed, slowing him virtually to a stop, his feet hit the ground harder than he expected, jarring his knee a little, but not so much that he collapsed under the weight of his landing.

The bungee held.

If he'd dropped straight down, he'd calculated an eighty-five percent chance of it snapping, but the curve of his descent spread the tension along the whole rope rather than a single section. He'd hoped to touch down seamlessly, exactly at the point he commenced walking, but the tough impact made him limp.

He left the homemade—and therefore untraceable—device to

the security services, and pulled his scarf down, hurried from behind the massive sculpture's plinth, and mingled with the crowd.

Trying to hide both the limp and the weight of his pack, he passed out through the open courtyard and linked arms with Bridget as she joined him. They became just another couple among hundreds of people.

Glancing behind, the museum doors were now closed and armed personnel—paramilitary cops, not security guards—manned the entrance.

Jules and Bridget dashed across the street. No one had spotted them, but it was only a matter of time. He couldn't fight with the bag on, and he couldn't expect Bridget to carry it.

"Okay, ready?" Bridget asked.

"For what?"

"Charlie's directing us. Can't you hear?"

Jules checked his ear. The subvocal bud was missing. "Damn, must've come out when I left the window."

"*Left the window.*" Bridget guided him into a small hat shop full of colorful headwear. She bade the elderly lady at the counter *hello* in Striovian, then carried on through the back into a cramped kitchen, ignoring the lady's protests. "You make falling three stories sound casual."

"I try my best."

Bridget rolled her eyes and depressed the fire exit's crash bar, taking them out into an alley where a blue Sierra Cosworth waited. "You try your best? Great. Now let me try mine."

CHAPTER
FIFTEEN

While Bridget slipped in behind the wheel and sparked the engine to life, Jules secured the rucksack in the rear's footwell, then hopped into the passenger seat. Bridget faced forward, cold and professional, as if she'd done this a hundred times. Her stern eyes focused ahead.

She crawled the car along the urban passage, wide enough for two cars of this size but narrowed by the presence of dumpsters and other detritus.

Careful. Don't draw attention.

To Jules, she said, "The sirens weren't for us. It's Toby on his way back. Military choppers are inbound." She gripped the wheel. Big breath. "Mission aborted. Charlie, talk to me."

Bridget pulled the ancient muscle car to the end of the alley and obeyed Charlie's instruction in her ear to turn right into a street lined with bars, small restaurants and takeout places offering gyros and kebabs and, oddly, cheesy fries. She kept the engine in the low revs, its growl pulsing, ready to roar.

Jules hadn't spoken in the minute since they'd started driving. That wasn't unusual for him, though. Annoying, sure, but not unusual.

Unfortunately for him, she needed to make small talk before broaching a more sensitive subject. "We'll have another chance."

"Sure."

"Maybe they'll find a solution."

"He's done." Jules looked out the window. "The plan was flawed."

"How so?"

They reached the junction, taking them farther from the castle, where Bridget turned left onto a channel leading to a dual carriageway—like a freeway back home—heading out of the city.

"Too many strands," Jules said. "Should have planned it longer."

"His court date was today." Bridget kept the car just below the dual carriageway's seventy-kilometers-per-hour speed limit, the two-liter turbo begging to be let loose. "Had to be now."

"Could've boosted him later. Alfonse could've sorted out a new identity, a solid one. Or we could've left him."

She'd heard some unemotional lines from Jules before, but this set off a hot lance of anger. "How can you *say* that?"

He turned to face her. "This was not about returning the Sumerian seals. This was about robbing the Striovians of theirs."

"No. No, Jules, I..."

"Think about your next words, Bridget. I know you're an honest person. I even got close to sticking around back when I left my bangle for you guys. But I know people in New York now. And while I get to chit-chat and shoot the breeze, or whatever the phrase is for inane small talk, you're the closest folk I got to actual *friends*. So don't lie to me."

Bridget had no idea he felt that way. Wasn't sure he felt *anything*. She swallowed back her annoyance. "It started with the seals—"

"Slow down."

She stared farther down the road, the city now behind them, fields spreading either side. A line of cops a half-mile away slowed traffic but didn't stop it completely. The searches appeared cordial, seemingly random.

"They're trying to spook us into running," Jules said. "Can't search us all."

"Think they'll pull us over?"

"There's like fifteen black dudes in this whole country. What do you think?"

"Charlie?"

Charlie asked her to stand by. Five seconds later, she said, "There's no turnoff on this side. You'll need to pull a yooey."

Yooey.

Short for "U-turn," Bridget figured, her language skills coming in handy yet again. "We have to turn around," she told Jules.

"They'll see."

"I got this."

"You sure?"

"In my town growing up, even rich kids know two things: hunting, and driving."

A quarter mile from the line of cars, the first gap in the fencing, she turned the wheel and mounted the grass at a non-conspicuous forty kph, unsure what that translated to in miles per hour. Felt like about twenty-five. She executed the maneuver smoothly, able to join the opposite direction without fuss. Both she and Jules craned to check the rear mirrors.

No one following.

Not yet, anyway.

"The seals," Jules said. "You were telling me how this wasn't a setup?"

Bridget kept alternating between the road ahead and the mirrors.

Charlie said, "Keep right, take the slip road. And I'd love to hear about this non-setup, too."

Bridget pulled off, just as the first blue lights commenced spinning a long way behind. "Gotta push this now."

As soon as the slip road bore a curve, Bridget popped the

clutch, dropped the stick a gear, and the acceleration pressed her back in the seat.

Blue and red lights flashed behind them, closer now, confirming the pursuit.

On a straight road devoid of buildings, penned in on either side by hedgerows, Bridget gunned the engine, and the turbo powered them to one-hundred-and-fifty kilometers per hour—around ninety-five mph.

"Damn, Bridge," Jules said. "You can see that bend up ahead, right?"

Instead of braking, Bridget dropped it a gear, lurched forward, but lost little torque. She took the bend and accelerated out of it, changing back up to fifth.

Gunfights turned her to Jello. A fistfight, well, she stayed out of the way. But this... she'd never had to perform like this for LORI before. Her vision, her reactions, her simple awareness surprised her. She even marveled at how swiftly the urban became rural out there.

"I didn't lie to you," Bridget said. "We really came here for the Sumerian seals, to return them and, sue me, claim the reward. We need cash to keep going."

She yanked the wheel and again dropped a gear to take a corner. No cops in sight.

She steered them back onto the straight. "But Toby looked into what kinda gift we could give, and he learned about them finding other seals. Ones *similar* to the Sumerians'. Toby gutted the fiction and when we worked out the truth, he *had* to see them. After what we found in India, how could we not?"

She waited for Jules to nod or acknowledge he understood. He said nothing, gave nothing away.

"We brought in Alfonse, convinced him the Sumerian seals were pre-biblical artifacts, but they'd be of interest to the Vatican. He made some calls, and yeah, they were interested. But the presence of the older seals, the permafrost ones—"

"Next field," Charlie said.

Bridget decelerated swiftly as an open gate to the right came into view, pressing Jules forward into his seatbelt, eliciting another, "Damn, Bridge."

She smiled at that. "The other seals gave us added incentive."

"To rob them," Jules said flatly.

The car juddered on the pitted track running alongside the field, which swung inward toward the center where a helicopter idled.

"To investigate them," Bridget said. "Toby wanted to talk them around. The backup plan… to take back the Sumerian seals… was just that. A backup. And we never got to use it."

"Until now."

Bridget supposed it was as good a time as any to ask, "Did you take some? Of the others?"

Jules stared at the chopper, at Dan and Harpal waving to them as the rotors warmed up. "No. I stayed on mission."

Bridget's jaw tensed. She adjusted her grip. "That's fine. Cool."

They pulled up. As soon as they got out, the cop cars streamed into the field. Four of them.

Two halted at the entrance, spilling officers who immediately drew their guns. They couldn't fire yet due to the lead cars rumbling directly at the escaping fugitives.

"Nice of you to make it." Dan ushered them on board.

"Here." Jules handed him the rucksack full of stone.

Dan's arm wavered only a second before he lifted it to his shoulder with relative ease.

In the helicopter, Bridget locked the belt across her, and Jules accepted the bag of seals back from Dan, placed it at his feet, and strapped himself in. Dan piled in straight after.

The lead cop cars pulled up fifty yards away. Their voices barely penetrated the engine and downdraft, but their handguns —aimed at the chopper—left little room for interpretation.

Still, Dan couldn't help twirling his finger near his ear and shrugging.

Can't hear you. Sorry.

The rotors were at full speed now, and with Harpal still pulling the belt across him, Dan lifted off.

Guns fired, and Bridget jumped in shock. She pulled her knees to her chest as her heart pounded faster than at any point at the wheel.

Bullets pinged off the hull, hit just behind the rear seats, but within seconds they were too high for an accurate shot from a pistol. The nose dipped, and soon, they were flying directly toward the border once more.

Their mission was a failure.

CHAPTER
SIXTEEN

TARASIVNA CASTLE

With his wrists secured in steel handcuffs behind his back, Toby Smith gave no resistance to the men gripping one arm apiece. They marched him from the vehicle into the elevator beside the loading dock. No one spoke.

Since returning to this central base, Toby had stewed for thirty minutes under the gaze of the pair, retreating into himself and sweating profusely. He tried to ignore the discomfort by reciting poetry in his head and replaying the things he'd learned so far. Mostly, he rehearsed how much he would yell at the Institute members for attempting such a foolhardy ploy as breaking him out of a secretive government facility—a government whose separation between police and State lurked between hazy and nonexistent.

As they were all so keen to remind him at times of great stress and disagreement, the Lost Origins Recovery Institute was not the military. That also meant standing orders like not risking jail to break someone else out were not exactly binding. If he won his freedom somehow, he planned on making them all sign a personal contract of sorts. One pledging to obey instructions like that from this day forward, a formal promise to one another, to which Toby believed they would adhere.

In the elevator, sweat trickled down Toby's back. His groin was moist too, perspiration spreading to his thighs, and he effected a waddle of sorts to fend off chafing.

Chafing.

Forget the chafing. The failed rescue might damn him to more extreme interrogation methods than a bit of red skin between his thighs.

The elevator doors split open, revealing Zimina Yanovna, now shod of her tactical gear, alongside the grizzled Igoravich.

"Toby," Zimina said. "I do not understand how you thought you would survive this."

"I planned nothing, I—" He halted his speech as Zimina raised a finger to her lips.

"This way."

The men accompanying him held tighter, one pinching his skin, so he cried out, "Ow," and when Zimina aimed a frown his way, the guy eased up. *Slightly.*

At the vault she took him to only days earlier—but now felt like weeks—Toby was not shocked to find technicians combing the place, the door wide open, and the shelves nearest the viewing window virtually empty.

He said, "Ah."

"Yes, Toby." Zimina wandered inside and barked in Striovian, clearing the room of everyone but her, Toby, and Igoravich. "As you say, *ah*. Although, I expect you know all about this, no?"

"I know nothing, Zimina—"

Igoravich clipped Toby around the back of the head. Zimina only narrowed her eyes rather than chastising him.

"General Yanovna." Toby winced at the sharp pain. "I'm sorry. If the incident outside was down to my team, my friends, I assure you I had nothing to do with it. The opposite, in fact. They should have left me to your judicial system. I've done nothing wrong, after all. Nothing... particularly criminal, anyway."

"You maintain your innocence? After *this*?" She strode to the vault door, arm lancing toward the shelves formerly stocked with Iraqi heritage. "They stole almost all of them."

Igoravich shoved Toby from behind. To keep from falling flat on his face, Toby trotted inside the storage unit and ran his gaze over the length of the room.

"Only the Sumerian ones," Toby said.

Zimina scowled, taking a deep breath. "You say that like it matters."

Toby feared antagonizing her; that would also antagonize the large gentleman who appeared to serve as her right-hand man since the incident. "I cannot say for sure my institute was not behind this. But if they were, they were simply repatriating goods looted *illegally* during an *illegal* invasion and sold on—*illegally*—for profit."

"And you do not *profit* from their return?"

Toby focused ahead where the Reaper Seal stood on its shelf. "We earn our money through honorable means."

"They were not interested in this?" Zimina slipped on a pair of cotton gloves and strode to the shelf where Toby's attention lay. "You talk of Iraq's plunder. What of ours? What of the many treasures taken from Striovia throughout the ages? From our founding Queen who journeyed to Egypt with gifts for Cleopatra, and fell prey to traitors in her absence, to the Justinian purge, the Vatican's conflict, right up to the Soviets stripping us of our very identities? Like this." She plucked the large seal from the shelf and returned to Toby. "Grabbed by the Romans as if it were theirs to possess. *This* is our heritage, Toby Smith. *It* is to be protected. If we do not, nothing will stop our powerful northern neighbor from absorbing us again."

Toby stared at the object in her hands, marveling again at the artistry and workmanship, but instead of cowering at her assertions, he said, "And it's still here. My people would not take anything they couldn't justify. Morally."

Zimina shook her head. "Morally." A glance at Igoravich. Back to Toby. "I wonder how their *morals* will serve them when I demand the maximum sentence for your crimes."

"You might suspect their involvement, but I have been incommunicado for days. I know your word holds a lot of sway over the courts, but you still have to prove my intent."

"Not for your original crimes."

"But I offered to cooperate!"

Zimina pushed past Toby and out into the anteroom, where she placed the larger seal onto the table in the center of the space. Igoravich gestured for Toby to join her, and he again obeyed.

She said, "Talk. Now."

Toby wanted to touch the artifact, but his hands remained bound. Less than an hour earlier, he had resigned himself to cooperation, so there was little in the way of a sting or a pang of guilt as he capitulated. "These things, the rock, the substance within... it does something. You cannot possibly comprehend how dangerous they can be."

"Why can I not comprehend it?"

"I have seen things recently for which I have extrapolated theories, but no solid explanation. Until we understand why similar objects like this behave as they do, there is no understanding."

"Because I am a meek little woman?" She adopted the soft, mocking tone he liked so much. Playful. Lacking the edge of the past few days.

"No, nothing to do with your gender—"

"Or because we are a dumb Eastern European nation, ready to lie down and be swallowed whole by the snake of Mother Russia?"

"Fine, I'll explain. But please do not allow your man here to strike me if you fail to believe me."

Zimina nodded.

Toby coughed, then commenced. "If this 'Reaper Seal' and the scroll case are formed of the same substance as an item we came into possession of recently, they hold properties no one can yet define. The items appear genetically coded to an individual, causing several possible reactions."

Zimina glanced from the seal to Toby, a deep frown forming. "What reactions?"

"A glow, for one." He shrugged somewhat helplessly, unable to corroborate his words. "There is also a violent reaction with saltwater. When in contact with both a gentleman we befriended and the ocean, the stone generates a kind of… power. Electricity. Uncontrolled thus far."

"Which gentleman did you befriend?" Zimina fluttered her eyelids. "Someone worthy of opening our scroll? I'd love to meet him."

"I know it's hard to believe." Toby had expected this response. He wished Jules had been there to show her, to prove there was more to his interest than simple profit. "But please, do not discard me."

"Discard you?" She nodded at the door. "Denis."

Plainly some pre-arranged order, the soldier marched to the door, closed it tight, and flicked off the lights. It left only the soft illumination from the storage unit's observation window.

"I'm sorry," Toby said for what felt like the millionth time. "But I am not someone who can activate this."

"Oh, I didn't expect you were."

In the dark room, Toby made out Zimina removing one glove.

She touched her bare skin to the cylindrical artifact. "Is the glow you mention something like this?"

The Reaper Seal lit up. A substance beneath the rocky exterior shone a bright green, streaming out in dazzling beams of light.

Toby's jaw literally gaped, his whole body slack, near weightless. "My… god…"

"Goddess, actually," Zimina said.

Toby's eyes bulged so much they almost escaped their sockets. "You are like Jules. Like the ancient shaman…"

"We calculated it was genetic but have not yet isolated the markers that react with the substance. We are not even sure if it is chemical or biological. The stones are inert without my living genetic tissue applied, so we cannot examine it without my touching. But if you remove something..."

"You must create a circuit with the item. Your living genetic material and your brainwaves. Or whatever quantum explanation there is for observing proton behavior."

In the green glow, Zimina frowned, the seal between her and Toby. "Quantum physics?"

"Yes." Toby's lungs behaved as if he'd run up four flights of stairs. "There is a famous experiment referred to as the 'slit test' where, if you fire light through two vertical slits and observe the pattern on a target on the other side, the photons land in a random pattern. But when the physicists moved away for a break, they allowed the experiment to run. When they returned, the photons had landed in the same shape as the two slits. Watching the experiment continue, they returned to their scattershot approach."

"I have heard of this. Vaguely. I thought it was just... fiction."

"May I posit that perhaps you have been using geologists? Chemists too? Not theoretical physicists."

"Still, they should have been aware of this possibility." Zimina turned her back, facing a blank wall, hand remaining on the seal. "Captain Igoravich, please unshackle Mr. Smith. *For the moment.*" As Igoravich unlocked the cuffs, Zimina said, "Toby, join me."

Toby went through the process of rubbing his wrists, flexing his elbows and rolling his shoulders as he moved beside the general, observing as she placed her other bare hand on the object.

In more defined quality than the clay impressions, the light projected the seal's image onto the wall. Again, Toby's mouth fell open.

The scene stretched over the surface in almost perfect detail, like an overexposed photograph or expertly built diorama. The Death character, his two nude companions, the worshiping masses, the crop... Zimina rotated the seal in her hands, the pictures emerging as they came into view. The sun turned into the circle pictograph with the zigzag blemish, clearly intentional by the artist.

It was more than a little frightening.

"I have long held the belief that these objects possess true power," Zimina intoned. "I can feel it coursing through my hands. It never fades. Never changes. If we can tap this energy, locate its source, maybe we will supplant oil from Russia and the Middle East. Or create something to make any would-be invader tremble."

Toby gazed up at Zimina, her attention fully upon the seal. "We hypothesize that a people who lived in isolated pockets of humanity created these objects. Savage beasts and humanity's oldest ancestors populated the world beyond theirs; no wonder they spent so little time venturing outside their intelligent communities. We are, however, certain their artifacts indicate *humans*, and probably share a common ancestor with us, having evolved independently. But we believe they were not about conquest. Or power. This is a story. Information. *Knowledge*."

"And as an old spy like you must know, knowledge most certainly brings power."

His standard response to an accusation of being a spy, former or current, was always denial, but he saw no point now. "If we can study these, if we work together, instead of prose-cuting me over some perceived insult, there may be more to learn."

"Lights." Zimina placed the seal back on the table and let go as Igoravich flicked the fluorescent tubes back on. "Toby. Your knowledge of these items is impressive, and I cannot believe your being here is a coincidence. You wanted to steal them. To interpret the pictures and make your map. You wanted to follow the path, wherever it leads, and you wanted to hoard this knowledge for yourself."

"No, I—" Toby caught himself in a lie, one Zimina would see through, so told the unfettered truth. "I was interested in these, yes, but I had no way to confirm it was what you just showed me.

I was curious. I would have asked for a loan, for a partnership. I am not a thief."

Zimina held herself still, hands braced either side of the Reaper Seal. "I wish I had left the old days behind. The days of threats from inside our country and out. But I think I knew, deep down, they would always return." Her glance at Igoravich was answered with a slow, respectful nod. "I *will* find out why, exactly, you want them. If they lead somewhere, to some greater knowledge of Striovian destiny, I *will* retrieve it."

She then produced the stone scroll container with the Latin inscription, seeming almost bored by it. When she clasped it with one hand, the dull glow emanated as Toby expected.

Zimina bowed her head, then swallowed. "I was never sure if it was worth the risk. If I should take the chance. So worried that it was hubris driving me, feeling foolish to think myself 'worthy.' We *believed* 'worthy' meant a quirk in DNA... but without cast iron *proof* of the DNA theory, we never dared try to open this. Order are orders, after all."

With her other hand, she twisted the 800-year-old artifact, and it popped open, splitting at the halfway point.

No fanfare.

No ceremony.

No acid dissolving the contents.

Just a look of glee from Zimina, who donned her cotton gloves again to fish out the parchment.

Toby almost reached out to stop her, to urge caution, but could not. He watched, helpless to intervene.

She unspooled the rolled paper-like item. "Latin again."

"May I?" Toby shuffled his feet in the least impatient way he could manage.

"Circulus ostendam in virtue Dominus."

"That's..."

"Thank you, Toby, but I can read Latin myself. And it makes sense, does it not?"

Toby wanted to approach, to appeal again to her sense of

reason, but it seemed a foolish move. She knew what it meant, as did Toby. But what fascinated him the most was not the Latin, but the scratched shapes scribbled above, which Zimina appeared to have ignored. It was a language he'd seen before, one that predated any known writing. Perhaps that was why the curator glossed over it in favor of what she knew.

"The circle will show the power of God." Zimina stood straight. Shoulders back, feet together. "Captain Igoravich. I need an audience with the President. I am exercising my option to re-enlist. I am no longer a ceremonial general. I will take up my post as a senior officer in the Striovian military. Effective immediately."

CHAPTER
SEVENTEEN
AUGUST 18, EVENING

SICILY

Jules saw Alfonse Luca as less of a big teddy bear than the ladies of LORI did. He was a real contradiction, a man who yearned to escape stereotyping yet bundled himself away surrounded by what people would expect from an ex-mafia don. Now retired to brew his own wine, perhaps Alfonse had aspired to that cliché and manufactured it, believing a new life would grant peace from the demons that surely plagued him.

But Bridget and Charlie treated him like an uncle who'd over-dosed on extrovert juice, while Jules, Dan, and Harpal stood back and allowed the three to greet one another with hugs and triple kisses.

"And the boys!" Alfonse boomed, his right hand straight out, his left positioned like an ax ready to descend upon the first handshake.

Jules took the hit, grasping the jowly Sicilian's right hand and pumping hard. He braced and, sure enough, the left slapped forth, trapping him in a double grip. The left hand retracted and patted Jules's shoulder.

"Good to see you, Alfonse," Jules said as brightly as he could.

Socializing still didn't come naturally, but another reason Jules held back, in ways Bridget and Charlie didn't, was that Alfonse needed to be the alpha male in any situation. If he was not, he retreated into himself and became more difficult to deal with. At least, that was Jules's read on him. Either consciously or subconsciously, Dan and Harpal acted the same way as Jules.

Both endured the alpha-handshakes, and all five followed Alfonse up the path to his villa in the center of his vineyard, each lugging a backpack.

The vineyard itself could have been cut from a Mediterranean postcard, sweeping lines of grapes surrounding a white-walled villa with a terracotta tile roof, all overlooking the ocean glittering in the distance. The only things ruining the vista were the half-dozen men patrolling with submachine guns and sidearms.

"Wine?" Alfonse offered as they passed into his wide-open kitchen, where a raft of wine glasses and a carafe of deep red waited.

Again, the scene was crafted, this time as the domain of a celebrity Italian chef. Although don't call Alfonse *Italian*. Ever.

"Thank you, no," Charlie said. "We've got a lot to talk about."

Alfonse pulled an exaggeratedly insulted face. "Come, come, it is my first crop!"

"Your wine?" Bridget said. "I thought it wouldn't be ready for another whole year."

Alfonse shrugged. "Organic grapes grow slower, but the fruit is so much sweeter."

"I'll take a glass," Jules said.

Alfonse beamed his way and boomed, "Wonderful!"

They needed Alfonse on side if he was to agree to their proposal.

Harpal also volunteered to try some, and Bridget joined him. Charlie eventually gave in, with only Dan abstaining.

"I'm more of a beer guy," he said.

Alfonse didn't seem perturbed now he'd roped in four-fifths of the team. They all drank together.

It was a little bitter, and Harpal did a good job of hiding his displeasure, while Bridget and Charlie managed a warm, "Mmmm," apiece. Jules remained neutral. He had no idea how to respond, finding the fruity kick not unpleasant.

Dan addressed Jules specifically. "So, how's that stuff corrupting your temple of a body?"

Jules threw him a grin. "Nicer than beer."

Alfonse took his time swallowing. Once he did, he gave his assessment. "Hmm. Not my best batch. But drinkable. Come. Let us move to the deck."

Outside the French doors to the patio, they settled on Alfonse's all-weather seating, clean cushions in place for the occasion. It was where the team had last assembled for Alfonse when he'd made them an offer. Now, they were the ones with the proposal. But first, business.

They each presented their bags, the heavy seals redistributed evenly depending on the strength of the Institute member, and they had been packed more carefully than during Jules's raid.

Alfonse unwrapped samples from each bag, laid them on the table, and examined one up close. "Marvelous. His Excellency will be pleased."

"You still giving these to the Pope?" Jules asked.

"Indirectly. My good friend, Cardinal Valdez, will take possession and inform his boss."

Charlie placed her glass down, half empty. "I'm sorry, Alfonse, but I have to ask. We thought these would be returned to Iraq."

Alfonse reached across Jules without apology and took Charlie's hands in his. "My dear, I am excited to bankroll these expeditions. But my penance for many, *many* misdeeds, no matter how excellent I was at them, is to serve *God*. I make no apologies for this." He released her hands and sat back, arms open, a cheery demeanor. "Friends, this world is falling apart. Our military man will have seen much to confirm this, yes?"

"Yeah, it's a dump." Dan sipped the water he settled for.

"Not quite yet." Alfonse chuckled for a single second, then his expression darkened. Jules sensed a longer speech approaching, and Alfonse duly delivered. "But it will be if we continue behaving the way *I* did for most of my life. Not caring for anyone but myself or my own family. This is why the world hurts now. This is why we have our Nazis rising again. Why Islamic terrorists think it is right to murder those who are *not like them.* And why governments of powerful countries impose their ways on weaker ones. These seals..." He swept his hand over the small cylinders before him. "They are a symbol of that chaos. A country invades another for no justifiable reason except to stamp on those people. No offense, Dan."

Dan, a veteran of that war, waved it off. He'd likely heard it before. Many times.

"But it does not stop there," Alfonse went on. "Some of the angry people in Baghdad, they regarded their own government as *'the other,'* the *not like them,* because they reigned above. Existed outside their lives. And because the government owned the museum, it was a beacon. Their revenge on their tyrant president was to plunder what they saw as his."

Jules was getting bored. Alfonse's monologues justifying his motives were, according to Dan on the way over, a regular appointment. As politely as he dared, Jules said, "Alfonse, can I just ask something?"

Alfonse gestured happily for Jules to proceed.

"Where does the Pope come into this?"

Alfonse's lips pressed together momentarily, perhaps considering if the interruption insulted him. He appeared to conclude it did not. "Good question, my friend." Alfonse stood, and the group let out a collective breath.

Perhaps Jules overstepped a mark. He had to work on this.

"The Pope," Alfonse said, re-wrapping the seals on the tabletop, "is an ambassador. Not only for Catholics, not only for Christianity as a whole... but for mankind. To people in Muslim countries, he embodies the West. He will return these items to Iraq. It will be as if the western Christian world has extended a hand in friendship, accepting the heritage of their Muslim cousins. If this gesture prevents just *one* angry young man in that part of the world from turning himself into a bomb, it is worth every penny. Every sacrifice."

Silence descended as Alfonse repacked the final seal.

"Toby," Jules said. "He's still in custody."

On his other side, Dan nudged Jules, trying to stop him speaking, from screwing up some form of manners that Jules couldn't see yet.

Alfonse nodded slowly, grimly. "Ah, yes, Toby."

"Leave no man behind," Jules said.

Dan bristled. "Hey, I told you about that crap. Don't say it unless you mean it."

"I want to get Toby."

"He means it's not interchangeable," Charlie said. "You make that promise for Toby, you make it for everyone."

Jules again didn't get the notion of a "code" to live by, a hard-wired philosophy, but he accepted some people believed in it. Military types, especially, needed that reassurance, that building of camaraderie.

"Sorry," Jules said. "I just wanna bring Toby out."

"Me too," Dan said.

The others nodded, focused on Alfonse, which the large Sicilian acknowledged.

"We can only think of one way to free him," Jules went on. "We need your help with that."

"I can help?"

"Thank you for funding his new legal team," Charlie said. "But I think their justice system is too tightly connected to the government. At best, the Brits can keep international pressure on them for a fair trial. But if *we* give them something in return, it'll be more likely to sway them. Jules has an idea he chose not to share with us yet."

"Anything." A sense of relief flowed from Alfonse. Maybe he genuinely felt guilty about Toby.

"The seals," Jules said. "They got others there. Different ones. Someone thought I'd automatically pick 'em up and bring 'em out." He looked pointedly at Bridget, who averted her eyes. "I didn't. They weren't the job."

"You could have ransomed them for Toby?" Alfonse said.

"Nah, I don't think they'd have gone for it."

"They wouldn't," Harpal said. "It'd make us the bad guys. They'd set the international antiquities cops on us in a heartbeat."

Alfonse squinted Harpal's way. "These other pieces..."

It was Bridget who piped up. "Those pieces were not part of the looting of the Museum of Baghdad. They're older. Dug out of permafrost, dating them to pre-Ice Age peoples, when it was thought the height of human ingenuity was the ability to bring down a mammoth, then boast about it in the form of a painting. It points to an older civilization, an intelligent one. Like the tomb. Like the bangles we used. The books we found."

Jules watched Bridget grow more uncomfortable, as she now had to admit something she hadn't wanted to before.

She repeated what she'd told Jules in the car, how Toby had come across these other seals, and excitedly added what she'd held back. "These bigger seals are similar in design to the Sumerian ones, but not identical. We think, when you place them together, you get a story. An instruction."

All watched her now, not just Jules.

"Toby wanted to take a look before telling us all about it," she said. "It was still a theory. But from what he showed me, the instruction was a message. Possibly... *possibly*..." She took a breath. "Possibly a map."

Deep breaths were inhaled around the table. Jules read their expressions as repressed anger and disappointment.

"I thought Toby was past keeping secrets," Charlie said.

"Old habits," Harpal replied.

Recriminations were pointless. Holding a grudge was pointless. What mattered was the *now*, and how this knowledge could help Toby.

Jules said, "Leading where?"

Bridget perked up, a chance to evade the ethical questions. "You know the Sumerian ones, and others like them, are used to finalize documents and seal chests with the sender's impression? The larger ones are much too big to use in such a way. We think they were for decoration, or to show a map or trail in relief. They'd dry the clay and paint it, giving the reader a clear impression. Jules, you saw..." Her words faded and she once more averted her gaze.

Jules didn't care about her guilt. He had thought maybe these people could be his first real friends, given all they'd been through, but they were just as illogical and duplicitous as those he'd acquainted himself with since returning to New York.

"I seen 'em," Jules said. "What's waiting for us?"

"I honestly don't know."

"Yeah, well, *honestly* ain't gonna cut it. You sent me in with incomplete intel. You hoped I'd go off book and take the other seals myself, and that fell flat. If you'd told me ahead of time, I coulda' worked something out, but you didn't. So, I gotta have more than that."

No one interrupted. Only Alfonse made any gesture of support, and that amounted to a patting of the air, trying to calm Jules.

"I can't say." Bridget swallowed what Jules guessed was a tear or two. "I don't know. We *can't* know. We just need to follow the trail, but—"

"But Jules didn't take the seals," Charlie finished for her.

Harpal glanced at Jules. "We don't have the intel we need."

Again, a thick silence descended as the group sat with their thoughts in the sunshine.

"It's plain old words when civilians say it," Dan said, "but I live it. *Leave no man behind*. It's a code made famous by the Marine Corps. I was a Ranger, but the principle applies. I want to rescue Toby. And I will. No matter what."

Harpal frowned. "What does that mean?"

"It means Alfonse has the contacts to get me a bunch of mercs. You guys head back to Brittany. Be my alibi. Watch stuff on my Netflix log-on, buy me some gear on my eBay account, have people from the town spot my car driving around. Bribe a barman to say I was there. Whatever."

"Dan, you don't have to," Jules said.

"These creeds are just a fancy saying to civilians, but it doesn't mean I can forget it."

"No." Jules took two sheets of plain folded paper from his back pocket. "I mean, you don't have to go all balls-out Rambo-commando to get Toby home." Jules unfolded the sheets and lay them flat, both legal pad-sized. "You guys forget I got a photographic memory?"

Everyone craned over the pencil sketches he'd made of the Reaper Seal and the inaccurate map of the world's northern hemisphere.

"We don't have the seals," Jules said. "But we got the map. If Alfonse is willing to back us, we're halfway there."

CHAPTER
EIGHTEEN
AUGUST 18, NOON

SRI SATHYA SAI HEART HOSPITAL - HIRUSH, INDIA

The hospital's triage station saw the unwashed masses of poor people, injured or writhing with illness, patiently waiting for a doctor. To the untrained eye, this would imply a mass outbreak or an accident had occurred, but Prihya Sibal understood it was just a Saturday. Nothing to do with the reason she'd been summoned.

And that question pressed heavily upon her: *why was she here?*

Closely followed by: *why the urgency?*

Dozens lined a waiting room, the stink of their sweat and bodily waste thick in the air, offset only marginally by the tang of disinfectant. These people worked, and to not work meant death, so ailments like cuts and nausea went untreated until the weekend, their symptoms and infections growing worse with every delay. Such was the way of the world.

Prihya held her gag reflex in check as she rushed through and waved a pass at the security guard, who buzzed her into the main building.

Here, the smell dissipated, but the wards on either side still contained what India's now unofficial caste system deemed *untouchables*, those born into poverty and destined to remain there, elevated to the positions of servants or cleaners if they were lucky.

It had only been in the past couple of decades that laws had been passed demanding even such lowly creatures as these be treated in hospitals when needed. And while Prihya knew, in her head, that such a system was wrong, she could not help but avert her eyes and increase her pace to be rid of them.

Prihya had few lofty ambitions in life. She was self-educated in the areas of true history, of alternative theories to the established order, and *officially* trained in the areas of architectural engineering and in search and rescue procedures. Her archaeology professor from the night school she attended still enjoyed sparring with her, at first dismissing her notions as conspiracy theorist nonsense and giving her a withering smile, as if feeling sorry for her inferior intellect. But she saw through his mask, inferred how he clearly found their debates engaging.

However, she was not one of those sad saps who bought into idiotic theories solely to separate herself from the establishment. She did not buy into the notion of flat earth, nor that aliens built the pyramids, nor of lizard creatures secretly running the world. But equally, she never assumed something was right just because it *sounded* right. If she evaluated it was true, or the possibility of truth weighed greater than a falsehood, the human race deserved to know.

Such aspects of our history should not be hoarded by those with power.

And now, she was a part of the cover-up.

There were several reasons for her agreeing to not go public, mainly that no one would believe her at present, anyway.

Photography was forbidden on the site where she currently worked, mobile phones confiscated upon arrival. Prihya's job was in her capacity as a structural expert, a troubleshooter in digging through avalanches and destroyed buildings. She was used to running rescue ops in the aftermath of earthquakes or construction accidents. It was only through pushing herself forward to gain experience on archaeological digs that meant she'd wound up there.

Throughout the careful digging, they had liberated artworks and writings that Prihya could not catalog herself, which was unusual. She could identify, if not translate, many ancient texts from her own part of the world and across Persia and Europe. This was a newly discovered language; one no modern person had seen before. It was all inventoried and shipped off by an odd British man with a hooked nose and an attitude that suggested he reigned over the territory like it was still the time of the Raj, and he'd soon be hopping on a boat home to report to Queen Victoria on how well the savages in India were serving her. He'd lasted a week before being recalled, a mere three days after they discovered the survivors.

It had been Prihya's sharp ears that located the two men: one conscious, one comatose. Limbs were crushed, a head cracked and lolling, but the hearts still pumped, so she'd organized the crew. After four hours of bracing the surrounding slabs and boulders, the workers freed the pair.

And both were placed under arrest.

On the fifth floor of the hospital, Prihya's pass allowed her through to the intensive care unit. The ward smelled more strongly of disinfectant than the fecal stench of below, and the genders were kept separate, although only by one corridor. Twelve beds in each ward held a prone figure, all hooked up to one machine or another, in varying degrees of consciousness. All was clean. No one moaned or coughed.

And no one questioned her as she passed through.

In the final room, at the dark end of the corridor, a police officer stood guard. He checked Prihya's ID and radioed inside. Someone within unlocked three bolts and the door opened.

Prihya stepped inside and a plain-clothes female officer— Prihya guessed that's what she was—patted her down while the male who opened the door watched. A quick discussion between the pair out of earshot ended with nods of agreement.

"Ten minutes." The woman departed, followed by her male colleague.

The door closed but did not lock, so Prihya decided the pair must be standing outside. All that was left was for her to figure out exactly what this place was, and why she'd been summoned.

The room was the size of one of the wards containing twelve beds, but it was almost vacant. The lights were out. The floor was so clean, the sheen reflected the pattern from the ceiling. Two beds stood against opposite walls, curtains pulled around both. Light from outside cast a dirty hue through the panes at the end, generating silhouettes onto both units, one large man lying flat and unmoving, while on the other side the occupant hit a button to raise himself to a sitting position with a loud whirring.

"Hello?" The man spoke with a light US accent which Prihya recognized partly because her own English teacher had been American, but she also remembered his voice from the site.

He was one of the people she'd pulled from the rubble.

She approached the curtain of the moving man, her footfalls squeaking rather than clopping, preparing herself mentally for whatever awaited her.

Both men had been truly messed up when she'd recovered them, closer to death than life. She couldn't believe either still lived, but it seemed they'd found a coffin or sarcophagus in which they'd hid. As the thousands of tons of temple and hillside crashed down, their salvation cracked and one side crumbled beneath the weight, chunks falling around them large enough to create air pockets, and to not pancake across the level. It was a miracle she'd witnessed before in other disasters, but never tired of.

This one, for some reason, was as much frightening as awe-inspiring. And although she'd sworn to never be intimidated by someone in power, and that she would reveal any truths the government or established archaeological order tried to suppress, this felt different. This was something she had to brave, to push on through.

She swept the curtain aside and stood at the end of the bed, her gaze firm, arms folded. "I'm here."

The bed's occupant had long blond hair and was tall and pale. His legs had been crushed and one arm too, all of which she had assumed would've been amputated.

He caught her staring at the shriveled limb. "Oh yes, the arm. Close one, that. They were going to lop it off, but I got the feeling back in my fingers after a day and had to insist they give it a chance. And now look." He curled the fingers into a half-fist. "Impressed?"

To Prihya, veteran of a dozen small and major incidents in which people lost their lives and their limbs long before she arrived on scene, moving those fingers was...

"Impossible," she said aloud.

The man didn't quite smile. It was more of a satisfied twist of the lips, a lizard spying a fly. It made Prihya step back.

"Please, Ms. Sibal," he said. "Although I am regenerating rather more quickly than the average Schmo or Joe, I am still at something of a disadvantage. My friend over there wasn't so fortunate."

Prihya glanced behind her, shocked to find the large man in the bed conscious, observing her without moving.

"They will be performing a third surgery on his spine later this week, but I'm sorry to say his speech function isn't quite what it was."

"He's conscious too?" Prihya said.

"But not without lasting damage. Isn't that correct, my friend?"

The man in the bed grunted.

The blond man said, "Time for sleep."

The patient opposite them closed his eyes.

The blond man cast his gaze away, first at the floor, then at Prihya. "I hear you are very bright. Inquisitive."

She wasn't entirely sure that she wanted to continue this conversation. Frankly, she'd be happy returning to the foothills to carry on pulling insignificant slates and stone fingers from the ground, keep her big mouth shut, and at the end of her contract forget everything she saw. No way was this a safe situation. No way was it right.

"Ask," the man said.

"Ask what?" She made sure her voice sounded firm, strong.

"The question you need to answer."

"How is your arm healing?"

"Oh, no, no, no. Not a boring one like that." He wagged the first finger on his all-but-crippled arm. "Ask the big question. *The* interesting one."

She could run, hit the door and tell the police officers she wanted to leave. They wouldn't try to stop her, would they?

And yet.

"What is that place?" she asked. "The one they pulled you from?"

"Hmm." The man traced a faint smile. "You're getting warmer, Ms. Sibal."

"Who built it?"

"Very warm."

She thought harder, splitting her brain between her escape route and pleasing a person who possessed enough sway to remove her from a government contract to visit him in a hospital bed.

She said, "What do you want with me?"

The man's good hand shot into the air with a thumbs up. "Congratulations, you win the star prize!"

Prihya swallowed back an odd sense of pride, hiding her reaction. No point showing him her true face yet. "What is the star prize?"

"I bought out your contract. You now have the option of returning to digging in the dirt or working with me."

"Doing what?"

"Many things. You're curious about the tomb you found me in? Who built it? Whether there are more out there?"

"Yes."

"There is a group of people I wish to destroy. Not physically, unless I have to, but I need them out of the game. They are competitors. Ruthless."

"The British?"

"God, no. They're pussycats. No, this is a private firm. They call themselves freelance archaeologists. The Lost Origins Recovery Institute. Have you heard of them?"

"No."

"They go by LORI for short, and they're *really* annoying. They're the ones who destroyed the tomb. I would like to see justice brought and I believe you have a skill set they might admire."

Prihya hadn't known of the sabotage when she'd commenced her dig. The authorities, and indeed the British man in charge, swore they did not know of any explosives. There were no witnesses except the villagers who'd lost their homes, and who were relocated to a patch of land bought anonymously by a foreigner whose only stipulation was they named the place Luca Town.

However, she'd found blasting caps during every layer of excavation. An opportunity to punish those responsible was the only thing more exciting than an offer to explore the history itself.

"How can I help?" she asked.

His eyes narrowed. "You accept? Just like that?"

"Of course not. I need to check on them myself. To be sure they are who you say."

"Good." He closed his eyes, and when he opened them, they were bloodshot. He'd suddenly gone dog tired. "You will be my eyes and ears out in the world while I recover. Once you learn all you need to about the Lost Origins people, our work will begin. Taking them out of the field and tracking the *true* history of the tomb. Officer Kahn will supply you with a profile, and your salary will be more than you might wish to negotiate."

"That's it?"

"Everything you need. Both digitally and in paper form." He closed his eyes again, words slurring. "I'll rest now. And wait for you to confirm... we will work together... soon."

Prihya watched his head loll to one side. She turned to leave but stopped to lower the man's bed and gently shift his head so he wouldn't wake with a stiff neck.

A huge salary.

Hunting rogue grave robbers.

Investigating an ancient mystery.

There was nothing about this that didn't strike Prihya as perfect. That was why she pledged to herself to take this slowly. To gather evidence and to make her own decision.

CHÂTEAU CACHÉ, BRITTANY

Bridget had never felt so isolated as when the team settled into the library's upper level at her parents' property in north-western France. Not that they were treating her badly, but something had changed, a tonal shift that she couldn't pinpoint.

She needed to put that aside.

Normally, they would set up in the study with its gentlemen's lounge style chairs and deep mahogany paneling or in the operations room housing Charlie's central computer—which she'd nicknamed the Demon Hub. Today, though, they needed a large wall, preferably white, and the library provided that.

They gathered on the other side of the ops room—the library mezzanine, looking out over the bookshelves stocked with thousands of books. It held more than a dozen rows of reference tomes, with older editions mixed in, and more valuable originals stored under lock and key. It was in this section where Toby rediscovered the Justinian Bible gifted to General Yanovna—an item they'd come across when purchasing other books from a trader in Berlin.

Once they were set up with a laptop and projector, Charlie

dimmed the lights and took center stage while Jules, Harpal, and Dan formed an audience with their backs to the main room.

"What Jules has drawn for us appears to be a map of the northern hemisphere." She tapped her computer tablet, and the projector sprang to life, a digitized image of Jules's sketch lighting up the wall. "As you can see, the land mass from Europe extends farther north than it should. There is no United Kingdom, and the mainland stretches up as far as Norway. Netherlands and Russia are much the same. The Atlantic also retreats east, making the northern United States and Canada appear larger than they do today."

She tapped the screen again, overlaying an up-to-date satellite image of the same area, translucent to determine where one ended and the other began.

"The UK *currently* commences near the tip of Jules's map, before the Atlantic shows up. The North Sea and English Channel are not present on the Striovian seal, which is why the sketch is different to how things actually are."

"Due to the map's age, yeah?" Jules said.

"Bridget?" Charlie said.

Bridget stood and took over the computer tablet. She wiped away the modern map and tapped her finger on where the East Coast of North America would start. "I won't go into the detail Toby usually inflicts on you, but let's just establish where we are in historical terms."

Harpal and Dan groaned theatrically, but Bridget noticed Jules simply staring at her.

"There's a period of time known as the Younger Dryas. It harks back to around 110,000 years ago when the ice sheets covering the north were hundreds of feet thick. Melting had started, but the Younger Dryas was the trigger for the earth to plunge back into a longer ice age. This lasted almost another 100,000 years."

"Didn't the Ice Age just cover the world?" Dan asked.

"No. Remember we talked about the great leap forward in human evolution?"

"Sure, when we started farming and stuff."

"Well, shortly before that, there is evidence of civilizations becoming more advanced. Just before the Younger Dryas, we find beads and even primitive jewelry. Humans were self-aware somewhere between 140,000 and 200,000 years ago. They traded. They lived in communities. And in that period approaching the Younger Dryas, when something happened to dampen the sun's strength, they were just starting to indicate progress."

"So not *shortly* before." Jules remained nonchalant, focused on Bridget. "The great leap forward was around 60,000 years ago. The first signs of evolving into civilization were 120,000 years ago. That's, like, twice as long as we've recognized civilization."

"She means in geological terms," Charlie said. "60,000 years is the blink of an eye compared with the Earth's age."

"Right," Bridget continued. "My point is that the Earth was warming up 110,000 years ago. But then either a meteor impacted, sending dust up into the atmosphere for thousands more years, or a whole load of volcanic activity did the same. Whatever the reason, the sun couldn't get through, and the world froze again. This meant the migrations of humans and their counterparts, like Neanderthals, got diverted. It even led to the first known humans arriving in the Americas."

"Sorry to be a grump," Dan said. "What does this have to do with the map and the dude with the scythe and the skull for a head?"

Bridget nodded, aware how impatient people got with unnecessary details, and brought up an old article in a scientific journal with the headline, *Dragon Quest, Interrupted.*

"The international press wasn't exactly swarming over it, so the only interested publications were the local news agencies, historical societies, and inflammatory nut-jobs."

The image showed a government official posing next to a long wooden box with its lid closed.

"During a hunt for dinosaur bones, or those of other prehistoric creatures, they got as far as a previously unknown layer of permafrost. In there, they came across a rectangle. It was three-dimensional and resembled a coffin. They had planned to go farther but were held up."

The image on the wall transformed into an excavation—black and white, with little to suggest the photographer was a professional. Beside it, Bridget flashed up a picture taken from inside a hole dozens of feet long and deep, a slice of land cut through to reveal layers of sediment and rock. The oddity was a rectangle approximately eight feet long.

Jules folded his arms over his chest. "So, if this dates back to the permafrost in that region, it must have been put in the ground before the thaw. Which was when?"

"If this man-made object was genuinely buried beneath the permafrost, it arrived there *before* the Younger Dryas."

Nobody spoke for a moment, each doing the math in their heads. Bridget assumed Jules had already worked it out but was unsure if speaking up would annoy anyone.

It was Charlie who piped up first. "Around 110,000 to 115,000 years ago."

Whistles emanated from both Dan and Harpal.

"Just 7,000 years is approaching an eternity in human development terms," Charlie added. "In just 2,000 years, we progressed from the earliest writing on stone tablets to building the Great Pyramids. In another 5,000, we landed on the moon."

"When we find out why they made the map," Bridget said. "We'll know more. Possibly radon-date the seals."

Jules, as ever, ingested the information. "So, if I'm guessing right, this is also the mummy we heard about, meaning it was more than just sticking a corpse in a box along with some possessions. But even setting aside mummification, just burying people in any sorta ritual way shouldn't happen 'til around 50,000 YA."

"Correct," Bridget said. "Which is when a certain race sprang up. Gave us writing and artifacts that tell a story. Essentially, the first modern humans."

"Okay," Harpal said, excitedly. "I know this. The Sumerians, right?"

"Right." Bridget displayed a photograph of one of the seals returned to Alfonse, four thin pictures of the scene taken from various angles. A goddess receiving tributes from humans. "And there is this one."

The next picture depicted a fatter drum-like seal, except this was solid, unlike the hollow ones that Jules described. It also displayed a series of lines that appeared to mean little.

Bridget used a laser pointer as she narrated. "Scholars hypothesized the marks were either maps denoting land as it should be divided in terms of crops, or nothing more than a pretty picture of some clouds. There was no manual, after all. But now we've seen the more detailed version..."

She switched to the blown-up projections of Jules's sketch. The similarity was unmistakable.

"I think whoever these people were who buried the oldest Striovian seals, they either survived to trade with the Sumerians in the Middle East, or they migrated as far as the Middle East, and the Sumerians found a similar batch."

"The Sumerians copied the pre-Ice Age people?"

"Not entirely *copied*," Charlie said. "A lot of the artwork in the Sumerians' is original. The vast majority, in fact, as far as we can tell. But it stands to reason if they either knew of this other race or discovered its remains, there would be some influence crossing over. An incorporation of ideas."

Harpal leaned forward. "Could the Sumerians be direct descendants?"

"Interesting question," Bridget said. "We would need to examine the mummy before we could even theorize—"

"It's not *interesting*," Jules said. "It's off topic. Again. What does *the map* mean?"

Bridget gathered her thoughts and returned to projecting

the original, overlaying the modern equivalent. "The map is accurate as of the time *before* the ice sheets melted, dating the seal to at least 12,000 BC, so they must have traveled extensively to get the scale right. But because it was found in permafrost that formed over 100,000 years ago, it seems correct that it would have represented that phase in geological time."

"What's the interesting bit?" Jules asked.

Bridget frowned. Jules's tone had changed in a way she'd never heard. Not aggressive; more like the way Toby would get when about to reveal something that made him sound smarter than he was.

Jules was *probing*.

Testing her knowledge.

She said, "I have to admit, I'm not sure. Maybe you could enlighten us?"

"Pull up my picture of the Grim Reaper and his girlfriends," Jules said.

Bridget stared at the screen in her hand for a moment too long, causing Charlie to take it from her and dab a dozen times, completing the task.

The traditional figure of the Grim Reaper appeared translucent on the wall, overlaying the pre-Ice Age map. Two naked women flanked Death, and an orb glowed in his left hand. That section of the picture lay on the right, with Jules interpreting the scene flowing left, toward the Americas. The people paying tribute bowed down in a row, with crops and vegetation behind. The sun shone overhead, its rays exaggerated into long lines filling the entire sky.

"You're sure this was all of it?" Charlie asked.

"There was a lot of detail," Jules said. "I definitely got most, but there were some other bits that I figured weren't important."

"That's not like you, Jules," Harpal said. "I thought you remembered *every*thing."

"I got every detail I need in here." Jules tapped his head.

"There's a few imperfections too. The sort you'd expect over time. I guessed they weren't intentional."

"What imperfections?" Bridget asked.

Jules examined the projection overlaid on the map. It was hard to read his expression, but Harpal was correct; Jules never skimped on relevant detail, at least in the short time Bridget had known him. He disregarded anything that he judged point-less, but since he now couldn't seem to dismiss the imperfec-tions as such, she figured he was racking his brain to recreate them.

Margarete entered, bringing pastries and a pot of fresh coffee. No one had asked her to do this, and it wasn't one of her duties. She was a housekeeper, a caretaker, and the only reason Bridget's parents hadn't brought in an outside company to take over cleaning and maintaining the place. Margarete almost came as part of the fixtures and fittings.

She stared for a long moment at the wall, tutted, and placed the tray down. Spoke in French. "Enjoy your food." A glance back at the figure of Death, and she addressed Bridget directly. "Is this what you do with your time? Messing with pagan art?"

"Thank you," Bridget answered in the same language. "We are exploring some artifacts. Nothing to be concerned about."

Jules stepped up to the wall, his shadow splayed across the map and the artwork. He produced a marker pen and drew a series of dots directly on the paint, teasing a gasp from everyone but Margarete. Jules paused to look over his shoulder where he found Margarete with a face like thunder and her hands on her hips.

"Hey." He nodded a greeting in her direction, flashed a smile, and went back to drawing on the wall.

Margarete scoffed and pointed from Bridget to the pen work. "That wall will need to be repainted." Then she shuffled out, tutting as she went.

Jules stood back, taking in the dots that led across the top third of the picture, with a series of scratches in the north-east section of modern Canada, along with an adjustment to the round sun, giving it a partial wavy line.

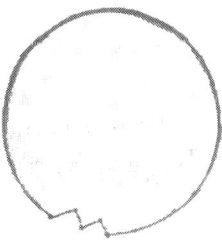

"Okay, Picasso," Dan said. "What does that mean?"

Something in Bridget stirred. A memory. It buzzed through her stomach, spreading through her limbs, and making her fingers jittery. "One minute."

She dashed away, down the spiral stairs to the main part of the library, flicking on a light as she passed the switches.

Toby liked to arrange the books not by area or by culture, but chronologically. Anything written at the time was simple to cross-reference with other parts of world history. It helped if they wanted to corroborate something like the Krakatoa eruption; heard in central Australia, its effect spread almost worldwide through tsunamis and sheer noise, the soundwave reaching Java, and blood red sunsets seen as far as Scandinavia and New York. Keeping accounts from 1883 together made sense, charting exactly what happened during that event.

However, what they were talking about today occurred long before any textbooks or journals would have been written, at least not those discovered to date. The only exceptions may have been unearthed in India earlier that year.

Ignoring her frustration at that particular episode, Bridget dug out an academic tome from the late 20th century. She leafed through, found the chapter she needed, and ran back upstairs.

She arrived on the mezzanine and laid the book down next to the projector, then opened it to a chapter regarding migration. With the eyes of the team upon her, she read quickly, flipped pages, eventually landing on a map similar to the one on the wall.

This one had zoomed in on the Arctic ice sheets, Greenland, and Northeastern Canada. She held it up for all to see, tracing her hand along a dotted line in the far north.

"I don't know about the lines coming out of the sun, but the others show the migration pattern of the first people to settle in North America. There is some debate about the exact genetic lineage, but they are broadly known as the Clovis People."

CHAPTER
TWENTY

STRIOVIAN AIRSPACE

The Ilyushin Il-76 soared at a far steeper angle than a civilian flight, popping Toby's ears within seconds of take-off. In another life, he'd gotten familiar with the old bird, a Soviet-era Airlifter capable of a forty-ton payload which held its own against the worst Siberian weather. Although the size of a commercial freighter, it could take off using short runways and unprepared frozen airstrips. But since the first of its kind was launched in 1971 and dumped out of commission in the mid-90s, Toby listened closely for any bolts shearing off or panels rusting away. None of the other passengers appeared to share his concerns, though.

Arranged in a single compartment, eight men and two women sat behind him in cracked leather chairs in two-by-two segments more akin to car seats than those on a passenger plane. Toby could feel the springs. The men and women were soldiers or highly trained law enforcement, decked out in heavy camo fatigues stripped of all insignias and anything that might ID them as Striovian.

This meant only one thing: they were venturing beyond their

borders on a mission for which their government might disavow them should they be caught. A "black op" in modern parlance.

One oddity Toby noted was the last names printed on their left chest pocket, names that appeared genuine through the brief exchanges during boarding—Holorov, Lukic, Benjamich. It took only a few seconds for him to understand they would be needed to ID the remains should any of them not make it home.

Stationed next to Toby, the captain called Igoravich took up more than his fair share of the double seats, his bicep spilling over and pushing Toby up against the side where he could only watch as they emerged from clouds into the night sky. Yanovna occupied a two-berth to herself. Like the troops behind, both showed zero emotion. That was until the Il-76 leveled out and all released their belts.

Yanovna stood and faced forward, into the space before them: thirty feet of storage had been converted into an IT hub of cobbled-together screens and workstations.

She spun to face her people, throwing a mere glance at Toby before speaking in Russian. "I believe in my country. I believe in doing all it takes for my people. This man..." She gestured to Toby. "Is accused of espionage. But in return for mercy, he is aiding our mission to arm us with a weapon that will deter the great oppressor from treating Striovia as it has Ukraine, and many other countries like it. I will never bow down again."

The troops replied as one with a deep-throated pledge in Striovian: *"Free forever. Slaves never!"*

Toby didn't know much Striovian, which is why he assumed Yanovna was speaking Russian, but he knew this pledge. Striovian children said it at school. Police spoke it at graduation. The army lived by it as a creed.

"Toby Smith is our prisoner, but he will interpret the maps and symbols that will secure our freedom for now and for future generations. Do not be fooled, though. He has friends who may be seeking the same as us. If they threaten our mission, I will not hesitate to authorize lethal force." She focused on Toby. "I will give Mr. Smith one chance to talk them down. If he fails, they die. Understood?"

Toby nodded meekly. The troops grunted, "*Yes, sir,*" the Striovian language having only one respectful word for addressing a senior officer.

Yanovna held her head high. "I will strategize with Captain Igoravich and interrogate the prisoner. We will set a course and you will be briefed presently. In the meantime, rest. Write your final messages, and all will soon become clear."

With a flick of Yanovna's chin, Igoravich pulled Toby's arm. Toby undid his seatbelt and stood, shuffling into the ops area with Igoravich and Yanovna.

"Final messages?" Toby said.

"We write a note at the beginning of each deployment," Yanovna replied. "If we make it home, we burn the note. We write a new one each time."

"No recycling? May I ask why?"

"Life changes," Igoravich answered for her. "We say different things for different times."

"Like Habib Masouli?"

Yanovna directed a sharp look at Toby. "When did you establish a connection to Masouli? Was it when you first saw the scroll?"

"A few moments ago." Toby had no reason to lie, but he assumed Yanovna would not automatically trust him. "It had completely slipped my mind. There were excavations in Scotland some years ago, but nothing of significance surfaced. Still, I looked into the documentation and legends from that time. A wise man, an advisor to King James the Fourth by the name of Habib Masouli, saw off some incursion, then entrusted a scroll to… I forget his name. The priest resident there..."

"Father Goswelt." Yanovna had clearly conducted her own research before departing.

"That sounds correct. He was supposed to take something to Rome, where the Pope had just declared the Americas to belong to

Spain and Portugal, or some such political appeasement. But that message… makes little sense. *The circle will show the power of God…"*

"Wait here." Yanovna indicated a padded chair on a rail beside a long bank of computer consoles, in which Toby planted himself. "This will not take long."

She signed into the first of several terminals and watched while it booted up. Toby counted six such machines.

Beside him, Igoravich watched too, that stone expression just observing.

Toby spoke too quietly for Yanovna to hear. "Unusual."

Igoravich turned his head only. "What is unusual?"

Keeping his voice low, Toby said, "General Yanovna. Striovia was always a very traditional country and is still quite conservative. How did a woman come to hold such a high rank and influence?"

"You think I don't like woman in charge?" The captain's tone remained low too, presumably unwilling to distract Yanovna in her task of bringing fifteen-year-old computers to life. "You think Striovia is like Syria? Like Iran?"

"No, not at all." Toby hated to play the misogynist card. But getting someone on side, if only in small increments, might save his life. "I just wonder what it's like for a man of vast experience and intelligence to take orders from a woman who has been a civilian for the past decade."

"One down." Yanovna moved to the next workstation.

"Do not try this," Igoravich said. "I am loyal. I obey orders."

"I know." Toby sensed he'd pushed this as far as he could for now. "And I respect that. My apologies for questioning you this way."

Igoravich appeared satisfied and returned to watching his General. However, Toby took heart from one aspect of their exchange: the captain did not alert Yanovna.

It meant Toby had wedged his foot in what he used to call "the door of doubt." It was step one in securing an asset. Make them worry, in just a small way, that their loyalty and commitment were misplaced.

Yanovna returned from the second terminal. "We are ready, Toby. You've had time to study the images. Tell me what you have deduced."

"It's a map," Toby said with a glance at Igoravich.

The man remained alert, staring straight ahead, but his eyes, the set of his jaw, had definitely softened.

Step one.

Usually, the process of turning an asset took weeks, sometimes months. Toby only had hours, possibly a day at the outside.

But as ever for a black op, they were moving quickly. Decisions needed to happen fast. Step two might present itself sooner than usual.

Toby said, "What do you know about the Clovis People?"

CHAPTER
TWENTY-ONE

CHÂTEAU CACHÉ, BRITTANY

"Clovis People," Jules said as Bridget stared, hoping for a reaction to what she felt was a revelatory deduction. "Thought they came in from the other side. The Bering Strait."

"Maybe. But we have located their remains on both coasts. Seems to imply they migrated from the north. Look."

She demonstrated on the map in her book how the ice sheets came down as far as Great Britain, Belgium, and most of Russia. The lines of migration flowed from the far east of Russia, across the frozen sea to north-western Canada. They also covered the far north of the Atlantic, stopping in the northeast.

Bridget went on, "Having driven up from Africa and Persia, settled in Europe during the warming period, they'll have bred and spread. Then, as the Younger Dryas hit them, they'd have had to learn to live with the cooler climate. As resources got scarce, mass migrations took place, spreading without realizing they lived on a sphere. So two tribes could easily have drifted west and east, while others still must have gone south. But this crossing here." She jabbed the red line on the page. "It matches Jules's dotted line there."

Everyone looked at the wall, then took their time returning to her book before settling on the wall again.

"How do we know about this route?" Dan asked.

"From archaeological digs, matching the style of artifacts, burial ceremonies, that sort of thing. There is new evidence that other peoples, genetically diverse humans, moved into North America around the same time. Meaning more than one group made a home there. Some ventured farther inland. But the Clovis either didn't move after finding suitable land or were incorporated into other tribes and bred their genes out of the pool."

"Could they have been wiped out?" Harpal asked.

Jules shook his head. "Whenever a civilization is wiped out, there tends to be a lotta smashed up skeletons and destroyed land."

"We've only found peaceful settlements," Bridget said. "At least, far as we can tell. Nothing indicating large-scale slaughter."

"Am I right thinking the big thing to take away," Harpal said, "is that whoever made the seals knew the Clovis People?"

"No," Jules and Bridget answered simultaneously.

Jules indicated for Bridget to go ahead.

She said, "The large cylindrical seals were found in 100,000-year-old permafrost. The Clovis People migrated around 20,000 years ago."

"So, how is this possible?" Charlie asked.

"Coincidence." Jules shrugged. "If one bunch of people used the only route available, stands to reason another group would."

"I agree." Bridget closed her book and stared at the wall. "Those scratches are interesting."

"There's that word again," Jules said. "Interesting. Is it really interesting this time?"

"That cluster." She indicated where Jules had sketched a grouping of smaller dots. "A kind of circle."

"In the middle of the approximate location of where the Clovis People settled," Charlie said.

"There are burial mounds and evidence of huge settlements

found all over that region. Could be important. But I'm no expert on the Clovis. I'll read up en route."

"En route?" Harpal said. "Where to?"

"Canada."

"We can't just go rock up in Canada," Dan said. "That's hundreds of square miles. What do you hope to do? Start digging at random and happen across another tomb?"

Bridget thought through the issue quickly. "Charlie, you've got your new LiDar equipment licensed, right?"

Charlie crossed her arms and squinted. "I hate to nit-pick, but LiDar is a brand name. What I've developed is high-frequency ground-penetrating radar. The Lear will be too fast, but you could strap it to a small prop plane, and it will cover five hundred square miles in, ooh, about a year."

"Toby doesn't have a year," Dan said.

Jules frowned. "Why not?"

"Because they know we're interested in the seals. Because Toby won't allow himself to be tortured when he can help interpret the images. Like we just did. We need to move. We need to try to narrow that search area and find whatever that map is pointing to."

"I'll load up with everything we have," Bridget said. "Learn on the way. Jules?"

"Sure." Jules stared at the scratches, unsettled at how intentional they looked. "I'm good at learning."

Charlie had already commenced searching online, both the public forums and Toby's own database. "I'll have Phil hire a local guide, someone who can maybe give us the lay of the land."

Lay of the land.

"That region." Jules referred to the map again, the part with the condensed cluster. "There's something we ain't seeing. Something special."

Charlie swapped out the map for a modern overlay. "Nothing."

"Adjust for continental drift."

Nobody moved. Even Charlie just hovered over the keyboard and mouse.

"Ain't much," Jules said. "Over 12,000 years, it's probably a couple hundred feet. Over 100,000..."

"I don't have that software," Charlie said.

Jules took over her laptop, ignoring her annoyed *hurrumph*. "Lots of volcanic activity in the time between ice ages and now. Lots of seismic business goin' on." He killed the sketches and zoomed in on the map, skewing the scale they'd established to match to the Reaper Seal and corresponding topography. "Means we might not see it in a couple of decades, but over that length of time..."

He switched to a satellite picture, then clicked and dragged the image around, searching quickly in a hundred-mile radius. The images burned into his mind's eye, discarding the useless ones, until he found a single possibility.

He said, "That reference looked intentional, small, specific."

"Instead of an X-marks-the-spot," Harpal said.

"Or a circle."

Jules zoomed back out from the geological feature, restoring the original scale, and overlaid the sketches from the Striovian seal—translucent so it could be compared and manipulated. He dragged the sketch into place, so it lined up with his hypothesized location. The dotted cluster matched it precisely.

Jules stood back, clicking for more information. "There you go. Mount Chepadu. What I bet is this is surrounded by old Clovis settlements."

An energy set in, Jules's certainty infecting the team. All stared, all twitchy, ready to go.

Harpal was the first to move for the door. "Guess that leaves me to fuel the jet. Wheels up in two hours."

PART THREE

"Discovery is seeing what everybody else has seen and thinking what nobody else has thought."

- Albert Szent-Gyorgyi

Nunavut Region
Canada

CHAPTER
TWENTY-TWO
AUGUST 19, 11:00 A.M. (EST)

CHEPADU DISTRICT, NORTH-EAST NUNAVUT REGION - CANADA

After landing at the airfield in Chepadu, Jules asked Harpal, "What's a jiffy?"

With everyone in chunky coats and hats, Jules and the four LORI members lugged a rucksack each and two crates between them across the tarmac of a tiny airport a hundred miles from the east coast of Nunavut, the northernmost region of Canada. Although the high altitude was absent snow, it had been visible on many of the taller hills as they flew in.

The temperature proved quite the shock to the system, a biting cold usually associated with frosty mornings, but the dry air left it fresh and—to Jules—fairly pleasant. Bridget shivered the moment the door opened and didn't stop as they made their way to the terminal—a grand-looking hut with a makeshift tower and a figure waving them over.

"A jiffy is a short unit of time," Harpal said. "Seconds, minutes, even hours. Depends on the context. Why?"

"Because he was eavesdropping," Charlie said. "That's rude, don't you know?"

Yes, he'd listened in as Charlie chatted to her husband, who'd made the arrangements for when they touched down. Phil had sourced a guide and, after delivering the man's resumé—Luther Gibson, 48, an official of Parks Canada, freelance consultant and speaker, divorced father of two teens, pays all his disposable income to their college funds, four years' military service—Charlie took the conversation off speakerphone. "Just exploratory," Charlie had assured Phil.

She couldn't know that for sure.

They had joked a little about how Luther's military service didn't count because it was Canadian. Although Jules had heard Americans and Brits joking about Canadians apologizing to enemies for popping a bullet in them or asking permission to bomb an airfield, he knew it was all in jest. But the jokes today had concealed something else—most likely Phil's discomfort at Charlie heading out into the field again.

"The Striovians are not about to launch an invasion of Canada," she'd told him. "We'll be in and out in a jiffy."

Almost at the remote terminal, Jules now shrugged at the accusation of rudeness. "Lots I ain't been told on this trip. Gotta keep myself informed."

"That wasn't intentional," Dan said.

Jules gave a pointed look toward Bridget. "No?"

Bridget huddled deeper into her coat and gave a muffled, "You want another apology?"

"I wanna get these damn books or statues or wherever the map's pointing us and get Toby free. Then I'm done."

The man waiting for them was dressed like every archaeologist from every archaeologist-starring movie ever made: khaki cargo pants, beige shirt, multi-pocketed brown-green vest, and a battered waxed fedora. He had a goatee beard, broad shoulders, and a paunch, and stood at least six feet. His gut wasn't huge but still sagged over a belt that held a badge denoting his position in Parks Canada. Jules almost missed the Glock 17 secured in a holster on one hip.

As Charlie placed one end of her radar crate down and

extended a hand, the man's paunch withdrew and his goatee spread with his smile.

"Luther Gibson." He shook Charlie's hand in a double grip.

"Good to meet you." Charlie slipped free and introduced everyone.

"Private archaeology foundation?" Luther said.

"Freelance archaeologists," Bridget corrected. "And we're real grateful you could make the time."

"Two teams," Dan said. "You okay accommodating that?"

Luther nodded. "Let's get set up."

The twin-prop plane swooped low over the forested hills, its airspeed faster than Charlie hoped for. No matter. It would still handle her ground-penetrating radar tech, now attached to its hull, which would feed to her iPad.

Luther had offered their own GPR, but she'd checked out Parks Canada's tech and found it wanting. "Besides," she'd added back at the airfield, "you've helped us out so much already. Temporary visas, transport, manpower."

Luther, with thin, balding hair which he spent way too long combing before firing up the engine, piloted the plane with Charlie riding shotgun, while Harpal and Bridget occupied the cramped rear. As well as the engine noise requiring them to wear headphones and mics to communicate, as the airspeed slowed to accommodate the GPR, every gust of wind buffeted the little plane, making it judder in a way that suggested it could plunge from the sky at any moment. Luther appeared calm, though, so Charlie took his lead.

The big problem she had with the setup was the subvocal earbud they all wore, something she promised Phil she wouldn't remove unless absolutely necessary, meant she heard whatever the rest of the group chatted about.

"So, it's Chepadu you're interested in," Luther said.

"Yes." Charlie kept an eye on the tablet computer in her lap, where the GPR results would feed through.

"You know we can't do anything big up there, right?"

Charlie looked up from the screen. "Why not?"

"Sacred land."

Bridget's crackly voice piped up. "I didn't read anything about that. This is a national park, not a burial ground. Not even close."

Luther seesawed his hand side to side. "Technically, yeah, but Parks Canada has to take a more holistic view of stuff like that. Trying to be respectful to all people, including my own."

"Your own?" Harpal said.

"I'm one-quarter Thule."

Charlie figured him as lily-white as she was, and you didn't get much whiter in the UK than Welsh. "Thule. Proto-Inuit, right?"

"Genetics show we mostly grew into the Inuit race, but some diverged in other directions. I'm one of them. Or my family is. Even if I wasn't part Thule, we can't just go digging willy-nilly on the hill."

Dan's voice grumbled through the earbud, the man himself still grounded. "Could've told us that before you took off."

Silence reigned for a moment.

Luther played with his hands on the controls, tightened his grip, then loosened it. He turned to Charlie. "Hey, listen, no big deal, but... there's a town. Ten miles east of here. Not much, but they serve a great steak. You eat steak?"

Charlie regretted leaving her wedding band in France, but she couldn't bear the risk of misplacing it. She rubbed the finger where it usually sat, but Luther didn't appear to notice. Nor did she think an outright rejection of him at this point would get them anywhere, especially since he hadn't asked her out directly.

"I eat steak," she said.

"Cool. I can recommend it." Luther checked some instruments.

"Here it comes," Dan said.

"Quiet," Charlie hissed, but it came through everyone's headphones.

Luther looked up. "Hmm?"

"Talking to myself." Charlie tapped her earphones. "The plane's so loud."

Luther appeared to accept that. "Yeah, but you wanted a slow plane. This is the slowest." He tapped a dial that didn't need tapping, then held the controller two-handed. "I could introduce you to the owner. Of the steak place, I mean." *Super casual.* "They do a thirty-two-ounce beauty. It's free if you finish every bit of meat."

Phil's voice arrived: "Hey, everyone, think I could kick this guy's arse?"

"Nothing to worry about," Dan replied. "Man's a slob. You could take him."

"Nah," Jules said, on the ground with Dan. "He's rocking a beer gut, but the way he moves… he knows his way through a fight."

"I was SAS," Phil said.

"Yeah, but your legs don't work. Think you'll get around that?"

"I carry a Ka-Bar knife under my seat. And a taser."

Jules went quiet, plainly considering the slight shifting of the odds. "Okay, you might have an edge."

Charlie would have happily torn them off a strip but didn't want to alert Luther to their secondary comms. It wasn't exactly legal to use such technology without a license there.

Bridget removed her headphones. "Charlie indicates there will be no steak date, no matter what."

Charlie fired her a thumbs up, then pointed out the front. "Is that Mount Chepadu?"

"Oh yes," Luther said. "There she is. Our favorite volcano."

•   •   •

The hut-come-terminal had reminded Jules of the airfields where he'd prep before a session of hurling himself out of a plane for whatever reason; skydiving, wingsuits, even HALO jumps. Those were something he had in common with Harpal, apparently, but they'd never gotten close enough to discuss it at length. But then, Jules learned his skills for practical reasons; Harpal was an adrenaline junkie.

Sparsely furnished, and absolutely intended for the specific business of shuttling professionals in and out of a remote area, it was where Jules and Dan remained while the others went up in the twin prop. There, they met a guy called Tommy. Who stank of marijuana.

As he packed one of several bags laid out, the shaggy-haired *dude* said, "Hey, you guys are gonna love Chepadu. It's totally cool. Snow and ice at the top, dead caldera full of endemic specimens, just gotta watch out for the landslides and bears."

While Dan made small talk, Jules picked up a pre-prepared pack and unlatched it.

"Hey, it's okay." Tommy waved him off. "I already did that one."

Jules unspooled the fabric, spilling it out on the floor. "I load my own 'chute."

Tommy took it well. "No worries, man. So how come you're with a bunch of stuffy old archaeologists?"

Jules avoided much of the conversation with Tommy by blanking him or replying with questions of his own—about the plane they'd be using, the fuel, the altitude. Their cover as wanting to skydive to the 2,000-foot-wide caldera of Mount Chepadu seemed to hold water, a dual expedition by the two American men to carry out this fun session after their academic friends had done their thing. Originally, Harpal planned to accompany Jules, but when it was plain Luther was more keyed into government channels than they realized—Parks Canada carrying similar heft as the US Environment Agency or the

National Park Service—they figured someone with Harpal's background was better placed.

Once they packed the chutes and retired to the break room, chatter remained minimal, surrounding Tommy's own love of the place—"Came up here from California to run a camp and never left. Went to college. Now I'm a professor!"—until Luther probed the possibility of a date with Charlie. With Phil still clued in from the UK, it gave Jules a momentary distraction of preparing himself mentally for what awaited.

Difficult to prepare for the unknown.

After reassuring Phil he wasn't about to lose Charlie to Luther, Jules stepped out of the hut. Wrapped up warm, his breath misting, he tapped the earbud to switch it off for some peace and quiet.

Unfortunately, Professor Tommy joined him. "Your buddy said you'd like the company."

Dan, Jules decided, would pay for that.

They needed to keep these people sweet so Jules's rudeness and deflection wouldn't work all day. He had to engage.

Urgh.

"Chepadu." Jules tapped into his reserves of patience. "How old is it?"

King of small talk.

"Few million," Tommy said. "Been extinct at least two million."

Meaning even the manufacturers of the 100,000-year-old seals would not have known it as an active danger.

"And it's a nature reserve," Jules said, "not an archaeological site, right?"

"Yeah. We got the Clovis history up here, y'know? The first people over the Bering Strait and all that. It's pretty high up, though, so you only get a few places where people lived. No central heating back then, yeah?" Tommy hugged himself, having popped out in just a wool hoodie. "You got the Inuit. Before them, the Thule. And don't get Luther talking about the Thule; you'd think he was a shaman or something. He's from Ontario."

Jules hated chatter. Irrelevant background bored him. But occasionally, it was useful. "You know plenty about it. The history of the land."

"Yeah. Like I said, I'm a professor." Tommy, who looked not much older than Jules, blew into his hands, then stuffed them in his pockets. "You got the Dorset before the Thule, and the Pre-Dorset before them, or the *Saqqaq* people, if you're being precise."

"Saqqaq?"

Tommy spelled it and paced, stamping his feet. "The Saqqaq are the real interesting ones—pre-Christian, like 2,000 B.C. We get Mormons up here sometimes, claiming to be religious scholars. Thinking the Saqqaq might be the Israelites who settled America. Looking for anything they can use to prove something about their religion."

Jules paced as well, mirroring body language more than keeping out the cold. He didn't want to let on that he knew more than he did; he was supposed to be a skydiver, adding to the casual nature of their subterfuge.

Casually, he asked, "They find anything?"

"Nah." Tommy waved him off. "If they did, you'd never hear the end of it. Mostly Thule stuff, a bit of the original Inuit settlers, some European bits. Hey, looks like they're done."

He pointed to a speck in the distant sky.

"Woo! Let's do this!" Tommy ran back inside to give Dan the good news.

CHAPTER
TWENTY-THREE

Before Tommy could whisk them off into the air, they needed to wait on Charlie's party as they disembarked and secured the equipment. The groan from their prospective pilot sounded like a teenager being refused a curfew extension. Not that Jules ever had that problem.

After his parents died, he'd never asked permission, barely even knew what his foster homes' curfews were. Certainly never listened if they'd told him. He'd had a mission; to locate the bangle stolen from his mother, a task the cops of New York didn't seem to care for.

Charlie and Bridget breezed into the terminal, and Dan showed them to the large area where they'd set up the parachutes. Harpal entered ahead of Luther, seemingly placating the man.

"We will get to the bottom of it, I promise," Harpal said. "We just need a couple of hours."

"Hours?" Luther replied, his eyes wild, his hand gestures imploring. "It'll take *years* of study."

"Let's try to shave a little time off that." Charlie set her tablet on the bench table and Dan brought her larger bag, which hadn't accompanied them. From there, she took a workstation laptop and opened it, booted it up immediately and paired it with the tablet via Bluetooth. "Gather round."

Jules and Dan stood at the back, taller than the others, while Charlie sat on a stool and presented the 3D rendering of Mount Chepadu and the surrounding topography. The mountain was less a classic cone with a depression at the top where the lava once spewed, and more like a single claw. The caldera was to the side, meaning when it last erupted it blasted at an angle instead of the familiar straight-up-in-the-air direction, leaving around two-thirds intact on the other side.

"The GPR eliminates trees and vegetation." Charlie repeating this was unnecessary in Jules's opinion, but he remained silent on the subject. "We did three passes, different angles, and the software knitted it all together."

"Please tell me it's hollow," Dan said. "Full of bookshelves and maybe little lizard people working as librarians."

Bridget fired him the stink-eye. "Not quite."

"It's impossible," Luther said. "We've mapped this region."

"But you didn't map it with this level of detail," Charlie said. "You haven't investigated the lava towers."

"We sampled the rock." Tommy leaned in toward the screen. "Whoa. That's funky."

Jules recognized the abnormality. It was clearer when Charlie tilted the graphic, swinging it around to explore. A fissure showed on the south side, a gash under the land burrowing deeper than the GPR could penetrate.

"It's about four feet wide," Charlie said. "Right under a lava tower."

"That's the Gorgon Block," Tommy said. "Right, Luther?"

Luther nodded, his eyes still as wide as a coke fiend's, like he'd forgotten to blink for the past five minutes. He blinked. "Yeah. Big round ball of long-dead rock. Guess it leaked out of that crack, stuck on the ledge, and never went anywhere."

Harpal's turn to frown and get closer to the screen. "How come no one ever saw it?"

Tommy scoffed. "It's boring by volcanologist standards. Whole thing has been dead for thousands of years."

"And we only searched for human settlements," Luther said. "Two hundred square miles. There are more settlements marking different peoples than anywhere else in Canada. Something attracted them to the general area. Relatively gentle terrain to get from the coast inland, but we didn't think they'd have a specific destination in mind."

"What kinda destination?" Jules asked.

"This." Charlie zoomed out of the graphic and flipped it so they were looking down from above. Twenty-two bright spots were highlighted. "Irregular constructions."

"Or rather, regular constructions," Bridget said. "Nature doesn't produce these shapes, except in isolated, highly coincidental freak occurrences. Rarely gives us more than one in a set place, and the fissure under the Gorgon Block is odd. A near-uniform width as deep as the radar can go."

"We found six settlements on our own," Luther said. "Need to get teams out here to unearth the others—"

"Tommy's taking us up first," Jules said.

"Right." Dan reached for his parachute and kit bag. "Me and Jules'll secure a perimeter and you guys join us soon as you can—"

"Wait, wait, wait." Luther broke away, his hands erratic again, standing to one side. He realized everyone was watching him. He sucked in his gut and spoke directly to Charlie. "No one is setting up any perimeter. I'm calling this in to Central. That mountain is off limits to anyone without government clearance. I'll be fired in a day!"

"Seriously?" Dan said.

"Seriously." Luther remained stationary, running his hand through his wispy hair as he appeared to be calculating a million things.

Dan glanced at Jules, tapping his ear.

Jules reactivated his comms and turned his back on Dan, who

paced slowly to the window looking out onto the unmanned airfield. Jules took the hint and, while Luther scrolled on his phone, shifted for the drinking fountain.

"I'll take Luther," Dan said. "You do the kid."

"I'm not *doing* anyone," Jules replied. "No one gets hurt here."

"Come on. This isn't the time for your Zen crap."

Jules didn't answer. Took a drink.

"Fine," Dan said. "Harpal, you online?"

"Yeah, I heard." Harpal's voice was virtually a whisper, and Bridget and Charlie appeared aware too, eyes twitching back and forth. "Government officials, though."

Harpal could handle himself in a fight, but Jules was better. He was also stronger, more able to control a subject when applying a sleeper hold. Luther was ex-military, and Tommy was an unknown quantity.

"Fine," Jules said. "You call it."

He circled back to where Tommy still marveled at the graphical representation of Mount Chepadu and watched in his peripheral vision as Dan stalked toward Luther.

Assaulting hired mercenaries was a simple choice for Jules; low-wage security guards made him uneasy, as did police, and he only indulged in that when in danger of being caught or if the benefits were too great to pass up. It had been a fluid ethical dilemma in the past—basic math as to whether it got him closer to the bangle. Now it was murkier, and Jules didn't like his newfound conscience one bit.

Dan was in position.

"Hey." Jules raised his chin, but resisted saying, *'sup*?

"Hey, Luther." Charlie stood and opened her coat, pulled her sweatshirt tight, and walked toward Luther. "You find someone to report to?"

Softer tone.

Accentuating the breasts.

Hips swaying ever so slightly.

Jules didn't understand flirting. He studied it, even used it occasionally. But all he learned was from textbooks, online tutorials, and observing and mimicking others. He knew it when he saw it, but simply didn't *get* it.

Charlie said, "Look, we understand you'll do what you have to do, but maybe it could wait? Until morning?"

"Is she flirting?" came Phil's voice. "That's her flirting voice."

"I think so," Jules said, away from Tommy.

"And she's awesome at it," Harpal added.

Luther lowered his phone. "I'm not sure."

"The sooner we get done here," Charlie said, "the sooner you get to show me that steak place."

Luther licked his lips—at the prospect of steak?

"Oh, she's flirting," Phil said. "Is she touching him?"

Charlie had stopped short of a coquettish finger twirl of her hair, no pouting. Even Jules knew that'd be too much in the flirting department.

"We only want to look." Charlie's Welsh accent drew front and center. "You can get us there overland, can't you? We lose the radar feeds, we say you were just showing us around, and *you* discovered one of the new settlements. Then there's more to find, too."

Luther considered it.

"Come on, boss-man," Tommy said. "Like the big guy suggested, drop these two in, then you bring up the rear."

"We *did* find it for you," Bridget said. "And we really need to see what's there. What's one day?"

Luther stared at his phone.

"We don't even want credit," Charlie said. "You put your name first on any papers, I'll give you the schematics of what we had and… we can add a little bonus onto the fee we agreed for your services if that helps. Say, another… twenty percent?"

Luther stroked his goatee. "Twenty-five. To help recruit more staff, you understand. *I* come with you. You do as *I* say. If *I* say it's time to go, it's *time to go*. Okay?"

"Thank you."

"And," Luther said, "*you* buy the steaks."

CHAPTER
TWENTY-FOUR
AUGUST 19, 2:15 P.M. (EST)

As the tiny plane climbed ever higher over the lush hills of the Nunavut highlands, Jules repacked his supply bag, a canvass rucksack which he strapped to his front, while his parachute took its place on his back. Having turned down the headphones and mic, he absorbed the sounds, the vibrations, reaching out with touch, auditory senses, smell—satisfied the afternoon was progressing well.

"Anything scare you?" Dan asked.

"Not much." Jules pulled the straps tight. "You?"

"I don't know if it's fear, but we're about to jump out of a plane into an area we don't know. Think we should decide what happens if we go off course?"

"I don't frighten easy 'cause I plan." Jules kept his gaze on the horizon, tilted close to 45 degrees as the plane climbed. "I work out every logical eventuality, and act accordingly."

"Okay, big-brain, what if you're off course on your landing? Big updraft blows you into a sidewind and you're halfway down the mountain?"

Jules remained nonplussed. "I'll walk up the mountain, adjust my timings, and pick up as soon as I can."

"Okay, what if I go off course, and you're all alone?"

Jules switched attention to Dan. "I'll cry a little. Then I'll remember why I split the C-4 between us instead of stashing it all in your pack like you wanted, and *then* I'll get on with the job. If you make it in time, great. If not..." He shrugged and returned to the horizon, now leveling out. "I'll be fine."

"Glad you'll be fine." Dan checked out the window, almost at the extinct volcano, and called to Tommy, "How long?"

"T-minus one minute, bro!" Tommy shouted back.

"Thanks, bro," Jules replied.

Dan mouthed the "bro?" back at him.

"Social norms," Jules said. "I'm getting better."

"That's up for debate." Dan made another check of his kit.

Jules did likewise, pulling the straps snug to his thighs, shoulders, and waist. Then he waited, happy that Dan remained silent.

Even big macho ex-spec-ops types had to find this hard. Dan was out of practice, as was Jules, but Jules's ability to retain minute detail usually extended to his muscle memory, too.

The equipment was in order.

His body was in acceptable condition.

His mind was clear.

The door opened. Air blasted the cabin.

"Go for it, man!" Tommy shouted.

Jules went for it. A standard pitch forward, midair roll as his stomach lurched due to the massive shift in gravity. As the air resistance gripped him, he evened out, the small control 'chute above making the effort minimal. Wind pummeled him as he dropped.

Although normally a pleasure dive would start at between 13,000 and 15,000 feet, the altimeter read 10,000; the plane would have taken ages to climb that high. Especially with the air so thin and cold.

Below, a green carpet with gray flecks spanned from one horizon to the other, minor gaps in foliage indicating low-lying towns in the distance. The blue of the ocean cast a vague hue even farther away, a flat line beneath the eastern sky.

Jules concentrated on where he was headed. The claw-like mound, higher than the surrounding landscape, acted as a beacon. The caldera to one side was the most sensible place to put down, leaving a half-hour hike to the Gorgon rock formation.

A quick glance behind showed Dan flying downward, catching him up. Jules checked his altimeter. 5,000 feet to go until he needed to pull the cord.

Dan leveled nearby, whooping and waving, a ridiculous grin on his face, his trim beard caked in frost. Double thumbs-up, and another whoop suggested he'd forgotten how banal Jules found these activities.

But Jules was trying to change. He considered flipping Dan the bird, a show of reverse camaraderie in which he'd witnessed several bro-types in New York engage, but, like sarcasm and flirting, he worried it might be misinterpreted. He settled for returning the gesture.

Couldn't bring himself to holler.

2,000 feet.

Both pulled their cords and floated in silence. Dan emitted some nervous relief laughter and Jules appreciated the beauty of a near-unspoiled landscape.

They landed on the lower edge of the caldera in snow, a light dusting that covered an icy crust. The far side reached another five hundred feet into the air like a static ocean wave, providing shelter for shrubs and trees which still bloomed. Variations on common species of birds similar to robins—endemic to this specific place—would be nesting now, making Jules happy that his idea to pose as extreme birdwatchers was argued down by Harpal; he'd have had to research even more than usual.

Dan spent several minutes admiring the panoramic vista, while Jules pulled his parachute back in, checked his insulated pants and made sure his coat was undamaged. Then he inventoried the equipment in his pack—the water, foldable shovels, and picks, the light bars, and the C-4 and detonators. One of the most stable explosives available, there was little risk in it going off accidentally, as long as the detonators were secure in their own packaging, which they were. Dan's pack was near-identical, but he'd only just started checking through it when Jules was ready to go.

"Need a hand?" Jules asked.

"Sure."

Jules clapped—a round of applause.

Dan stared a moment before completing the repacking of his parachute. "When did you start making jokes?"

Jules ceased clapping. "Three months ago. It's supposed to help us bond. Is it working?"

"Not really."

Jules waited patiently, then led the way, using a plus-sized cellphone's GPS to guide them.

Both men jogged easily down the terrain. There were only sporadic paths, beaten out by carabao and smaller animals, possibly the odd bear—although Tommy assured them they hadn't seen a bear in years.

"Still," Tommy had added before takeoff, "whenever we're out there, on the ground, we're under orders to carry a gun big enough to take down a bear. Government doesn't take chances."

The temperature fluctuated so often there that snowmelt flowed down, then froze before the ground could absorb it, leading to swathes where it was as much ice underfoot as rock, slowing progress. If those hardy plants and trees had learned to live there, Jules could navigate it.

With only minimal slipping and sliding, the pair found a more well-used trail and sped up.

After five minutes, Dan just had to annoy Jules by speaking. "You haven't checked the map in a while."

"I'm capable of recreating a 100,000-year-old diorama that I glimpsed for a single minute," Jules said. "I think I can follow a modern GPS without much trouble."

"Really?" Dan said. "Around a mountain?"

"It's a volcano."

"Any reason you're slowing down?"

Jules slowed more, trotting to a stop. Surrounded by trees, unable to see the shape of the land, meant Jules had little to go by except instinct and their approximate location compared to their starting point. He took out his phone to check the map. "If it makes you feel better..."

Dan looked at it, too. "We head down here, then hairpin back to the Gorgon formation."

"Or we don't."

"What are you thinking? Cross country?"

The volcano was steep where they stood. Simple enough navigating by the route tramped by man and beast but improvising off that track was a risk.

"Broken ankle ends the expedition pretty quick," Dan said.

"Then don't break an ankle."

"Wait—"

Impatient, Jules shot off through trees. The land's incline steepened more than he'd expected, but he barely slowed, dashing in tight "S" shapes, leaping onto rocks and sliding down their smooth sides, springing onto low-lying branches, skirting shrubs and scattering flocks of birds with his sudden appearance. A larger mound loomed, and he was about to scale it to see where he was when he recognized the mangled outcrop—a photo shown to them before they left.

"I'm here," he said.

The Gorgon Block reminded Jules of an elephant's head without a trunk, all lumps and bumps and ugly as hell. Eighteen feet high, black, and set at the edge of a clearing surrounded by trees, mostly younger red oaks.

A steep trail led in from the opposite direction down the hill, which skirted a sheer face of gray stretching eleven feet at its shortest point, as if holding back the land from collapsing over it. After the clearing, a series of gnarled red oaks guarded the other descent, one, in particular, growing at such an angle that where the ground had eroded, huge roots coiled on the slope like a python, forming a cave of its own.

Dan arrived, filthy and out of breath.

"Took a few stumbles?" Jules asked.

"Next time, I'm navigating."

Jules smiled, wondering if he should attempt another reverse insult, something to show he held nothing against Dan for his late arrival. Time to take a chance. "Come on, we both know you're only in this team to shoot guns and blow stuff up. So, go for it. Let's get inside whatever this bad boy's hiding."

Dan just stared a moment, as he did at the peak. Then he laughed and slapped Jules's shoulder. "Gimme that C-4."

TWENTY-FIVE

AUGUST 19, 3:00 P.M. (EST)

ILYUSHIN IL-76 AIRLIFTER

Private Zefirova Victoriovna was aged twenty-one when she first encountered the Mikhailovic-Dunham MkIII satellite system. Three days after graduating from the military academy with scores only the top twenty men commonly achieved, her commanding officer showed her into a darkened room full of women older than her. It was an introduction to the next five years of her life.

Despite someone as illustrious as Zimina Yanovna achieving high rank, and indeed planning and executing the revolution that freed their people, women were still treated like china teacups—if they were lucky. Diseased whores if they were unlucky. But Zefirova aspired to emulate Yanovna, and effect change from within. The only way was to play the game and position herself to push Striovia into the 21st century.

Five years.

Five years of learning, watching, waiting. Of immersing herself in the workings of both the Striovian Army and the Mikhailovic-Dunham communications satellite—a GPS and cellphone relay to the rest of the world, but a high-tech observation platform to those with clearance.

Understanding was key.

It was necessary to feel the satellite's moods and foibles, its intricacies, and failings, like calming a troublesome child that meant no harm by its tantrums or uncontrollable ticks and swearing. She had embraced it fully and became the only expert worth a mention, which was great in terms of pay and a certain prestige—for an army private. But less great for her promotion prospects.

So, when the opportunity arose to serve on a live operation with the great General Yanovna herself, Zefirova argued her case strongly. When her CO refused, she'd pointed out how angry General Yanovna may be if they sent an underling when the foremost mind in this technology was available.

One thing Zefirova never expected was for the mission to be a covert op in a sovereign nation, which made today even more special.

Logged in to the terminal in the belly of their mobile operations center, isolated in concentration, Zefirova had repositioned the MkIII satellite over the Canadian province of Nunavut. She'd traced the transponder from the Learjet owned by the Lost Origins Recovery Institute—a terrorist organization seeking to undermine the Striovian State—and monitored it both remotely and in real-time images. Retaining the satellite's path, she switched from a geosynchronous orbit to a faulty booster purge, sending it halfway around the world, rendering many car navigation systems and certain cell phone functions useless until an EU satellite picked up the slack.

Once Zefirova informed the general where the Lear had landed, the Airlifter changed course over the Atlantic, heading south of the region under a diplomatic banner. With a pre-arranged flight plan and diplomatic credentials, no law enforcement could search the plane, nor question anyone on board. They could refuel without interference, make contingency plans based on Zefirova's intel, and be on their way.

The Mikhailovic-Dunham spied on the two trips by Luther Gibson's airplane and picked up at least two people infiltrating Mount Chepadu by parachute, one of three possible destinations Yanovna's prisoner had pinpointed.

Shortly after, another group departed the Parks Canada facility on what appeared to be ATV quad bikes. Heading again for the former volcano.

After relaying this information to the general, Zefirova added, "I mean no disrespect, but may I make an observation? One you can disregard if I am lacking facts, but I would like to voice this."

Yanovna's reply came through her earphones. "If it is relevant, go ahead."

Zefirova split the feed into four segments: one wide, encompassing maybe fifty square miles; one close up on where she last saw the incursion pair land; another on the quad bikes closing in on a location on the eastern side of Mount Chepadu; and, finally, the section following the civilian helicopter containing General Yanovna, Captain Igoravich, the prisoner Toby Smith, and a three-strong unit.

"I saw the images your artifact produced," Zefirova said, surprised at the time about how candid the general had been. "And the clues you shared with us all. When I think of that and compare it to the landscape the terrorists are hiding in… there is only one possible destination."

A quiet moment passed before General Yanovna answered. "That is why we are on our way."

Zefirova swallowed, unsure how the next suggestion would be taken if the general had not already figured it out. A man, certainly, would view the notion from a twenty-five-year-old female private badly, but Zefirova trusted Yanovna. "General, if there is no other likely destination in the region, your prisoner was lying about the other two. Looking at this land in detail, from these angles… I believe he was stalling."

PASSENGER HELICOPTER, AIRSPACE OVER NUNAVUT

Zimina Yanovna thanked the young comms officer, asked her name to remember it properly, and signed off to address the problem she posed.

"We had a deal, Toby."

"Whatever do you mean?" Toby replied. "I have been nothing but cooperative."

The passenger helicopter chartered through the embassy in Washington was more luxurious than most military vehicles. It seated her and Toby easily in the first row, with Lukic and Holorov on the bench seat behind. Igoravich and Benjamich were at the controls.

Toby did his best to look insulted and confused, but Yanovna didn't buy it.

"Stalling?" she said. "Did you think we would not find out?"

"I did no such thing." He seemed earnest. But then, spies—and former spies—were experts in denial and subterfuge. "I assure you, I am being completely honest."

"Toby, let me be clear. Stalling tactics will only work if you can keep us away from the map's target indefinitely. Your team would have to get there first, remove what they find, and escape before we arrive."

Toby said nothing, but a faint crease on his forehead gave away his concern. Already working the scenarios, seeing where she was going with this.

"We know, Toby. We know they are at Mount Chepadu. And they have enough of a head start to beat us to whatever is buried there."

Toby, his hands free since he posed no risk at this point, bit his thumbnail.

"If they beat us to what we seek," Yanovna said, "it may not end well for them."

Toby lowered his thumb and sighed. "I can talk to them." He looked straight at Yanovna. "If they have what you're looking for,

I can get them to stand down before any violence becomes necessary."

"Violence," Lukic said from the back.

Toby glanced at the man.

Lukic had a knife in one hand, pointing it at Toby. "You betray General, I gut you. Like rabbit."

"Rabbit," Holorov said beside him. "I like rabbit."

"I give you spy's foot." Lukic slapped his friend's shoulder. "Good luck charm, yes?"

Both men laughed. Yanovna grinned at Toby's discomfort.

She appeared about to speak when Igoravich squeezed through from the helicopter's front section. "We are coming up on the area now, from south-west. Dropping to fifty feet above the canopy. The mountain will conceal our approach."

A soft *whumph* sounded, audible over the rotor wash, alerting all but Toby.

He seemed to sense a change in the cabin, though. "Is there a problem?"

"That was an explosion, Toby," Yanovna said. "They must be close. I cannot let anyone have this power. It is mine. It is Striovia's salvation. This means you get *one* chance to save them. Talk them out of doing something that will get them killed. Or you all die."

MOUNT CHEPADU, NUNAVUT REGION

An explosion rippled across the slopes, shaking the forest and making Bridget jump out of her skin. "Dan, you ass."

Leading the convoy through the national park, Luther pulled to a halt and raised his hand. Everyone pulled up.

He pointed at Charlie, angrily at first, then bit it back to mild annoyance. "Was that your people?"

"Maybe." Charlie offered an innocent smile. "I'll give them some grief when we meet up. Is it this way?"

Charlie hauled ahead through the trees, drawing a grimace from the Parks Canada guide as he revved the quad bike and followed.

The trails were clearly laid out, marked on manual maps and the GPS units attached to the bikes' handlebars. Some were routes taken by amateur enthusiasts who'd be happy coming away with one of tens of thousands of arrowheads or shards of pottery scattered about the land up there, while others were more exploratory in nature. Luther claimed his team regularly beat out new ingress points to the volcanic slopes as fresh clusters of artifacts turned up. The section dominated by the formation nicknamed *the*

Gorgon Block was always considered too rocky, too hardscrabble to turn up anything of interest. There was no reason a pre-industrial tribe would venture up there, except maybe as a lookout spot.

Bridget still suffered the sting of Jules's comments. Despite his apparent emotional retardation, he plainly felt betrayed in a deeper way than she'd realized back in Striovia. He'd even fired a barb at Charlie about her misleading Phil on the possible dangers. A lie by omission was often seen as a cost of doing business within LORI, compartmentalizing certain facets to keep the whole intact. Toby was especially economical in things that might incriminate.

Plausible deniability.

That was always his reasoning. The only thing he and Bridget kept from the team had been a possibility that the seals from the mummified body may have been much older than first believed. The map was not on their radar until Toby delved deeper. And yes, they did finalize the decision to undertake that mission based on Dan's history—his being on duty when the Museum of Baghdad got ransacked. But Bridget *had* to see that map. Had to explore what might be waiting.

Knowledge.

Enlightenment.

Truth…?

Knowledge for the sake of knowledge.

What was wrong with that?

Another explosion tore through the air, and again Luther pulled to a halt. Charlie, still ahead, glanced back and slowed, dropping back to join them.

His arms tense, Luther stared at Harpal this time, having gotten nowhere with Charlie. "Are your friends stupid, or just suicidal?"

Harpal removed his helmet and rubbed his hair, sweating lightly in the winter chill. They all were. He said, "A bit of both, I reckon."

"This isn't funny." Luther jabbed a finger toward the peak, the steepest rise some way off in the foothills. "We're still about twenty minutes out, but if they don't stop blasting, we're going back."

Harpal followed Luther's finger up to where a faint line of smoke twisted skyward. "I'm not sure. Might be best to let them get on with it."

Although Bridget didn't turn the man's eye the way Charlie did—and make no mistake, Bridget would be giving Charlie her own portion of grief about that flirting nonsense back there—she seemed to keep his attention when she spoke. Perhaps it was her credentials, which they'd cited when obtaining permits for entry.

"They won't risk damaging anything," Bridget said. "They're real good at this."

"I'm not worried about them destroying artifacts." Luther simmered more than when he'd spoken to Charlie. "First, it's ridiculous to think you'll find anything in that crack beneath the surface. But mostly, dislodging one of those big chunks of ice is a risk. And landslides aren't exactly unheard of. The constant freezing and melting makes it on the unstable side."

"O-kay," Harpal said. "So, there might be an *element* of risk."

"I'll see if the sat phone's working." Bridget dismounted and rummaged in her backpack, turning away from Luther.

She didn't want him seeing they'd been in touch with Dan and Jules all along, connected through the satellite phone that fed via a sub-relay carried in Charlie's pack. One of two. Dan kept the other in his rucksack to enhance the signal and increase battery life.

Bridget lifted the phone to one ear and touched the bud in her other. Paused as if waiting for the other end to pick up. "Hi, Jules, yeah, it's me. You hear me okay?"

"Yep," Jules replied through the bud.

Everyone would hear except Luther as Bridget said, "Listen, there's some concern about possible landslides. Maybe an avalanche?"

No reply. She pictured him staring up at the towering mountain. Applying logic. Thinking it through.

"One more," Dan said.

"Let's wait," Jules said.

But it was too late. Another huge boom split the air. Bridget and the three near her ducked and then stared up the slope. She half expected a cascade of snow and rock to come hurtling down on them.

"Last one," she said firmly and pretended to hang up.

As she returned to Luther, Jules called Dan *a dumb ape* and explained the dust and trickle of rocks placed them in danger. He voiced how annoyed he was at himself for not analyzing that possibility, but all they could do now was hang tight and hope nothing critical gave way.

"Tommy, you there?" Luther said. There must have been a reply because he went on, "You got the monitors up on the north and east faces? Good. Yeah, it was just these cowboys messing around. Any more activity, you let us know, okay?" He hung up. Addressed the group. "We stay on the bikes for ten more minutes, then it's another ten hiking. But before we go on, I gotta explain something." He pulled his belt up, adjusted his shirt, and puffed up his chest. "As an official of Parks Canada, I have the power to place anyone under arrest on this land. If you break any more laws, that's exactly what I'll do. And using explosives without a license is against the law." He touched the Glock in its holster but withdrew his hand quickly. "Understand?"

"I'm sorry." Charlie had to keep him sweet without more flirting. "It won't happen again.

Dan spent the next twenty minutes feeling extremely clever indeed.

He put a proposal to Jules, who worked something out in his head, applied logic, and agreed to help Dan with the idea; *better safe than sorry.*

Once the rest of the Institute rocked up on foot, he and Jules were the picture of innocence.

"Hey," Jules said.

Charlie breathed heavily and put her hands on her hips, gazing at the clearing. After explaining that the ATVs wouldn't make it up that final stretch, she said, "Tell me you found the entrance."

"Over here." Jules led the way.

Bridget pushed in front of the others, striding toward the Gorgon Block and the five-foot-wide crater blasted out of the hillside a few feet above it. In the crater lay a hole granting entry to the gash in the mountainside.

"Had to dig, too." Dan's arms still ached from the effort. "But we're through into an empty space. Narrow, though."

Bridget leaned over the hole, which was no longer smoking, and the dust was clear. "Oh, my."

Dan didn't need to see. He and Jules had tossed glowsticks down there and observed how the same colored rock as the Gorgon had set in place faded in size the farther in it got. The cavern widened enough for an average person to walk through.

Now they all had a view, Dan tapped Harpal. Pulled him to one side. "You itching to go down there?"

"Not really," Harpal said. "But I'll admit I'm curious. If you found this by accident, it'd just be a cave. But those old seals pointing here..."

"How about you shore up the rear with me?"

"Why?"

"To guard the entrance."

"Who from?" Harpal asked.

"From whoever."

"Carabao? Squirrels?"

Dan lowered his voice. "It's either chasing away rabid squirrels or listening to *them* geek out over whatever cave paintings they find."

Harpal raised his hands, miming a weapon braced at his

shoulder, and aimed into the trees. "Got one looking at us funny. I'll keep an eye on him."

"That's my man."

Still regretting the absence of firearms, Dan announced to the others that he and Harpal were sticking around there, which brooked no argument.

"It shouldn't be possible." Luther sounded breathless, gazing inside. "I have to see this."

Harpal joined Dan again, his subvocal unit off. "So, when they're gone, how about you tell me why we need to be guarding a perimeter?"

Perhaps Dan was just being paranoid. But he was sure he heard something that shouldn't be there, something that might spell trouble. Better he shared it only with Harpal so the specialists could do their thing.

Jules concealed his excitement at delving into this regular-looking gash in a natural environment. From the moment he tossed in the first glowstick, it was clear there was something *un*natural about the fissure.

Excitement led to rash choices, though, as it had when he'd left Dan to blow stuff up. He wanted this over with, to locate whatever remnants—if anything—lay beneath their feet. Then they'd bargain for Toby's freedom and Jules could get back to reducing his pastry intake to one every other day, weaning himself down to one per week.

They kitted themselves out, omitting unnecessary bulk while shoring up anything that would give them light. Having left Charlie's relay pods behind to save on weight, comms would die beyond a certain point. Back in the UK, Phil logged off for this phase, with Dan promising to fill him in on anything he needed to know. It'd preserve battery life too.

Similarly, Jules had left most of his regular equipment on the plane. He'd brought one of his bungee cords with its retracted grappling hook inside a baton which he now fixed to his belt, and Dan caught him squishing a tennis-ball-sized brick of C-4, which he secured inside his sock.

The balding sad sack of a midlife crisis from Parks Canada had forbidden more explosions, but the prospect of waiting days for access to blocked caverns sent Jules into an impatient tantrum.

Internally.

Partly his natural, hard-wired impatience, but mostly that the Striovians possessed the seal. *And* they also had Toby. Everything they needed to mount their own expedition.

Before they could commence exploring, Luther continued trying to take charge, so Charlie humored him as he gave directions. They all had to keep their helmets on, which they'd brought with them from the stashed bikes, and he instigated a buddy system, immediately pairing himself with Charlie and Bridget with Jules.

Jules couldn't read Bridget's tight expression—it was conflicted, for sure. Worried? Guilty?

Didn't matter.

What mattered was the objective. Anything else was mission creep.

Luther and Charlie took point, eased themselves down into the crater, and disappeared into the longer tunnel. Jules and Bridget followed, landing on lava hardened a million years ago. Jules crouched alongside his buddy, keeping her within touching distance until the cavern opened out into a rough triangular shape. It was like walking through a Toblerone.

They lost contact with Dan after fifty feet. The hillside was too dense for the satellite signal to penetrate, and once the scattering of glowsticks was behind them, only head torches and handheld flashlights enabled them to see.

Jules touched the walls every so often, rough with millennia of seepage, the occasional root snaking through, and only a smattering of bugs that scurried into the holes burrowed to reach this spot.

Miniature explorers.

The passage could have been natural. Descending steadily, it boasted no flat surfaces, nothing polished or constructed. But one thing gave it away as perhaps not being forged by nature.

"It's too consistent." Luther echoed Jules's conclusion. "Here, deeper, it's even flatter." The man might have been a bit hopeless in the personality department, but he was no fool. He used a trowel from a pouch on his belt to scrape at the soil to the left.

"Careful there," Bridget said. "We don't know how stable this is."

"The size of the passageway, it's just right for—" He stopped talking, cutting himself off. Ceased moving entirely.

Charlie froze beside the man. "Oh... my... god."

Bridget had been silent until now but rushed forward alongside Jules. "What is it?"

When Jules took in what Charlie and Luther's lights had found, the muscles in his face went slack. His eyes must have been wide, and all four just stared.

"That's more impressive than a cave painting," Jules said.

CHAPTER
TWENTY-SEVEN

Harpal observed Dan patrolling back and forth, his right hand constantly positioning itself close to his heart, thumb extended and fingers searching for a grip, as if he'd been wielding an assault rifle pointed at the floor that had suddenly dissolved.

There'd been no time for a firearms pickup, and Charlie had worried that smuggled items would land them in a Canadian jail right after evading a Striovian one. As a business with a legitimate use for explosives, the C-4 was licensed and her other tech was covered by international carnets, but importing guns was a big no-no.

Plus, they shouldn't need them.

No one knew if the Striovians would act on the same information, Jules placing the chances as fifty-fifty at best. But now they had Toby, someone with knowledge of an ancient people who shouldn't exist, and able to confirm the seals' age was correct, not some mistake in the radon dating process.

If they tortured Toby—a possibility that Harpal ranked at far better than fifty-fifty—he might hold out for a time. But Yanovna was a smart woman; she was as smart as Toby, and as ruthless as Dan. The only reason they'd have for not exploring the regions laid out in the seals would be that humans—intelligent humans—

did not evolve for millennia after the seals' supposed construction. A paranoid government would not sanction an infiltration of a foreign land based on that, yet would be unwilling to share this intelligence with others.

"They're coming," Harpal said.

"I know." Again, Dan's finger searched for a trigger guard on which to rest. He frowned, settling his hand on the knife on his belt. "Think they'll ask to join in nicely?"

Harpal gazed out over the canopy of green, the mist fading into view many miles away. "Nah. We need to get out as soon as we know what's down there."

"Agreed."

"You know, if logic dictates there's potential for physical danger, that puts you in charge. Toby's standing policy. *Man-at-arms is responsible for avoiding firefights or getting us out of them*."

"You'll support that? If it comes to voting?"

"Sure."

Dan turned a slow 360-degrees, watching everything, maybe expecting a commando unit to leap out at any second. "Because Bridget's blind to anything but the endgame, and Charlie won't admit it, but she'd be lost without Toby."

"Jules is a logic guy," Harpal said. "He'll come around."

"You think my gut and your experience'll be enough?"

"It'll have to be."

Jules's heart rate rarely rose without some serious cardiovascular stimulation, so when he felt his blood pounding at the sight, he guessed the others must be stunned into the frozen poses they now held.

The gap Luther had scraped in the earth exposed a metallic surface the size of a dinner plate. It gleamed like silver. When they all joined in shaving the surrounding mud and soil, they uncovered a whole section without end, meaning the metal must have extended way beyond, maybe even along the whole wall.

Charlie and Luther attacked it like starving refugees presented with bread for the first time in weeks. They wiped at the surface, uncovering lines, markings, similar lettering to what they'd witnessed in India earlier that year.

"Is it the Indus precursor?" Charlie asked, following a line Luther cleaned up with a small brush.

"No," Jules said, the language etched in his memory. "Not the same. But derived from the same source."

"You're sure?"

Bridget agreed with Jules. "Unless they're the same people and had a much bigger alphabet."

Jules moved closer, squinting to take it in. "And chose not to repeat any of the same words here as over there—"

"Okay, I get it," Charlie said.

The exposed section spanned floor to ceiling, and five feet eight inches at its widest point. The words ran at the top and bottom with diagrams in between—a landmass by the looks of it.

"Oh my god," Luther said for the seventh time, panting like a dog at every cleaned-up area that presented a new series of lines. "How can this *be* here?"

"A guess?" Jules said. "Generally, I don't do guessing. But that's all I got."

"I'll take it."

"The lava flow and Gorgon formation is millions of years old. It'd have followed a channel. Whoever built this burrowed around the channel 'cause the earth was weaker."

"But *why*? Why leave… *this*?"

Bridget marveled at it, a flat hand tracing the letters rather than the illustration. "Because they knew their time was limited. A tribe of humans whose intelligence grew independently of the majority of the others. I have a hypothesis on that, something Toby and I were working on—"

"Another thing you chose not to share," Jules said.

"We hadn't formulated it yet." Bridget took her hand away, her chin down. "It's like getting a paper ready for peer review. It's not ready for others to see. When we work out the kinks, we'll be fully open."

"Yeah, well, right now..." Jules stood back, that part of the wall as clean as it'd get without washing it.

The others followed his lead.

In their lights, the lines between the upper and lower texts were undoubtedly a map similar to the one that had sent them there.

"Can't be," Luther said.

Jules pressed his lips together and fought the urge churning in his gut. If he didn't speak, though, things would never change and only get worse. "Okay, you gotta stop that."

Luther turned his head and in Jules's lamplight appeared to not understand. "Stop what?"

"Saying it can't be true, it can't be here, it's not possible. With your own eyes, man, it's *right there*."

"I know, I—"

"So quit wasting your breath and all our time and start thinking straight. You're a professional. Act like it." Jules then returned his attention to the drawing.

Luther stammered a second, stopping only when Charlie placed a hand on his shoulder.

She said, "Jules gets ratty when people add unnecessary garnish to a situation. But he's right. This looks kind of familiar, but—"

"The East Coast." Luther stepped to the wall, allowing Charlie's hand to fall away. He traced the intricate lines, the flashlights shining back off the dull metallic surface showing him almost hypnotized.

"The Canadian eastern coast?" Bridget said.

"US. The current East Coast. It's the Laurentide ice sheet. The lower end. When did you say these people lived?"

"We can't say when they evolved. Just that, whoever they were, their gene pool was small. Must have died out long before modern humans. Our own ancestors evolved—"

"Are we talking more than 20,000 years?"

"More than likely, they lived closer to fifty. Certainly, more than 30,000."

Luther closed his eyes. Jules couldn't see his face properly—a consequence of the lamplights not being focused—but when he started laughing, the other three just waited. "It's the Laurentide ice sheet. Showing the southernmost point of the 2,000-meter-thick glaciers that covered North America." He rushed to the opposite wall, stabbing with the trowel as if attempting to murder it. Clumps of sod and earth fell away to the metal beneath, creating a gap the size of a saucepan lid. "More here. Of course, there is."

Again, Jules cast his mind back to the approach to the tomb they discovered in India. That one displayed murals carved into the stone, with evidence it had been painted over for clarity. That artwork told stories, ones that appeared to reflect modern legends, of floods, great warriors, mythical weapons. The photos he took had fascinated the others, especially Toby, but they never shared their ideas with Jules. Until now.

"They chronicled their lives," Bridget said. "If they were explorers, there's no reason they wouldn't have been cartographers too. Maps would've been essential."

"And they understood inter-generational knowledge," Jules said. "Passing it down. Like... *witnesses* to the world around them."

"Witnesses." Bridget sighed. "That was one of the things Toby and I discussed. Like their mission was to preserve something. Preserve their knowledge for the future."

"Meaning, if they made a map to this place, they must've stashed a buncha other stuff here."

"You have a map?" Luther said.

"So, this might be another library." Bridget's speech pattern sped up, her face shadowed, but the big grin plain in her voice. "We'd have more to work with."

"I don't think it's a library," Jules said.

"Why not?"

Jules shone his head torch and the flashlight between the ice age map and the new gap in the wall. "Let's move on."

"No way," Luther said. "We have to examine this, figure out what it—"

"The pictures ain't the reason they built this place." Jules wandered away, expecting them to follow but not caring if they did or not.

Luther was the first to catch up. "Then what *is* the reason?"

"Not sure yet. Hoping I'm wrong but hoping I'm right too. It'll make sense."

The women trailed them now too.

Jules said, "You like talking. Tell us about that ice sheet. Why it might be important."

Luther relented. "You sound like a New Yorker."

"Brooklyn."

"Ever visit Manhattan? Long Island?"

"Sure. I live in Manhattan."

"New York became the city it is today because of its harbor, but that only formed between 13,000 and 18,000 years ago. The ice sheets stretched that far south and melted sometime during that period. Lots of thawing and re-freezing over the next 7,000 years, y'follow?"

"Yeah, I know all that." Jules didn't need a rehash of the Younger Dryas or other basic history lessons. "How's it relate to New York?"

"You understand what the *Pleistocene Epoch* means?"

"The combination of two Greek words," Bridget said. "*Pleistos*, meaning 'most' and *kainos*, meaning 'new' or 'recent.' The most recent age."

"Right. The end of the Pleistocene Epoch saw all that ice change and formed the massive bay we know today. Back then, it was basically a lake, with a natural geological barrier between the Hudson and the sea, which was much farther out, okay?"

"Okay," Charlie said.

"But the number of mammoth remains we've found, and rocks not indigenous to that area, points to a massive geological event. There are boulders in Central Park that originate hundreds of miles north. When the ice melted around 18,000 years ago, the Adirondack Mountains held millions of cubic feet of water, like a reservoir. But as more meltwater from the north flowed in over thousands of years, the banks burst, sending a million-and-a-half cubic feet *per second* spilling toward the sea."

"That a precise calculation?" Jules asked.

"It'd need to be that high if it was going to rip so much from the land—animals, boulders, sediment."

"That's more than the Mississippi at its peak," Bridget said. "The same melting period that flooded Doggerland."

"What's Doggerland?" Jules asked.

"You don't know Doggerland?" Bridget's tone was almost playful, but then she appeared to remember who she was talking to. "Right. You probably never had a *logical reason* to learn about Doggerland. Doesn't matter right now. Why don't you listen to Luther about your hometown?"

"Listen to Luther," Charlie said. "Like a radio phone-in show."

Luther allowed a little laugh before going on. "The water from up north flooded the Champlain Valley and burst across what is now New York City." His hand gestures became grand, as if delivering a lecture to a bored audience. "It crashed through the natural barriers and swept all this debris in its path, mammoths, trees, and any primitive people living there. It'd have grown too fast for them to move out of the way."

"The Verrazano Bridge." Jules kept his tone neutral but swallowed back a hint of sadness at thoughts of the bridge; his father drove Jules and his mom across it the night the pair died. "Suspension bridge connecting Staten Island and Brooklyn. It crosses the Narrows."

"Exactly," Luther said. "As the original glacier formed, it carried boulders hundreds of miles. When the glacier melted, streams full of sand and sediment burst through the barrier that once separated the Verrazano side from the Narrows. It formed a water plain. Without this event, without all that sediment and rock, Long Island wouldn't exist."

"Sure, cool." Jules had been taking in all Luther said, but also calculating their route, the shape of it. "You make it sound like something special."

"You don't think it's special?"

"It's interesting, I guess, but not as interesting as this passage. Unless you got something else to add."

"I do." Luther adopted that haughty tone again, a gesture he must have utilized when expressing just how gosh-darn in charge he was. "That map back there? It showed land features that no one would witness for thousands of years. It's not exact, but that drawing actually shows the area Long Island would inhabit. They saw the land where the sediment would create a larger landmass which wouldn't be seen for centuries. This is… *impossible*."

But it was plain Luther accepted the truth. He had the same goofy look Bridget expressed when learning something new. Jules just hoped he wouldn't demonstrate the same loss of perspective she'd undergone these last few months.

Dan snapped his attention to a noise that few people would recognize, trying to orient himself in relation to the sound.

"What's up?" Harpal asked.

"Too many hills. Sounded like… an explosion. Or a landslip."

Harpal turned to check up the hill. "Might we have loosened something? That Luther guy was worried about it."

Light was fading, day heading for twilight. The shape of the land there didn't give them a view of the peak above. But Dan wasn't concerned there.

"No," Dan replied. "I've heard detonations in mountainous regions before. Afghanistan. When it's coming at you in a straight line, the concussive blast spreads through the ground. The sound is cushioned off the surrounding land, and here there's trees as well as soil and rock. It'd be softer."

"I didn't hear anything."

"You're not listening for it."

"And you are?"

Dan looked at him, tried not to sound like an ass. "I never stop listening for it. Once you know it, picking up on that sort of thing is second nature."

"You're sure?"

Dan scanned all he could see again, using binoculars, trying to spot the telltale curl of smoke. "I'm sure. Someone set off ordnance. It was an explosion."

CHAPTER
TWENTY-EIGHT

Luther's conclusion appeared to impress the others, but Jules was trying to work out how to deliver his own news. Luther didn't seem like an alpha in any area except this one, impressing people only by his knowledge and his middle-management position in Parks Canada.

But did they need his help beyond this trip? Now they were there, did it matter if they hurt his feelings?

"It's a spiral," Jules said. "Man-made."

Sure enough, Luther replied defensively. "What is?"

"This place. We been turning steadily left for the past twenty minutes. The floor might've been carved out of a lava tube originally, but we left that behind a while ago. Far as I can tell, it's as close to geometrically perfect as you can get." He angled his hand to the left, shining his light to emphasize the curve ahead.

"This is incredible." Bridget breathed harder, struggling to keep a lid on her excitement. "It could be another library, another repository of knowledge. More important than Alexandria, more than Aradia, more than—"

"It's a mine, Bridget." Jules couldn't stand to see her build up her hopes any higher. "It's a functional tunnel. It'll lead to a core."

Although it was Bridget who said, "What?" as if Jules was

insane, he picked up vibes from the others that they didn't believe him.

"I got a theory on what they were mining, too."

"But you won't tell us?" Charlie said.

"You guys love when Toby holds back, so why don't I keep you in suspense? Pass the time."

Then the corridor ended. In their lights, it expanded out a hundred feet into a wide space like an underground parking lot. Only this was completely open, no pillars, and was roughly circular, the ceiling twenty feet over their heads. The dark gobbled up the flashlight beams, snagged every so often on items discarded around the edges.

"Careful." Jules stood forward, arms out to signal the others should halt.

"What's wrong?" Bridget asked—eager, impatient.

"Charlie can explain basic engineering better than me."

"There are no supports," Charlie said.

Jules ventured in a half dozen feet and crouched to touch a circle of rough material embedded in the floor. "Wood." He looked back, dazzling Charlie with his headlight and lowering it slightly. "There *used* to be supports in here."

"But tens of thousands of years will rot it," Luther said.

"Whispers," Charlies said. "No baritones, no big noises." She pointed at Luther. "No digging." To the others, she said, "The first sign of any subsidence, we retreat. Quickly, but soft footfalls."

Luther shook his head. "You're just going in there? No way. We need to make it safe, bring in—"

No one listened, pulling on gloves and opening their packs. Jules snapped a glowstick, dropped it, and moved toward the middle of the hundred-foot chamber, laying a rod of light every ten feet. Bridget did the same, heading right along the perimeter, and Charlie went left until they gave decent illumination to the near-impenetrable dark.

In order to complete his lighting duty, Jules ignored what lay at the center, returning to the two women only when he'd reached the other side. The small items scattered around the edge were familiar by today's and Neolithic standards: tools in the form of ax heads, picks, even something resembling a beaker, metallic in nature.

"They'd need smelting skills." Charlie's voice became a whisper. "Again, tens of thousands of years too early."

"And they've never shown up before," Bridget said, equally softly.

Jules set off toward the center. "You like that, you're gonna love this."

In the middle of the room, Luther was already there, having abandoned his concerns in favor of curiosity.

It seemed anything made of wood had rotted away. Jules hypothesized the outer edge had been lined with shelves once upon a time, while in the center stood a block of metal, square, four feet on each side; a plain chest, browned with centuries or, more likely, millennia of corrosion, but somehow still in one piece.

Luther kneeled and eased off the lid, the covering having rested on the top rather than connected by a hinge.

As Jules, Bridget, and Charlie reached the box, Luther was removing what looked like a stone blade. Curved. Dark with greenish flecks.

"Lemme see that." Jules relieved him of the object and showed the others.

"Hey, I wasn't done with that." Luther stood, put his hands on his hips and puffed up his chest again. "Do I need to remind you that I am in charge here—"

"Shhh." Charlie pressed a finger to his lips. "Please." Whispering now. "We've seen something like this before."

"Not quite like this." Jules turned it over in his gloved hands, aiming his light across it. "The rock's just like my mom's bangle. The green flecks're pretty clear. But the surface..."

Bridget ran her hand over it. "Smooth. Like it's been coated in something."

"Glass," Jules said. "Not perfect. It's got marks on it. Scratches.

And this end..." He showed her the thicker area, the opposite end to the tapered point, where a crude molded bracket enveloped a shard of black pulp. "Imagine the blade attached to the top of a pole."

Bridget spent exactly four seconds in silence, touching the glass-encased rock blade. "A scythe. It'd have been a scythe."

"A *scythe*?" Luther's voice rose, but he caught himself. "Farming is only a couple of thousand years old. What would this mean?"

"It's not a practical tool," Bridget said. "More like the Grim Reaper's possession."

"No orb," Jules said. "I was expecting an orb."

"Orb?" Luther said. "Reaper? What the hell are you—Oh, fine, this is *over*. You played me. All this. Lies."

Jules would've liked to say he could sympathize with the man, but he'd been a part of the deception.

Did that make him as bad as Bridget and Toby for lying to the team? To him?

"Why forge a scythe that couldn't be sharp enough for anything practical?" Jules asked.

"Ceremonial?" Bridget suggested.

"Looks like the bangle."

Bridget stared a moment longer. "Take off your glove."

"Bridge..." Charlie said, a warning undertone.

Luther threw up his hands and blew out his cheeks. "Okay, so no one is listening to me."

"Your voice," Charlie hissed.

"Oh, screw this." Luther walked backward, not quite shouting, but certainly louder than anyone was comfortable with. "Screw the steak. You played me, and I don't appreciate that. If you'd told me the truth, I could've been helpful. Now... this is my land. My country. I'm getting all the damn credit for it, and you lot are going to jail."

Jules was now sure Luther felt bad. It was the man's work, his passion, and they'd bulldozed in, manipulated him. He could be a problem. Dan being outside meant it wouldn't be a problem for long, but hey.

"Luther." Jules removed one glove. "Wait and listen. I'm gonna show you somethin', and you can't freak. Okay? The secret we're keeping from you."

Luther paused, nodded his lamp toward Jules's bare hand. "Make it fast. Make it good."

Jules couldn't touch the rock directly but could poke out the pulpy remains of whatever once served as a pole or handle and find the rough surface beneath. "Watch."

Jules pushed beyond the old wood and pressed his finger against the rock. The flecks inside lit up.

Luther's mouth opened, gaping there as he took two tentative steps toward Jules. "My..."

A soft, grainy trickling noise silenced them all, like sand poured over a slab. They couldn't pinpoint it. All glanced around, searching for the possible breach. Trails of dry dirt, as fine as smoke, ghosted from the ceiling, caught in lamplights and the glowsticks' wan illumination.

No words needed, they proceeded for the exit, feet as soft as they could manage. They were almost at the doorway to the triangular corridor when a huge, chest-thumping *throom* echoed across the space.

The rear of the cavern plumed with dust. Clouds billowed. Jules detected a tremor that did not bode well for stability.

From the direction of the collapse, red lines danced in the gloom, lasers falling on the torsos of the four archaeologists. No one knew where to go, what to do.

Jules retracted the finger that triggered the light and held still; Bridget froze next to him, one hand on his arm. Charlie stood beside Luther, and Luther reached for the pistol on his belt.

"Don't." Charlie gripped the man's wrist, keeping the gun in its holster.

Gradually, the figures emerged from a five-foot-wide hole in the far wall: three troops in black, submachine guns aimed with laser sights, night vision goggles over their faces along with hard masks on their mouths and noses. They wore filters rather than being hooked up to oxygen. Next came a woman in the same operational gear and a bearded man with a scarred face, who manhandled Toby Smith himself. All wore the dust masks.

So. They'd done it.

The Striovians had found them.

CHÂTEAU CACHÉ, BRITTANY, FRANCE

Prihya Sibal traveled to France on Valerio's dime. She'd never accessed an expense account before and never expected to. Certainly not a bottomless one. The black Amex card had no limit, and, therefore, neither did she. Drawing out cash was simple too, advised by the man in the hospital to take what she needed, to spend what she had to, and they would pay her salary on top; and it was a salary to make the greediest banker on the planet blush.

Being paid so handsomely to perform a task she'd have accepted for the cost of her expenditure alone seemed wrong, so she was sure to be diligent.

Okay, she flew in business class, but that was as much for privacy as indulgence, so she could review the papers procured and printed from various sources regarding the Lost Origins Recovery Institute and make notes accordingly.

There wasn't a lot.

The group consisted of spirits, floating through the realms of fringe archaeology, areas Prihya herself had skirted. Tombs associated with out-of-place objects—or "ooparts"—and with obscure kings and queens, making sense of legends from world folklore, and preserving lost books.

But only in the abstract.

No rumor mills featured Toby Smith or Charlie Locke. Almost as if someone constantly searched for any mention of them and scrubbed these references from the web. It was only Valerio Conchin's connections to various governments that furnished her with the handful of incidents related to their stated goal: to return historical artifacts to their points of origin.

The number of close calls with the law in half a dozen countries across Asia, the Middle East, and Africa suggested they didn't always follow the rules. Most recently, they were suspected of breaking and entering at the UK's Windsor Castle, and the theft of a priceless object from a Mongolian museum in the wake of a mass shooting.

Could LORI have been responsible for that attack, like terrorists? Used it as cover for the theft, even?

From all she'd read about them, they seemed devious and reckless, but not evil. Yet she could not write off the possibility. If they were scrubbing the internet of rumors concerning them, surely, they could have deleted similar incidents of terror.

That this atrocity occurred just days before the collapse of the structure in India spoke volumes. There was more to this group than a bold mission statement.

Their associate, Jules Sibeko, was far easier to locate.

Pictures of him on mugshots showed a handsome black man. His expression seemed almost cocky. Fleeting glimpses suspected to be him on CCTV made him look like a costumed vigilante from a comic book; he was always masked, but she was in no doubt it was him. A young orphan, gymnast, martial arts expert.

Thief.

Like LORI's stated aim, he'd spent much of his life stealing artifacts from those who didn't deserve them, taking a payday usually, but oddly obsessed with a bangle of unknown origin.

Something old, dating back to the Roman occupation of the Middle East.

It was frustrating to possess so little research material. That was why she'd flown out there in the first place, why she'd splashed out on the business class ticket.

Her other indulgence to date had been when she'd landed in Paris. *Shopping*.

She was a serious businesswoman now; looking the part and preparing for any eventuality was half her job description.

She spent one night in a mid-range hotel to get over the jet lag, to pick up business wear, field clothes, and footwear, and get a haircut. Then she hired a BMW to make the drive out to Brittany, where she tracked down the château.

Not *officially* the group's headquarters, but when Prihya confirmed Bridget Carson of LORI was the same Bridget Carson, daughter of the Carson Corporation's CEO, she identified the company's properties in the region. With so much secrecy surrounding it—scrubbed from Google Earth, from all mapping apps, and under an observation order from the British government—it made sense that this was their center of operations.

Prihya drove the BMW to the gate and spent a short while watching the house several hundred yards up the driveway—not a royal mansion, sure, but certainly huge in Prihya's experience.

She pressed the intercom. A woman answered in French. Prihya apologized and asked if the woman spoke English or German, the extent of Prihya's multilingual abilities.

"I speak English," the voice said.

Although Prihya was fluent in English, she carried a Hindi accent, so was sure to enunciate clearly. "I have an appointment with Mr. Smith. To discuss the origin of an item he came into possession of recently."

No reply.

"Hello?" Prihya said. "Mademoiselle?"

"It is *madame*," the woman replied tersely. "And Mr. Smith has been unexpectedly delayed. He will not be available for the fore-seeable future."

Unexpectedly delayed.

Not arrested in a foreign country and his team scattered who-knew-where. Using the contacts and log-on names for the dark web, Prihya had learned that the team's Learjet departed French airspace but not a destination, nor how many people were on it.

"May I speak with Mr. Smith's alternate?" Prihya asked. "It is quite urgent."

"What is the urgent message?"

"Not a message. But information. Concerning their latest expedition."

A pause then, "Please come back tomorrow."

Prihya had expected obstruction but planned for it. She'd talked her way into plenty of educational institutions and parties, trying to reach professors of conventional archaeology to discuss new evidence she'd uncovered, or to challenge a paper they'd published which contained blatant inaccuracies. Or lies.

She said, "Perhaps I could come in and wait while you contact Mr. Smith or one of the Lost Origins Recovery Institute. I fear they made a mistake in their calculations. It could have... it could have placed them in danger."

The intercom opened, someone on the other end pressing it but not speaking. It then died again.

Prihya activated the line, her accent strengthening as she sped up her words, hoping to convey the severity. "If you don't let me in so we can try to contact the team urgently, I'll have to send a message to Ms. Carson's father in America. I would prefer not to do this, but I am sure he will understand his daughter's privacy is important." Prihya paused for effect, regulated her voice to the lighter accent. "I only wish to explain my part in their expedition. If you do not believe me, or you do not consider my information worthy of disturbing them, then I will leave without trouble."

Prihya let go of the button.

The speaker crackled and stayed silent for a long few seconds.

Then the woman said, "Drive up to the main door. I am armed. Do not try anything."

"Thank you, *madame*," Prihya said.

The gate trundled open, and she drove the rented BMW into the heart of her target's operation.

INSIDE MOUNT CHEPADU, NUNAVUT REGION

"Do not try to deceive me again." General Yanovna marched through the fading smoke and dust, secure in the knowledge that the only firearms in the room now belonged to her men.

Having searched Jules Sibeko, Charlie Locke, and Bridget Carson, they relieved the man identifying himself as *Captain Gibson* of the Glock 17 he carried.

Happy with security, Yanovna turned her attention to her surroundings. "This is just like the mine we excavated in Striovia. Where we found the mummy and the seals that led us here."

With Toby Smith's insight—something she'd never admit out loud.

"This is an act of war," Gibson said.

Yanovna had sized him up already: a doughy man hiding a good build, yet his words lacked conviction. A middle manager in an enforcement agency who needed to feel like a big man, someone in control. Most likely, with a disappointing personal life. His assertiveness might have worked with a lesser person, but then he had no idea Yanovna was the architect of a revolution and cared little for protestations like that. "If we kill you all and leave without a trace, there will be no war. If you cooperate, and we let you live, mentioning this will ruin you. Make you appear a failure. Is this what you want?"

The man's jaw clenched.

Yanovna read his impotence as ascent. "Very good. Now you were saying something about a danger?"

She was talking to the dark-haired woman, Charlie Locke. The woman who'd expressed fears of a cave-in.

"Look at the floor." Locke pointed at what looked like a black stump. Then another. "They once held up the roof. The tunnels in here have been reinforced, dug into triangles, and lined with metal panels. But here..."

Yanovna checked around. She didn't worry about the *look-behind-you* play while Lukic and Holorov occupied the group in a crossfire should they try anything. And Toby was still their hostage, flanked by Igoravich and Benjamich.

It was correct that what appeared to be ancient supports stained the earthen floor and ceiling, and the hole that her men had blown into the wall bore more cracks along the surface than she was comfortable with. There was damage to the roof around the space, but they'd only blown away a landslip—a second entrance before being filled in.

That in itself suggested subsidence had occurred at some point.

Having accessed the mine from a million-or-more-years-old lava tube on the opposite side of the mountain, Yanovna had expected everything to be as safe as the salt mine in Striovia. The tunnels there were a different shape with no supports, while those back home came with conventional struts and posts. Younger, she realized, if these pillars had rotted to nothing.

She said, "Give me what you found, and we can part ways as friends."

"You can see all we have here." Locke kept glancing at Toby as she spoke. "We'll clear out. Just leave us with Toby."

"I am not in a position to free a prisoner," Yanovna said. "And why would I? When I can take what I want, anyway?"

"We know what you're looking for," Bridget said. "We can show you something you won't believe."

If Toby thought his subtle chopping motion with one hand—a signal to the Carson girl to stop talking—went unnoticed, he was sorely mistaken. His crestfallen expression in the low light of the flashlights meant he knew he was caught.

"Zimina," Toby said. Igoravich backhanded him lightly on the side of the head. "I mean, *General*. You promised."

"I did promise, didn't I?" She had to balance the honor of keeping her word with strength in front of the troops. "Speak. Persuade them to cooperate."

Toby straightened himself. The suit he'd been dressed in was filthy and there was no tie, but he adjusted his shirt buttons, anyway. "Bridget, Charlie, I'm sorry. Zimin— *General Yanovna* knows about the special properties in the seals. She knows of the active shards and that a certain branch of humanity grew its intelligence faster than others. She understands this. And she wants to know what they concealed here. If you have found something, please… she gave her word none of you will be harmed if you cooperate. And the general is an honorable woman."

Yanovna held on Toby, assessing if he relayed any codes in either what he said or the tone he used. A little robotic in nature, she thought, but she did not believe he'd betrayed her. She turned her attention to the one called Bridget. "What is it? Show me now."

A scratching wafted across the room. No, not a scratching. A rasp and a patter; dry soil shifting at the back of the cavern where they blew the debris. Just a small displacement from the ceiling.

"Okay." Gibson attempted his leadership bluster again. "We all go topside. This place could collapse any moment."

"We can gather as much as possible." Bridget stepped out of position, aiming for the center. "Even if it doesn't seem important, we have to try."

Yanovna held up a hand and the soldier on the left—Lukic—advanced, gun aimed higher. Bridget stopped mid-stride, hands up. She backed up to her previous position, eyes still on the collection of tools discarded around the center of the space.

"Come on, *please*," Gibson said as a trickle of soil fell closer to them. "We have to *leave*."

Gibson was clearly not a part of this. The three spies who sought to rob Striovia of its rightful heritage exchanged glances, ignoring Gibson, and lingered on the African-looking one —Sibeko.

Yanovna approached, staying out of the beams from the two weapons trained on the thieves. By Sibeko's feet lay a dark slab shaped in a crescent. She'd missed it at first, but now they seemed eager to get out. Following Toby's plea, they weren't hiding it.

"Pass that to me," Yanovna ordered. "Slowly."

Sibeko made large, languid, and deliberate gestures to retrieve it. "Gonna step forward if that's okay."

Yanovna beckoned him. "Now."

He needed just one stride to place the object in her hands.

Not a full crescent as she first thought. It weighed as much as one of the larger seals, and in the flashlights, she noted identical flecks and stones inside a glass-like outer coating. This could only be cut from the same substance as the permafrost items. She was tempted to dissect it here, now, to get answers immediately. Her only disappointment was that it resembled more a farming implement than a weapon.

With a glance at Locke and Bridget, Sibeko received nods in response. "This rock does something weird. I can show you."

"That isn't necessary," Toby said.

Confusion crossed the faces of his minions.

"You said cooperate," Sibeko said. "You want that, I want outta here."

Another shift of earth signaled even Igoravich to make sideways glances all around. A clump beside their improvised entry point slapped to the floor and plumed into a dry cloud.

"General," Toby said. "This can be examined topside."

Yanovna ignored him, holding the item near her face, her palms stroking the surface, marveling at its beauty. "This is where our seals came from."

"Yeah, I figured that." Sibeko rejoined the others, shrugged specifically at Bridget. "This mine. The seals pointed us here. Harvesting images. They weren't just about crops. It's where they found or made the rocks for the Striovian seals, my mom's greenstone bangle, and that scythe thing."

Yanovna perked up. "You have other objects?"

"Yeah, they're special. Certain genetic signatures. I'll show you, then we can get goin', okay?"

The young man opened his hand, asking for the stone blade.

Is he able to do what I can do?

"Allow me." Yanovna had located the spot where a shaft would be inserted and pressed two fingers inside. The stones, like fine jewels, sparkled, bathing the cavern in a dazzling glow. "Is this what you had in mind?"

The three spies flinched and stepped back. Bridget's hand found her mouth, while Charlie Locke's lips parted as she attempted to quash her surprise. Gibson glanced between the clear exit point and the hole that now cracked deeper into the structure.

Sibeko watched the light show, his posture tight, eyes unblinking. That was all the reaction he gave, though. Yanovna even allowed him to glide gradually toward her, his gaze held on the glass-encased rock.

"It's brighter than mine." He looked up at Yanovna. "You're more bonded to it than me. Figure that's why I didn't see the map."

Yanovna cautioned herself to appear unsurprised. All should appear planned. "Tell me. About the map."

Sibeko pointed around the room. "I mean... *this* map."

Staring at the glow itself had kept Yanovna from seeing around her. When she followed Sibeko's finger, concealing her surprise was no longer an option. "Everyone, turn off your lamps."

Darkness descended at her order, leaving only the glowsticks' soft hue and the laser sights from her soldiers' weapons.

The curved artifact projected fine lines onto the cavern walls. Close to a modern hologram in appearance, they shimmered in the center of a green diorama, a schematic depicting land masses —familiar yet warped. Like the seal's rendering of the northern hemisphere.

As Yanovna shifted it into a position resembling a contemporary globe, her fingers felt fat and clumsy. With their shadows, it couldn't be depicted clearly.

"Ma'am." Sibeko addressed her in a softer tone than earlier. "May I?" He held his hand at her elbow, asking permission to touch her.

Yanovna acquiesced. "Try nothing. Or you die."

Jules placed one palm on her wrist, the other on her elbow, and eased the scythe blade over her head, then adjusted her grip. The diorama expanded, spread over the roof instead of all around as the seal had behaved. Now she understood.

Without words, she allowed Sibeko to guide her to the center of the room, close to where more showers of dirt were cracking free.

"We don't got much time," Sibeko said.

"Then be quick." Yanovna removed one finger from the bracket.

Sibeko stuck his own in there, accompanying hers, touching their digits together and pressing against the hard surface. The image bloomed over the roof. What had been bright before was now high definition. It incorporated the same area, a top-down map of planet Earth with the North Pole at the center. The massive Arctic ice sheet dominated, with a reaper inlaid in the middle of the Atlantic Ocean.

Floating there.

The Reaper's scythe pointed at North America, landing—she

guessed—on this very spot, while his other hand held an orb like the one depicted on the seal. It glowed with power, striations emanating like a spider's legs, ending at points within land masses drawn by people who lived alongside humanity's hardiest ancestors. Although approximate based on her own picture of the modern globe, it appeared one line ended around Striovia, perhaps the salt mine or the dig that unearthed their mummy. One stretched toward India, one to China. One extended all the way back to America, while another stopped in Western Europe, near where she estimated the UK sat today. The three southern-most spider legs disappeared out of view, though, to where the image distorted.

They twisted the blade lengthways, revealing the illustration continued south over the equator. Where it ended might indicate another stash of artifacts, weapons, more rocks of this odd nature, a nature she had to embrace and explore.

Energy.

A weaponized agent.

It didn't matter. It was hers. And nothing would block her from obtaining it.

Circulus ostendam in virtue Dominus - the circle will show the power of God.

A thump drew everyone's attention. A *whoomph* and a billowing cloud of dirt rushed from the ingress point, the cleared landslip replenished from above. But it didn't stop there.

A gash opened a third of the way into the cavern, showering earth.

"Can we run now?" Sibeko said.

"I think so." Yanovna slipped the artifact free, killing the light, and flicking her head torch on. "Go, now!" She pulled up her dust mask and sprinted, the object cradled in one arm.

Locke and Bridget were closest to the exit, but Gibson charged past, shouldering Locke out of the way. The two women dashed through without pause, though, while Lukic and Holorov stationed themselves on either side. As soon as Yanovna made it through with Jules at her heels, the pair followed. Igoravich and Benjamich half-carried Toby as the earth rained down.

Just yards from safety, clouds of brown and black enveloped all three.

Bridget cried out, "Toby!"

Continuing backward, away from the billowing center of the mine, Yanovna fought the lump in her throat, dreading the prospect of losing men under her command. Igoravich had been there since the beginning, a good man turning on his own father for the glory of Striovian independence.

He would be missed most of all.

The three burst through the doorway, barreling onward, coated in filth and grime, but not stopping either. Toby's legs pinwheeled, touching the ground, teeth gritted with the effort but propelled by the two military men.

Claps of thunder shook the walls as the unsupported roof collapsed, and a fast-growing fog forced all upward at a full sprint. Even with the masks, it would be hard to breathe, and the spies and thieves had no apparatus at all. Eventually, they slowed, and took stock of the fine mist of dust particles that had chased them up the passage.

In less than thirty seconds, the cavern was gone.

CHAPTER
THIRTY-ONE

Bridget's legs weakened as they tramped back up the ancient passageway. She was lightheaded. Waves of cold alternated with heat throughout her body, and she accepted Jules's arm for support.

While he could compartmentalize this, Bridget never did. She'd come under fire before, and her reactions had gotten quicker, her flight response less rigid. Yet almost losing Toby still trilled inside her.

General Yanovna kept pace with her and Jules, having ordered only one light to remain active; aimed at the ground to highlight the route, it was only enough to prevent walking into a wall. The lead soldier—Igoravich, Yanovna had called him—used night vision goggles to sweep ten yards ahead of them, his gun aimed and ready.

Charlie accompanied Toby alongside Luther, who hadn't spoken a word since his show of panic during their escape from the cavern. Two soldiers shadowed Yanovna while the final one brought up the rear—as if someone might sneak up behind them, which seemed ludicrous to Bridget.

A discipline in enemy territory?

"I don't get it," Bridget said.

"Get what?" Jules asked.

"Silence." Yanovna remained close to Jules, on the other side of Bridget.

Bridget had little knowledge of the general beyond what Toby had given her before they imprisoned him. He spoke in glowing terms, a collegiate relationship which he'd hoped might have touched on friendship. The hard edge to the woman indicated there was far more to her than a retired general pursuing a passion for ancient history.

"What don't you get?" Yanovna asked.

Bridget's legs strengthened now, although she coughed a tickle from her throat. "You talked about weapons. Power. We've never found anything like that."

"Light requires energy. Genetically coded, quantum connections, according to your Toby. It may be the biggest leap forward the world has seen in decades. New power leads to new technology, and always new weapons."

"You're certain the light in the stones can generate fuel?" Jules said. "Means it's gotta express energy on its own. Something combustible. Ain't never heard of that."

Yanovna patted her zipped pocket. "I have it on good authority."

Toby joined them from behind. "The message in the scroll may not mean the power you need."

"How can it be anything else?" Yanovna lowered her arm.

"What scroll?" Jules asked.

"Show us?" Toby said. "Please? We may be able to offer a little insight."

Yanovna shook her head slowly. "And why would I do that?"

"Because there's more to the Latin on that paper, and Bridget is an expert in languages."

Bridget slowed momentarily, unsure if she wanted to collaborate this way, but trusted Toby knew what he was doing.

Yanovna fished a folded slip of paper from her pocket and flicked it open. Modern paper, meaning she had scanned the original and printed it for reference. Still walking, she shone the flash-light on it.

"*Circulus ostendam in virtue Dominus,*" Bridget read. "The circle will show the power of God."

"We know this," Yanovna said. "You wish to contribute insight? Do so now."

Bridget spotted why Toby was so eager for her to lay eyes on it: the letters above, which would have appeared as nothing more than a pattern to most observers, meant a lot more to her. This was the language of one of the books they retrieved. Of the people who built the tomb and repository in India.

"Jules." Bridget gestured for him to look.

He did. "Yeah, Latin. Looks like power to me."

Bridget couldn't make him ingest the other writing and could only hope he noticed.

"Still," she said, "Latin is a funny language. Multiple mean-ings depending on tense and usage."

Yanovna folded the paper and placed it back in her pocket. "Quantum physics, if we unlock the mysteries using this material, will gift us defenses more powerful than anything Russia can aim our way. *The power of God.* Maybe even more potent than their nuclear arsenal."

Bridget couldn't imagine something like that being good for anyone, and while she wanted to shout the woman down, she could see it made sense from Yanovna's perspective. "Russia doesn't want to destroy Striovia. They want to absorb it."

"Like Crimea," Yanovna said. "I will not allow that."

"And you'll bring it all down?" Jules said. "Soon as anyone says boo to you."

Yanovna again brought the stone blade to her light. "I cannot imagine how much work went into this." The general held it to one side, prompting Jules to squint closer. Not much light to see by. "Etching the imperfections into the glass, over this odd shape. Surely a ball, an orb like the one carried by the death figure, would be better."

"Designed specifically for that room," Jules said. "Roof had a bulge to it. Like a dome, but too shallow to stand alone. Carved out, not built. Needed the struts. Still..." He stroked the glass surface. "They had to redo the dimensions, calculate it so it all split down the middle. Computer could pull it together now, but just using a brain to work it out... that's an avalanche of intelligence right there."

Bridget hoped Jules wasn't applying his logic too heavily. He'd gone his own way before, his tunnel vision causing him to side with—or to use—competitors in the hunt for other items. If LORI appeared to be failing, it was conceivable he'd throw in with Yanovna.

His mission: to get Toby free and return the Sumerian seals to the rightful owners.

So far, they'd accomplished the repatriation of those items stolen from Baghdad, which left freeing Toby. And when Jules had an objective to achieve, he didn't care much about other destinations, about side quests like where maps pointed; he didn't share her sleepless nights as she analyzed one theory after another to decode the books and source their origins. He'd more than likely be happy to get Toby back to France, then go finish applying for that job he'd mentioned, whatever it was.

They paused at the wall map carved out of the metal lining the tunnel. Yanovna switched on a second flashlight to examine it.

"I think they wanted us to follow them," Bridget said.

Yanovna shifted her light to Bridget's face. "I'm sorry?"

"These people, whoever they were... they made a point to witness everything. Understood the ice sheets were melting."

Yanovna returned to the map on the wall. "This spans the whole corridor?"

"We'd need to excavate to be sure," Luther replied, butting in. "But we picked this spot at random. Seems likely to be more of the same."

"They stored their knowledge in high peaks," Bridget said.

"Entombed art, literature, stories about their world. All lost over time."

"You believe I am a fool for trying to arm our nation?" Yanovna said.

"No." Bridget arched her back, searching for words that might get through to the general—and to Jules—without offending or drawing more scorn. "I think they wanted future generations to learn what they knew. Maybe their own descendants, or other intelligent species. But everything I've seen is like... an invitation."

"The images of death?" Jules said. "Bit of a blow to the head, ain't it?"

"We see death because of the modern depictions of that reaper figure. This pre-dates our concept of the Grim Reaper from the Four Horsemen. In all of these, he's holding a scythe and that ball, which could be anything. An actual artifact or the power of the sun. Could be about farming, growing food and storing it for the winter. It's *knowledge*. Accounts of the past. A gift from them to us."

Yanovna gave a tentative smile, then switched off her second flashlight and walked on. All took up the pace again.

Bridget wished the general had been in India to see the things in the tomb, in the repository, before it was destroyed. She was a scholar as well as a military figure. Heck, maybe Yanovna could have been their savior. If Bridget had been more like her, they'd have saved more than a few old books they could barely understand, let alone translate.

Yanovna really could have been a pioneer in this quest.

Perhaps she still could be.

"Toby told us you're an honorable person," Bridget said. "You want cooperation for us to have any chance of freeing Toby."

"I promised only my recommendation to our justice system," Yanovna said. "I will not set free a threat to our security unless the courts say so. They must weigh his sins against his usefulness to the State."

The tunnel was coming to an end, back to where they started, and Igoravich held up a fist to halt the group.

Had he heard Dan and Harpal up above? Or just standard practice like the rear guard? There'd been no mention of the others, so presumably their knowledge of LORI's expedition didn't stretch to firm numbers.

Bridget just hoped no one did anything dumb. Maybe this wouldn't have to end in a fight; Dan and Harpal were unarmed, after all.

"We can see where the map leads," Bridget said. "If it's just more stone tablets or books or whatever, you'll have to be satisfied with that. We'll cooperate with you, help work out the origins. If it relates to your country, you're a hero. If it really is weapons or can be used as weapons, you take them home and shore up your defenses."

Igoravich reached the entry hole and signaled one of the other soldiers to join him. Both hopped out, and Bridget immediately grew concerned about their two friends.

Out there.

Hiding, hopefully.

Do nothing stupid, Dan. You too, Harpal. You're not as indestructible as you think.

She'd almost lost Toby back there. She couldn't cope with more peril.

"Might work," Jules said. "I ain't against it, but there's more to consider. Toby goes one way, you guys go the other. Or stick together." He shrugged. "Explosive mix, whatever."

Again, Bridget picked up on something unsettling about the way Jules spoke. Was he really going to abandon them if it meant Toby was out of harm's way?

Igoravich called back down, "Clear," and Yanovna led the line to the exit.

She climbed out first while the remaining soldiers ushered the others out into the early evening. Although nearly dark, the moon cast a light that made Bridget blink after being in the near blackness for so long. Seeing so far in the distance felt odd, but she shook the feeling away. Checking her watch, she found it was eight p.m.

No sign of Dan or Harpal.

Hopefully, they'd be holding tight, gathering information on the enemy. Both were highly skilled, with Dan able to take down pretty much anyone they'd come across, one against one. She'd never seen him against four armed soldiers, though.

Jules paced in a tight circle. "Where do we head next?"

Bridget thought about speaking up, mentioning the two out there, loudly, so they'd have to surrender. But the longer they stayed hidden, the longer Bridget worried a fight was about to break out that they just couldn't win.

Igoravich ordered one soldier—Lukic, it sounded like—to radio back to base. At least, Bridget thought that's what the order was, but she only caught some of it.

They set up near the Gorgon rock with one monitoring the group at all times, huddling them together a few feet away. They checked guns, stripped a radio from a backpack, and Yanovna consulted with Igoravich out of earshot.

"We have a long walk," Yanovna said after they discussed their options. "Our transport is the other side of the mountain. But we will call reinforcements. Then we leave."

"Together?" Bridget asked.

"Charlie, Luther," Jules said. "The ATV path."

Charlie and Luther glanced the same way: down the path up which they walked earlier. Toby did the same.

"What's that mean?" Bridget asked.

A *thunk* sounded nearby, the opposite side to the Gorgon Block. Lukic stepped around to investigate, sidearm drawn.

Bridget couldn't see what caused the noise, but the soldier suddenly called out, pointing, and—

An ear-splitting boom rang out. An explosion, tearing across the ground, blew Lukic off his feet, the power ripping him apart. Blood sprayed. Limbs flew in several directions.

Partially shielded by the Gorgon, the shockwave threw Yanovna over, while a second soldier screamed in pain, his arm bloody from shrapnel. Igoravich and the final guy prepped themselves for more attacks.

All they got, though, was another explosion, this one much farther away.

"What the hell is going on?" Bridget shouted.

"You will all die for this." Yanovna retrieved the submachine gun abandoned by the dead man and armed it, aiming at Toby first.

"Wait," Toby pleaded. "Just wait."

"No more." Yanovna firmed up the stock on her shoulder, her reluctance plain. But resolve descended.

Then a deep tremble spread over the ground.

"Avalanche," Luther said.

"What?" The general's hesitation lengthened, curious now.

A growl vibrated from hundreds of feet away, up toward the peak.

Luther pointed frantically. "Avalanche!"

"ATV track!" Jules said. "Now."

Harpal sprang out of nowhere, the foliage having concealed his approach. He landed a kick in Yanovna's side and whipped the gun from her.

Jules's hand gripped Bridget's arm and yanked her forward.

The trees higher up swayed and danced, and the thunder grew louder. Only one thing this could be, and it wasn't good.

There hadn't been time for a plan, and it surprised Jules as much as anybody that Dan and Harpal followed his hints. Dropping phrases such as *an avalanche of intelligence* and *explosive mix* and even *you'll bring it all down* wasn't a foolproof idea, but they'd evidently decoded his suggestions.

Harpal was the first to make it into the open, disarming Yanovna and catching her unaware. Dan sprang from the opposite end, surprising Benjamich with a huge uppercut elbow and swiping the machine gun he was holding. He immediately turned it on Holorov and Igoravich, cutting Holorov down but missing the captain.

Jules had to move. He was right behind Harpal, Charlie, Bridget, and Toby. Luther was already gone, but LORI didn't want to leave. The track up which they came, where the ATVs waited farther down, was sheltered if the landslip proved too big—and the wave of air blowing down from up high certainly indicated a heavy load.

"GO!" Dan yelled, checking the bodies of the men downed so far and sweeping the radius of his position for the others.

Yanovna was on her knees, a snarl to her. She still held the scythe blade. Jules moved to return for it, but Toby said, "Just go. Leave it with her."

They had seconds to decide.

"Zimina," Toby called as they started jogging. "Run! Go! I'm sorry. I never meant it to happen this way."

As a slurry of stones burst through the tree line, Dan had Yanovna cold.

Toby again: "No, Dan, not her!"

Jules was stuck midway between Dan and the fleeing group, with all parties telling him to go, to run, to head down the safer route. The last of them disappeared into the deeper forest.

Jules and Dan checked up the hill. Bigger rubble crashed through, and Dan took shelter by the Gorgon, keeping Yanovna in his sight. Jules shifted closer to the escape route.

Dan's gun drooped, pointing at Yanovna's sidearm. "Drop your weapon and you can run."

"Generous of you." Igoravich emerged close to Jules, a Lebedev PL-15 pistol aimed at his head. Must have circled around. "Now you put down weapon."

Dan hesitated.

Jules said, "Four seconds."

"You not make demands."

"*Two* until we all have to run."

Yanovna twigged what he meant. "Go! Everyone go!"

Based on the wind rush ahead of the main bulk of the avalanche, Jules was only two more seconds out. It was enough time for Dan to sprint backward, for Yanovna and Igoravich to rejoin each other and dive into the hole leading to the mine, and for Jules to flee the other way, following the others down the track.

Rock and ice and chunks of hard-packed snow blasted out of the trees, crushing dozens as it cascaded in a huge mass.

The subvocal kicked in.

Dan: "Keep going. Get everyone to safety."

Jules stuck to the track, pressed up against the natural wall, smaller debris peppering him while the bigger lumps and boulders bounced over.

"Stay where you are," Jules replied. "Wait right there. Dig in!"

"Go. Look after—" But the comms cut off.

Jules could only charge onward, keeping to the side until he reached the end of the landslide's range. He kept jogging backward as he rounded the ridge, the way to safety, staring back, watching as thousands of tons of rock and earth and ice tumbled and settled.

The rumbling eased. The vibrations lessened. No further huge chunks followed. Reduced to dust and trickles of pebbles, the ground appeared replenished, a fresh layer forming atop the old.

No sign of Dan, though.

No sign of life.

A new landscape, beneath which a man Jules had hardly gotten to know was buried. He shouldn't have felt a loss there, but he couldn't help it.

The subvocal equipment had failed at some point, and Jules couldn't even call for assistance in retrieving the body. All he could do was drop his shoulders, wander along the path, and plan on how to break the news to Dan's friends.

A *whump-whump-whump* cut off his thoughts.

Helicopter.

It came closer, louder, building in noise until it hurtled overhead. Jules himself pinned to a tree, crabbing around the trunk to evade anyone looking out.

Not a military model, but big, fast. A large civilian vehicle with skids and a regular cockpit. No external guns.

"Jules?" Charlie's voice crackled through his earbud. "Are you with Dan? His comms unit is dead, but yours looks okay. What's going on?"

The helicopter hovered over the Gorgon rock, now half buried in a landslip. It pivoted steadily. One person hung out of one door, searching the area—the last known coordinates of the Striovian troops.

The man hanging out the door disappeared inside, then stretched back out, this time the harness on his belt clear even from Jules's distance. The man produced a sizable machine gun and fired in blaring bursts of three.

"Jules!" came Charlie again. "Are you with Dan? Is that racket you two?"

He focused on the blindside of the Gorgon, right where the hillside fell away steeply. There, the roots of a red oak overhung the contours so massively that its python-like roots formed a cave.

Dan.

They were firing at *Dan*.

"Jules!" came Bridget's pained voice. "Please, you and Dan, get back here. We're ready to go."

"Get outta here," Jules said. "I'm gonna be a little late."

And as his mind calculated the best route, Jules's legs were already pounding. Against all logic, against all good sense, he sprinted *toward* the firefight.

CHAPTER
THIRTY-THREE

At least it wasn't a gunship.

As Jules skirted the clearing upon the newly settled ground, he collected six stones somewhat smaller than baseballs, ones with hard edges and angular peaks. He had no firearms, no weapons of any kind. Dan returned fire only with potshots, which kept the hovering vehicle from overwhelming him straight away. He wouldn't hold out long, though.

And Jules's idea had no practical application beyond a distraction. Hopefully, it'd be enough.

Near the high end of the clearing, he ran the numbers. Physics.

The angle of approach is twenty-eight degrees, increasing to thirty-five.

Kinetic energy against gravitational potential energy—mass multiplied by the earth's gravitational field strength, multiplied by the height of an object propelled into the air.

Add in his own momentum, and — damn.

He wasn't familiar with the helicopter's schematics, so couldn't calculate the downdraft precisely. Just estimate its weight and go from there.

"I hate guessing." Jules slipped his grappling hook and baton from the loop of cloth in his pants leg, freed six feet of bungee rope, and coiled it like a lasso.

He took off running—a rock in one hand, baton in the other— toward the helicopter hovering the near the bottom end of the clearing. Downhill, he had less control over his speed, so headed in a diagonal. The spare rocks stashed in his jacket pockets knocked against his body. He hurdled smashed logs dragged from the forest, ran up the side of natural outcrops, and leaped to the next; then, he barreled forward until he had the momentum to use the Gorgon rock as a ramp.

The machine gun still fired at the ground, at Dan's foxhole.

Fighting both gravity and the chopper's downdraft, letting the cord unspool, he sprang into the air directly beneath the vehicle. Once under its belly, he flung the grappling hook.

It snagged the skid and Jules had to adjust his grip, his calculation out by about nine inches, forcing him to wrap the elastic cord around his forearm. As expected, the helicopter jerked down a fraction while his momentum swung him out. Onward. To the point where he saw the gunman in the doorway stumble.

The gunman's head stiffened, lowlight goggles pointed at Jules as this new arrival on the chopper drifted out on the end of a rope that stretched to its apex. The Striovian gunner struggled to bring his heavy automatic weapon around, a knock-off of an American M60.

It was enough time for Jules to retract his arm and hurl the jagged, baseball-sized rock.

The projectile struck its target in the glass visor, the *crack* just audible over the rotor wash.

Then Jules pitched back the other way, using his legs like a kid on a swing for more distance, rummaging in his pocket for another rock.

Now aware of their stowaway, the helicopter banked. Jules twisted in midair and shifted his weight, changing direction. This time, he hurtled toward the front of the chopper, rising at the end of his swing, the six feet of cord stretching to nine feet below the cockpit.

He threw the rock.

It ricocheted off the reinforced glass without cracking it, just leaving a white mark. Still enough to startle the pilot, though. He spun his stick sideways, descending rapidly.

It didn't seem intentional to Jules, more a slip of control, but it was effective, as losing altitude sent Jules toward the Gorgon Block at speed. He had no choice.

A thrust of his feet allowed him to rise over the fast-approaching volcanic outcrop, but he'd be on the ground in the next half-second. He let go of his rope, continuing the kick into a backward somersault.

As the helicopter passed over him, adjusting its dive into a swoop, Jules landed harder than he wanted, rolling, tumbling aside and hoping the spike of pain up his left ankle wasn't anything serious.

"Jules!" Dan yelled. "What the hell!"

Jules had landed on the part of the hill with the giant red oak where Dan appeared to be half buried. Scurrying over that way, listening for the chopper's return, Jules endured the bolts firing up his ankle, but it wasn't broken.

He found Dan had done just as expected. He'd used the cave-like root formation as cover, sheltering him from the worst of the boulders and ice chunks that carried on down the slope, but coated him with soil and logs and other scraps of wood.

Unable to escape farther than a couple of feet out of the hole, his head was bleeding in two places—front and back—and his left arm bore a gash from shoulder to elbow. His eyes were wild. Blood pooled in his mouth. "Move!"

The helicopter banked again, gearing up for another run.

Dan shoved Jules aside and aimed, firing a burst of three. His shots hit home, impacting the cockpit and forcing the pilot to swerve out of sight.

"My foot's stuck," Dan said. "Can't get to it. Just get out of here."

Jules already figured Dan was in a seated position. Some roots had given way, and the landslide caught him out.

"Any C-4 left?" Jules asked.

"Can't reach my pack." Dan pointed to the largest snakelike root where the backpack lay. "Nothing left anyway. Just the last detonators."

Jules then remembered his own stash, pulling the small scoop of C-4 from his sock. Dan grinned.

Staying off his ankle, with the helicopter's rotor getting louder every second, Jules scrambled for Dan's pack.

There were two men inside the incoming vehicle, but he couldn't tell if they had another set of night-vis goggles. Dan's gunfire had startled them, but they were regrouping.

Jules found the pack and pulled it free. Opened it.

One detonator.

Scrambling back to Dan, he checked his own phone, linked to the electronic switches via one of Charlie's own apps.

"Nice," Dan said. "Think you can make that throw?"

"What throw?" Jules scrabbled at the debris burying Dan to his waist.

"Into the bird."

"That'd kill them." Jules got down to Dan's leg.

"Yeah. *They're* trying to kill *us*."

Jules halted only long enough to say, "I can't kill," before resuming.

"It's self-defense, man. You'll kill *me* if you don't. You'll kill *yourself*."

Jules had explained his philosophy on taking lives when they'd met months earlier. *Life is sacred*. All life. And if Jules couldn't master a situation without killing, he would feel unworthy of living on.

There was always an alternative.

But Dan was a soldier, hardened against such notions. Collateral damage was inevitable. Bad guys and good guys. Black hats and white hats. To Dan, it was a scale, a balancing act; do more good than bad, and he slept easy.

Jules never bought into that. "Got a knife?" he asked.

Gunfire burst through the trees, the incoming soldiers using the canopy as cover. Probably infrared picking up their body heat. Inaccurate, though, bullets passing through branches and at a longer range than before. The wash shifted foliage, too, and the moonlight gave away its position.

"One sec." Dan returned fire, single-shot mode. Four bullets, and the vehicle banked again. "You are not blowing my leg off."

"No, I'm not." Jules got to the offending blockage. "The force of the falling stones and soil pulled you along, and now it's packed in tight."

"Yeah, kinda guessed that."

"Wasn't talking to you. Just working something out."

"How to not blow my leg off?"

"Among other things, yeah. Now quit whining. They'll be back in around five seconds."

Jules traced the root along the contour and, eight feet from Dan, he dug with his hand under the fresh, loosely packed ground. He formed a hole an inch wider than his arm. A swift calculation confirmed using all the C-4 too close would likely not only blow Dan's foot clean off but his leg and possibly left arm and half his skull too.

Not good.

Jules halved the small block and inserted the detonator. He set the charge, then slid it down his hole.

Dan's gun blasted again, and the helicopter flew out of sight. "Hurry it up. They know my ammo won't last forever."

"How long *will* it last?"

"About zero minutes. I'm out."

"Then cover your ears." Jules lay on the ground, hugging Dan, a shield against the blast.

"Hey, watch it." Dan clearly didn't want to be coddled, but ceased arguing, time being so limited, and covered his ears.

Jules found the frequency, pressed one ear to his shoulder and stuffed a finger in the other.

The helicopter returned, banking to expose the gunner.

And Jules set off the C-4.

The explosion sufficed to send the chopper away again, loud enough to thump Jules's eardrums to numbness and showering both men with stones, soil, and splintered wood.

Jules rolled off and reached into the ditch he'd scraped along Dan's legs. The blockage shifted but didn't clear.

"It's looser." Dan pulled at his limb, a grimace filling his whole face. His head bled heavily.

"Quit that. I just need a minute." Jules plunged his hand deeper, pushing hard.

"Don't think we've got that long."

The rotor wash moved the trees, coming in from another angle.

Jules's fingers scraped. His shoulders strained, pushing against the soil, the stones, the splinters of wood.

The downdraft penetrated the foliage.

"Damn it, Jules, run!" Dan cried.

"Not even close to thinking about that." Jules pulled out his hand and switched to his foot. He kicked at the sod and felt the root shift.

The helicopter circled over them, losing altitude for a better angle. They'd been probing the pair on the ground, assessing ammo, their willingness and ability to fire.

Jules's next kick sent the root up and over Dan's foot, the explosive having disconnected the wood several feet away.

Now it was free of the crushing debris, Dan yanked his leg out.

As the gunfire rattled once again, both he and Jules rolled first sideways, then down. Bullets chewed the ground where they'd been, while the forest gave decent cover.

Dan, limping, one hand to his face, tumbled head over heels, crunching onto his back, then bouncing onto his front; he was in no shape for a pursuit like this.

With their attention on the seemingly easy target, Jules fished out another two rocks and ran uphill in an arc. Like Dan, he limped, but kept the pain compartmentalized, a non-broken bone able to take his weight. And since the helicopter could only hover in the clearing, he took advantage of the trees, coming out lower than he'd hoped, but got off a decent throw.

His first jagged stone pinged off the body, the second hit the gunner on the arm. That guy pointed angrily, plainly yelling an order, because the chopper turned.

It turned Jules's way.

Jules lined up his final rock.

He was impotent against that machine but might just cause enough of a delay to allow Dan to escape.

The gunner prepared his shot.

Jules threw the rock—one final, futile act of defiance. The projectile flew hard and arrow straight. It impacted the cockpit as intended.

And the helicopter exploded.

Not total destruction like a missile strike, but the windshield cleaved clean off, shattered under the force of a blast. A second one ripped into the vehicle's body, and a third pulped the pilot.

The helicopter devolved into a spin. No control. Hurtling for Jules's position by blind luck.

Jules took a running jump, leaping out over the slope's gradient for distance. He dropped down farther than he swept out, landing and flattening himself to the opposite side of the nearest tree trunk.

The helicopter smashed into the ground nose-first, pancaking the lead section, and shattering the rotor blades. Shards of metal twisted and spun, several whistling past Jules's hiding spot, while the remainder of the vehicle ripped apart and flipped into the forest.

There would be no survivors.

Charlie came running from the direction of the ATV route, wielding the biggest shotgun Jules had seen outside a poaching gang in Kenya.

Luther's bear gun.

She kept it trained on the wreckage, switching its range to assess the possible ambush points of the Gorgon Block and various boulders until she reached Jules.

"Nice timing," he said.

"Luther took a little persuading to give it up," Charlie said.

… whenever we're out there, on the ground, we're under orders to carry a gun big enough to take down a bear…

"Where's Dan?" she asked. "Is he okay?"

"Let's go find out."

CHAPTER
THIRTY-FOUR

Now they weren't running, and the day had passed fully into night, the winter cold descending with a vengeance, making shivering the norm.

Ignoring his minor sprain, Jules led Charlie in the direction he'd last seen Dan running and falling. Now it seemed the danger was passed, both switched their lights back on, calling for their missing teammate. Sweeping their flashlights in a methodical grid, they found him thirty yards away, leaning on a trunk, conscious, but hurting.

He grunted rather than shouted his position, having taken a longer fall than Jules had noticed while facing down the helicopter.

"Gotta get him outta here," Jules said. "They'll be back, looking for survivors."

"Yes, but not for a while." Charlie stroked Dan's hair, avoiding the cuts. "You okay, big fella? Let's get you sorted out."

They had no first aid kit but cobbled together a splint for the man's foot—branches and the straps from a pack, cut with Charlie's knife. Jules wadded up his own undershirt to act as a compress to the gash on Dan's scalp. However, as he applied it, one wound appeared worse than he first thought; it wasn't from a passing cut, but Dan had been hit hard in that part of the head, near the back. The soft part.

Jules told Charlie, and she checked Dan's pupils using her flashlight.

"Concussion," Charlie said. "Mild, but he'll need a doctor."

"Nah, I'm fine." Dan slurred his words like a drunk.

Charlie eased off Dan's coat and tore off his left sleeve to check the gash on his arm. She used the sleeve as a bandage. Even without field medic experience, Jules could tell it was a light wound, unlike the one on his head.

Once Dan was mobile, the pair supported him on either side, staggering to clamber down the slope to what could charitably be described as a trail. Jules allowed Charlie to set the pace, her bullet wound only months old and would still be tender, the scar tissue likely to tear if she over-extended.

Jules didn't mind so much; his own ankle wasn't in great shape, but he'd got off lightly compared to the other pair.

As the trio picked their way with Dan doing his best to struggle on, Jules suggested a dead weight might be better and offered to render him unconscious if Charlie agreed. Dan told Jules he was welcome to try. Charlie declined the offer.

Instead, she passed the time explaining that the group was rabbiting, largely due to lack of equipment. Toby had expected Yanovna to capture Dan and Jules, and if they made it out of Canada, Toby would bargain for their lives, exchanging his own if necessary, or perhaps using the books recovered from India as a makeweight.

It was around that point that Bridget demanded Luther call in his people; law enforcement, the army, the air force, whatever. But the guide was only interested in putting as much distance as possible between himself and the gunfire chattering from the hillside. Unfortunately for Luther, Charlie had spotted the case attached to the side of his ATV and recalled the mention of bears up there. The guy refused to entertain returning, so Charlie charmed the gun from him—if switching from flirting to threats was charming—and ordered him to get the rest of them back to base.

The tale, although pointless from a tactical point of view, staved off the cold for a little while. The shrinking elevation helped some too. But Dan was finding it increasingly difficult to walk, straining and refusing to give in to exhaustion, nausea, or pain, all of which Jules read in him with every step. Charlie pushed on harder and for longer than Jules expected, but she was fading. Not that either injured party would admit it.

"Let's build a fire," Jules said.

"I can make it." Dan gripped Jules's shoulder. "We keep going."

Jules glanced from him to Charlie and back again. "It's a half-day hike to the airfield without a concussed sack of testosterone on my back. And it's night. Gonna be below zero soon. You insist on *making it*, you kill us both too." He maintained eye contact.

The forest spoke in chirps and rustles. Dan's lips thinned. Hard to tell in the lamplight, but they appeared pale too, verging on blue.

"Let's make a fire," he said.

Flames were a risk, what with a Striovian black ops team in the vicinity, but Jules worked the odds. A couple of factors meant they fell within acceptable parameters.

First, the troops attacked using a civilian helicopter with only two men and one large gun on board, meaning they possessed little ordnance. That made sense since it was a last-minute mission on foreign soil, executed by a country not renowned for its international military exceptionalism.

Then there were the missing officers, General Yanovna and Captain Igoravich. Jules had spotted them returning underground before the avalanche hit, meaning they were likely still alive. Any additional manpower would be dedicated to digging them out.

Finally, they'd been heading downhill for an hour and

winding randomly in the direction they needed to go, with Jules's internal compass guiding them. Jules knew where they were in a general sense, but in the dark, even his picture-perfect memory couldn't pinpoint them. When the sun rose, he'd be able to cross-reference it with the time and crossmatch it to Mount Chepadu's location to establish an exact route.

For now, though, they warmed themselves by the fire.

After they shared Charlie's half-canteen of water, Charlie managed to sleep, the trek exhausting her in her still-recovering state, while Dan pretended to snooze—*pretended*, because Jules knew Dan wouldn't sleep recognizing he had a concussion.

Jules meditated instead, silently staring into the fire to center himself and take his mind off the hunger that had made itself known.

"You don't kill." Dan's words were still slow, but no longer slurred.

Jules broke with the mindful moment and saw Dan was half slumped against a rock, heaving his leg into a more comfortable position.

"No," Jules said. "Aikido. Subduing your enemy quickly and kindly."

"Kindly." Dan coughed, softening the noise as Charlie slept. "Even in a situation where you could die in return."

"Even if."

"You're complicated." Dan switched his weight to his other buttock, pressing a palm into his back.

"Need a massage?" Jules asked.

"Yeah, but excuse me if I wait 'til we're back to civilization."

Jules never got offended at people saying no to him. He couldn't understand why others took the words *no thanks* personally. "How am I complicated?"

"Mr. Logic defies logic over a principle in some obscure martial art."

Jules was an expert in Krav Maga, a fighting art developed by the Israeli army, alongside being proficient in Taekwondo, and a master of Aikido. The latter meant turning his opponents' strength against them, utilizing only what he needed to win—a martial art only effective when performed by someone of true skill. "Aikido came to me when I was real troubled. Champion in tough contests, but this was different. Meant something. Mastering all of it, including the theoretical side... it was as important as kicking ass."

"And the theoretical side doesn't let you kill? Like a doctor."

"Right."

"And that works for you?"

"I'm still here, ain't I?"

Dan paused to think but wasn't letting it go yet. "Would your teachers approve if some psycho killed you when you could've defended yourself?"

Jules stared at the flames. "I don't know. It's not their business, anyway. It's mine."

Dan chuckled to himself, which made him cough again. "It's a phobia."

Jules twisted to him. Said nothing.

"Aww, man, I'm right." Dan laughed now, keeping the volume down. "Mr. Logical Android has a *phobia*. Killing people, even in self-defense. You can't do it."

Jules stared at the ground. "Killing one person, killing a hundred. What's the difference? What happens if I overstep that line once and don't stop? When do I start making the decision to take a life? Only when I'm in trouble? Or when someone else is? Just because I know the person in danger, do I really have the right to kill someone who's threatening 'em?

"What about if some drunk's throwing punches at me in a bar? He could theoretically kill me with one lucky blow, so am I justified killing that asshole? It's a line I don't wanna cross. Maybe I will one day." He looked back to Dan. "But if I lose myself there, I don't know if I'll ever come back."

Dan's amused expression slipped into a soft, contemplative

slump, monitoring the fire and the swarm of sparks that spat from a pocket of moist wood.

"We were never going to return the seals," he said.

"The Sumerian ones? We already did."

"The others." Dan blinked slowly. "I didn't know Toby and Bridget agreed anything ahead of time, but those bangles of yours scared the crap out of Toby."

"Thought they wanted a new branch of study."

"LORI exists basically to skew the conventional. To make small but significant discoveries the mainstream isn't interested in. It started as returning stolen loot to its rightful place, but now that part of the business is just a means to an end. You know I was stationed in Baghdad when the museum got looted?"

"No."

"No one gave a crap about it. While I was guarding some hotel full of surrendered government workers, the Sumerian seals were on their way out of that basement. I landed guard duty at the museum after the worst of the looting, got to know the workers. Kind of what made me interested in this stuff."

"That why you started doing security for these digs?"

"Joined the private sector after I served out, yeah. Volunteered for anything like that. Toby poached me, and here I am. Returned the seals to their rightful owner and having to guess what my boss is up to with a bunch of other seals."

Jules gazed into the same spot in the fire. "They suspected the seals would light up when I touched them."

"Never said anything before we went in the first time. Just Toby and Bridget. Charlie's used to it, and she's ex-military like me, so need-to-know missions are a way of life. Harpal is former MI6, so was probably on board with it too."

"Why're you telling me this?"

"To give Bridget a break. They weren't certain. But they knew if the seals had the same powers as your bangles, they shouldn't be in the hands of a paranoid nation proven to help themselves to stolen artifacts to push their own agenda."

Jules didn't buy it. "The rocks react violently to saltwater. Striovia is landlocked. What's the danger?"

Dan adjusted his position again, drawing a wince as he settled. "Who's to say saltwater is the only thing it reacts with?"

Jules thought it was unlikely but had no proof one way or the other. "So, Toby and Bridget were going to confiscate them?"

"I don't know for sure. But Toby wants to understand these rocks, and Bridget has been obsessed with the books and the origins of the people who built that tomb in India. There's still no direct evidence of who they were."

Jules had thought about that a lot throughout the months since he'd parted ways, leaving the Aradia and Ruby Rock bangles in their care. His TV shows and home improvements blocked out the mystery for a time, but he kept coming back to it. "They shoulda' clued me in. Let me make that decision."

The fire snapped and crackled. Creatures scurried yards away, a bird calling in the distance.

"You made a decision," Dan said. "You left the Striovian seals where they were. And then they came after us. That was *their* decision."

"And you killed them." Jules faced Dan, not accusing him, not judging him. Just a statement. "Is that how you live with it?"

"I guess. They know what they sign up to. Their families too. And illegal incursions like today are voluntary, well paid. I'm a soldier, they're soldiers. Me or them."

Jules understood the logic but had never accepted the conclusion. It started with the Aikido teachings, the basics bringing him peace during a tumultuous period of his life, so he'd thrown all in with the philosophy. Never leaving dead bodies behind him was useful too, in that he was a low priority fugitive in places where his face was known.

But now, maybe Dan was right. Had it become a phobia?

Was it a weakness?

Or a strength?

While he had the skill and intelligence to avoid taking lives in most circumstances, he was around seventy-five percent sure that if Charlie hadn't stepped in, he would not have survived the helicopter encounter.

"By the way, thank you," Dan said.

"What for?"

"Coming back for me."

Jules bowed his head, still mesmerized by the fire. "You're important to the group. You risked your life to save us."

"My job."

"My choice." Jules sensed Dan had more to say, but it wasn't needed.

Not that it stopped Dan from continuing. "I told you back in France… leave no man behind… that's a creed to live by, not empty words."

"I know."

"So..." Dan leaned a long way over, supporting himself on one hand, the other extended, palm out.

Jules reached and Dan grasped his hand, thumbs-first.

"Thanks," Dan said again. "It really means something, man."

"We don't need to bro-hug or anything, do we?"

Dan disengaged with another quiet laugh. "Nah, not yet. Maybe next time."

Jules smiled. "Let's hope that won't be needed, then."

"Amen."

Jules placed a couple more logs on the fire and lay down, figuring he'd have a decent ninety minutes before the flames died and the cold would wake him.

"Jules? Dan?" It was Toby's voice directly in Jules's ear.

He sat up. "Thought this thing wasn't transmitting no more."

Dan asked through his frown and hand gestures, *What's up?*

"You're almost out of power—" A crackle cut Toby off for a second. Then, "Tommy and Luther matched our frequency. Where are you?"

Jules described their approximate heading away from Mount

Chepadu, while Dan roused Charlie, who'd removed her earpiece entirely.

"Is everyone okay out there?" Bridget chimed in.

"Fine," Jules said. "Bit chilly."

"We're sending a chopper," Toby said. "Then we have work to do."

"Work? We found the place."

"No, we found the *starting point*." Bridget sounded way too enthused. "Next stop is Doggerland."

"We're going to Doggerland?" Jules said.

Dan was now upright, sat with Charlie, watching Jules intently. He asked, "Where's Doggerland?"

Charlie perked up, alert and eager to join in. "Doggerland..." She grinned. "Is about four hundred feet below the North Sea."

CHAPTER
THIRTY-FIVE
AUGUST 21, 07:00 P.M

ILYUSHIN IL-76, EASTERN ALASKAN AIRSPACE

Although many nations feared annexation by the Russian Federation, the Striovian government maintained good diplomatic relations with influencers from that country, not least so they could keep the power on. It allowed Private Zefirova Victoriovna to open encrypted channels between the Striovian energy minister—a strong ally to General Yanovna—and Piotr Kolorov, head of the Kolorov family's business empire, driven mainly by oil. Not only did she charter a helicopter from the remote US territory of Alaska into Canada, but she also shipped out their in-house disaster recovery team, an essential cog in any mechanism that involved drilling and fracking.

Zefirova didn't want to think about the cost. She guessed the government valued Zimina Yanovna more than gold, though.

They'd lost contact with the general as a landslide hit, and a combination of radio broadcasts and fuzzy visuals from the Mikhailovic-Dunham MkIII satellite played out a gunfight and the loss of at least five men. Possibly the general and the captain, too.

Weak signals had followed, suggesting someone survived. The crew on board the Ilyushin Il-76—still flying under diplomatic transponder codes—had no way of discerning their meaning or exact location but knew there were tunnels on that mountain. That gave them hope.

The crews had arrived at first light and dug for three hours until making a verifiable contact. The team pulled General Yanovna and Captain Igoravich from their sanctuary—hungry, weak, and fuming—and transported them back to Alaska where Zefirova had landed, again under diplomatic cover. The local FBI office was not impressed, though, so was sending agents to check out the passengers and "offer assistance" with their mission.

Luckily, "local" in Alaska meant a thirty-hour trip, so Yanovna and Igoravich had time to get cleaned and patched up, eat two meals, grab plenty of sleep in a comfortable bunk, and be on their way before the Federal agents even arrived. The others remained on board the plane, and American hamburgers delivered with Yanovna's compliments alleviated a spot of sagging morale.

When Yanovna and Igoravich were discharged by the complex's medical team and stepped back into the Airlifter, they appeared fresh, with scratches and bruises, but otherwise, they walked tall and strong. Clothes were donated by those at the oil company's airfield, so both the general and captain looked like civilians. But that didn't matter. They were back.

As well as Zefirova, the four others stood to salute their leaders. Yanovna and Igoravich returned the salutes, and Igoravich dropped his, marched stiffly to a locker and opened it by dialing a combination on the padlock.

From there, he took seven shot glasses and handed them out, filling them with the finest vodka from Striovia—$500 US per bottle. All held the shots aloft and Yanovna called the names of the men who'd died the previous day. They drank their vodka in one and shouted the names back.

Yanovna tossed the glass back to Igoravich and added her own final contribution to the prayer. "They will be avenged."

Now, fully fueled and untouchable by the authorities, despite several threats of a fighter "escort," they were headed to coordinates provided by the general, the origins of which no one questioned. It was not until they were over international waters that an encrypted message arrived labeled *Top Secret*. General Yanovna retired to a workstation at the end of the bank of monitors, donned her headphones, and thunder descended across her face.

Yanovna kept her voice low so as not to alert the comms specialist that she was in disagreement with their President. But the man's chief of staff, Nicholai Rostov, stared out at her. The President could not risk even the slightest association with this mission, a condition Yanovna herself insisted upon, but she did not doubt Nicholai's order came directly from the top.

"You lost a prisoner, General. He is free to roam the world with our secrets. You violated sovereign lands and were unable to recover the bodies of your comrades."

"They have no identifying documents," Yanovna said. "Our uniforms are Chinese imports, and the guns are black market Ukrainian. It will not come back on Striovia."

"And the families will have no bodies to bury."

Yanovna had no reply to that.

"Your relic hunt is over. Bring back the artifact and we will work on this from our facility in Losnesh."

"Because you gave Kolorov's doctors authority over when I could leave, the spies now have a two-day head start. They have regrouped, employed others to help. I must intercept them."

"What you must do, General, as ordered by your President, is return for debriefing, and to resume your work as Curator of Striovian Antiquities and Historical Heritage."

That was her official title. "I am still a general."

"You will not be." The chief of staff dipped his chin and picked his words carefully. "General, I admire you and am grateful for all you have done, all you have sacrificed for our nation. But if your plane is not back on Striovian soil within fourteen hours, the President will strip you of all military rank *and* your government post. Am I clear?"

Yanovna flashed to the cowardly assassination of Lukic by Toby's pet attack dog, the assault on Benjamich that rendered him unconscious for when the avalanche hit, and the murder of Holorov with one of their own weapons. Toby brought this upon them, and she understood how much Toby cared for that Institute of his. He all but begged her to spare them.

No more.

No more begging.

"If the trade winds are kind," Yanovna said, "the plane will touch down in under fourteen hours."

"Good, General. I look forward to—"

She cut him off. "Oops."

Yanovna stared at the blank screen, her fist curled tight, her jaw and lips stone.

Then she stood and wandered over to Zefirova Victoriovna, loosening herself up. "You performed extremely well. I understand you are one of our foremost experts in satellite operations."

"I am, General."

"And quick thinking. I might not have considered using a corrupt oligarch to our advantage."

Private Victoriovna appeared to be blushing. "You are too kind. I did my duty."

"I need a satellite error to send us off course by a few degrees. Can you handle this?"

"How many degrees?"

Yanovna pulled up a chair and leaned closer to Victoriovna. "Captain Igoravich and I wish to bail out over western France. The Brittany region. You will then have the pilot correct your path to the north and you may continue to land in Striovia, or..."

Yanovna left the choice hanging, hoping she was on the same wavelength.

Victoriovna did not disappoint. "I will gather as much portable equipment as possible, General. Let us work out a rendezvous before you depart."

CHAPTER
THIRTY-SIX
AUGUST 21, 5 P.M. (GMT)

WINDSOR CASTLE, UNITED KINGDOM

Colin Waterston read and re-read the extraordinarily ballsy request from Toby Smith.

He and his ragamuffin bunch of so-called "freelance archaeologists" were requesting temporary visas for two of their number —Jules Sibeko and Dan Vincent. Bridget Carson was already imbued with dual citizenship, despite Colin's effort to have it revoked following their unconscionable actions earlier in the year. Unfortunately, Ms. Carson's parents had friends in some rather low places. As for the others, Charlotte Locke, Harpal Singh, and Toby himself were UK born and bred, so he could not keep them from entering these shores. But since the flag from immigration sprang up as soon as Sibeko and Vincent were input, Colin was alerted.

Eventually.

The reason it took the best part of a day and a half to reach him was exactly what he was trying to discuss with the Home Office as he strode from Windsor Castle's Round Tower through a gilded hall currently undergoing a minor renovation. Phone growing sweatier with every moment and papers flapping along, he was getting nowhere with a low-level clerk who did not recognize Colin's authority in the matter. In fact, the clerk seemed utterly baffled as to why the curator to the country's royal family might be concerned about a standard immigration request. The flag was not terror or hate crime related, just a general warning to check deeper background on recent movements.

It was the recent movements that Colin was interested in. And he was growing rather exasperated. "One of the people traveling with the applicants was, until recently, a prisoner of the Striovian government. Toby Smith. Look him up. We have received no notice of his release, and your colleagues in the Foreign Office have been petitioning to see our man since we learned of a violent incident that postponed his court date."

The clerk stuttered. "But why—"

"Did you check my clearance ID code?" Which Colin had now issued more than once.

"Yes, it's fine, but—"

"Then answer my questions." Colin exited the hall and pushed through into a corridor with a painting on the wall every three meters—each a foreigner of noble blood, most a distant relative of the queen or her extended family. "Where have they been? What have they done? What law enforcement flags are there?"

"None, sir. They were in Canada until recently, invited by the Parks Canada association. They're responsible for maintaining the national parks and the heritage of—"

"I know who Parks Canada are." Colin tramped up a stone spiral staircase. "I'm just highly suspicious of the attentional request. For accommodation in Scotland."

"That's where they said they'd be based, sir."

Colin breezed through an anteroom, clicking his fingers at the fresh-faced young man seated at the only desk. He didn't slow as he entered his office. "I have only one option, don't I?"

Colin hung up and waited for Simon to close the door behind them both. Then, as his assistant nervously smoothed his tie and suit, he went straight to the source.

Although Toby had attempted to alter phone numbers several times, he was someone Colin just had to keep an eye on. It took Toby four rings to answer. Colin put him on speaker so Simon could hear.

"Toby, it's Colin. How are you? Striovians change their minds, did they?"

"I'm very well, thank you," Toby said. "Glad you picked up my request."

"You can sneak Yanks in and out of Britain all day, Toby. Was this really to grab my attention?"

"You know me too well." The smile in Toby's voice was almost audible. "I'm surprised it took you so long to call."

"Austerity, Toby. You appreciate how it is. So, am I correct thinking you're in Montrose?"

"Nearby. You realize what I'm looking for?"

Colin had been afraid of Toby getting free and causing trouble. Simon's clouded face indicated the lad knew why Colin had appeared in such a terrible mood. "You saw the seals?"

"And you already know all about them?" Toby said.

"Not all, no. The Striovians are secretive. I'm surprised they gave up the Sumerian ones so eagerly. Apparently, the Pope has praised their cooperation. Your doing?"

"In a manner of speaking."

Colin settled back in his chair but couldn't get comfortable. "Why are you back here?"

"Sightseeing. And maybe a little digging and probing."

Colin pinched the bridge of his nose, cautious about what he could and couldn't say.

Although he held great sway over affairs of state, he accepted his authority was somewhat nebulous, his official job description ill-defined, and could embarrass the government if he overstepped or if they made his security clearance public.

"Toby, don't make me come to Scotland. Just tell me what you need. If it's nothing that might undermine the royals or the PM, I can look the other way."

Again, Colin could practically hear the smile as the conversation went Toby's way. Simon Pickard sat forward.

"A few years ago, there were some explorations relating to Doggerland," Toby said. "Scans, probes, and the like. Gave you the most detailed map of the area. Any chance of a loan?"

Colin had to regulate his tone. Sound calm. Give nothing away. "Montrose. Doggerland. Toby, I hope you and your undereducated bunch aren't going to sully Britain's name. If you are still wanted by Striovia—"

"They are taken care of," Toby said. "What I'm interested in are the detailed Doggerland scans, which are subject to freedom of information requests, I believe. And I know there was significant activity in this area after the Indians decided they no longer required you on the Aradia dig."

Colin bristled, his memory of that dig differing significantly from the accounts by many on the scene. He'd never acted condescending in his life. He treated everyone fairly. It was a rule of his, and something he demanded from all his underlings—top brass and lower-class staff alike.

"With your record," Colin said, "and your suspected breaking and entering of Windsor Castle this year, I cannot grant your request. You're welcome to appeal, but that will take several weeks. Maybe months."

"What was going on up in Montrose, Colin? Is there a link to Doggerland and the church your people excavated two months ago?"

"Nothing," Colin said. "You will stay away from the Crown's property, and I forbid you from setting foot on Doggerland itself."

"I had to try," Toby said. "Colin, we both know there is something here. If there wasn't, you wouldn't have been bothered enough to call personally. And as long as I don't break any laws, even you don't have the authority to detain me."

Toby hung up.

Colin Waterston slammed a paperweight down on his mahogany desk, the crystal sphere seated in a wooden base sending a dull pain through his wrist and up to his elbow. "How the hell did they find out about Doggerland?"

Having grown accustomed to his boss's occasional outbursts, Simon Pickard reacted with only a blink, his hands clasped firmly in his lap, a mirror of Colin's own manner. "I think it's common knowledge, sir. There are books and papers—"

"I don't mean its existence, I mean... what does that blasted Institute of Toby's want with it? They don't do anything without either cause to believe the official record is wrong, or if there's some injustice been committed."

"Injustice?"

"Yes, yes, their sanctimonious sense of right and wrong. Returning artifacts to where they think they belong rather than who legally owns them." He shoved the paperweight with two fingers. "These things changed hands dozens of times during their heyday, so what's the problem?"

"And the other thing? What's in the scans of the area he's interested in?"

Colin straightened first the papers on his desk, then his hair, his physical reaction to the news about Toby's location having dislodged several carefully gelled strands. "Nothing. It's a drowned swamp. Neolithic settlement." He concentrated on replacing the paperweight *just so*. In the right light, clouds swam within. "Toby has it in his head that the ancient world holds more interest than flint tools, cave paintings, and breeding with Neanderthals."

"Such as what?"

Satisfied with his reorganization, Colin looked up at Simon. "Such as nothing. It's a fantasy."

"You asked how they found out, though. Does that mean—"

"It means that a British national has broken out of custody from one of our allies, and I am sure a deportation request will soon follow. Irrespective of his fantasies—and no matter what you thought you heard from me, they *are* fantasies—we need to arrest him for his own good." Colin pointed at the door. "Now alert the

Home Office. We may need some backup on this. We must stop him from making a mockery of the United Kingdom."

"Shame, then." Simon turned to leave.

"What is?"

Simon stopped and faced his boss again. "Shame Doggerland lies under international waters."

CHAPTER
THIRTY-SEVEN
AUGUST 21, 9:30 P.M. (GMT)

CHÂTEAU CACHÉ, BRITTANY, FRANCE

General Yanovna aimed her handgun into another room, finding this one empty as well. She had faced the prospect of storming Toby's base of operations and found it distasteful. Risky, even. So, discovering the place empty was a surprise. It meant they'd already moved on, perhaps well ahead of her. But it was the absence of a major alarm system that set her nerves on fire.

Before the revolution that freed her country from the yoke of the Soviets, Yanovna was as fit as any man under her command. She gave everything, and concluded her reward—a job to pursue her passions—was well deserved. No husband, no children, no family to speak of, she'd grown close with the brothers, sisters, and offspring of tight allies. She was "Aunt Zimina" to dozens of kids around the country. One thing she'd never left behind, though, was her fitness.

The high altitude, low open—HALO—drop had admitted her and Igoravich to France before the airplane changed direction to get back on course, and it terrified her as much as the first time she'd trained in the infiltration technique. She was out of practice and relied on Igoravich's experience to guide her through.

Not bad for a fifty-six-year-old woman.

Fifteen acres of open land were dotted with the occasional tree, while a stream running through the middle of the property fed from an underground channel leading to hills many miles away, and to a small cottage that was clearly occupied.

Under the cover of darkness, they had made their approach to the house, which appeared dark and therefore empty. Armed with black market submachine guns, sidearms, and an assortment of equipment, their infrared goggles revealed the crisscross of alarm triggers invisible to the naked eye, and—she suspected—able to differentiate between human and animal. Motion-sensitive lights were only activated if the pair got too close, and they could hide in the trough carved out by the stream while Igoravich pinpointed the sensors. He indicated the blind spot and said he would remain watching and come for her if anything went wrong.

Accessing the ground-floor window was straightforward, the layout easy to navigate in the dark. It seemed odd that they'd leave it this way, which was what made her suspicious enough to strap the knock-off MP5 submachine gun tight to her back and pull her pistol.

Now, she led with it around each corner. Still no alarm.

She stalked into a library and finally sensed a presence. Someone else *was* there.

Would she be so fortunate as to find Toby in his favorite chair, smoking a pipe and reading Chaucer?

Only one light shone, this one at the far end; the shuffling of feet and pages meant a person was working or looking for some bedtime literature.

Silently, Yanovna skirted the near wall, gun out, her goggles switched off and folded over her head on a hinge. With her throat mic, she updated Igoravich. He tapped twice to acknowledge her.

At the final aisle, she glided over the polished wooden floor, only glancing at the collection of literature that rivaled her President's, and certainly overshadowed her own.

She remained unsure how many she faced there but was

certain she would shoot the big thug—Dan Vincent—the first opportunity she got. No questions, no smart remarks, just a bullet through his skull. Then she'd interrogate Toby and his other pets. Certainly, it'd be one in the knee for Toby himself to demonstrate she was serious.

She reached the end of the lane and poked her head around as briefly as possible.

Someone had set up on the floor: a single cushion, an angle-poise lamp creating the light she'd spotted, and four books weighted open to specific pages with other volumes laid across them. Two massive sheets of paper were taped to the bookcase ahead of the cushion—one a printed map, the other hand-drawn.

Yanovna advanced, wishing she had a suppressor on the pistol.

She halted and cocked her head.

Listened.

Nothing. Not even a light scuff of a shoe.

Placing one foot soundlessly after the other, gun extended, Yanovna made her approach, scanning each aisle of books as she went. Reaching the study nest, she held her aim in the direction she hadn't cleared yet and risked looking at the map.

The UK, with northern and Western Europe, and some odd contours off the British coast. The hand-drawn one showed the same contours with scribblings Yanovna could not read.

It resembled the map she'd illuminated when touching the Reaper Seal and when activating the scythe head, the contours where one striation from the reaper's orb ended.

It was a map of prehistory.

If she could use this mysterious destination to help her people, she would. There would be no need to compromise with the Russians, and certainly no capitulation, as she suspected her President might surrender to if the energy situation deteriorated further. Even if she had to kill all of Toby's minions or spend the rest of her life in prison.

Notes on the desk caught her eye, variations on the Latin note from Habib Masouli's scroll.

Circulus ostendam in virtue Dominus.

Dominus = noun or proper noun? Jehovah, God, or "a" god?

Power = light?

It was as if the group were re-translating the Latin phrase. As if she may have been wrong. But Toby agreed with her interpretation of the words.

Or did he?

Was it another deception?

"Who are you?" came an accented voice.

Yanovna snapped away from the papers and dropped into a shooting stance. She nearly pulled the trigger, but the stranger matched none of the files on Toby's people. "Who are *you*?"

The dark Asian woman—a girl really, no more than twenty-eight, possibly thirty—held still, arms by her side, a book in each hand. Her hair was loose, and she was wearing pajamas—a girl enjoying a sleepover. "I'm… not supposed to be there either."

Indian accent. So, the writing Yanovna couldn't understand could've been Hindi, or one of the other languages from that part of the world. The girl had immediately attempted to bond with Yanovna—the *I'm not supposed to be here either*—meaning she was afraid but eager to pretend she wasn't. Like this was normal.

It took Yanovna a moment to figure out why she believed her.

"Did you deactivate the alarms?" Yanovna asked.

"Yes. I left a bug in the system when the housekeeper let me in a few days ago to talk about Toby and his people. A present from my employer. I can come and go."

"Who is your employer?"

The girl stared at the gun. "I can't say. I don't… I don't really know. He has an interest in this Lost Origins group, though. As you appear to."

"Were they here?"

"I watched the house yesterday and today. They flew out this afternoon."

Yanovna kept the gun steady. "Your name."

"Prihya."

"You are not one of Toby's?"

The girl swallowed. "No. They robbed and destroyed a site of huge importance to my country. And I think they are preparing to rob another. Something belonging to people I do not fully understand. The Lost Origins group calls this race... *the Witnesses*. I want them brought to justice."

"Do you know what this place is?" Yanovna twitched her head toward the maps.

"Doggerland," Prihya said.

Yanovna lowered the pistol but didn't holster it. "Tell me about why it is special. Something unknown in public. And maybe I shall share what *I* have discovered."

PART FOUR

"There is a dark side in all of us. And for us 'bad' people, the bad side dominates. I think there is a great sadness in villains..."

- Christopher Lee

Map of Doggerland
The North Sea

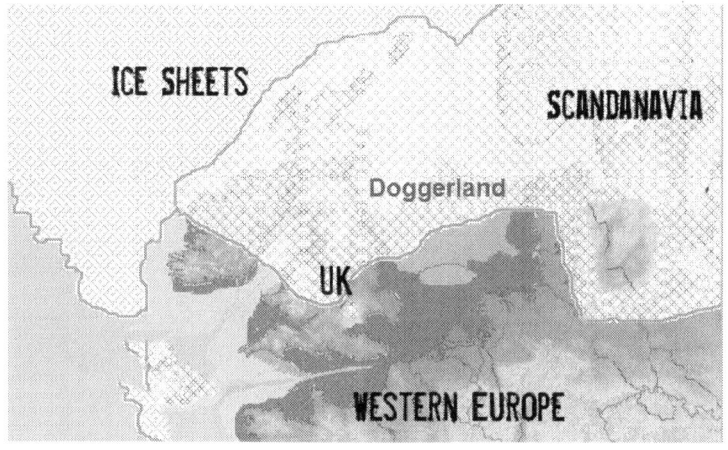

CHAPTER
THIRTY-EIGHT
AUGUST 22, 7:00 A.M. (GMT)

THE *NY BAKKE TO*, THE NORTH SEA

Enjoying the sharpness of a crisp, clear morning, Luther Gibson stood at the bobbing prow of the *Ny Bakke To*, a scientific research vessel he'd hired through a Norwegian colleague, someone he met at a convention in Helsinki three years earlier. Dr. Jan Jansson had been only too happy to oblige.

They had spent an evening drinking too much fine red wine— three bottles between them—and stayed up way too late, comparing stories and marveling at the similarities in ancient remains between the regions of northern Europe and northern Canada. They concluded it was only to be expected, given that geology and fauna were the driving forces in population migration, not politics or war or borders. When the ice sheets melted in Canada, they melted in Scandinavia.

The pair had bonded over a monster hangover and enjoyed a firm friendship in which they even visited with one another's families. Until, that is, Luther's wife decided she could no longer tolerate the harsh conditions of small-town winters, growing jealous of the silly crushes imbued by college girls upon her husband—crushes he absolutely *never* took advantage of—and demanded Luther choose between her and his career.

He chose work on principle, offended she could think to control him, using the children to intimidate him, like a club held over his head. It was only when he struggled to find another age-appropriate woman willing to share his bed that he saw he'd made a mistake.

Hubris had guided him to assume his brain and his sheer manliness would land him plenty of mates before settling down with an ex-swimsuit model or former Olympic athlete. Unfortu-nately, times had changed. Manly men were no longer *de-rigeur,* although a certain assertiveness appeared preferable. And impres-sionable college girls, whom he *could* attract—albeit in dwindling numbers compared to previous years—did nothing for him except boost his ego.

Luther was so confused.

He'd shelved all that in favor of dating slowly but surely, his weight gain playing havoc with his self-confidence. Re-learning the scene came next, trying to decipher the female mind in prepa-ration for when a specimen showed up with whom he had suffi-cient points in common. Charlie Locke had seemed ideal.

Until she turned out to be married.

From then on, Luther used his position to elbow his way into this group's expedition.

It had been *his* choice, his *mistake,* to prioritize his work over family, a decision he had to live with and cling onto the rare morsels of positivity that happened his way. As the split grew more bitter, so too did his wife's accusations—accusations of cheating and unreasonable behavior that filtered to his kids, who blamed him for everything. They didn't want to see him anymore because of what they perceived he'd done to their mother. And those truly positive moments in his work arose along far less frequently.

Perhaps his mistakes all led to this moment, though. If those *decisions* paved the way to the greatest discovery in anthropology, he might at least *start* to impress them. Could he return as the dad they needed instead of the dad they thought they were stuck with?

In return for covering up the battle on Mount Chepadu and, more importantly, *temporarily* concealing what lay beneath, Charlie and her gang had to be completely honest with him and include him in any finds. He could help, too, promising cooperation and access to a boat. They'd agreed, and Luther had retrospectively written up the bangs and explosions heard in the distance of several towns as exploratory blasting. His deputy in the Chepadu region, the deceptively able Tommy, would hold things down while Luther accompanied these freelance consultants to what might prove a joint discovery of significant interest: a race pre-dating the Paleo-Eskimo culture, Canada's oldest residents, believed to date back to 2500 B.C.

There were older *inhabitants*, of course. The recent find of a settlement on Triquet Island dated to around 10,000 years before the pyramids of Egypt, but there was no evidence of an actual thriving civilization surrounding it. What Luther promised his superiors was an organized people even older than Triquet. He just didn't get too deep into *how much* older.

It was difficult enough to comprehend, let alone explain.

Around the size of a medium fishing trawler, the *Ny Bakke To* came with a minimum crew of three—a captain at the wheel, an engineer to keep it running, and a Norwegian safety official. Well-equipped with clean workstations and sterile labs, enough anchor chain to park them in five-hundred-meter-deep seas, plus facilities for the crew to chill and travel like passengers on a tour boat, it was ideal for LORI to hire it via some Italian shell company. The boat's name translated as *New Ground Two*—ironic in this case, given the 100,000-year-old ground they were seeking. It was in one of the breakout rooms where Luther and Toby were to lead the final staff meeting.

"The official Doggerland story is simple." Luther pressed a button on a presentation aid, pulling up a map on the room's impressive 60-inch HD screen, a computer simulation loaned by Dr. Jansson. It depicted northern Europe, specifically Great Britain and Scandinavia, in their current form. "This is the area we're looking in today. The North Sea. But in the Younger Dryas, it'd look more like this."

He switched the view to an artist's impression of the same section of Europe with the sea removed.

Jules raised his hand. "We know this. I read it in a book while you guys were arranging transport."

"Let's just reacquaint ourselves," Toby said. "We don't all have a photographic memory. From here, we can pick up what to do next."

Jules folded his arms.

Dan did likewise. The larger man's head was held together with plastic strips, his left foot protected by a hard, plastic boot. He gave a big yawn. "Okay, it's education time."

"And it might be more important than you realize," Bridget, the southern belle, said. "So, pay attention."

Luther went on. "Throughout the Pleistocene Epoch, or 'most recent' epoch, the last ice age meant Mesolithic Britain was occupied by hunter-gatherers. *This* prehistoric land..." Luther tapped the screen with a pen. "Was larger than the modern United Kingdom and joined Britain to mainland Europe. Its northernmost coast was a few miles north of what was now Montrose, on the east coast of Scotland."

"Hence mine and Bridget's advance recce there," Toby said. "It was fun winding up Colin Waterston, but as expected, he would not cooperate. Alas, nor were there any experts locally who could help figure out what Colin's people are hiding. *If* there is anything to uncover on the UK mainland, we'll have to investigate the hard way."

Luther's finger traced an area on the screen from the east of England to the Netherlands, splaying his fingers as he did. "Some people, like my friend Dr. Jansson, call this wide plain *Nordseeland*, or 'Northsealand.' We mostly know it as Doggerland.

"People lived here as they did any fertile place. Hunted it, produced children, and fished on the edges. But, like the creation of New York's landscape, the end of the Younger Dryas melted the ice sheets. 8,000 years ago, the North Sea was rising gradually over the landscape, which forced away its inhabitants. But we think the huge disruption that created New York Harbor also triggered a tsunami that wiped Doggerland off the map for good."

"Resulting in another flood myth," Jules said. When Luther watched him in silence, the lad elaborated. "Oh, you want me to recap with stuff we already know, too? Okay, no problem. We've seen more flood myths in every culture we come across than we know what to do with. Difference with these volcano guys we're hoping to ID is, they seem to exist in a time when humans couldn't paint, let alone think about the future." Jules blinked toward Toby. "How was that? Did I do it right?"

Toby cleared his throat. "Yes, that was fine. Luther. Please."

"Are we still calling them *the Witnesses*?" Bridget asked before Luther could pick it up. "I liked that name."

They'd discussed that at length, getting irritated at calling them, *these people, whoever they were*, so came up with a title. The Witnesses had stuck.

"I like that too," Luther said. "*Witnesses*. But the people who settled here, Mesolithic humans, lived through massive environmental change without the levels of intelligence on display under Mount Chepadu, with the sea swallowing all the land low enough to flood." Luther pressed the button again, and the graphic showed blue creeping back over the plains, returning it to the original picture. "We still see evidence near modern coastlines. In fact, during the Middle Ages, societies interpreted clusters of ancient tree trunks as proof of the Biblical flood. Unfortunately, there are people who still point to them today."

Jules's eyes hooded in exaggerated boredom. "And…?"

"And you're up," Toby said.

"Great." Jules stood and toggled the laptop to his own sketch of what he'd observed projected onto the roof of the mine's unstable chamber. "The ice sheets are still in place at this point, but the maps these *Witness* dudes produced are stupidly accurate."

Luther had never met anyone like this kid. Jules talked like the kind of slacker that hangs out with his pals on street corners playing tinny rap music from his phone and leering at girls as they passed. He also didn't like to socialize much, and Luther detected a lingering tension between the lad and Bridget. Jules had even announced his departure as soon as Charlie confirmed there was no arrest warrant for Toby Smith, planning to leave them with the drawing and nothing else. But Toby apparently talked Jules into seeing it through.

No wonder.

If what Luther had seen the youngster do in the cavern was real—his touch activating the metallic flecks inside the artifact—then, of course, he should stick around.

"I did this as best I could," Jules continued, and switched to the same picture, but manipulated the land masses in increments. It twisted the Grim Reaper and the circle-and-zigzag/sun image a little too, but the lines emitting from what they assumed was a representation of the sun landed in the same landscapes. "Charlie did the math and used the same formula for the continental drift that made the Reaper Seal wrong by a few miles. Should look like this today."

"*Under* the North Sea," Luther said.

"Yeah, sorry, I thought we were all there already. Anyone *not* clear that we're on a boat, heading for a landmark three hundred feet under the surface? Anyone?" Jules narrowed his eyes Luther's way, then returned to the others. "So, looking at a couple of factors, namely the light ending here..." He tapped a point in the far north of Doggerland. "It's now five miles off the coast of Scotland."

"Not quite international waters," Harpal said.

"No, but UN agreements allow innocent passage through

territorial seas," Dan said. "So, we're good as long as we don't have weapons or drugs. Which we don't."

The ex-military man had argued with both Luther and Toby about his fitness, and about bringing guns with him, but the penalty in the UK would be even harsher than in Canada. He seemed especially worried given his leg injury, but it shouldn't hamper him too much under the water.

"It's also a hill," Jules continued. "Ain't many of 'em for the Neolithic guys to climb, this being a low-lying plain and all, but these Witness folks like to stash things in the highest land available."

Harpal had a question. "If the main part of the land is 300 feet down, how deep is this?"

"Peak's eighty feet below the surface."

"That doesn't tell the whole story," Toby said.

"Right." Bridget sat forward. "We get underwater landscapes all over the ocean floor. Mountains, canyons, rolling hills, and valleys. All amazing. And we've all recovered fantastic things from sunken ships, lost cities, and land reclaimed by the sea."

Luther had learned they were all as experienced in scuba diving as he was, such was the nature of their work.

"The ocean would erode a simple mound," Bridget said. "But for something to remain in place like the hill we identified from older records, it has to be solid."

Luther accepted they were probably correct, but if he followed them blindly, they might sideline him. "And you re-ran the figures?"

"Yes." Jules again dead-eyed Luther. "Separately. Bridget and Toby went fishing for up-to-date scans of the area, while me and Charlie calculated the end of that light beam. Both found the peak here by ourselves, so we figure it's the bullseye."

Luther disregarded the attitude. He was jointly in charge there, and he would ask what he liked. "And what about that mainland trip? What's in Montrose?"

Toby took a breath before answering. Obviously used to being the one to push the agenda, the older man's patience was wearing thin. "I don't know exactly. There was a flurry of activity several years ago. The proximity of that activity to the Doggerland peak set off my coincidence radar. When you combine that with the scroll in Zimina Yanovna's possession, it *can't* be a coincidence. The only historically significant period I can think of involving that church out there is when the Lairds of Dun feared King James the Fourth was overstepping his bounds. They thought he was going to start taking their land, so formed a rebellion of sorts."

"Rebellion," Dan said. "Like your girlfriend."

Even Luther knew Dan was referring to Yanovna.

Toby waved off the comment. "Fear of losing everything to a more powerful interloper? General Yanovna fought hard for independence. What would you do, Dan, if your country was under threat of a takeover by a tyrannical regime? Your second amendment was specifically created for its citizens to fight against such threats—domestic or foreign, was it not?"

Dan patted the area where his sidearm should sit. "Sure was."

"And how much collateral damage would you allow to defend your country? I'm sure a ragtag group of archaeologists wouldn't faze you in the slightest."

Dan let his hand drop. "Think the general will keep coming?"

"I have a source that says she was recalled home," Harpal said. "*Could* she try again? Sure, if they consider us a threat. And Toby is still a wanted man there."

"What about this church?" Luther asked.

"The church we visited on a hilltop outside Montrose," Toby said. "It has an interesting history—"

"A relevant, interesting history?" Jules said. "Beyond the stuff about the scroll you already told us about?"

"It might have—"

"Then how 'bout we leave the lesson 'til it's relevant?"

"*I* might have something relevant," Bridget said.

All turned to her.

"The Latin text on the scroll from this church reads, 'The circle will show the power of God.' But when I compare the Latin script to the writing above—"

"Writing you can't translate," Jules said.

"Writing I hadn't been able to translate until now. Or at least, I can translate a bit."

Luther's checks on the redhead showed her to be a linguist, something of a savant who would've been a handy codebreaker before the advent of the supercomputer. Even she struggled with this, though.

"It's not an exact science, so it's still not clear. I was onto something back home before we left, but… I know Latin and I know Indus. Indus evolved from an older language, which has comparisons to the writing in the books we got from India. There are details to the words, to the slant of certain lines. I thought it was nothing at first, but there's a consistency to it, a… nuance in meaning. Changing things from singular to plural, from a verb to a noun. When we use a word like 'run,' it can be a noun or a verb. We add 'to' or 'a' so it becomes 'she likes *to* run' or 'she went for *a* run.' In this written form, they slant the word at a different angle."

Luther hadn't seen the paper, but Jules and his photographic memory had. He'd scribbled the Latin and the odd squiggles for Bridget, who had disappeared until it was time to depart. Presumably, she was working on this, along with other texts they hadn't shared.

She said, "I used the Latin-Indus translations as a kind of Rosetta Key and applied that to the writing on the scroll. I still can't give you a definitive translation, but educated guesswork means Habib Masouli's interpretation was wrong. Because the Romans and Britons had their God—capital G—they assumed anything to do with a deity was Him. But if you discount this, since the concept of Jehovah and Jesus wasn't around during the Witnesses' time, you switch it to a noun. The circle will show the power of '*a*' god. Small G. Or even… it's odd, but I think they wrote the word Masouli took as 'God' but conjugated it into a

verb. 'To god.' So, the circle enables people to *act* like a god?"
Bridget swayed her head, shaking away the guesswork.

"Or '*the*' god," Jules said.

They all switched from Bridget to Jules.

He shrugged. "I learned some Indus after I got back to the States. Just outta curiosity."

Luther wasn't familiar with Indus; he was barely competent in Latin. "So, what's the conclusion? Is it a message about power?"

"I can't say yet," Bridget replied. "There are too many permutations. Circle might be a cycle or a circuit, but I need to study it more."

"Circuit." Charlie stood and stared at the screen, then clicked her fingers as if seeing the pictograph for the first time. "The circle, the wavy line. It's... almost like a modern symbol used in electrical schematics. Power."

"Could just as easily be the sun." Jules moved his finger in a horizontal zigzag, tracing the pattern. "Or the sea."

Toby placed one hand in the other. "Well, Bridget, it looks like we have several threads to tug at."

Bridget bobbed her head and shifted aside. "I'll start tugging while you guys are below in Harpal's snazzy new swimsuits."

"Harpal got us some swimsuits?" Dan said. "That's nice of him."

"Oh yeah." Charlie pointed at Harpal. "The swimsuits, maestro."

The "swimsuits" were state-of–the-bloody-art wetsuits, helmets able to switch from clear to infrared for short periods, and breathing apparatus that cost Harpal a major favor from a woman in the Royal Navy which he would have preferred to save for a stickier situation. She'd put him in touch with the manufacturer who agreed a rush order—enough gear for all seven, just in case. The material was brown and green, like the company's branding, although they were thicker than usual, better insulated, and the breathers lasted longer than regular tanks at deeper depths. The helmets also encompassed the whole head like an astronaut.

Dan, Jules, and Harpal stripped to their trunks and donned rash vests before pulling on the wetsuit legs.

Sexist as it may have seemed, the currents under the *Ny Bakke Tʋ* would be brutal, so it came down to strength, meaning the three strongest team members got to dive. Even with his bum leg —not broken but gashed and strained—Dan was a more sensible candidate than Bridget, Toby, or Charlie. Given Dan's recent recovery from his head wound, Luther had argued that he should accompany the LORI men, which was fine with Harpal. However, Charlie forbade him from touching one of the three ground penetrating radar pucks that she'd recalibrated for underwater work.

Luther withdrew to sulk.

On deck, Charlie selected a GPR puck—a block the size of a house brick with a sturdy handle and a wrist strap. "People have mapped this seabed using sonar and radar, and some snazzy bollocks you don't need to know about."

"Appreciate that," Jules said. "8,000 years of sediment, fish poop and rotting corpses and plants, not to mention two hundred years of human pollution. You certain it'll even make it to the rock surface?"

"To get the most out of my GPR, it's just like on the plane. Get as close as you can, move over the target area in a grid, and we'll pick up the feed." Charlie referenced iPads in a dry bag to one side. "Thanks to Harpal's resources, you'll also have limited radio comms. A relay box gets lowered along with you, so the signal and your comms get transmitted up the hardwire to us."

Once Dan, Jules, and Harpal were snug in the wetsuits with only their helmets to go, Charlie handed them a portable unit each. She then showed them how to strap the devices to their wrists and hook a second line to their belts. Harpal found it heavy, but figured it'd move easier under the water.

Dan slapped Jules's shoulder. "Ready for the fun bit?"

"I'm not keen on fun underwater," Jules said.

"Need me to hold your hand? I can get you a blankie if you want."

Jules caught Harpal's eye. "Is he like this with you?"

"All the time."

"Great."

From the moment Jules came on the scene earlier that year and kicked Dan's ass in an alleyway, Dan had always cast suspicion on him, questioning the guy's motives and temperament. Since Canada, Dan appeared to have warmed to him somewhat.

Bridget said, "If this place follows the other sites, there will be two entrances. One much higher than the other."

"So, start at the top of this mound and wind around it."

"Dangerous going too deep," Jules said.

Harpal spotted something unusual—a hesitancy in Jules normally absent; either he did something because it was necessary, or he said no because it was pointless. There wasn't much gray with him.

"You don't want to go," Harpal said.

"I'm going. I'm the best placed to make a success of it, but visibility's gonna be low. Going's gonna be tough. And I ain't convinced we'll find anything with these." He hefted the hand-held GPR puck.

"Not what I meant." Harpal's intuition was probably his best feature, his ability to read an asset or a room, to pick up on tails, on the body language of someone nearby who may be aggressive or a little too inquisitive. "I mean you're scared."

Jules gave the team a once-over, holding a beat longer on Dan before replying to Harpal. "I became an expert-level diver for practical reasons, but always hated it. Nothing instinctive about it."

"You jump off buildings using a piece of elastic," Dan said.

"That's got fixed parameters. Gravity, my weight, the tensile strength of the rope. Water ain't logical. Ain't much you can plan. It's dangerous. I've always been able to adapt when things go wrong, but I been closer to death more often under the water than out of it. Anything goes even slightly bad, I abort. Every time."

"Good plan." Charlie touched the point on her side where she was shot. "I wish I was coming with you, but I'm not risking it. Any sign of danger, and there's plenty to be had, abort is exactly what we do. Clear?"

Before anyone could agree, Bridget added, "But only if there's a threat to life. We can't risk losing what's down there."

A look passed between Charlie and Toby, another for Harpal to pick up on; it was something he'd observed a lot the past couple of days and couldn't shake. He was in no doubt the pair was worried about Bridget in some way.

The *slap-slap* of flippers introduced the arrival of Luther Gibson. He'd poured himself into the wetsuit Harpal gave him down below and donned the helmet. "I'm ready. How about you guys?"

CHAPTER
THIRTY-NINE

AUGUST 22, 7:40 A.M. (GMT)

ROYAL NAVY FRIGATE, THE NORTH SEA

Colin hated Toby Smith.

Okay, that was a bit strong. He didn't *hate* the man. But he was mightily suspicious of anything his former mentor got up to, especially around historically important areas linked to the monarchy. It made Toby a source of great frustration.

He'd been a headache for the House of Windsor even when he used to work for them, having decided one day that some treasures obtained during the rule of the Empire should be returned to the cultures from which they were removed. Or "stolen" as Toby put it. He'd pitched the idea one day that it would serve as a grand diplomatic gesture, improve Britain's standing in the world. The powers that be had disagreed, stating rightly that historical artifacts such as the Elgin Marbles were obtained during a time of legitimate government. When Toby tried to back-channel several items through the diplomatic service, he was unceremoniously dismissed from his post.

Much to his star student's shock and disappointment.

It was for this reason—Toby's mentorship—that Colin found extreme action against the man awkward and distasteful. Yet always necessary. Toby's recklessness would land him in jail one day, and Colin was honor-bound to slap on the cuffs. His former mentor's idiotic plans, his desire to discover something long theorized but never proven, might even get him killed. Him *and* his scruffy team.

So, no, Colin didn't truly *hate* the man.

But he *would* arrest him.

As he huddled in the darkened operations room of a Navy frigate alongside Simon Pickard on the lad's first field trip, Colin monitored the feed from a surveillance drone piloted from the mainland. The lieutenant commander assigned to them had only ceased asking questions when ordered to by his captain, herself unaccustomed to taxiing representatives of her majesty's government around the North Sea and therefore obeying orders and nothing more. Clearing the ops room was another bone of contention, but Colin assured the captain he'd vacate the place should the Belgians invade.

"As I feared," Colin said. "His damn fantasies."

"Sir, you still haven't told me what these odd theories are," Simon said. "Perhaps if you share—"

"They're irrelevant." Colin didn't look up from the screen showing the small science vessel they'd tracked from Norway once the ex-MI5 agent—Singh's—passport pinged on a records check. "We just need to stop them doing anything that might place themselves or someone else in danger."

"They're two hours away from us, with legitimate papers to be here," the lieutenant commander said. With a single earphone and mic, he looked like a backing singer for a naval-themed dance troupe. "We don't have any authority over them."

Colin found the lack of imagination in this new generation quite troublesome. He sometimes wondered how, exactly, they circumvented any of the ridiculous rules set up to protect innocent people. When the same rules protected those who were a threat to the UK, surely agents like himself, and this lieutenant commander, were honor-bound to seek loopholes and throw those threats into a big hole from which there would be no escape.

"There are international piracy laws, are there not?" Colin suggested.

The lieutenant commander, whose name Colin failed to remember, paced two steps and turned, running one hand over his short hair. "But if there are no other vessels under threat, that won't wash." Another two steps. "They're not pirates, not terrorists, not smuggling people. But you say they're a threat. Without evidence."

"I have evidence," Colin said. "I'm just not at liberty to share it."

They watched the screen, the zoom from 5,000 feet unable to ID faces, but Colin spotted Toby's squat frame. The usual two females flanked him, and four men donned what looked like scuba gear. There must have been other crew, but—

"Five?" Simon said.

"What's that?" Colin asked.

"Five men, total. I assume they're men. Toby Smith, and four in wetsuits. We only have three others, aside from Smith: Dan Vincent, Harpal Singh, and that yank Jules Sibeko. Who's the other?"

"Must be Luther Gibson," Colin said. "He hired the boat out of Telemark in Norway. That's where we picked up Singh's passport."

The lieutenant commander listened to the single earphone, his brows knitting together.

"A random search," Simon suggested. "There are laws that allow the Navy to board vessels in our waters. Human traffickers, drugs..."

Colin rubbed his chin. "We'd need a plausible excuse. The lieutenant commander and captain are merely tolerating our presence and won't risk an investigation. If we arrow straight for a boat and find Toby up to no good, our route will look like we targeted him."

"Which we are."

"Exactly. Not randomly. We need a more subtle approach."

"Mr. Waterston," the lieutenant commander said. Colin would *have* to learn the man's name. "There's another vessel approaching. Thirty minutes out."

"From us?" Colin asked.

"From them." The Navy man pointed at the surveillance screen, having zoomed out to show miles of ocean. Sure enough, a second boat approached on an intercept course with Toby's.

"Who are they?" Simon asked.

"I'm not a hundred percent sure," Colin said. "But I have my suspicions."

The lieutenant commander used his pacing to stand beside Colin. "This *may* allow us to intervene."

Colin brightened. "How so?"

"We know British civilians are on board the Ny Bakke To, and there's an unidentified ship approaching them at speed. It wouldn't be unreasonable to suspect piracy in this case."

"In British waters?"

"Low level, and not usually our concern, but it happens. And this other vessel has no transponder signal, meaning it isn't merchant or naval or a fishing boat. That alone is sufficient to involve ourselves."

Colin smiled. Perhaps he'd underestimated the young officer. "What's your name, son?"

"Garrett," the lieutenant commander said.

"How far away?"

"At full speed, we'll intercept in two hours."

"In that case, Lieutenant Commander Garrett, let's fall back."

"Fall back?" Again, the copper-haired lieutenant commander appeared confused.

Colin found the next part of his job difficult. When liaising with Interpol or other law enforcement, Colin's colleagues in the British Foreign Office and security services paved the way for him to plan and even lead investigations abroad. Diplomacy, and the need for keeping Colin's involvement a secret, meant those other agencies happily took the credit for bringing down any criminals. The commandeering of British agencies was more troublesome because they discovered exactly who Colin was and questioned why a royal curator should be allowed to take command of their facilities.

"Call your captain," Colin said. "I need her to order a course to Perth Harbor in Scotland."

"What's in Perth?" Garrett asked.

"Nothing, just a harbor. We're only plotting a course. We're actually heading for Montrose. I'll explain all once your captain objects, calls her superiors, and then begrudgingly follows my instructions. So how about we stop gabbing and get to work?"

CHAPTER
FORTY
AUGUST 22, 7:45 A.M. (GMT)

THE *HAIFA SPLENDIDE*, THE NORTH SEA

General Yanovna now commanded a crew of four, who came with the converted fishing trawler which Igoravich picked up via a former Cold War ally turned smuggler. Prior to departing the Airlifter over France, Igoravich also sourced six mercenaries out of Ukraine, part of an underground militia of ex-military preparing for a ground invasion by Russia. A payment from Yanovna's slush fund allowed them swift egress from their borders to rendezvous with the *Haifa Splendide* in France.

On top of the muscle, Yanovna enjoyed the company of an able and willing partner in the Indian girl, Prihya Sibal. It was, oddly, Prihya who had secured a weapons delivery but refused to reveal her source. If Yanovna read the girl correctly, Prihya didn't actually *know* who the source was; a proxy for someone with deep pockets and a long reach.

For now, it didn't matter.

"Thirty minutes," Igoravich reported in Striovian, joining Yanovna and Prihya on the mezzanine deck outside the bridge. "Another party is already holding steady over the coordinates."

"Toby." Yanovna seethed at speaking the man's name. She

switched to English, so Prihya didn't find them suspicious. "Slow approach. I want to observe them first. Make sure the men are ready."

"Yes, General." Igoravich, too, spoke English, although his vocabulary was not as accomplished. "Will we attack as soon as we can?"

"We take the boat. If we act too hard, we may lose anything they have learned."

Igoravich pointed an open hand to Prihya. "We have our expert, do we not?"

"I am not as versed as Toby Smith." Prihya's accent came through thick and heavy, even to Yanovna's ears. "I know things, yes, and my employer has resources, but I agree with General Yanovna. Let's see how much they know."

Since sharing with Prihya her ability to sync herself to both the Reaper Seal and the scythe head, Yanovna spent hours trying to pinpoint the exact location of the next mine. *If* it was a mine.

Prihya had talked about a tomb which had become a repository of writing and art, of carvings and engravings never observed in any historical record. She also calculated the shift of tectonic plates, reassessing the original coordinates closer to the UK coastline. With Zefirova Victoriovna monitoring the area via satellite, Yanovna had a distinct advantage over Toby and his killers.

Igoravich dipped his head in agreement. "Then we will prepare for boarding other ship." About to leave, he stopped and raised a finger, then lowered it.

"You wish to say something?" Yanovna said.

"General, just a word to caution."

Yanovna lifted her chin to listen.

"Toby Smith," Igoravich said. "He is your friend and he betray you. I know is hard. But we are here for Striovia. Five men give lives. I risk jail. You too. And Private Victoriovna is helping from ground. She will see court martial if caught."

"And I appreciate the support. It is necessary. What is your caution?"

"If we cannot get revenge on Toby Smith, we keep our mission, yes?"

"Of course."

"We take weapons. Go home. Plead mercy to President. And maybe, he spare us from treason."

Yanovna sensed Prihya's discomfort. A captain worrying over his general's state of mind, about her intentions, would do that. "Denis, we will never put Striovia second. If we face jail for bringing home something to protect our borders, jail is the sacrifice we must make. If it is death, then we die knowing we preserved our country's way of life."

"What if...?" Igoravich held his tongue.

"We are rogue agents, Captain Igoravich. Speak freely."

"General, if you are wrong... if no weapon is here for us... what then?"

Yanovna allowed a smile. A pat of her deputy's arm. "Then we are in Great Britain. Bastion of human rights. We will seek asylum from the torture that awaits us at home."

Igoravich's posture slumped an inch or so, but he accepted her words. "I will prepare men."

With a salute, he left Yanovna and Prihya alone, tramping down the metal staircase to where the mercenaries had been cleaning and familiarizing themselves with the weapons—British and American firearms smuggled out of the Middle East some years ago.

"Why do you believe it is a weapon?" Prihya asked. "Toby called these people Witnesses. Not warriors."

Yanovna leaned on the rail, absorbing the wind blowing her hair straight back and the spray in her face as she gazed at the horizon, craning for their destination to appear. "The message in the scroll, transported alongside maps. It speaks of power."

"The translations are not exact. From Bridget Carson's incomplete notes, they speculate the other lines are a language. One the wise man in Montrose mistranslated. The power could be light. Or knowledge. The circle could be the cycle. A crop cycle or a cycle of seasons. Master this, and you have the power to reproduce, which falls in line with the fertility goddess we see on—"

"The people are something we do not understand yet." Yanovna was growing irritated at her conclusions being repeatedly questioned. "*Or* their stones. The seals we found, and then the stone scythe that pointed us here... if not a direct weapon, there is *power*. Something we can use. I still do not see how this is possible, but I accept the reality."

"A people whose science is different from our own," Prihya said. "A branch of humanity who somehow grew their intelligence outside the Toba Catastrophe."

Yanovna had been a professor of antiquities, became the foremost expert in her country, but despite studying human evolution as much as anyone, it was a rudimentary knowledge. She only dug deeper when the age of the mummy and its seals were proven. "How did one event trigger better thinking, though? Better brains?"

Prihya had been cagey about chatting with Yanovna, a lack of *complete* trust, but an uneasy alliance meant neutral subjects came easy. "An eruption of the Toba super volcano in the Pacific 75,000 years ago was so big, its effects stretched over most of the planet. Ash, methane. Some think its cooling effects delayed the ice melts. But mainly, it killed stupid humans. Brute strength was not enough to be the alphas anymore. Clever humans found new ways to survive and passed on that intelligence to their offspring. The offspring learned more, and the cleverest survived again to pass on *those* genes."

Yanovna laughed. "So, intelligence is an accident."

"*All* evolution is an accident." Prihya gazed at the ocean. "If a different tribe went through that process in an isolated landmass —a unique event making intelligence more important to survival than strength—there is no reason they couldn't have accelerated their brains over thousands of years before Toba."

Yanovna imagined the sequence as a speeded-up montage of Red Indian-types from TV when she was young, breeding and building, painting, then writing. "Then when they reach the point where they ask what else is out there, they explore?"

Prihya shrugged and turned back to Yanovna. "It appears to be what Toby Smith and Bridget Carson are theorizing at the house in Brittany. I ran through their other notes, not just the most recent. I see many flaws in their logic. It is not impossible, but their evidence is flimsy."

"And unimportant," Yanovna said. "We will soon learn what these Witnesses can do to help us. Power, light, knowledge. Cycles or circles. At the very least, it will rid Striovia of an enemy of the State when I kill Toby Smith, and your employer has one less competitor to worry about."

It surprised Prihya how well the traffickers had kitted out this boat: satellite communications, radar, and a well-maintained engine and body. And she was glad of it; this was the first time she'd traveled on a boat on the open sea.

When she left the general to her musings to nip below for a cup of tea, she battled the twin notions she'd been carrying since the previous evening: General Yanovna was an enemy of the enemy, but did that make her a friend?

The clandestine nature of Prihya's work had been tantalizing at first, while the unlimited credit card and cash on hand made her feel like a female James Bond. Not to mention the gadget—just a cell phone, essentially, left in the vicinity of the main alarm panel, which acted as a conduit for some hacker in North Korea to access and disable.

That was straight-up thrilling.

Then there was the breaking and entering aspect, which she studied and practiced some years ago, but never failed to make her nervous with each attempt. The first night of roaming LORI's château had been nerve-wracking and uncomfortable, her clothes tight and burglar-chic—hence the pajamas on the second night.

But this, now, was the part that both thrilled her and scared her the most.

Having made a loose agreement with the general through their mutual need to locate and understand the Lost Origins Recovery Institute, Prihya still kept secrets.

Likewise, Yanovna only shared her ability to make a rock light up after Prihya revealed the project notes made by Toby Smith and Bridget Carson relating to what they termed the Aradia bangle and the effect the touch of someone called Jules had on it. The notes, she explained to Yanovna, were available the same way she deactivated the alarms—by wirelessly tapping the system. The safe was hidden, though, and Prihya hadn't had time to explore fully yet, so accessing that part of the house had to wait.

Then Yanovna described what Toby Smith and his people had done in Canada—killing five of the general's men and stealing a map to hidden artifacts belonging to Striovia—and that was really all Prihya needed to hear.

It helped with her assessment of the freelancers, specifically whether they worked for good or ill, but she hadn't observed these events for herself—it wasn't *evidence*; just conjecture. She wanted what was best for mankind, so if they turned out to be harmless, she would reject the money, the resources, and the prestige she'd experienced so far.

At least, she hoped she'd have the strength to turn it down.

This would be a mission where Prihya could observe LORI under pressure, study how they worked, and decide what quality of people they were.

Prihya made tea in the galley, stared down one of the two leering mercenaries who were downing some energy drink or another, then retired to a private bunk. She sipped her tea for a few seconds, then slipped the cell phone she'd told no one about from her sock; she held down the number seven.

It appeared to be an old Nokia, one of the first to popularize mobile devices, which made calls and sent text messages, and little else. That speed dial on seven went to a voicemail, the owner of which never answered, but it required her to leave at the minimum a daily progress report plus any significant happenings. She assumed the details got back to her employer fairly quickly.

"I have made an ally," she said. "General Yanovna. Fugitive from Striovia. We received the package for her assistants. I am going to observe her interactions with the Lost Origins people and try not to interfere. If there are items of significant interest, I will attempt to acquire them on your behalf."

Then Prihya gave their current coordinates, hung up, and drank her tea. The culmination of her assignment there, and therefore the rest of her life, would commence before the day ended.

CHAPTER
FORTY-ONE

UNDER THE NORTH SEA, 5 MILES EAST OF MONTROSE

Because all concerned were accomplished divers, and there being no insurance forms to complete, Jules was mercifully spared a long lecture on how to work the air tanks and weights, and there was no need to recap on hand signals. This was partly because their spaceman-like helmets allowed them to speak clearly, something Jules hadn't experienced in his years exploring wrecks and probing for cities lost off the coasts of places like Greece and Italy.

They went through weather conditions and the dangers posed by the freezing temperatures of the North Sea even in summer, but Harpal assured them the insulation was sufficient for all but the worst Arctic temperatures. It left the so-called action dudes to explore the seabed.

Action dudes was Charlie's phrase, and it wasn't polite.

Visibility was poor. Their shoulder-mounted flashlights just about kept each other in sight, but unlike the Mediterranean and Caribbean where Jules did most of his dives, even relatively clear conditions like today only gave them twenty feet. Only ten feet down, their view blurred into shapes and movement. They could barely see the anchor chain or the comms cable. And that was only after the first minute.

For every three-to-four feet they dived in their loose diamond formation, Jules equalized his pressure by swallowing, and the monitor in the helmet accounted for the plummeting temperature which kept the visor from steaming up.

"Thirty feet." Jules checked his gage

"Confirmed," Charlie replied in the speaker by Jules's ear. "Thirty feet."

He glanced at the box attached to Dan, pulling the comms relay with them. Jules wanted to go quicker, but there was no rush. Rushing would make them sloppy. And the current gripped them from the moment they hit ten feet, thrashing them around as if trying to buck them out of the water. Every couple of yards, pressure hit them like a side-wind, tides having a major effect this close to shore.

"Forty feet," he said.

"Confirmed. Forty feet."

Bridget's tone came over the speaker, languid yet rapid-fire, an odd oxymoron. "Can you see anything yet?"

Darkness loomed below. Above, the light from a clear day dappled the sea like a dull skyscape, but there was enough swirling microbial matter to track their path from the surface, disturbed by their mass. They'd seen few fish except for a school of cod, a smattering of jellyfish, and a dead crab tumbling by. They were saving the infrared mode—a watered-down version of military-style night vision goggles—for when they really needed it, given the short battery life.

"Fifty feet," Jules said. "Nothing yet."

"Confirmed. Fifty feet," Charlie answered.

The current sideswiped Jules harder than before and he twisted to stay in place. A quick check on the others showed they'd weathered the shift in motion, too. *OK* signs came from each of them.

"I'm fine," Luther said. "That was a strong one."

"What was?" Bridget asked. "Are you okay?"

Jules shook his head. "Just a little wave. Nothing to worry about."

"You're at sixty feet," Toby said cautiously. "How does it look?"

"Dark." Jules checked above him. Nothing visible except a dull blanket of daylight; even the boat was difficult to make out. He brought his arm around with the dive computer showing the depth gage. "Fifty-eight, but sure, let's go with sixty."

Luther had dipped ahead of them, against the agreement that they'd sink as one tight group. "I see it," he said.

"Wait there," Dan said.

Dan took off faster, and Jules and Harpal sped up to catch them, the pressure squeezing, the need to equalize more urgent.

Luther halted in mid-swim as Dan grabbed his shoulder.

"It's no joke down here," Dan said. "You don't run off."

Luther pointed at his own chest. "I have fifteen years' experience of waters like this—"

"Others don't," Toby said over comms. "You going off risks their lives too. Think about that."

It wasn't easy to see facial expressions, but Jules read the bob of Luther's shoulders as compliance.

"Sorry," the Canadian said.

That signaled them all to reform into the loose diamond and continue down.

A dome of shadow darker than its surroundings materialized ahead, growing larger as they hit seventy feet and Jules almost forgot to report in. Almost.

"It's there," Jules said after the formalities. "I'm turning on the ground penetrating radar. Let's see what we got."

He carried out the instructions issued above—essentially an on-off switch, then aim—and Dan and Harpal followed suit.

"Luther, sit back," Jules said. "Need your eyes. Make sure we're all level and ain't about to hit something that might damage us."

"Of course." Luther's tone was more conciliatory than it had been.

"Eighty-two feet." Jules floated above the surface, so large it stretched for the whole of his field of vision as if he'd touched down on the bottom of the ocean.

Not usually given to amazement and wonder, he could not resist pushing his hand into the loose sandy floor and feeling around. He almost imagined grasping a handle purely by luck and twisting it to gain entrance to some long-lost hall of treasures.

Although Bridget made it clear how much she regretted the destruction in India, and how LORI were forbidden from getting within one hundred miles of the site, Jules had kept his own curiosity hidden. He'd compartmentalized it as best he could. The past was the past and lingering on regrets was poison to the soul. He'd never expected to get another chance, though, and throughout the time when freeing Toby was at the forefront of his mind, his subconscious nagged at him.

A second chance.

He withdrew his hand and retreated from the swirling muck that his motion displaced. "Ready?"

"Ready," Harpal said.

"Ready," Dan said.

"I'm in position." A good ten feet away, Luther gave the OK sign.

As planned, they each aimed their GPR pucks at the ground and backed away from one another, sweeping their arms from side to side to capture the greatest surface area possible.

With Luther directing them, they covered it slowly but methodically until they reached the drop-off. From there, the underwater hill sloped downward, and the trio swam circles around the feature, descending in a choreographed dance.

Jules imagined the puck as a spray paint can, and their objective was to cover the seabed in a whole new color. The deeper they went, the darker the surroundings, the wider the hill grew, and the farther away from one another they swam. Each of them kept at least one set of lights in sight and followed Luther's directions when they strayed.

Being unable to see the results was incredibly boring. Jules just hoped it was more interesting up top.

Shadowed by the main tower on the *Ny Bakke To*, Bridget held her breath as she watched the first images roll across the screen. The workstation held the tech receiving data from below, both the comms and the radar results.

As the action dudes progressed, the hill began to take shape on the screen: flat land initially, then a shallow dome.

Once they'd made contact with solid mass, Bridget tore herself from studying the line of text, from connecting vague similarities and dismissing the least likely, and concentrated on what they could physically prove.

Knitting together each of the three pucks and linking to their GPS units, Charlie's software created a 3-D landscape in multiple rainbow colors—the contours of the hardscrabble surface beneath the sand and ocean detritus. Bridget only sort-of heard the conversations below, and barely noticed the bobbing and roll of the boat. It took all she had to pry her eyes away to meet Toby's. He'd been saying her name.

"Sorry, yes?"

"Bridget, you do know this may be a wild goose chase, don't you?" Toby said.

Bridget returned to the monitor—an iPad retina screen inserted into Charlie's portable unit. "I know, but... just the geological feature being here means we're on the right track."

"He means," Charlie said, "this could be nothing more than an instruction. Everything we've seen is agricultural."

"I know that." Bridget heard her own voice, extending her words into "Ahh knowww thayat," and clamped her mouth shut, concentrating.

She watched the seabed come to life, not even entertaining the possibility of their doom-laden conversations over the past few days. The hypotheses ranged from another repository of knowledge to a library, to nothing more than fertile ground on which to plant crops—100,000 years before organized farming was known to exist.

It made sense, given the symbology of harvest and life. One thing they agreed on was that the robed figure with the scythe was not representative of death, the way it had been depicted in the Middle Ages and apocalyptic literature.

"There!" Bridget pointed to a dark spot on the mapping software.

"It's nothing." Charlie had explained how it worked, but Bridget took little notice.

Bridget understood the technology's function above ground, so assumed it would work the same underwater. The only major difference was the three-pronged sweep of sonic emissions instead of a single wide arc.

"Jules," Charlie said. "Back up two meters."

A pause, then the dark spot that looked like a portal to Bridget was filled in like the rest of the graphic. Bridget absorbed the heavy cloud of disappointment and continued to watch.

Occasionally, a dark line intruded on the consistent contours of purple and green and orange, but upon investigation, it turned out to be a car wheel, or a panel door, or even a box full of hardware tools fallen from a ship decades ago.

Forty-five minutes passed, in between which the men came up for replacement air after the first thirty, leaving the comms relay as their marker to resume. Air must have been low again now, despite the high-tech equipment, and Bridget had given up on watching every millimeter of graphics and taken to stretching and leaning over the side.

"Can I head down there?" she asked. "I'm not exactly doing much up here."

"There are only three pucks," Charlie said.

"And yet Luther's allowed."

Charlie muted the two-way. "Luther is an arse, lass. He wants to be Mr. Leader, let him. He has stuff to prove to himself. You don't. So, unless they come across a signpost they need translating, you stick around here."

Bridget huffed and puffed some more but stopped short of an all-out tantrum. She was better than that. Just needed to see. Needed to *be* there. Needed to—

"Back up," Toby said.

It was the first interruption Toby had made, most of them coming from Charlie and Bridget. Mostly Bridget.

Harpal said, "How's that?"

From Harpal's puck, the image on the screen rolled one spot into a darker hue. A straight edge grew more distinct, and as Harpal maintained his position, a corner formed.

"Everyone freeze where you are," Charlie said. "Harpal. Pull back. Then keep aiming it there."

"Not that easy," Harpal said. "I'm being tossed about a bit here."

They'd expected tough currents, to be pulled this way and that, but so far, they'd coped fine. It was exhausting in mild seas, though, so Bridget could only imagine what it was like down there.

Charlie took to the keyboard, tabbing to a screen of code and tweaking the settings. "Two more minutes."

The monitor switched back to the 3-D landscaping program, revealing a tighter frame and more detail.

"My god." Charlie's hand touched her chin, lips parted. "There's something here."

Bridget got closer to the image, now definitely rectangular in shape.

"Could be modern debris," Toby said.

"Guys," Charlie said, "on Harpal's aim, let's see what we've got there. About seven feet long, you're looking for a rectangle."

"Like a door?" Jules said.

Bridget detected a rise in his voice, a hint of anticipation, of excitement. She knew he suppressed a lot, and the fascination with ancient people was one of those—a fascination she shared.

"Dig," she said. "Come on. Let's see it."

Toby said her name again, as if to urge caution on her expectations—yes, *again*.

"Can't see a thing," Dan said. "Too much fog."

"Just wait," Bridget said. "The disturbed sediment will fall away. Give it a minute."

Silence returned. An occasional heavy breath. Luther offered to try instead, and Dan refused to make way.

Jules said, "I can feel something."

"We're through to the surface crust," Dan said. "Just got to clear the air. Well, you know, the water."

Then more silence.

"Murky." Luther filled the awkwardness of waiting in silence. After another minute, he said, "Fifteen percent."

"Pardon?" That sounded like Jules.

"Fifteen percent," Luther said again. "The air tank. It's down to—"

"Oh, man..." Harpal cut him off. "Everyone flick to infrared a sec."

"What is it?" Bridget asked. "What do you see?"

Nobody spoke, presumably following Harpal's instruction.

"It ain't something that fell off a ship," Jules said.

Bridget could barely keep from screaming, from crying out, from exploding. "What *is* it?"

Again, no one answered.

"We need more air," Harpal said.

"And I think we'll need an engineer," Jules added.

"Know anyone available?" Dan said.

Charlie sat back in her chair.

Bridget couldn't believe no one was describing it to her. If she ranted and shouted, it'd give Toby more ammunition with which to admonish her, but if there was something in front of Jules that he couldn't figure out, Bridget definitely wanted to see it.

"What are we facing?" Toby asked.

"I can't believe it," Luther said breathlessly. Swimming up now along with the others. "It's incredible. I've never seen anything like it. It's an engineering marvel."

And, Bridget realized with a sinking feeling to her stomach, *everyone else gets to see it before me.*

CHAPTER
FORTY-TWO

This time it would be different. No half-truths, no lying by omission, no misleading assurances. The only remotely manipulative thing Charlie did was to pull on her wetsuit before placing the face-to-face satellite call with Phil. She hoped it would make him see that she was ready to depart and remind him she was an able diver with plenty of experience.

Unlike in Canada, Phil had not been keyed into their comms throughout the dive. Usually, when it was a simple satellite uplink and a relay, it was better to keep him there, but today it was more important to concentrate on maintaining contact between the surface and those below.

He hadn't found out about the gunplay on Mount Chepadu until Charlie arrived for a twenty-four-hour layover in their Greenwich home—shortly before she rejoined the Institute in Norway. He'd been unusually quiet, although their three kids, Joan, Alexander, and Boadie, were less restrained as they all enjoyed their chaotic family time. It was harder than ever to leave.

And he was unusually quiet now too, facing out from the monitor, brow tense but face bright. "Of course you're going down there. You're needed."

"That's it?" Charlie said. "I'm needed."

"You know your body. If you say the wound won't get worse, I'll trust that."

Charlie, alone at the workstation while Toby and Bridget helped the action dudes restock on air, chewed her lip. "You don't want me to go."

"Of course, I don't," Phil said. "I want you here. Doing the job you *told* me you'd be doing for Toby: researching from a chair in the home office we spent a fortune converting. Not gallivanting around, shooting down helicopters. But you know what's needed out there, and you know what's waiting for you. If Toby's crusade is more important, I have to accept that."

"Phil, that's not—"

"Not what? Fair?" He slapped his hands down. They landed out of sight, but they'd have hit the arms of his wheelchair. "I know what fair is, Charlie. Fair is understanding the dangers posed and knowing when to quit. We're not indestructible. No matter how many wins we've got behind us. All it takes is one screw-up, one miscalculation."

Charlie's head spun for a moment, her chest cold. "Phil, I'll—"

"Be careful, yeah, I know you will." He looked down, sighed through his nose. "You're there, I'm here. You know the risk, and you know you'll be missed." His eyes popped back to the screen. "If it means that much, I won't try to stop you. I *can't* stop you. But remember who's waiting if— *when* you get back. I love you."

Phil hit a key to hang up, his image replaced by a placeholder of a family photo, a pile-on pose with the kids, loving that they got to jump on their parents on the tiny lawn of their home.

Charlie never got to say "I love you" back, and she wanted to punch the screen for that. Probably would punch Phil when she got home.

If she got home.

Having taken shrapnel on an expedition with LORI, Phil's spinal injury was a constant reminder to her and the others that the dangers were real. Death or serious harm was only one poor decision away. Phil would never forbid her outright—she wasn't the type of woman who responded well to ultimatums—but she understood his concerns.

Understood them but pushed them to the back of her mind.

With the dudes having departed below, she quickly ran the checks on her kit. When Toby and Bridget returned, they did a second sweep, and then she was in the freezing water. The cold crippled her for a split second before the suit did its job, and she got her bearings to right herself. The four-month-old bullet wound still ached occasionally, especially during exercise and strain such as the escape on Mount Chepadu. In the cold ocean, it puckered tight, as if the body was adding more protection from the body's idiotic owner.

Several minutes passed as she ran the numbers—ten feet… twenty… thirty—with Toby and Bridget acknowledging her. To preserve air, chatter remained zero until she got to the right spot, and even then, it was a subdued reunion with little talk.

Lights from the suits cut through the murk and glowsticks lit up the excavated patch of basalt crust through the silt and sediment. The current and intangible nature of the seabed meant it swirled and shifted and didn't take kindly to people digging nearby. That they'd found this on a shallow angle helped, but it was far less clear than on her computer simulation.

Occasional fishes darted by to investigate, and to distract Charlie, then shot off, startled by the glare.

Charlie accepted a trowel from Dan and pushed herself to the slab. On the screen, it had been delineated, but in person she needed to jam her fingers in to trace the outline.

And it *was* an outline. A definite straight edge connected to three others—a rectangular door-like shape with no handle.

"Definitely man-made," she said.

"I think we figured that," Jules said.

"Is that essential speech?"

"It has longer-term benefits of reminding everyone—"

"I'll take that as a *no*, then."

Jules must have decided her logic was stronger, because he

quietened before joining her. The others remained back, lighting the scene only.

"How old is it?" Bridget asked.

"I can barely see it," Charlie said.

"Use infrared."

"There's a one-hour battery pack at ten meters," Harpal said. "Much less at a-hundred-and-some feet."

"Ten minutes, max," Jules said.

"Agreed," Toby put in. "Be frugal."

An invisible hand eased Charlie and Jules out of the way and the lights went haywire as the three others seemingly felt it too; a sweep of sea current disturbed the excavation, such as it was.

Once they righted themselves, Charlie said, "Let's clear more of it. Make it a little easier."

They concentrated on the top part first, then the sides, taking fifteen minutes and draining another half tank of air apiece. They floated using the shallowest of breaths, waiting for more of the disturbances to clear, switching to infrared for thirty seconds.

An eerie green and black visage greeted Charlie, but it did its job, cutting through the muck and particulate to show the outline of what had to be a door. Or a rectangular stone plug. She also spotted a round indentation near the bottom edge.

No, not round. Not perfectly round. A circle. With a wavy line. *Again.*

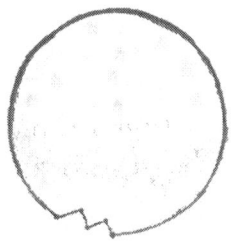

Switching back to regular vision, Jules must have had the same idea as he got closer, joining Charlie.

"No doubts?" he asked.

"None," she said.

Both anchored themselves one-handed, using their fingers in the outer groove, and examined that space between "door" and bedrock.

Jules poked it.

Charlie ran her hand along the groove. It felt…

"Squidgy," Jules said.

"Is that a technical term?" Charlie asked.

"I don't know anything about technical. I know hard. I know squidgy. This is squidgy."

Charlie continued around, this part of the hole less foggy than the freshly disturbed sections, but her gouging more dirt out of the depression churned the water with more sediment. Jules's visor turned green, showing he was in infrared mode, trying to see more than she could.

"We know these folks were advanced." Jules returned his faceplate to transparent. "All that's separating 'em from the ape people is their brains. *Intelligence.* Ain't got flying cars or lasers, right?"

"As far as we know," Bridget replied.

"Everything we have found suggests that's correct," Toby said. "They have advanced intelligence and access to this rock with odd properties. But nothing suggests they accessed anything we don't know was available at that time. They simply used resources more wisely."

"Why?" Dan asked, drifting closer along with the others. "What you got there?"

As Charlie combined her visual check with her touch, she understood why Jules asked about the Witnesses' tech and resources. Her heart thumped faster and the ache in her side intensified. "It's rubber. They sealed this door using what feels like *rubber*."

. . .

Bridget sat back, staring at the sky, her long red hair falling free behind her chair. Another incredible discovery about the Witnesses. Back upright, she locked eyes with Toby, who returned a similarly impressed expression.

"The books we rescued from India," she said. "They were treated with some chemical, an oil that we haven't been able to ID. Could it be that?"

"From the brief tests I conducted, it appeared natural," Charlie replied, her voice still full of wonder. "A resin derived from plant life."

"Rubber comes from trees," Luther said. "Couldn't this?"

"Takes a massive amount of chemicals to turn it into something like this," Jules said. "Long process, and highly technical. Can't brew it in a cauldron or smelt."

"Plants evolve and die out like animals do," Luther replied. "If this is natural, like rubber, it could just be an organic substance that they could mix without mass chemicals. Anything's possible on that front."

"I mean, sure, given time, maybe you could get a rubber-like substance, but… not this." Jules sounded uncharacteristically enthused, baffled, even thrilled. "It's like… oh, man, that's cool."

"What is?" Toby asked. "What's *cool*?"

"The seawater," Charlie answered for him. "It's as if it helps solidify the substance. Jules just cut a piece away and the surrounding parts grew back. Filled in like… like wet sand collapsing back in on itself."

Bridget pictured it and shook her head, teeth virtually grinding. "Any writing? Anything?"

While they checked, Toby sounded even more excited than Charlie and Jules. "You know what this means, don't you?"

"What what means? This door? We won't know until they check what was left."

"Its existence, in this form, leaves a very broad hint, though."

Toby lowered his chin, lips pursed, playing the professor again—a manner he'd subdued since returning from Striovian custody. "The fact this door is waterproofed, but also accessible. Instead of sealing it permanently."

Bridget ran with it.

A millennia-old race.

Intelligent.

With things to say.

Already proven a desire to preserve their knowledge and stories.

"Are you there yet?" Toby asked.

"They didn't just *map* the world," Bridget said. "They *knew* the ice sheets were melting. They predicted the flood would cover this part of the planet."

Toby grinned. "So, they created this place before the hominids populated the land, and long before the sea took it over."

"Why? If they knew it would be flooded?"

"Maybe when it was built, they didn't know for sure, but made this correction as a safeguard. In India, they crafted a door that repelled sea water, but the sea never reached that point."

Bridget now tag-teamed him. "Oh, yes, they didn't have calculators or computer modeling, and no way to be sure just how much the meltwater would affect their repositories. So, they put in contingencies." Her skin tingled, and she fanned herself to cool the rush of blood to her face. "They wanted their descendants to see who they were. So, they gave them an entrance."

"Wait," Jules said, who'd evidently been listening. "You saying the witnesses expected to die out? So made a freaking watertight entrance?"

"Don't be stupid," Luther said. "No way, not even they could make something like that. Could they?"

"Like an airlock," Charlie said.

"That might be a little too much." Toby pulled his mouth to one side in a wry manner. "Even for our ancient friends."

"Hey!" came a guy's shout from up top. The *Ny Bakke To's*

bridge was on a raised platform toward the center of the boat, and Bridget recognized the call from the skipper, his Scandinavian accent nothing more than a lilt in his English. He made his way to the rail over their workstation. "Are we expecting more scientists?"

"No," Bridget replied. "Why?"

"There is another boat. Does not look like coastguard or a fishing boat."

Bridget stood first, checking where the skipper was pointing. Toby joined her.

"Are they heading right for us?" Toby asked.

"Not precisely," the skipper replied. "But I see them a while ago. They wait, they come closer. Wait, come closer. Now they are on this way."

Toby held still, and Bridget's chest thumped hard.

"Hello?" the skipper said. "If trouble is coming, bring your people up. We leave."

"We can't," Bridget said. "No one knows we're here. Even the Striovians—"

"If it's them, we need to go," Toby said.

"If it's them, they'll beat us to the vault, or whatever is down there."

"The Striovians are coming?" Luther said.

"We don't know that," Bridget answered.

"Captain," Toby said, "how long do we have?"

"Until they reach us?" The skipper shrugged, his eyes on the ocean. "Twenty minutes at this pace."

"Charlie," Toby said. "Work out what we need to know. Then hide it as best you can. We may need to evac."

"No maybe," Dan said. "We got no way to fight back. If that boat doesn't identify itself in five minutes, we go."

CHAPTER
FORTY-THREE

Below, Jules was close to talking to himself out loud. Simple logic was usually sufficient to keep his natural curiosity in line and prevent mission creep.

In the past, when he had a single-minded aim, that was easy. But this had been multi-stranded from the beginning: the infiltration, the rescue of Toby, retrieval of the stolen seals. Then he'd got sideswiped when he learned of Bridget's deception by omission; he should have walked away then, left the group to their own business. But he owed a debt, having been the driving force in locating his late mother's bangle and freeing him from that obsession.

With Toby out of custody, he'd somehow allowed their need to know everything about all they touched to leech inside him, to infect him in a way he never had been infected before.

Perhaps that crazy billionaire had been right?

Valerio Conchin had gotten inside Jules's head once, and planted a worm that hadn't exactly grown, but wriggled and probed. That the Reaper Seal dated to the same era as his mother's bangle hinted at deeper answers, at understanding what it was, why it was created, and why his mother and father were willing to die to protect it.

He'd allowed this to expand, to advance beyond the straightforward, which was why he was under the North Sea, staring at an engineering marvel.

Should they go in?

Or retreat and assess if the newcomers up top were friendly?

Which seemed unlikely.

"I know how to open it," Charlie announced.

Jules had a couple of ideas but wasn't certain of any.

"I just don't know if we should," she added.

"Worried about flooding it?" Luther asked.

"Just do it," Dan said. "We came with nothing, we go home with nothing. Or something. Either way, things stay the same or they get better. Easy logic."

"That's not the logic," Jules said.

"Okay, let Dr. Spock examine the patient," Harpal said.

Jules frowned but didn't veer away from what they were now certain was a door. "What could a pediatrician do here?"

"*What?* I never mentioned a pediatrician."

"Dr. Spock was a famous pediatrician and author who died in 1998. If you're referring to the Star Trek character called Spock, he wasn't a doctor. Just Mister."

Bridget came on the air with an amused tone. "Was *Mister* Spock a pedant as well as a logic monster?"

A couple of chuckles.

"Any more news on that incoming boat?" Jules asked.

"They slowed," Toby said. "Still coming, though."

"They ain't friendly. They're checking us out, seeing if we got weapons."

"Okay, decision time," Dan said. "Open up or get out. I'm thinking we rabbit."

"We can't," Bridget said. "If they get to it first..."

No one needed to hear the end of that sentence. If the Striovians got there first, LORI lost any leverage of trading what they found for Toby's pardon. If Toby received no pardon, he'd be a wanted man in Striovia, and they would utilize all their diplomatic clout to have him returned to them for a show trial.

"If we flood it, we lose it all," Charlie said.

"You're the engineer," Jules said. "But I play the odds. Why create a watertight seal that you can open underwater if it wasn't designed to be opened?"

Everyone bobbed in place, Charlie gripping the circular groove near the lower end of the door while Jules kept his fingers in the straight channel. It was difficult, so it was no wonder those floating freely were moving so much.

"You're sure?" Charlie said.

"No," Jules replied. "That's why it involves odds, not facts."

Bridget came through again. "Close it fast if it looks bad, okay?"

"I'm doing it." Charlie spread one hand over the circle, the other with her fingers in the furrow between the door and the seafloor's crust. With one knee on the surface, she pulled herself tight and pushed on the circular shape.

Nothing.

"It's like a suction cup," Jules said, realizing what she'd concluded.

"Right." Charlie was out of breath already. "The bugger won't move."

Jules butted in, flicking to infrared a moment. "Twist it too."

Charlie did as instructed, and Jules held her in place for a better grip. Through her, he detected movement in the stone as it ground into the door itself. Jules lay his hand over hers and lent his added strength, giving a slight twist, pushing it the final stretch.

The rubber-like seal broke.

Seawater rushed around them, sucked into the void beyond like a plug pulled from a bath. The barrier had cracked for the first time in… no one could know. Since before Jules's earliest ancestor walked upright, that was for sure.

The flow was intense, churning the loose sediment from the

exposed basalt, trying to pull Jules and Charlie in, forcing them to push against the outer crust to remain stable. The three men a few feet away undoubtedly felt it too, with Dan and Harpal wobbling and Luther actively turning a full circle before righting himself.

And then it was over.

The relative calm returned, a miasma of sediment and particulate glowing in the flashlights. All Jules heard was the group's collective breathing and a faint intermittent beep.

"What is it?" Bridget asked excitedly.

"It's gotta wait," Jules said. "Charlie's air's dipped under ten percent."

Charlie checked the readout on her dive computer and confirmed. "Eight percent. Guess I'm using more than you fellas."

"Your injury makes you breathe more. The exertion of opening the door tipped it over. I'm twelve percent. Anyone else low?"

"Twenty-two," Harpal said.

Dan was twenty and Luther sixteen.

"Time to refuel," Toby said.

"Last trip," Harpal said. "Only had enough for a couple of dives each."

Jules now sensed the finger hold he'd maintained throughout —it was easier to grip. He twisted and set his visor to infrared and saw what he'd hoped. "It's open."

Instead of waiting, discussing, chattering away about odds and theorizing about who built it, Jules braced against the hard surface and pushed the door.

It swung open on an unseen mechanism, possibly a counterweight or pulley system. Gasps came through his helmet, but Jules gazed inside. Faint green glows entered his peripheral vision, the others improving their own sight to peer through the murk.

It was a spherical cavity, big enough to hold two family saloon cars, now full of water. Facing them, another stone door bore a carving like an infinity sign on its end.

Jules had seen it before, representing the two bangles that opened the tomb in India. Except this was a carving, not a hole.

"My god," Charlie said. "It *is* a bloody airlock, after all."

"We've found it, Bridget." Jules couldn't help speaking quickly, unable to fight the energy fluttering around his stomach. "We've found what they pointed us toward. You gotta get down here. Harps, please say you got enough tanks for Bridge, man."

"If someone else waits topside, sure," Harpal said, a bubbly lightness to his tone. "Wouldn't want our southern princess to miss out on the treasure."

"Hear that, Bridge?" Jules said. With no reply, he spoke again. "Bridget? You there?"

"Go!" came a fragmented voice—not Toby, not Bridget. A man. Accented. "Go now!"

The captain of the *Ny Bakke To*.

Jules said, "Damn it, they're here."

All flicked their infrared off.

Dan pointed his flashlight upward. Nothing visible up top. "We can surprise them."

"They know we're here," Jules said. "Only decision now is surrender, or..." He pointed at the door inside the primitive airlock. "Or we carry on."

CHAPTER
FORTY-FOUR

Yanovna boarded the *Ny Bakke To* on a gangplank laid between the vessels by Igoravich, dripping in his wetsuit alongside the two Ukrainian commandos.

Although there was a chance someone below might spot the military men snorkeling over the surface, the North Sea was dark and cold, and if they were near the seabed, she would expect low visibility. Besides, by the time anyone noticed the incursion, it would be too late.

The cautious approach worked, and with eyes on the smugglers' trawler, the commandos were able to board the *Ny Bakke To* and sweep the deck and bridge with zero casualties to either side.

"I do not want anyone harmed," the general told the gathered crewmen as they knelt beside Toby Smith and Bridget Carson. "I am not a pirate. I come seeking items betrothed to Striovia long ago—"

"Striovia wasn't even a country back then," Toby said.

Igoravich motioned to strike him again. The constant punishment made Igoravich resemble some bargain basement villain, so Yanovna stopped him with a twitch of her wrist. Hitting Toby was a pointless gesture.

"There *were* no countries when these seals were buried," Yanovna said. "The very concept of borders was as alien to a creature back then as ripping down borders would be to us. But we do not live in those days. We live now. Which is why anything found within our country is ours. Therefore, any *legacy* of those items is ours, too."

"British territorial waters extend twelve miles off the coast." Toby kept his hands on his head but maintained a fixed, fiery stare on Yanovna. "You have no claim on something a mere five miles out. You can *see* the country you're stealing from."

Yanovna crouched to her haunches, level with the little man. She cast a glance at Bridget, the redhead with the freckles and the sparkly green eyes, with her elbows pinned in tight as if trying to make herself a smaller target. The girl seemed unable to speak. She visibly trembled as one of the mercenaries paced the line.

"And what was your plan, Toby?" Yanovna asked. "My old friend? My colleague? To trade what you find for your life? For a pardon from our President?"

Toby wavered minutely, but it was enough.

"So, you were willing to steal from your own country?" she said. "Does that not make you a traitor? A selfish one at that?"

"We'd have shared what we learned first," Bridget blurted.

Yanovna snapped her head back that way, amused at the girl's hunched shoulders and head hanging down, unwilling to make eye contact even when speaking to the general.

"You can have the books," the girl said. "Or whatever is down there. But we found it. We just want to see." Finally, she turned her face to Yanovna's, eyes damp. "Me. It's me. It was always me. I needed to know. I persuaded Toby to keep it from the others because I knew they wouldn't risk everything on a hunch. And the seals—the ones in the permafrost—I thought they'd hold clues, something to follow, but I never expected such detail." A tear escaped her and ran to the end of her nose before falling to the deck. Her eyes followed it and remained there. "Jules called it knowledge for the sake of knowledge. But it's more than that. It's… important."

Yanovna cupped Bridget's chin. Toby tensed, but Yanovna drew Bridget's face up without hurting her. "You are a child. I bet you have seen little of war, of the true brutality of the world. Never lived under the fear of being killed for saying the wrong thing, for being seen with the wrong person… so scared you are almost afraid to think your own thoughts. I will never live like that again."

She stood and found Prihya Sibal had joined them, standing by the gangplank that linked the two boats. Hands clasped before her, she briefly closed her eyes when Yanovna beckoned her over, then strode forward, her breaths deep and calm.

"This is your target," Yanovna said. "Toby Smith of the Lost Origins Recovery Institute. Cute, no?"

Again, Toby fired his defiant glare back. "Who are you?"

"Doesn't matter," Prihya said. "General, where are the others?"

Yanovna picked up a faint catch in the young woman's voice. Concern. Fear. This was supposed to be reconnaissance for her, not a military exercise.

"Below," Yanovna said. "Correct, Toby?"

Toby stared, a prisoner of war resigned to defeat, yet clinging to a gossamer thread of courage.

Yanovna faced Prihya. "We are in the correct place, Prihya. Your calculations were accurate. And I suspect they have found a way into this… mine. Or whatever use they had for this part of the land." She stood over Toby, Igoravich at her shoulder. "And they are making arrangements to steal what rightfully belongs to us as we speak, no?"

"There are no weapons." Again, the copper-haired girl summoned the strength to speak, her words tainted with fear.

"Then what would an ancient people with such power over the forces of nature hide from primitive humans? What would they hide in places only accessible by individuals with superior intelligence?"

"Art," Bridget said. "Knowledge. Historical accounts of themselves and the world. There are no weapons here."

"Let us investigate, Zimina," Toby said. "I swear we'll share the find. Whatever it is."

Yanovna saw for a moment the good man who Toby used to be —the man who had tried and failed to repatriate items taken by the British Empire from around the world. The man who'd made her laugh during video calls and whom, she suspected, had a hand in filtering information to her rebellion during the Cold War years.

But the past was unimportant in all ways except to inform the present.

And she would not return to that past. Ever.

Only now mattered.

"I cannot," Yanovna said. "I will take it by force if necessary. And if you surrender to my custody, I will leave your people alive if I can. But if they resist, I will not hesitate to kill them as surely as they killed my men in Canada."

"Blame *me* for that, Zimina."

"Oh, I do, Toby. I do. It is why I make you this offer. Take it, and most of you walk away."

"You don't trust me," Toby said. "But you trust hired mercenaries?"

Yanovna took in the Ukrainians, two of whom understood enough English to listen in, and smiled at the thought. The other two back on the trawler were watching out of earshot.

"They stand shoulder to shoulder with Striovia," Yanovna said. "Fully prepared for battle if needed. Money, yes, but pride too. If there is a chance my mission here helps deter Russia from taking over Striovia, if I can offer protection to other nations under threat, they will be there for me. And they bring other things, too."

"Like what?"

"This boat is a smuggling boat, Toby. And we are exploring an undersea tomb. What do you think they bring?"

"Oh, crap," Bridget said, almost amusingly. "You've got a submarine, haven't you?"

CHAPTER
FORTY-FIVE

With only minutes of air left, Jules made a decision for them. "I'm going in. Come with me, or swim up top and hope they don't blow your head off." He drifted through the doorway.

"You don't even know how that works," Luther said.

Charlie heaved herself forward, swimming into the spherical chamber, lopsided, her wound noticeably giving her trouble. "We'll work it out."

"I got a fair idea how they built it," Jules said. "But everyone who's comin', you gotta come now."

Dan and Harpal, seemingly needing no discussion, joined Charlie and Jules.

"Luther, this ain't a contest," Jules said. "Come with us or take your chances. Five seconds."

Luther debated with himself a beat longer, then swam into the space with the others.

"Lights out," Charlie said. "I just need the one. Jules, you with me on this?"

She flicked over to the green visor, which prompted the men to follow suit, and all but Jules's flashlight went off. The night vision required only low light to function, but it did require some.

Jules pulled the door closed over them, its top "hinge" a

molded pivot with a longer slab continuing into the round room that acted as a seesaw-style counterweight. It didn't seal tight, but their improved sight revealed the circular "handle" used to release the pressure and suction of the rubber-like resin had been depressed this side. It made sense the reverse would perform the opposite task.

Simple, really.

Jules pushed the door as snug to the frame as he could, then told Dan to give the stone dial a shove. Charlie didn't object, demonstrating Jules was likely correct about the injury hobbling her somewhat.

Dan pushed and twisted, and slowly but surely got movement out of it.

A minute passed, gradual progress every few seconds. Even through the suits, a sucking noise sounded until the mechanism was fully depressed.

"Now what?" Luther asked.

"Now, we go in." Jules floated over, his world eerie green, finding the off-center rendering partway between the number eight and the infinity sign.

"What are you doing?" Harpal said.

"Hoping we don't need some stone jewelry to get in here."

Luther pushed by and pressed the symbol. When nothing happened, he tried the same on each corner of the door. "It's stuck fast. And I'm betting we can't get out the way we came—"

"You just don't have the touch," Charlie said.

"I don't... look, I hate to be rude, but I need some answers. I've been lied to, misled, sidelined... promised a date over steaks..."

Charlie's expression was invisible, but her shoulders sagged momentarily.

"And the only reason I'm here," Luther said, "is because I threatened you with calling the authorities. But this is my expedition too. So, please, stop playing games and get us out of here."

"Huh," Jules said. "Claustrophobic, much?"

"Now. If you don't mind."

Jules removed one glove, the icy water almost burning his skin. The shock proved just how well-insulated Harpal's suits were.

He then touched his hand to the symbol on the inner door and the shape lit up green. The tiny flecks of metallic ore glowed as they had with the Aradia bangle and the scythe blade. He pressed on the surface, which gave a click, like a latch unlocking.

A hiss.

Then the current commenced, sucking water through a crack between door and rock, speeding up as Jules eased it open so the gap got bigger.

Within seconds, the chamber emptied, leaving the five of them standing with flashlights popping on as they preserved their night vision batteries.

Before them, beyond the door that opened the same way as the outer one, stretched a long, triangle-shaped passageway, far taller than the door. Between the chamber and the corridor, a six-foot-wide gap had drunk the water, with a narrow footbridge that appeared undamaged when the seawater flushed over it. The floor was faintly domed, with gutters built along the sides to channel away any excess, akin to a bowling alley. No *real* drainage, although the chasm before them more than likely acted as a soak-away.

"Think we can breathe?" Luther asked.

"Umm, yeah," Dan replied.

Jules hadn't heard him remove the helmet, but it now hung off the back of his wetsuit. Jules disconnected his own, inhaling a dry atmosphere, no odors he could detect, and only the recent water they introduced as moisture. "Either there's limited air, or they got another way to keep it down here. Let's hope it's vented."

"What's the difference?" Charlie asked.

"If it's air from back then, it could have bugs we ain't adapted to. Bacteria, viruses..."

"This isn't 100,000-year-old air." Luther took a couple of exaggeratedly loud breaths. "Must have another way to circulate it."

"So, we be careful." Hiding his limp, Dan took point over the footbridge and into the hallway, its pinnacle eight feet from the lowest part of the floor.

All followed and when Jules pushed the slab on the far side, acting as a seesaw counterweight like the outer door, the inner door to the airlock swung closed. No one tried to stop it. A hiss signaled the inner door was now tight again.

Jules figured it was better than someone stumbling into the outer door; as advanced as this was for its age, he doubted there were fail-safes.

They stashed their helmets on their backs via the clasps and angled their lights so the shadows didn't splay too far or jazz anyone's view. Then, leaving their flippers and air tanks near the entrance and using the plastic sock-like inners as shoes, they ventured deeper into the structure, following Dan's lead.

It was plain his foot still troubled him, but he made a minimal fuss, keeping his limp only slight. Still, a bum ankle was the least of their problems.

Hundreds of feet beneath the surface...

Millions of gallons of water held at bay by two stone slabs...

In tunnels burrowed or shored up by ancient hands...

Leading... somewhere...

Jules's heart pounded as if he'd run a marathon. This wasn't like India. At least back there, he'd had a guide who knew more than him, a person who needed Jules to complete his own plan, so offered a layer of protection absent there. This place, this *mine*, he supposed, since it was shaped like the previous discovery, was as safe as the millennia of wear and tear would allow.

He said nothing of his fears, though. The others' silence spoke that they were scared too.

The walls were rough but close to smooth. Untreated. No metal plates or panels, no carvings, no murals. No encroaching of nature. Just a passage undeniably carved using precision tools.

A dark shape gaped to the right.

Jules shone his light that way. Another corridor, similar to this one. "Wanna check it out?"

"No," Dan said. "I want to find somewhere we can bed down and ambush whoever comes after us."

"You're assuming they'll follow," Charlie said.

"They followed us all the way to Canada," Harpal said. "Think this'll stop them?"

Jules pictured the outer entrance. "Might be covered over."

"We left the comms relay dangling," Dan said. "Unless Toby or the skipper managed to move the boat, they know roughly where we are. Toby'll cave to save Bridget, so they'll find us. Only a matter of time. Jules, gimme something."

Dan was a better strategist than any of them, and Jules had little to add.

"I'd get the lay of the land first," he said. "If there's something we can use as a weapon, great."

"And this corridor? What is it? Where's it going to lead?"

"No idea."

They walked farther, ignoring the off-shooting path, scanning the walls for words, paintings, carvings... anything that might give them a clue where they were, or where they were headed.

"It's a spiral again," Jules said.

Harpal was nearest to him. "Spiral? What's the big deal about spirals?"

"Spiral forms appear everywhere in nature. And in the geometry of old scientists and clever folk like that. Math, physics. They call it the Fibonacci numbers, or the Golden Spiral. Same proportions in pine cones, nautilus shells, sunflowers. Dunno if it's relevant here. I can't map it exactly—even I ain't that good—but the feeling I get, and in the other mine, is this is a spiral."

"DNA helix, maybe?" Charlie said, excited.

"Nice try, but no, that's different. These folks, they're clever. They're engineers. Not biologists." Jules paused by another offshoot and peered in, his light spearing the darkness.

This time, he stepped inside. After a few feet, it inclined at a steady thirty-five degrees.

"Hey," Dan called.

Jules figured they should be used to him by now and didn't respond—as rude as that might seem. *Rude* might've been a good way to go, though, considering how friendly Dan had gotten the past couple of days.

Since exemplifying something Dan valued—that damn creed of his—he appeared to be trying to befriend Jules. Asking his opinion, trusting his instinct, paying him compliments.

Not that Jules disliked the man; he'd just prefer to work out whether he was sticking around first. No point in making friends if he planned to cut ties after this. And he planned to do just that.

He had projects. A bona fide *job* to apply for. Coffee and pastries to handle.

The corridor hit a dead end; just a rocky point, tied off. It was shaped like a bench, hewn from the earth as the passages had been.

He headed back, catching expectant looks in his torchlight. "Nothing to write home about. Dead end."

They pushed on, the spiral construction getting more obvious as it descended, the left-turning progress tighter as they grew warmer, the atmosphere heavier. Every hundred feet or so, they discovered new branches off this central walkway, six of them in total, each identical. It was an incline, ending in a bench seat, and not much else.

"Theory?" Dan asked Jules.

"Pointless," Jules said.

"The tunnels?"

"Theories at this stage. I got nothing you can use."

"I could use some brain power," Charlie said.

Jules had been thirsty and tired for the past twenty minutes, and they'd last taken on water just before Charlie joined them in the sea. Harpal, Charlie, and Luther looked especially tired. Dan appeared to be faring better, but that could be his superior fitness or his machismo. All pushed on, but Jules slowed the pace.

"I'm guessing here," Jules said. "At first, I thought they might've been exploring other places for the airlock thing, but there's too many. Closest I seen to this before is when folks had ceremonial stuff going on. Special places to store statues, relics, crap they thought was magic. The little tables or benches at the end could've been where they put stuff that was important to them. A holy book, one of those seals, the general's weapon, whatever. But like I said, just guessing."

The corridor leveled out, and Jules held his arms out to halt them all.

"What?" Luther said, his voice a touch croaky. "What is it?"

Jules swept his flashlight back and forth across the ground. "So far as I can tell, the walkway we just came down was pretty much the same as the Fibonacci Ratio. If we get time to bring some equipment down here, I'll confirm it one way or another." He shone his beam at the roof where he found the triangular point missing, instead starting to smooth out, reaching higher, like the beginning of a more regular dome. "But it's stopped."

"What has?" Harpal asked.

"The turns. It ain't as tight as a nautilus shell, but it's come to an end. We dropped maybe a hundred feet, so we're close to the sea floor outside the mound. I think we're where we need to be. Oh yeah, we're where we need to be." He stood still, motioning his light from side to side.

A hole in the floor identical to the one at the airlock stood before them, a trench descending deeper than Jules could see. It spanned six and a half feet and stretched wall to wall, interrupted only by a footbridge three feet wide. Jules tested the finger of stone, finding it as firm as the floor on which he stood.

He chanced his whole weight.

An intake of breath came from those behind him.

"It's solid," Jules said. "Part of the ground."

He crossed it, keeping a pool of light between his feet and the floor in front of him. Once he reached the other side, he again redistributed the beam to take in his surroundings. But it wasn't powerful enough.

"Hey, everyone get over here." Jules swept the flashlight overhead, its reach touching a roof which he calculated to around twenty-two feet—about the size of a two-story house. Domed, though, so it likely went higher.

The others made it in across and shone their lights in different directions, finding a series of walls ahead, facing them end-on. Ten feet high, only three inches wide—more like screens, really—ending long before the ceiling. They formed channels like miniature streets, four entry points, and each as smooth as black marble.

"What is that?" Charlie said. "A... library or something? Like we saw before?"

Dan scanned the scene. "I don't see any shelves."

"How much night vision have we got left?" Luther asked, checking his own battery. "Probably five minutes here."

Jules flicked on his own dive computer, which linked to all the gadgets that Harpal had armed them with. He might get three minutes. Charlie had five, and Dan and Harpal were closer to Luther with seven and eight minutes, respectively.

"Gimme a boost." Jules patted Dan on the chest and pointed at the end of the closest wall, then backed up.

Dan complied and threaded his fingers together like a cradle. Jules jogged forward, placed one foot in Dan's hands, and the big man lifted him up the ten-foot monolith, where he pulled himself to the top.

Wobbling only for a second as he rose to his full height, Jules balanced on the three-inch-wide perch like a tightrope walker.

Everyone shone their flashlights at him, which was annoying. He waved them off. When he could stand without being blinded, he pulled his helmet back over his face and switched the visor to night vision.

The whole cavern opened to him. The ends of the walls did

indeed reach far deeper inside, where they formed a jumble of wide passages, angular conduits that turned back on themselves before rerouting forward again. Every ten yards, a roughly hewn pillar resembling a pale tree trunk connected the floor to the roof.

"Damn." Jules crouched without dropping back down. "It's a maze."

General Yanovna had hoped the group would return with their bounty so she could liberate them of it and make her way home with the prisoner who'd escaped her, and the future of her country secured. They'd been too long, though, meaning they'd either drowned or found an access point to a structure built to keep out the floodwater described by Prihya.

Once the decision was taken and calls made to enact the solution, it took Yanovna and the three Ukrainian mercenaries a full fifteen minutes to pour themselves into the wetsuits provided by the smugglers, and another fifteen minutes for one of the former special forces soldiers to run through the apparatus. They shouldn't need it for more than a few minutes, but her heart thumped that bit harder as she learned.

There were no PADI courses there, and although Yanovna was a strong swimmer in a pool, Striovia was landlocked with only a handful of beautiful lakes, so scuba diving was not a common hobby. It was downright dangerous, in fact, and not something for amateurs, certainly not after one classroom-based lesson. But she could leave nothing to chance; she needed to be there in person.

Yanovna demanded Toby and Bridget accompany her on the next stage, meaning they had to don their own gear while the general received her crash course.

Once all were ready, they departed the *Ny Bakke To* for the trawler, Toby and Bridget reluctant under the guns. When a helicopter formed a dot in the distance, near the sliver of color that denoted the mainland, Yanovna was ready.

"You have your orders," she told Igoravich, one eye briefly

drifting to Prihya. "Keep our expert safe and be ready for phase two."

"Of course, General." Igoravich stood to attention and saluted.

Yanovna returned the salute and stood easy as a Ukrainian piloted the submersible—a converted tourist vessel intended for sightseeing but used now for shipping migrants and other human cargo from boat to shore. Docked in the space where the netting and fishing mechanisms would normally be staged, the mini sub was black, the size of a school bus, containing equipment Yanovna had questioned when she first saw it but was now glad of. The top hatch was open, ready for them.

"You do not have to do this," Toby said. "I promise we will share our finds. You deserve to access it."

"I am sorry, Toby," Yanovna replied. "Truly. But it has to be this way."

CHAPTER
FORTY-SIX

Within a minute of stern focus, Jules had memorized the maze's layout before testing something.

It was risky up there, operating on gut instinct alone. But he needed to know. The others needed him to find out.

He stepped forward. His full weight on the next section of wall. And this confirmed why it would be impractical for all of them to climb up and traverse the field this way.

A concealed pressure-point in the wall activated and a section of floor in the correct trail fell away. Three feet of seemingly solid rock crumbled.

Dan was the first to notice. "What the hell was *that*?"

His night vision tech now dead, Jules retreated and jumped down. "Intelligence. It's a puzzle."

"What, they're testing us?" Luther said.

"Seems a bit… petty," Charlie said.

Jules shone his flashlight at the new gap. "During their existence, the Witnesses were presumably the smartest race out there. Head and shoulders over the next cleverest. They recognized proto humans as growing. Improving. Those surviving the massive climate changes *had* to be. This is their way of passing on their knowledge. When a species is smart enough."

"Like rats," Harpal said.

"The screen walls are connected to something that obliterates the structure of the ground. Problem is, it's been there for so long, maybe the ground ain't as stable as it was."

"Could we go up top?" Dan suggested. "Just let the traps fall?"

"Dunno how much it'll affect the walls we'd be standing on."

"Massive domino game," Harpal said. "With a long fall at the end."

"So, lead the way," Charlie said. "You're our bloodhound now."

Yanovna fidgeted all the way down, the pressure in her ears unexpectedly painful as they descended in the bare-bones vehicle. She saw Toby and Bridget equalize by holding their noses and mouths and blowing. This hurt more but cleared the bunged-up feeling.

While the physical effects of the dive proved unpleasant, she was happy when the submersible made easy work of following LORI's comms cable, and the LiDar unit Prihya insisted they steal from the Institute's HQ made locating the door simple. With the camera feeding images back to the surface, Prihya worked out that this was exactly what they were looking for, that the circular carving must be the key. But when she came up empty on the practicalities, it took Toby's reluctant cooperation to reveal what he'd heard from his team.

He successfully stalled them for a good ten minutes.

Two of the three Ukrainians exited the bus-sized sub's airlock to open the door, which took much trial and error, but they eventually gained access. Toby explained all he'd heard so far, and when the symbol he recognized from their expedition earlier this year appeared on the inner door, Yanovna had to accept that she was the only one who'd be able to open it.

The prep for her dive, and to take Toby and Bridget with her, took even longer than she'd expected, but they exited one at a time, one man returning for an item in a watertight box which Yanovna suggested might be helpful.

They then followed the path that Yanovna assumed the other four had taken: sealing the outer barrier, her touch activating the minerals or elements woven throughout the inner door, the draining of the water, and the traversing of the small bridge into the triangular corridor.

She could tell the Ukrainians, all kitted out for full low light vision, were stunned but trying to remain neutral.

All she'd warned them of was that it was an archaeological site with items of potentially world-changing nature—something that would help see off any aggressive neighbor.

They remained mute as they unpacked the quadcopter drone and set up their night vision goggles, issuing another to Yanovna.

As the door closed behind them on some sort of counterweight slab, the drone took off, hovering almost silently midway between the floor and the top of the roof, then shooting off into the dark with a soft purr. Its own night vision camera transmitted back to the second mercenary's phone.

"We will map the layout first, General," the man controlling the drone said. "Then we know what waits for us."

It flew for what seemed like an age, before its reactions got sluggish at the edge of its range, revealing the scale of the place.

"Bring the rest of the equipment," Yanovna said. "I cannot risk waiting any longer."

Jules gathered the others by the gap formed when he'd tried to cheat the maze; it was about three feet wide and easy to hop across. But if he'd taken two steps, that would have been six feet, then nine, then twelve. Who knew at what point the wall on which he'd be standing would tip over with nothing to support it?

And who knew how stable the opposite side was?

Tens of thousands of years, possibly more.

That it took so long to discover this place bothered Jules deeply. But that was a question for another time. Right now, he was considering sending Luther across first, the person he had the least affinity with and would feel the least guilt about if he died.

That was his old way of thinking, though. He needed to lead the way.

The other thing he'd shelve to consider later was at what point he became a leader.

He took a running leap at the gap, landing a good couple of feet farther than strictly necessary. When nothing fell away, he tested every step of the way back to the hole.

Solid.

"Okay, get over here," he said.

Mr. Leadership, giving orders.

It wasn't a massive surprise when they obeyed. First Charlie, who grunted as she landed.

Jules appraised her a second, but she waved him off with a "Don't worry. I'm fine."

Luther came next, landing hard. One of his feet cracked the ground and sent fine gravel tumbling into the dark below. Jules yanked him away from the edge, flinging him toward Charlie, who steadied the guy, reassuring him with a touch that he was safe.

As feared, it wasn't the once-firm platform of its original design.

Jules kneeled and peered over, light extended in there. A hollow void with flickers and tiny flashes was coming back at him; a reflection from a layer of water lying at an indeterminate depth, its distance and perspective making it impossible to guess how far a person would fall—at least a hundred feet.

Perhaps even all the way to the lower seabed.

"Okay, big jumps, guys." Jules backed up and held a hand ready to receive the next person across.

Dan made a good leap considering his bad ankle, with Jules

ready to grab him if the ground gave way. Other than a shudder that dislodged a trickle of collapsed stone, all was well.

Then Harpal gave himself several paces to make his jump. It was the push-off that crumbled under his standing foot.

He cried out, his momentum cut off, and he dropped.

Jules dove for the floor, reaching, his torso over the edge.

He swung his arm down hard.

His palm slapped against Harpal's forearm. Harpal gripped Jules's. Both slipped, halting at the wrist.

With eyes flicking side to side and quick breaths, Harpal's head checked everywhere around them. "I'm here. I'm alive." He heaved up his other hand to double his hold.

"Yeah," Jules said. "I got you."

The ledge on which Jules lay cracked, then disintegrated beneath him. He seemed to float for a tenth of a second, then his stomach flew up into his throat. His brain spun, and he dropped toward oblivion.

Except, he halted with a jolt; something had curled around his legs.

Dan.

Bear-hugging Jules around the legs, he strained to hold the pair below him. "Come… *on!*"

Jules's cold assessment came quickly: the next segment designed to fall through as a failsafe against maze cheats had crumbled under the added pressure, leaving them suspended in a chasm so vast that, even with his lights swinging back and forth, he couldn't see the end.

Both Luther and Charlie reached Dan, helping him heave at Jules and Harpal. They ascended only inches.

While Harpal swore over and over and over, Jules checked his surroundings, specifically the underside of the maze; it appeared to be one large slab a foot thick, possibly a natural formation adapted by hands powered by an imagination that made him jealous. Mechanics beneath molded as dark rods linked the marble screen walls to the structure down there, triggers to destroy the stone holding the walls in place. On top of that, the correct path to follow was shored up by plinths stretching across to the pillars which Jules had originally assumed held up the roof. But it appeared they were designed to keep the floor hanging from the ceiling, leaving any route with no plinth and no pillar brittle, a death sentence for the dim-witted.

They rose a long way with the next pull, Jules now lying with his hips on the ground. Another huge effort and Jules felt a further crack in the floor.

"Faster," Jules said.

They complied, pulling harder, and as Jules made it fully to solid-*ish* ground, he rolled, summoned every ounce of strength, and pulled Harpal over him for Dan to receive and pull back.

The floor collapsed no more.

A six-foot gap remained, with this side's section delicate, a section they scrambled away from.

"Well, that was a lot harder than I expected," Jules said. "Let's go."

"Go?" Luther said. "With more... *tests* like this?"

Jules was finding the man's whining grating now, making his hands jittery as he pushed on without waiting. "We haven't passed this one yet."

Once they got moving, everyone but Dan asked at least once if Jules was sure he knew where he was going. When Luther—the final one to ask—got his question in, Jules kept going forward but said, "I sketched not one but two complex maps from memory. You think I can't pick my way through a maze?"

"One wrong turn," Luther said, "and we're toast."

"I know. Except, I'm in the lead, and I ain't making any wrong turns, so quit yapping."

They went on for another couple of minutes in silence. Jules found Dan walking beside him at one point and whispered to him to keep an eye on Charlie, to which Dan agreed.

It was partly to keep Dan's new camaraderie to a minimum, but mostly, Jules noted Charlie continuing to wince. He didn't waste his breath, knowing she'd deny anything was wrong, but that didn't mean someone couldn't be there if she got worse.

"It's… incredible," Charlie said.

They'd said that a lot already, but the longer they spent amid the polished black puzzle, the clearer it became that this was a truly remarkable feat.

"Wish Bridget could see it," Jules said.

"And Toby," Charlie replied. "His life's work is here. Justified…"

"And me," Luther said. "I mean, I can see it, but… it's just thrown everything I know out. Every paper I've written… useless."

Like Dan, Harpal was never an expert in archaeological matters, but he'd obviously picked up enough to understand the implications. "It must have taken centuries."

"Why?" Dan asked. "If they were super advanced?"

"It took semi-modern man hundreds of years to construct the cathedrals we see today."

"La Sagrada Familiar in Barcelona," Jules said. "Still being built."

"If it's even older than what we've found to date," Dan said, "do we have to consider a *much* more advanced race? Like…?"

"Like what, Dan?" Charlie asked in an amused tone.

"Don't make me say it."

"Go on, Dan." Harpal poked Dan in the shoulder. "Say it."

Dan made a big deal of the sigh that followed. "Fine. Aliens."

Charlie giggled. Luther snorted derisively.

Jules shook his head. "Nah, we ain't had aliens visiting. Check out the *Fermi* paradox. That'll set you right."

"What's that?" Dan asked.

"Do you really want me to start lecturing you all about extinction events? Dark forest theory? Dyson Spheres? Because I can if you want."

"Are we nearly done here?" Luther asked. "How far now?"

"Two corners."

They wandered left in silence, then right, emerging at an expanse wider than when they'd started. The tunnel ahead gaped like an aircraft hangar, gradually narrowing to the size of a regular mine shaft.

"What are we betting this goes all the way to the mainland?" Charlie asked.

"It does," came a man's plummy aristocratic voice from the dark.

A light turned on in the passage. Then a second, and then four more. Portable arc lights flickered and crackled to life, flooding the cavern with radiance as bright as day.

When the spots in Jules's eyes dissipated, Colin Waterston was advancing slowly toward them, backed up by four men and two women in Navy uniforms. And, despite being a small cadre of military personnel surprising them from a darkened alcove, each one of them looked utterly ridiculous.

Dan actually burst out laughing.

Harpal sniggered.

While Charlie and Luther stepped back, hands half-raised, Jules kept his amusement to himself. "Nice wheels."

The seven people intercepting them had reached this point on *Segways*—those two-wheeled vehicles ridden standing up.

"They may look a little uncouth," Colin said. "But they are efficient and highly effective." He signaled the naval troops to dismount. "Arrest them all."

CHAPTER
FORTY-SEVEN

The naval team aimed Heckler & Koch MP5A3 submachine guns —Royal Marine weapons. Although these were not Marines, they would've had them in the armory. Still a touch sluggish thanks to his recent misadventures, Dan pegged them as either frigate or destroyer personnel in their blues, commandeered on the fly as Colin struggled to contain something that might cause a headache for the British Royal Family.

Or rather, *the government*, which was Colin's true assignment, according to Toby.

Only the red-haired guy wearing the lieutenant commander insignia appeared conflicted, though. No bravado, just doing what he had to do.

The others spread wide in a C-formation and wielded their guns like pros, ready to open fire if any of the group with their arms in the air so much as blinked.

"Weapons on the floor," the lieutenant commander ordered.

"We ain't armed," Jules said.

"Search them," Colin said. "And it might not *look* like a weapon." He pointed at Jules. "Especially that one."

The man who stepped forward to execute the search paused. "Sir, you know they're all in wetsuits."

More sniggering from Harpal and Charlie.

Colin exhaled with an impatient huff, an open hand toward the group. "They have *belts*, don't they?"

Dan felt sorry for this team. Under the command of a man who wasn't their CO, who was definitely making stuff up, and who made the sort of flamboyant hand gestures when issuing orders that Dan associated with divas whose showbiz lives elevated them above mere mortals.

As the seaman checked the team's belts, removing the trowels and picks, and confiscating the helmets stashed on their backs, Jules stared at the hawk-nosed man with an expression Dan recognized. He recognized it because he and the rest of LORI had been on the receiving end more than once.

This squint, this faint smile from Jules, normally meant his mind was anywhere but complying with the situation at hand. A sideways glance at Dan meant he would do something.

Perhaps Dan should have understood Jules's intent by instinct. Another day, without the headache caused by the pressure exacerbating his head injury, he would have twigged to it. For now, Dan just hoped it wouldn't involve too much running.

"You seen what's in here?" Jules asked.

"We explored this facility fully over a decade ago," Colin said. "Then, thanks to your Indian misadventure, we swept it again more recently. There is nothing more to find."

"So, you managed to decipher the writing on the marble wall round that first corner?"

It was Colin's turn to stare back at Jules. "There is no writing."

"If you got the touch, there's writing." Jules waggled his fingers.

There had been no symbols or letters, but Dan saw what Jules was doing—planting doubt, hopefully splitting the team. The problem was that although Dan would happily take out a hired merc or private contractor in the employ of the bad guy, or a soldier engaged in an illegal black op on foreign soil, Jules, Dan, and Luther were technically foreign nationals accessing Great Britain without visas. These were Royal Navy personnel, armed forces, defending their country. He couldn't kill or even seriously injure one of them.

Okay, maybe he'd knock Colin out, given the chance. If necessary.

Or for fun.

They had to play this carefully.

Colin didn't reply to Jules straight away. No snarky quip, no condescending dismissal. Dan had no idea how much Jules shared with the man when he'd sold LORI out to him—before Jules accepted they were on his side. Colin was as clued in as Toby, though, so if he didn't know artifacts with such properties as the bangles and seals existed, Dan would be astonished.

"Show me," Colin said.

The curator dismounted his Segway and stepped through the middle of the six military personnel, tapping the lieutenant commander on the shoulder as he passed. The officer partially lowered his H&K but kept it ready, accompanying Colin on his flank. Colin gestured for Jules to step over the footbridge, meaning Dan had to shift out of the way, nearer the armed sailors —the closest being a kid in his early twenties, not much older than Jules.

The kid eyed Dan.

Harpal had apparently picked up on something going on too, as he'd widened the gap between himself and Charlie, while Luther held still, his body half-shielding Charlie's in a sweet gesture of faux masculinity. Charlie would appreciate it, though, Dan was sure.

Heh-heh-heh.

Jules walked across the bridge, arms free and easy in that laconic gait of his, and toward one of the five incorrect paths, one of which gaped as if someone had already ventured upon it.

"Is this a trick?" Colin asked.

Jules stood motionless with his toes on the boundary between the safe zone and the section Dan expected would crumble under the weight of a man.

"I asked a question," Colin said. "Is this a trick?"

The red-haired lieutenant commander sidestepped, weapon still at half-mast.

Colin exhaled impatiently through his nose and crossed to Jules, stepping in front of the gun.

Jules grabbed Colin and shoved him into the maze.

The officer snapped the H&K into action.

"No." Colin gasped, eyes wide, frozen like a cartoon character in midair.

The ground beneath his feet spiderwebbed then fell away.

Colin dropped.

Enough to distract the gunners' attention.

The lieutenant commander reached instinctively and snagged Colin with one hand, but the weight of the man dragged him down. Jules grabbed the seaman's gun arm and held Colin by his suit's shoulder.

No one was falling to their death today.

"Stand down!" called one of the women, gliding forward in a shooting stance.

"Yes," Jules said to Colin. "It was a trick. *Dan.*"

Dan had already inched closer, his man focused on the situation with Jules. About to snatch the weapon and attack its owner, Dan heard a fluttering noise—alien enough to reconsider the element of surprise.

"Dan?" Jules's tone became urgent. "I can't hold this guy off-balance forever."

The youngster closest to Dan twigged something was up, and took two steps back, his barrel trained specifically on the former Ranger.

Dan pointed above the maze walls. "What the hell is that?"

"Uh-uh, sir," Dan's personal guard said, shaking his head. "Won't be falling for that."

"Is that one of ours, Charlie?"

Charlie followed Dan's finger to the quadcopter flying quietly over the narrow black walls. "No, we didn't bring a drone on this one."

"It's mine," came General Yanovna's voice from the path Jules led them through.

From that same point, two armed men emerged in crouching positions. They used the walls as cover, pinned tight, leaving them better positioned than the naval personnel.

Dan ID'd them as mercs in a second.

A third rushed out and covered Jules, the lieutenant commander and the prone Colin, who was still waggling his feet over a potentially fatal fall.

"Three seconds, Dan," Jules said. "Three seconds sooner, and we'd have controlled this situation."

Jules was right. Dan's reaction was poor, amateurish. He blamed the headache, but could have been thinking too much, worried about hurting one of the Navy people, or worse, engineering a fatal mistake.

"Come." The command from the third gunman was simple, non-negotiable.

Jules released the officer, and the pair pulled Colin up, leaving him on his knees, virtually hyperventilating as he gathered himself.

The British were crouched lower now, stocks at their shoulders, ready to fire. Tenser than before, they trained their sights on the newcomers.

The third mercenary kept his hostages covered.

No one was giving in. No one speaking. All awaited orders.

"Well, this is *really* annoying," Jules said.

CHAPTER
FORTY-EIGHT

Yanovna stayed hidden, her sidearm on Toby and Bridget. "I have your people here, too."

She poked Toby with her free hand.

"Bridget and I are fine," he called.

"They are not 'my' people," came an Englishman's reply. "All the same, if you could surrender, that would be preferable. We outnumber you, outgun you, and our personnel are trained by one of the best armed forces in the world."

The fear in the man's voice was palpable. He was not a military commander, Yanovna was certain.

She signaled Toby and Bridget to move forward, slopping out into the open in their green and brown wetsuits between her two gunmen in black. Yanovna remained behind cover.

Toby seemed cowed, as he had back in Striovia when he'd agreed to help beat his team to the Reaper Seal's destination. But the girl, Bridget, demonstrated a lot more steel than she had earlier—as if witnessing the maze had pushed aside all sense of danger that the men accompanying them would not fire a bullet through her head with one order from the general.

They'd mapped the route thanks to the drone's elevated position, and with their goggles needed no additional light, just guiding Toby and Bridget with shoves and pokes. While they made their way there, Zefirova Victoriovna had tracked the diverted frigate by satellite to a deep bay near a town called Montrose and followed the launch from the frigate to the mainland, along with the personnel who disappeared into a coastal landmark not usually associated with naval maneuvers. It was clear they had another destination in mind.

Once in position from this side of the mission, Yanovna had watched the drone footage, amused as Toby's people attempted to bluff the Navy into letting them free. But once they'd spotted the drone's presence, she had to join the conversation.

Yanovna risked a peek beyond the wall she now used as cover. "You have the manpower. We have the position. And hostages."

"There's no need for this," Toby said. "We… we are not your enemy."

"No. My enemy is barracked a swift tank ride from my border. My enemy violates my territory weekly, probing for weak spots, monitoring our resolve. My enemy is at the gates, and the West does nothing to stop it except slap the wrists of rich Russians who already have enough wealth in their trouser pockets to make such actions worthless. I need what you are hiding."

"Once you go this route," Toby said, "there is no turning back."

"Toby is correct," the other Englishman said. "You are already on sovereign soil. We cannot allow you access to the repository."

"Repository." Bridget's head remained down, but a bright smile lit her face, again seemingly forgetting the peril she was in. "So, there *was* something here." She raised her head. "Was it books? Art?"

Yanovna admired the young woman's passion. But what she'd seen in the seals, in the projected image from the stone scythe, was not mere literature. "No one goes to these lengths to protect *books*. The maps were a test. The location of the entrance. The maze. Habib Masouli's scroll. All of it. Only the worthy can take what they hid here."

The Englishman's eyebrows arched. "You found the message from Masouli to the Pope?"

"He, and the seals from the ancient Witnesses, have bequeathed the prize to me."

"Sadly," the Englishman replied, regaining his composure, "the Alabama belle is correct. Your 'prize' is nothing but sculptures and friezes. The interest ends at the fascination."

Yanovna's free hand curled into a fist. "I do not believe you."

"Zimina, please," Toby said. "Just retreat. Take me with you. Colin will let you go. I will surrender to your custody and maintain our previous agreement. I'll plead guilty, help you unravel all the things you need to know about the seals."

"Too late."

Those words sent two of the Navy people scurrying, and one of her guys by the maze exit prepared to fire.

"Hold." Yanovna checked the situation.

What had actually happened was the British pair had acted to usher the civilians aside, allowing a clearer view of the standoff.

"There is another entry point," Yanovna said. "*Colin.* Toby used your name. Is that who is in charge here?"

"I am." The tremble in Colin's voice made him faintly higher pitched. He composed himself, returning to what a man should sound like. "And if you leave, yes, you can go unharmed."

Yanovna's face creased, her mouth turning down, and a buildup of pressure hit her behind the eyes. She spoke, *explaining,* loudly enough for all to hear. "I last faced a decision like this when the Soviets ruled. Weeks before we made our final move against them, we discovered one of my key deputies... he was feeding information to the enemy."

She noted Toby's eyes flicker to her, then down to the floor. Yes, he'd been one of those who helped them. She was positive about that.

"When this man's family was spirited away one night, it seems he was ordered to carry on as normal. To come to meetings, to help plan our next move. But I knew about him. Others close to me knew about him. And why he was turning on us."

She swallowed, the memory as fresh as if it was last week.

"If I let the man live, it would have weakened our cause. But executing him meant the Soviets would know they had lost their mole. They would have no more use for the man's family."

Toby's eyes were closed. "Zimina, please, these people have families, too."

"Would the Soviets kill my man's family or release them to grieve over the traitor's death?"

No one replied. A distant growl sounded.

"I never learned that family's fate," Yanovna said. "Never heard of them again and did not seek them out. But the decision to terminate the spy in our midst was not even a struggle. One family, or one country."

She looked out again. The sailors took it in turns to keep their eyes forward and to check behind, up the passage where the growl of engines echoed out of the darkness.

"One unit of decent, honorable naval troops," she said. "Or lose my country."

"General," Jules Sibeko said. "Don't. We can help you get what they've hidden. Colin, explain it. Tell her."

"Too late."

"Zimina, it isn't too late," Toby said. "Please. I will *help*. I will cooperate. I can get you more than you have. More than what's in Colin's hideaway."

"You don't even know what he's hiding," Yanovna said.

"I do!"

Toby's outburst drew a slow turn of the head from Bridget, her lips parted slightly, and a frown etched on her brow.

"You… know?" she said.

"*Habib Masouli*," Toby said, loud enough for Colin to hear. "I did some thinking on the way here. I mentioned the Lairds of Dun to my friends. That they sacked villages and towns to show King James IV that they would resist his takeover of their lands. But there was more at stake. It was why he acted so quickly to quash them there when other regions were left to burn. The King of Scotland couldn't let them get their hands on it. On what was discovered during that time."

"What, Toby?" Yanovna said. "What was discovered?"

Bridget's head gradually turned back to the front, not saying a word.

The engines ceased growing louder, held at a set point, rumbling in the dark. No one knew where to turn, where to aim, so settled with two at the rear, the others up front.

"It was a time of exploration," Toby said. "A new world had been plundered and Columbus returned to Portugal with several ships. Hundreds of people, with tales of discoveries no one was ready for. But Habib Masouli's associates knew all about those things, had passed them down through generations." Toby wet his lips. "I do not know exactly what is hidden, but it was important enough to protect this small hamlet called Lish. On the coast. Where a Middle Eastern man preached the word of God for decades before he died. Passing on the parish to its former cleric."

Yanovna understood. "People knew about these artifacts. Hundreds of years ago... and hid them... found this place. The entrance from the other side... it's there. They *hid* them... because they could not risk the power falling into unfriendly hands. Only *worthy* hands." She calmed, absolutely certain of her sad duty, of what had to happen. "I am sorry."

"Ain't happening," Jules said. "Colin, do something now."

Yanovna's lip twisted, then righted itself. "I never wanted to be a tyrant."

"Then don't be," Toby said.

Yanovna firmed her finger on the trigger guard, unclipping a two-way radio from her belt. She stepped out, unwilling to be a leader who cowered while her people risked everything.

Checking on the two mercenaries holding fast by the exit, she picked up on their adrenaline rush, their anticipation of the fight.

If she was honest with herself, it would always come down to this.

She keyed the radio. "Execute."

And the soldiers who'd left their bikes idling and snuck up in the dark tunnel opened fire.

CHAPTER
FORTY-NINE

Jules sprang forward, parried the soldier's gun, and continued that momentum to fling the mercenary aside, hammering his elbow into the man's head to change direction sharply.

The soldier who'd been guarding Jules, Colin, and the Royal Navy guy had visibly concentrated on the man in uniform, a more obvious threat, so Jules had made micro movements to ease himself toward the guard. He'd gotten within striking distance when the shooting began.

The Navy people returned fire, but they were out in the open, while Dan and the others had been moved aside, the wall allowing them some measure of cover. Three of the six sailors were cut down in seconds before their colleagues mounted a reply. Running sideways, rolling, having to defend from two directions.

Jules hefted the weapon and aimed at the pair flanking the maze exit.

Still can't kill.

Maybe Dan was right. Maybe what started as honor had become a phobia. Every synapse in Jules's brain fizzed and crackled, telling him to go for the head before they realized they were compromised.

"Shoot them!" Colin Waterston cried.

That drew their attention, leaving Jules with no choice but to pull the trigger.

The first knee popped like a bag of blood, the man screaming in pain. His pal jerked back, then yanked the wounded man with him.

The red-haired lieutenant commander was on his feet, but the deafening firefight continued, and he couldn't see which way to turn. "Give me my gun."

"One sec." Jules assessed his options. "I ain't done yet."

He fired the H&K into the second part of the maze where Colin had fallen. That section crumbled readily, and he shot up the next, too.

"What are you doing?" Colin said.

Jules tossed the weapon to the lieutenant commander. "Dominoes."

He rushed at the officer. Before the man could react, Jules climbed him like a ladder and pushed off to reach the top of that screen wall.

Forming an easy target should anyone spot him, he trotted forward, activating more pressure points. His actions destroyed parts of the walkway in the next dead-end channel, as well as the ones he shot up. It left little holding this part of the wall in place.

Shifting his bodyweight, the marble panel toppled toward Yanovna.

As his gut swam upward, Jules yelled, "Toby! Bridget! Run!"

Jules leaped sideways to the next panel, prompting another section to disintegrate. The first smashed into the one adjacent, cracking it off at the halfway point. That half tumbled into the next—where Jules and Bridget were held.

"Move!" Jules yelled.

Three figures sprinted out—Yanovna, Toby, and Bridget—followed by a third dragging his friend. The walls crashed down like—yes—dominoes. Assembled in sections like the floor, it was only the first few feet of marble-like stone that succumbed, but the dust and cracks filled the air.

More gunfire from below. The lieutenant commander killed both the wounded mercenary and his buddy, then turned his weapon on General Yanovna.

"No!" Jules was more concerned the man would hit Toby or Bridget than kill someone.

He pushed off from the broken wall and cleared the nine-foot gap, landed beside the sailor, and slapped the gun upward.

Colin reached for Jules, but Jules parried and secured him in a painful wrist lock, easing him to the floor.

Aside, the final two Navy people fell, blasts from Yanovna's sidearm hitting them in the head as she aimed from behind Toby and Bridget.

Dan and Harpal dove from cover, sliding on their bellies, trying to reach guns dropped by the dead British people.

Jules had expected Charlie to do the same, but she leaned on the wall, a hand to her lower stomach. She was in pain.

The open expanse gave no cover—not Dan, not Toby, not Bridget... and not General Yanovna. But she didn't need it.

She pointed her gun at Toby. "I am sorry it has to be this way. But I cannot surrender now."

The lieutenant commander aimed again, and Jules didn't try to stop him. He was already springing over the chasm between the maze and the exit tunnel.

But Yanovna noticed the gun and yanked Bridget in front of her as she strode along—a human shield—then returned to Toby.

It only took a second. Less than that. Jules rolled to the tools removed from their belts and came up with a rock hammer—a thick, dull item that acted as a pick rather than a weapon. Despite the absence of an edge, with the right technique, it was heavy enough to fly straight.

And that's exactly what happened, launched from Jules's fingers, and impacting Yanovna's pistol, flinging it aside with a single discharge that left Toby cringing but unharmed. Maybe a burst eardrum.

It all took a matter of seconds.

Then Dan had his hands on a submachine gun. Harpal too.

As bullets chewed the ground before them, they returned fire. Joined by the lieutenant commander holding fast by the unconscious mercenary and Colin, they reduced the gunfire from the cave ahead.

Yanovna screamed in anger and kicked Toby in the face, keeping hold of her human shield in Bridget.

Virtually carrying her hostage, Yanovna ran hard for the exit where her men picked their shots more carefully.

Dan sprayed the ground with lead, plainly going for her feet, but the gun clicked empty. As he rolled to the next body, Harpal took over, firing single rounds at the fleeing general.

Jules got into a crouch to take off after them too, but a cluster of bullets impacted nearby. He hit the floor and used a mercenary's corpse as cover, making himself as small as possible.

All he could do was watch as Yanovna disappeared into the dark with Bridget.

Except she didn't disappear entirely. She stopped just at the periphery of one of the arc lights, pulling something from her pocket.

A small metal box like a Zippo.

"Follow me," she shouted, "we cut you down. And I slit this one's throat."

"No!" Bridget screamed. "Don't do it! *Please!*"

Don't do what? Jules wondered.

"I really am sorry." Yanovna hit a button on the little box.

A muffled *bang* echoed from somewhere deep within the structure.

"She's blown the doors," Jules said.

And as the general retreated into the passage with her hostage, Jules yelled, "Follow me!" and ran in the opposite direction —*toward* the explosion.

CHAPTER
FIFTY

Running was frustratingly difficult. Charlie didn't think the wound had torn or bled externally, but there were other things to consider. The underlying muscle had been punctured and, during her convalescence, knitted itself together—but evidently not fully yet. She estimated her current state to be the equivalent of jogging with a soft tissue injury. Except that hers was in her abdomen.

Still, it was up to her to snap Toby back to the here and now and highlighted what Yanovna had done. "She's got Bridget. We can't go after them—it's a bottleneck in there. And she's damaged the outer wall."

"Then why are you running toward it?" Colin demanded.

Jules returned from the maze where he'd run to seconds earlier. "You guys coming? It's either stay here and die, follow the general and die, or scrape together about a five percent chance of living and come with me."

Toby stared with shell-shocked eyes. "Maths."

"Math. Now, I can get you through the maze, but if you wanna take your chances, go for it."

They set off, first climbing over the felled sections of wall. Charlie and Dan hobbled slightly, and Toby needed some urging.

Colin puffed up his chest and cheeks in protest, but Luther said, "I don't know who you are, but I'd follow them if I were you."

The lieutenant commander, who introduced himself as Garrett, set off before Colin, and the curator sniffed in distaste at the physical nature of scrambling over rubble. He brought up the rear, and it was up to Charlie to tell him to hurry.

"Hurry?" Colin said. "Toward the incoming water?"

"If she'd blown the hatch fully," Charlie said, "a huge torrent would be here already, filling that corridor. We still have a chance. But this structure? Unstable."

As if on cue, the floor gave off a crack, which spurred Colin on.

Once on the trail winding in a long line, Colin could not help himself. "This is unacceptable. You let that woman go. She is going to locate something that we need to conceal from—"

"Time to cut this off," Garrett said. "You're a civilian. This is now a military matter."

Colin bristled but proceeded with the confidence of a man in authority. "I think you'll find you're under orders to acquiesce to my command."

"The scope of our orders was to accompany you, make sure you stay alive, and to protect the British Isles from a serious criminal endeavor. It never said anything about foreign soldiers, never said anything about secret passages and mazes, and it sure as hell never said anything about getting my people killed."

"This is a war. And they bravely gave their lives for—"

"They were *my* people," Garrett said. "Four years I've known them. And they're dead. Because of your orders. Now, I'm classifying this as an aggressive foreign incursion. That makes it a military matter, and outside the orders passed down to my captain. Stay out of my way."

Garrett pushed past the gobsmacked Colin.

Charlie said, "I like him."

Dan limped along while Harpal kept urging Toby onward; having barely spoken a word, Charlie wanted to take him aside, but there wasn't time.

At the end of the path, the powerful lights by the exit—presumably set up years earlier to facilitate exploration—reached the limit of their illumination, casting shadows into a twilight zone of empty space.

They had to leap across the six-foot gap—simple for most of the men, who took a running jump, sticking to the edges where it was more stable. Even Colin proved shockingly spry for a stiff in a suit and $1,000 shoes.

But Charlie and Toby would struggle.

"Charlie..." Toby trailed off as if he didn't really have anything to say.

"Come on, we'll catch you," Jules said.

Ahead, a slurry of water dribbled from the corridor. Not a massive wave, but there was definitely damage out there.

They would need Charlie.

She patted Toby on the back. "Go on, you can do it."

"I can't, Charlie." He looked up at her with sad puppy dog eyes. "You go."

"Charlie," Jules said. "He'll make it."

"I'll take care of him," Harpal said. "If there's a chance you can fix it, go."

"Stay and we all die," Jules said.

Charlie needed no more than that. She pressed her palm on her stomach, stemming the pain of the damaged muscle enough to convince her brain everything was fine. Momentarily, anyway.

Then she launched and flung herself over a gap she would normally have mastered without a second thought. Arms forward, feet out.

She landed.

But the lance of pain up her side doubled her over. She staggered. Her foot found the void, and she dropped.

A strong arm intercepted her, its meaty hand around her wrist.

Dan.

"You never said you were having problems." Dan pulled her to safety. "We're gonna have words about that later."

"Sorry." Charlie didn't pause, just nodded at Dan's leg. "Help Harpal with Toby?"

"Will do."

Charlie, Jules, and Luther turned their flashlights on and dashed up the stream of water cascading along the corridor, leaving the others. Charlie had to hold her side, pressing on it to keep going, to keep from vomiting.

"Go on ahead," she said. "I'll catch up."

"No, we stick together." Jules sloshed over to sling an arm around her waist from the left.

"I don't need that action dude code of honor, Jules. Get up there. Take Luther and use him."

"And me." Garrett jogged up out of the dark, his only light a flashlight mounted on his H&K—absent Colin for now.

"Get her other side," Jules said.

Garrett handed the gun to Luther, and—as the guy in better shape—took the weight on Charlie's right. Between him and Jules, and the strain Charlie managed on her own, they double-timed it up the passageway. At first, the tight spiral was more obvious this time, then the curve grew looser. The water got deeper, swirling around the curves. Garrett and Jules sweated, and Charlie could hear Luther breathing heavily behind.

They kept going, though.

When they reached the top, the source of the leak, Charlie's whole body went cold.

Using hefty tools and parts of metal commandeered from some mechanical vehicle—either the boat above or some submersible—Yanovna's people had propped open the inner door to the airlock, wedging a crowbar and a massive spanner in the top part of the counterweight slab to prevent it closing. Less pressure than holding up the weight of the main door.

Seawater had filled the soak-away hole with the footbridge where the remnants usually drained into and spilled over the lip. It gushed in through the ten-inch gap at the bottom of the door but didn't flow around every part of the open frame. The tanks and flippers they'd left behind were gone; either washed away by the not-insignificant discharge from the airlock or tossed down the soak-away by Yanovna and her people.

"The outer door isn't completely blown," Charlie said. "She must have only used a small amount of explosive. There's still time."

"There." Luther went to the wedged crowbar.

"No!" Jules and Charlie said together.

"Leave it for now," Charlie said.

"Why?" Garrett asked. "We need to stop it flooding."

"Quick lesson, so listen fast." Charlie got as close as she could, jamming her torch into the partially open door. The flow around her feet was powerful, a waterfall trying to sweep her away. She got a decent view inside, shining the beam to examine the damage. "If we close this inner door, it'll stop the flooding. But that means we'll have to wait out the Striovians and let them get what they want. I assume that's not on the cards."

"Not if we can help it," Garrett said.

"If Toby and Bridget had been straight with us from the start, we wouldn't have this choice," Jules said.

"Not the time, Jules." Charlie kept herself from yelling. "If we close the inner door, we'll be as safe as the design allows, but we can't get out except through the other end."

"It also might not hold that long," Jules said. "Place ain't perfect."

"*But*—if we get that outer door closed first, we can remove the wedge on the inner one, and restore its functionality." She saw the problem. "This side, they wedged the counterweight. The outside door, they blew that section. Probably thought it'd blow the whole thing open. But the pressure from outside on the counterweight and the main door keeps the flow lighter." She visualized the mechanism, how it had to work. "I need a strong pair of arms."

"I'll help," Luther said.

"No, I will," Jules said.

Charlie pointed at the tools jamming the inner door, too jittery to slow down. "I need someone with timing to make this work."

Jules frowned. "Is that a black thing?"

"I said *timing*, not *rhythm*. And I don't want you to dance. I want you to wait for my signal, then close it up."

"What'll your signal be?"

"Me and Luther'll come rushing out of that water-filled hole."

"Can I help?" Garrett asked.

"Stick with Jules. I might need dragging out."

"Got it."

"I need more room," Charlie said.

"You mean *I* do." Luther touched his stomach.

Charlie smiled. "I don't like to be rude."

Jules prepared to remove the tools, bare-handed, so the mechanism reacted to his touch. He wrapped his fingers over the lip at the top end. Again, the symbol lit up and allowed Jules to manipulate the door's movement.

Widening the gap sped up the flow momentarily, but it was enough to get Charlie and Luther inside.

Pitch black except for the swords of torch beams, Charlie found the seesaw back and forth remarkable; a failsafe that played with the billions of tons of water above, the pressure of it simultaneously trying to open and close the device. Right now, open was winning.

"We need to close it properly," Charlie said. "Reactivate the seal."

With water pouring in more steadily, Charlie pushed against that section, and Luther joined her. It narrowed the entry flow but didn't halt it.

Luther strained. Turned. Pressed his back against the stone door. "I… can't…"

"It's too much." Charlie's mouth thickened, her tongue fat. Unable to speak properly for a moment. "We can't close it without…"

"What?" Luther said. "Without another person? Get that soldier in here—"

"No." Charlie placed one hand on Luther's arm. "Do me a favor?"

"Of course. Anything."

"Go out and get me that crowbar."

Luther nodded and got on his backside, sliding out under the additional inches that Jules gave them.

Charlie stood waist-deep, staring at the broken door, the counterweight keeping the whole thing from collapsing in. For now. For maybe the next five minutes.

She pictured her children, her husband, and forged it into her mind, vowing it would be her last thought, the final thing she saw. "Jules, close your door."

"What?" Jules replied. "No."

"I've got the crowbar," Luther called back.

"Don't need it," Charlie said. "You wait there. I've got this."

Nothing happened.

"Jules, close the damn door," she said.

"What's she doing?" Luther asked on the other side, his face appearing at the smaller end of the gap.

"She's equalizing the pressure," Jules said. "She can close the outer door if the airlock floods."

All Charlie had to do was wait for the roiling incoming water to stop, then push the seal back into place, and the seal would reattach itself. Between three and five minutes.

She'd be moving by touch and the minuscule amount of sight she'd have, thanks to the helmet on her suit.

She might survive. If the air lasted out.

"Charlie." Luther returned, easing himself in through the gap.

"What are you doing here? Get out."

Luther turned his head from her torchlight, but she didn't think it was due to the brightness. "Just… if I don't make it out…" Now he brought his eyes back to her. "You're a good, strong person, Charlie. I'm sorry for being a dick. Tell my kids that, okay? Tell them... Dad's sorry for being a dick."

Charlie shivered—cold, surprised, scared. "Luther, what—?"

"Sorry, ma'am." Garrett appeared from the same place, rushing through faster than Luther had. He unfolded himself with her knees in his arms, scooping her up.

"No." Charlie slapped at him—his chest, his shoulders, his face. "Don't you dare!"

"Orders, ma'am." Garrett ducked down, back under the door, bringing Charlie out.

Panic washed through her. No way should someone else do this. No way would she allow it.

It had to be her.

Squirming out of Garrett's grasp, she pawed at the door to be let back in, but Jules was already closing it.

"Sorry," Jules said. "He's got better lung capacity, less injury, more chance of survival."

Charlie beat her hands as its edges fell flush to the frame. She could do no more. The airlock was sealed tight.

CHAPTER
FIFTY-ONE

So, this is what it feels like to be noble, Luther thought.

He wasn't even scared, which was odd. He'd been scared most of his life, certainly since his wife discovered how much he preferred the company of other women. Not cheating, per se, but hanging out with them. Younger women made him feel good.

Before he'd quit exercising and started feeling sorry for himself, he was one of those professors on whom the girls often crushed, as well as some of the boys. And despite him never touching them, not once straying from his marriage vows or university policy, he could not deny they swelled his ego to the point of bursting.

It was wrong.

Encouraging that behavior... feigning oblivion as these young women hung on his every word and dismissing his wife's worries to her face as paranoia while secretly accepting she was right—and enjoying the thrill of tricking her too.

What a dick.

What an absolute dick.

Why it took being secreted in the back of beyond to reflect on that behavior, he couldn't say; buried in the work of identifying tribal movements, getting excited about a new burial site, theorizing over a joint and a beer with Tommy about the possibilities of what humanity had achieved a mere 8,000 years ago.

Then in waltzes this goddess called Charlie, with her flowing hair, leading him on—leading this dick of a man by the nose—to facilitate a discovery that dwarfed anything in his life to date.

It put things into perspective.

As the water level reached his chest, he pulled on his helmet, breathed what little he captured in his suit, and reasoned he might *not* die there.

Again, it didn't bother him.

A bigger picture had emerged, one in which he viewed himself front and center. He'd seen things the past few days that he'd never imagined, a secret history of a people no one considered might exist. Sure, there were the rumors, the idiots who thought certain advanced races learned their trade from aliens or from a prior civilization while the powers that be covered it up—idiots who might not be a million miles away in their theories.

When conspiracy theory becomes conspiracy fact.

Not quite a full-on cover-up, just lacking evidence... as long as that English guy couldn't keep covering up the find, out of fear.

Now they had the evidence, would it herald a scramble for more? Would it turn the archaeological communities on their heads?

Quite possibly.

The surface crept up, meeting Luther's chin.

He wouldn't be there to witness it, but he'd been a part of triggering it... unless Charlie and her people died down there. If they got shot or drowned, or suffocated, or starved to death…

Luther only had a pocket of air left in his helmet. He felt the pull in his chest—suffocating—and remembered now that the helmet expelled the air to cycle in the supply from the tanks, meaning the majority of the CO_2 would leave him.

He gulped in those last morsels. Big breaths filled his lungs to capacity. Then he exhaled, saturating the sacs within as much as he could before finally holding his breath and sensing through the stillness that the chamber was completely full.

He opened his eyes, thankful for the visor, but everything blurred. Only one murky ray of light—no more infrared. He knew roughly where he needed to be, so the brief rush of visual in his flashlight's beam brought him to the circle that should reseal the cavity. He closed his eyes, breathing now impossible.

From what he understood, the charge damaged the counter-weight, so the seal should be intact unless the heat warped it. In which case, they'd have to take their chances with the Striovians or hope the sea poured in slowly enough to allow them to wait out the raid on the mainland.

With the water now equal inside as out, he heaved the counterweight slab up with his shoulders until the door fully closed. Then he located the circle sticking out this way and pushed it upward.

The door's lip extended too far out. This partially opened a gap between slab and frame.

Damn.

He pulled it back using the circle, so the corners sat flush.

From Charlie's explanation earlier, this part of the mechanism functioned like a plunger or the lever on a suction cup, pushing out the air to make the rubber seal tight. It was so hard, though, grinding against the millennia. And his lungs protested already.

Turn it.

That had helped open it. He expected it'd helped close it too but had paid little attention.

He let out a bubble of air which exited his breathing tube, tricking his lungs into thinking they were about to inhale again. His nose stung with the change in pressure, a trickle invading the nasal passage.

The stone turned. He pushed again, twisting. The door held in place.

Needing to *breathe.*

Just one tiny breath for strength.

But that would kill him instantly. And that would mean everyone died. Or the Striovian general won.

Sweat dribbled down his face, stinging his eyes, forcing them closed. He summoned all his strength, all his focus, and pushed and twisted.

The hissing in his ears came to him like music, and he wondered if he was high on what little CO_2 remained. It wasn't literally music, but with every centimeter he depressed the stone, the better it sounded.

Hissssss.

Hissss.

Hiss.

Hs.

Then he was out of energy, his face—his whole body—drenched. The circle felt flush to the surface, and he could not go on.

As promised, he kicked off and pushed to the inner door. He pounded on it, but under the water, it was like working in slow motion. No way would anyone hear him. Not that he expected them to.

Jules had calculated the airlock chamber would take two minutes to fill, then two minutes for Luther to close the door and activate the seal. Luther asked for an extra minute to be certain. He promised them he'd held his breath for longer than that in the past, free-diving wrecks in the Caribbean, and would be fine.

But that was a lie.

He'd heard of free divers going six minutes, although he had no idea how long he'd been under now.

All he had to do was not breathe. If he passed out, they might revive him.

It was possible, he supposed.

Suddenly, he shot downward, the whoop of his stomach, the release of his body, the sensation that of a rollercoaster plummeting.

He rolled along, bright lights over his eyelids, hands pawing at him.

Voices.

"Are you okay?"

"Hey, you did it."

"That was crazy."

Luther's helmet flew off, and he coughed, almost surprised it was just the single cough. Must have done a decent job there.

He wiped his sweaty face, but his hand came away dry.

That's when he realized.

That's when he saw who the voices belonged to.

A hazy light, darkness closing in from the outer frame.

"You did it, Daddy," the girl said—twelve-year-old Rachel, not the sixteen-year-old who refused his calls.

"You saved them." That was Tony, aged eleven, just a year younger than his sister, but far more a child than she was, and another who believed Luther cheated on his mother, then abandoned them when the going got tough.

"I did it for you," Luther said.

"I understand," a woman's voice replied.

Luther's ex-wife morphed into shape before him, her arm around the two kids.

"I'm sorry," he said. "I hope you have an amazing life."

As the darkness closed in, his family smiled back at him, proud at last.

CHAPTER
FIFTY-TWO

After the five minutes they agreed, Jules opened the inner door enough to drain it. As before, water cascaded out, flowing down the corridor over the saturated soak-away hole. He felt Luther thump up against the barrier, and Charlie must have heard it because she immediately shouted to get him out.

She'd protested for the first minute after Jules sealed Luther in. Then she was silent, boiling in anger at him, at Garrett, at Luther himself.

As soon as the outpouring eased enough to prevent washing them all away, Garrett rushed to the door, and Jules pulled it open farther. The Navy man dragged Luther out, heaving him over the footbridge and to the side where it was flat, flipped him on his back, and removed his helmet. Charlie positioned herself to commence chest compressions while Garrett checked Luther's airways.

CPR commenced. Garrett blew into the man's mouth. Charlie locked her elbows and pumped. She squeaked in pain.

"Let me." Jules joined them.

"No." Charlie leaned her full weight into every compression, wincing each time. "It has to be me."

Jules had seen a few dead bodies, and he'd already added Luther's to that list.

"I'm stronger," Jules said.

When Charlie completed her round of compressions, Garrett nipped Luther's nose and blew into his mouth again. Jules took over the chest.

Charlie wiped tears from her cheeks. "Why didn't you let me?"

Jules kept the rhythm. "You won't like it."

"What won't I like, Jules? Was it math again?"

"Math. But yes, basically."

Charlie shook her head. Garrett exhaled hard into Luther.

Jules recommenced pumping. "I didn't know if he lied about his lungs and the free diving, but I gave it a seventy-five percent chance of him being dishonest."

"But you still let him go."

"With good reason."

Charlie beat her fist once on Luther's chest as Jules paused for another breath from Garrett.

"What reason?" she asked. "Because I have *kids*? A *husband*? He could've had them back, too."

Jules attended to the dead man again. "You weren't strong enough."

Charlie sat back, her gaze numb on Luther. "Not..."

"Told you you wouldn't like it." Jules paused, waited for the breath. He started again. "I'm the only one who could work the inner door. Garrett's needed so the Navy don't blow us up. And you're struggling to perform CPR, let alone push that seal closed. Luther was the only option."

Charlie pulled her knees up to her chest, forehead resting on them. Crying. Not arguing.

They stayed like that a long time, continuing the futile act of trying to revive Luther. Jules broke two of the man's ribs in the process, showing Charlie they were doing all they could. Twelve cycles passed before she cut them off.

"It's over," she said.

In a hospital drama, it would be the point where the doctor named a time of death, but they just sat there in silence.

When the lights came wobbling up the track, the ground was still wet, but no water flowed. Dan and Harpal, Toby between them, all stared at the body.

They stayed silent as Charlie told them how Luther had saved them all.

Jules wasn't unfeeling. He was sad for the loss. Sad that Luther had such potential—enthusiasm, knowledge, passion for the discoveries—and lost it all to what Jules diagnosed as mild depression, closing himself off from the world in that remote spot. Jules had planned on recommending a touch of therapy, but now he'd never get the chance, and that was an emptiness he'd handle with logic.

Luther's death allowed more to live.

Math.

The sadness inside Jules intensified. He didn't know why, didn't care, something to do with irony or another opportunity missed. It made the man's death harder, somehow, and the deepening silence appeared to affect the others the same way.

"What do we do now?" Harpal asked.

"We get Bridget back," Jules said simply. "No more secrets, though. No more half-truths. We need to know everything if we're gonna stop 'em."

Many times in his past, Toby had lost those he cared for. Luther wasn't a major stain on his soul, but he regretted the death all the same. A gesture like that, giving one's life to save people Toby loved, would not be forgotten. He had to push that away for the moment, though.

One of those people was imperiled right now.

Three hours earlier, he still hoped for the general's humanity to outweigh her paranoia and fears. But seeing her coldly order the murder of those seamen, despite how much she disliked it, meant there was no turning back for her. No redemption except in the company of others who shared her belief that her country was under threat, and in the endgame of protecting what she valued most.

It justified the means.

"We must get our stories straight." Colin emerged from the three men holding the flashlights. "The mercenaries came through, tried to kill us all, and this man bravely gave his life."

"Yeah, that's *actually* what happened," Jules said.

"Very well." Colin, ever the peacock, straightened his disheveled suit. "Then we must return to the mainland and—"

"We're going up," Toby said.

"Up?"

"Or we surrender to General Yanovna."

Toby didn't care much for Colin's opinion. The team was hard to read in the torch beams, though.

"You have less air than you need in those helmets." Lieutenant Commander Garrett checked their masks over. "You might make it, but you have to rise slowly. Let out a few air bubbles every twenty seconds and make sure you don't go faster than the bubbles."

Like the others with Harpal's resourced suits, Toby had retained his own helmet. When he arrived with Yanovna, he and Bridget had to leave the tanks and flippers behind, meaning it had all been washed away along with the advance party's kit.

"We'll go back," Garrett said. "Mr. Waterston and I can't exit this deep. If the cold doesn't kill us, the pressure will pop our eyeballs. Your air in the masks should give you the edge in timing, too."

Toby stared at the helmet dangling from his fingers—same as the others'.

"Let me stay," Dan said. "We got guns, we got the know-how."

"How's the foot?" Jules asked.

"Fine," Dan replied.

"He limped all the way up," Harpal said.

"Tattletale."

"Or, here's an idea. Maybe you should *think* for a change." Harpal rarely got annoyed, or rather, he rarely let it show, so it was unusual to see an outburst like that. "You're hurt, Charlie's hurt, Bridget's missing. Toby is… I don't know what Toby is, and the best chance we have is to get this idiot to the surface." He hooked his thumb at Colin.

"I'm sorry, do you mean me?" Colin said. "I couldn't possibly."

He *was* in a regular suit, not a wetsuit.

"Then bugger off," Harpal said.

"Come on, Harps." Charlie straightened in her sitting position. "We need to decide here. Do we drag Colin up using Luther's suit?"

Colin appeared horrified, and Garrett poured water on the proposal. "Wouldn't be feasible. Luther is shorter than Mr. Waterston, and his bulk…" Garrett held his tongue, apparently uncomfortable fat-shaming a dead man. "Sorry, but… the wetsuit needs to be tight."

"*We* all go," Jules said. "Simple decision. Flank 'em. Colin and Toby know where they're headed, so it's one in each group. Toby comes up top, Colin guides whoever stays from this side. Carefully. Don't matter who that is, but a guy limping ain't gonna be too effective."

"Screw you," Dan said.

Jules ignored the comment. "We go in the other side. We pick up Bridget quick as we can and bug out ASAP. They see we ain't a threat, we live. They'll retreat to international waters first chance they get."

"Excuse me," Colin said, "but we cannot allow a foreign government to seize the Crown's property."

"Don't worry, we'll call the cops soon as we can."

"That is not what I mean." Colin cleared his throat. "Garrett, you and I will return to the mainland and order a strike on the grounds—"

"You bloody will not," Harpal said.

"We can get Bridget clear," Dan agreed.

Garrett stood aside, next to Jules. Perhaps a subconscious move, perhaps not. "We have to give them a chance."

"You work for me," Colin said.

"I really don't." Garrett pointed his torch at Luther. "If he's going to be the last good guy to die today, we let them try to get their girl back."

"You do not understand—"

"What I understand," Dan said, pressing himself against Colin, making him step back, "is you won't be calling in any drone strikes until Bridget's safe. Clear?"

Toby shone a light on Charlie, who had sounded a little croaky.

"There's this place too," Harpal said. "Do we leave it? Explore it more later?"

"Ain't important right now," Jules said. "We get out, we get Bridget, we go home. Anythin' about the foreign invasion or raids, I don't care."

"Math again, Jules?" Dan said.

"People trump books. People trump funky mazes and whatever tablets and glowing rocks Basil Fawlty here's hiding back in Montrose."

"Would Bridget agree?" Charlie asked weakly.

"Don't matter. She don't get a vote in this."

Breathing all around. Lights dipped.

"*We* vote," Harpal said.

"No." Toby found his voice now. He'd stood back and watched, stood back and listened as they argued and debated the tangible versus the philosophical. And there was no other call to make. "The Lost Origins Recovery Institute has never been a democracy. *I* am in charge, and *I* make the final decisions. Is knowledge for the sake of knowledge worth it? Someone already lost their life. And while I don't know exactly what Colin is hiding, whatever *is* there… do we trust it in the hands of politicians? Do we trust it in the hands of Colin?"

"That is monstrously unfair," Colin said.

"This isn't a democracy," Toby said again. "Charlie and I founded this group together. We've lost people along the way, but we've made it this far. If you want to discover the same things we do, we're glad to have you. If not, we can all go our separate ways. But we have *never* been closer to achieving what we set out to."

Charlie struggled to her feet, shaky. "We're going for it?"

"Of course." Toby landed his light on people as his spoke. "Harpal, you're in better shape than Dan, and you can fire a gun. You'll accompany Colin and Lieutenant Commander Garrett and ensure nothing resembling an airstrike is ordered. The rest of us will return to the research vessel and pursue Zimina's people to the mainland. Jules, your unique touch will be needed once we get there. Dan will put his brace back on, then he'll go with you."

"Muscle?" Jules asked.

"Muscle, yes," Toby said. "Charlie, I need you to get comms back up and keep everyone talking. Meanwhile, I'll attempt to decipher what Colin has locked in his metaphorical basement."

Dan pointed the submachine gun at Colin. "How about we just ask him?"

"Why do you think?" Toby asked.

Dan said nothing.

Colin pulled his ruined jacket tight and lifted his chin. "I won't say."

"Because he don't know," Jules said.

"Correct," Toby said. "That's the reason it's all still here, in a ruined church. The reason the objects of Zimina's desire are here and not in some dark high-tech corner of the British Isles is that they don't know what they have. They can't even access it."

Colin's lips pinched and his brows knitted together. "That's…

ludicrous. They might not be located somewhere you can just drop in and find them, but *of course,* I know—"

Dan lowered the gun.

"We have one more puzzle to solve." Toby pulled a helmet up over Charlie's head. "Let's hope we make it before Zimina."

PART FIVE

"To the wise, life is a problem; to the fool, a solution."

- Marcus Aurelius

CHAPTER
FIFTY-THREE

Once in the primitive airlock, Jules found exiting was far easier than closing it. The seal broke with minimal effort, spilling water inside alarmingly quickly, but steadily enough to avoid crushing them. Already equalized to the depth—which would have killed Colin and Lieutenant Commander Garrett—the foursome took a moment to acclimatize, then pushed open the door fully. When used for its correct purpose, the slab appeared to swing and sway as intended, taking both Jules and Dan to dislodge it thanks to the damaged counterweight. But ultimately, they opened the hatch.

There was no time to close it fully, instead pushing it into the frame and partially turning the "plunger." No one could follow them, but they'd agreed before commencing that they'd return to fix it once the situation with Bridget resolved.

Jules wasn't entirely sure of the purpose since everything of interest had been removed already, but even he had a vague feeling he'd like to understand that structure better.

In someone with a real passion for this sort of thing, it would burn inside them to explore it. Not least how that maze really worked; if the airlock had been a marvel, the test of intelligence in that chamber was utter genius.

In a tight group, they swam up as instructed, using the comms line and anchor chain as a guide—both miraculously still in place. They followed Garrett's instruction to expel small amounts as they rose, never moving faster than the air bubbles, no matter how tempted they might have been.

Jules noticed Charlie and Toby struggling and squeezed Dan's shoulder. They separated, Dan holding Toby's hand, Jules with Charlie's.

Jules's lungs hurt from the effort and swimming got harder the more air they let out. Their natural buoyancy reduced. Soon, his thighs ached with kicking so hard, and their rise fell behind the bubbles, causing Toby to panic and Dan to wrap his arms around the man and fall back.

There was nothing Jules could do.

Charlie protested weakly, pointing at them, but as he mimicked Dan's position in embracing her, she could not fight him.

They broke the surface and Jules snapped off his helmet, bathing his lungs in sweet, sweet air. As he forced himself to take the smallest breaths possible, he released Charlie, too. There was no gasp, no massive inhalation. She just lay there in his arms, eyes fluttering.

"Hey!" He waved at the *Ny Bakke To*, the only vessel present. "Hey, a little help!"

But there was no reply.

Charlie appeared gray. Jules checked she was breathing, then scissored his legs, pulling her on her back as a lifeguard would swaddle a troubled swimmer.

At the boat, the ladder hung down, but there was still no sign of Dan and Toby.

Jules's energy was virtually zero. He hadn't eaten or drunk anything in hours, and after everything he'd done down below— not to mention the oxygen starvation—he lacked the strength to get Charlie onboard. And with the *Ny Bakke To's* crew presumably killed by the mercenaries, there was no help.

He splashed water on Charlie's face. "Hey, you hear me?"

Her head bobbing away from the drips showed she was semi-conscious.

"Okay, listen, I'll be back." Jules pulled a rope from the side of the boat, the loops holding life rings that doubled as buffers when docking. "Hold tight."

He wrapped her up in the life ring and rope, and she opened her eyes, making a move to accommodate the binding. She breathed out a timid command: "Go... help... them."

Jules held her gaze for a second and nodded. He emptied his helmet of water and pulled it on, now replenished with a few lungfuls of air, and ducked under.

He turned and faced downward, back the way they came—again, using the comms cable and anchor as a rough guide.

This time, instead of losing buoyancy, he had to fight against the pull for the surface, arms and legs like Jello as he dragged himself toward the flashlights hovering several feet down.

When he got there, he'd spent the air in his mask, running on empty, on the final gulp he managed to take.

Dan hadn't let go, but Toby still struggled. They'd ascended a little farther but demanded Jules's added strength to pull them upward. This close to the surface, they were no longer worried about the bends, so it was a case of moving as fast as possible.

Bursting into the regular atmosphere again, Dan moved aside while Jules released the catch from Toby's helmet first, a *pop* sounding as the region around Toby's head returned to normal.

Unlike Charlie, Toby was fully conscious, eyes bugging as he gasped a massive breath. It rushed inside him too fast and once Jules got his own helmet off, he had to hold on to Toby, encouraging him to take smaller breaths.

Dan was demonstrably exhausted, lying on his back, bobbing in the sea as he recovered.

Toby eventually slowed down, panic easing but trembling, nonetheless.

"Where's Charlie?" Dan asked.

"Left her..." Jules checked the base of the ladder where he'd been unable to lift her out. "Oh, no, here! Take Toby."

Jules swam over, prepared to go under again, hoping his body would take it.

But a sinking feeling in his gut told him he was too late. She'd passed out, drowned, and it was his fault.

"Don't move," came a woman's voice. Accented. Indian, possibly.

Jules turned in place to find, staring down at him from the port side of the *Ny Bakke To*, a woman in her later twenties, holding a Russian-made pistol. Jules couldn't see what she was aiming at.

"I have your friend, the woman," the newcomer said. "She is not in good shape. Give me any trouble, or fail to cooperate, and I will kill her."

FORMER HAMLET OF LISH, SCOTTISH MAINLAND, UK

Montrose itself lay a couple of miles away from where General Yanovna emerged with the four mercenaries, Captain Igoravich, and their prize asset, Bridget Carson. A prize not only because of Toby's clear affection for her, but because she was the daughter of oil-rich Americans—leading to a lack of political will to sink whatever boat they made their escape on, or blow a plane out of the sky before returning to Striovian territory. She'd be released unharmed once they got home, of course; diplomacy would demand it.

If they were cornered, though, Yanovna would not hesitate to exact her revenge, killing Toby's princess as his people had murdered her men.

This location was a mystery to Yanovna. She hadn't been certain of trusting Prihya, especially when the girl insisted she take no further part in the military aspect of the mission and wait behind to fulfill her own assignment. But Prihya had been spot on with everything else so far. Satellite imagery confirmed she was still on Yanovna's side.

According to the mercenaries who followed Victoriovna's

Mikhailovic-Dunham satellite images, they landed their launch half a mile from the former settlement known as "Lish", then infiltrated the territory along the rocky coastline. They already knew the main frigate had turned close to Montrose, then sent their own platoon in a cutter away from the Navy's official route to Perth, giving the Ukrainian strike team an easy target.

As predicted, Lish was now nothing more than a low-end footnote in the National Trust's catalog of properties in the region, with a faintly interesting ruin up a steep hill with what Yanovna expected were impressive views over the North Sea. Its only noteworthy entry in the annals of the region's history was a brief flirtation with destruction and its consequential liberation by the king of the time.

The strike team had found the entrance to be a modern installation, a stainless-steel door no larger than what you'd get in an average house, concealed behind a facade of rocks and trees atop a cliff face that sloped down toward a pebble beach. It required passwords and handprints to unlock. There was no public access to the beach and signs proclaimed the land private property belonging to the Department of Defense, warning of unexploded ordnance being present. Any access points to the beach, and therefore the hidden door, bordered the hill on which the church stood.

The man in charge, Colin, had stationed four guards, whose lack of experience showed in the simplicity with which they were overwhelmed and—sadly—killed by the Ukrainians. Yanovna had told them minimal casualties, not zero.

There really was no turning back now.

They commandeered the two bikes at the entrance, apparently placed there to travel the five miles into the center of the structure along an unremarkable passageway. At some point, the silly electric vehicles had replaced the bikes—the fumes underground with no vents must have been unpleasant. Or the UK authorities included them as part of their attempts to reduce their carbon footprint.

Now Yanovna emerged on the cliffside and, after pausing a

moment to reflect on the deaths of the four sailors whose bodies were lined up respectfully near the entrance, she followed the restricted path up into the open. She called Private Victoriovna via sat phone, who confirmed the area was free of trouble. The only people nearby were the two Ukrainians who did not venture deep into the tunnels, instead, holding the three crew from the *Ny Bakke To* in place.

Making four hostages in total, should they be needed.

"General," Igoravich said. "How should we proceed?"

"Proceed off the cliff," Bridget said. "I don't know what you think is here, but—"

"What is here," Yanovna said, "is whatever this facility was designed to hide. It is too much technology for there to be nothing. It is far, far more than a curiosity."

The sat phone rang. Yanovna answered.

Zefirova Victoriovna said, "The frigate is moving again. Coming back your way."

"How far?"

"Ninety minutes maybe. Two hours at the most."

Yanovna thanked her and hung up. "Igoravich, leave two stationed here in case the survivors try to escape this way. I want the crew and this one..." She poked Bridget in the arm. "With us at the church. If the legends Ms. Sibal uncovered are correct, we may need extra hands."

CHAPTER
FIFTY-FIVE
4:45 P.M

THE *NY BAKKE TO*, THE NORTH SEA

Jules was in no shape to refuse the Indian woman's orders. He climbed the ladder and helped Toby, who was, in turn, pushed up by Dan. The older man collapsed on the deck as the woman with the gun backed up to keep out of arm's reach and to maintain her range. Charlie sat, leaning against her workstation containing a blank screen.

Jules sank to his knees, and when Dan made it over, he followed suit.

"Where are the others?" the woman asked.

Jules pointed a floppy arm in the general direction of the coast. "They went the other way."

"You're not Striovian," Charlie said.

"I am not," the woman with the gun replied.

"And you're not a soldier," Dan said.

Jules had concluded the same. While she knew how to hold a gun, it was not a natural extension of her.

"I am here of my own choice," she said. "I need to know why you are looking for the orb."

"What orb?" Jules said.

"The Orb of King James the Fourth," Toby said.

Toby was lying on his back, arms flat, his breaths coming deep and slow.

"What the hell is this?" Jules said. "I thought you—"

"I didn't know for sure. Just a suspicion." Toby turned only his head, apparently too exhausted to move anything else. "No one knows what it is, what it does, or even if it exists. But we are about to find out."

"Hear that?" Charlie said. Like Toby, she appeared too tired to lift more than a single limb at once, in this case leaning her head to one side.

"Hear what?" the woman said.

"Helicopter."

"Do not try to trick me."

"She isn't," Jules said. "Look."

"A playground trick?"

"Take another couple of steps back, honey," Dan said. "None of us can reach you before you pull the trigger."

The woman checked around her, then moved backward, gun trained between the seated, dripping wet people on the deck. Then she risked a look over one shoulder.

In truth, Jules could have thrown the flashlight at her, then rushed her, but it wasn't necessary. There really was a helicopter heading their way, a speck in the distance.

"That's my husband." Charlie sat straighter, her hand to her old wound. "You told me you'd researched us. Then you know my military background, *and* my husband's. He's calling in the cavalry."

The woman couldn't decide where to look. "Call them back. Call them off."

Charlie shook her head. "Standing order, m'dear. Basic failsafe. I don't make contact for two hours, he sends a gunship."

"Call them off."

"Nope."

"It's over," Jules said. "Why aren't you telling us your name and what you want? Guessing you're the general's expert I heard 'em mention, but you stuck around for some reason. Meaning you ain't interested in a buncha murdering hired guns or what they're after. You're interested in *us*. Right?"

She didn't reply.

Dan shifted his weight to curl a leg under himself. With the gun whipped around to him, he added, "The general sure didn't leave you to keep guard or kill us. So, let's work this out."

"You are thieves," the woman said. "Responsible for the destruction of a holy site in my country."

Jules put it together. "The tomb. You're wanting revenge for a tomb?"

"I want justice."

Toby mustered enough strength to sit upright. "And what of justice for the sailors General Yanovna killed?"

"She... killed?" The woman's brow knitted together. "She said it was a peaceful mission."

"With all those guns?" Dan said. "People died today. And if you're helping them, you're culpable."

"Got a way off this boat?" Charlie asked.

"I have the boat." The woman pointed the gun at the bridge.

Jules pitched the flashlight like a throwing knife.

It hit the woman's gun hand, drawing a yelp of pain, a gunshot, and then Jules was upon her, clearing the distance in double the time it would normally take him. He gambled she wouldn't recover from the surprise before he reached her, and he was correct, lifting her gun arm skyward and over-rotating her hand to release the weapon to him.

Satisfied and slow, he didn't see the kick to his gut before it impacted.

The woman hit him in the neck with the side of her hand, then aimed another kick at his knee. He stepped over that one, a little dazed from the neck strike, but with her off-balance, he redirected the force from her missed kick to make her slip on her butt. From there, he gave himself space and aimed the gun at her.

She snarled at him. "Do it. My people will find you."

Jules looked at Dan. "Pretty sure even you wouldn't execute someone like this."

Dan waved his hand back and forth as he stood. "I dunno. If she suckered me as good as she suckered you, I could be tempted."

Toby found his feet, and he and Dan struggled over to the workstation, which they turned back on and opened the cooler alongside.

Charlie waited where she was.

Toby took water from the cooler one bottle at a time, and Dan tossed them to Charlie and Jules in turn.

It tasted so good going down. All four drank greedily.

"What's your name?" Jules asked.

"Prihya," the woman replied. "And you will not get away with this."

The helicopter was louder now, almost upon them.

Prihya checked on it. Laughed briefly. "Not exactly a gunship."

Jules checked, too. It had indeed been a bluff by Charlie. It was a rescue chopper, kitted out with skids that could land on the water. She wasn't bluffing about Phil sending it, though. That really was a standing failsafe. LORI lacked the influence to call in the army at a moment's notice, but plenty to report a boat in trouble.

"Just need to refuel ourselves," Jules said. "Then we get back to work. What's the word, Toby?"

Toby was staring at the computer screen, seemingly unblinking. "It's a message. From Colin. Oh, my, this can't be good."

CHAPTER
FIFTY-SIX
4:45 P.M

CHURCH OF LISH

The mercenary brought the two men before her with a note of caution. They surrendered too easily, so the Ukrainian who accompanied them said.

The church was not quite a ruin, but it was beyond use as a place of worship. Hollowed out, all fixtures in the nave absent except a few doors to locked rooms remained. A visitor center equipped with computer hardware from the 1990s was the most secure aspect and yielded little of interest. Beyond the nave was a twisting series of passages and rooms but stuck to the general crucifix shape she was used to, having visited and explored dozens of similar structures. If Prihya's research was as accurate as the rest of her analysis so far, there would be a room within a room, perhaps a staircase into the caves. If they couldn't find it, they would begin blasting, using the hostages to keep the Navy, or police should they be alerted, at bay.

But the pair who emerged from the complex beneath the ocean —the man she now knew to be Great Britain's Royal Curator Colin Waterston and Lieutenant Commander Garrett of the Royal Navy—appeared far too compliant.

Standing in the center of the church under one Ukrainian's gun, Colin's eye wandered to the hostages held by the two other mercenaries on one side, then to Igoravich on the other, and back to Yanovna. He kept his chin high and British upper lip stiff. "I wish to negotiate."

"Yes?" It was amusing to Yanovna that men in utterly compromised positions always sought a way out by bargaining. "What could you offer?"

"Your life." The curator pulled up his right sleeve to reveal a watch of some impressive value. "If I do not call within the next ten minutes, a drone strike has been ordered on this very location."

"Interesting." Yanovna glanced at Igoravich and smiled. Back to Colin. "Your laws prevent armed forces from firing on your own civilians without a serious threat. Like a nuclear bomb about to go off. And this is most certainly not a nuclear bomb. Or is it?"

"You are invaders. The rules of engagement are clear. To deter further incursion, collateral damage may result. Unfortunate, but still." He paced, making Igoravich twitch toward his weapon. "You might all escape here if you leave now. But make no mistake, there will be no negotiation with the people who come for us. *None.*"

"Where is the cave?" Yanovna asked.

Colin stuttered, mouth working as if insulted about something. "I… I do not know what in the world you are talking about."

"We know there is something under our feet. A place of worship from long before Christ was hung on that cross. Your ancestors built this church to hide what lay beneath, and please do not bother to deny this."

"In that case, Lieutenant Commander, if you wouldn't mind."

The Navy man quickly shoved the Ukrainian, then threw a punch at Igoravich.

But Igoravich was Striovian Special Forces, trained in two martial arts and a lifetime of street fighting during the harshest period in the country's history. Even with his somewhat advanced years, and despite the naval officer summoning a perfectly serviceable punch, it was simple for Igoravich to sidestep, parry, and reply with three blows of his own before breaking the man's nose with the butt of his pistol.

By that point, Colin had already run, his gait like an ungainly emu or ostrich—so comical the pair of mercenaries watching the hostages just blinked as if they couldn't quite believe their eyes.

"Well?" Yanovna said.

"I will go." Igoravich took off at a jog as Colin fled inside the annex housing the visitor center. "He cannot stay in there forever."

Infuriatingly, the door had been shot up, presumably to check it for access to the caverns below. Quite how they worked out even that little nugget, Colin couldn't say. What he could say was that the metal shutter he now rattled down out of its scrolled housing wouldn't hold out long with only the latch on the inside. There were similar shutters on the windows to the glass booth, decommissioned months earlier due to his own investigation there, and the public received the story that Health & Safety had condemned the place until repairs could be carried out.

Still stocked with frightfully cheap souvenirs and trinkets, there also remained a computer running Windows XP. So low was the priority of this ruin, the National Trust didn't even consider it worthy of a system that could do more than process sales transactions and transmit the odd email.

Stripped of all electronics before they reached the surface, as predicted by Garrett, it was Colin's plan to use the only connected unit outside the access tunnel for several miles. Unfortunately, however, a Windows XP computer would run at Windows XP speeds. And that would be a snail's pace.

"Come out, Mister," came the deep voice through the shutters.

The bang of metal on metal rattled through the semi-darkness. "You cannot hide."

The Windows logo vanished. The blue screen showed, then a digital landscape, followed by a trashcan icon.

Come on, you infernal machine!

A gunshot sounded outside. The bullet must have been aimed at a lock because something crunched near the base of a window shutter and shook the steel panels.

The next half-dozen icons appeared as the computer slowly booted.

"Faster, damn you," Colin said.

Another gunshot. Another rattle. Another taunt: "Come out, Mr. British Man. I can come in and kill you. Or you come. Alive."

The blocky blue "e" for *Explorer* appeared in the taskbar and Colin used the mouse to click it. A window popped up and spent several seconds populating.

"One more chance," the big Striovian captain called. "I give you thirty seconds." A third gunshot rang out. "Okay, twenty."

Colin should use this opportunity to alert his superiors or the anti-terror police in Edinburgh, but they would take too long; they'd have to verify his government ID, then send it up the chain of command, before formulating a plan, and then pulling personnel together to execute a rescue.

Colin input a series of numbers memorized a long time ago, the code for a place on the web that his former mentor betrothed to him. Where most civilian websites start with "www." or more commonly now "https:" all websites are actually lines of code, with numbers and dots denoting the destination, like complex coordinates. With the Navy frigate already engaged and on its way from Perth, young Simon on board documenting proceedings, and law enforcement aware of "maneuvers" in the area, there was only one person he could call upon for assistance.

He accessed the website and selected the "share" button on a file he'd backed up there—the most secure cloud storage site in the UK. He added several words and numbers to the mail note and hit *send*.

The shutter flew up and Colin flicked off the screen, standing with his hands over his head. "Don't shoot, I'm coming."

And he hated calling on Toby for anything. Between this "surrender" plan—cobbled together by the Asian lad still hiding in the tunnel—and asking his former mentor to save his life... well, Colin feared he'd never hear the end of it. *If* it came off, naturally.

THE *NY BAKKE TO*, THE NORTH SEA

"It's a message," Toby said. "From Colin. Oh, my, this can't be good."

While Jules kept watch on Prihya, Charlie struggled over and virtually fell into the chair at her station. Both Toby and Charlie looked it over.

"A web link," Charlie said. "I'll run a check on it first. Satellite is receiving okay."

"This is..." Toby clicked the link, much to Charlie's shock. "Don't worry, I know what this is. It's not a virus."

The click brought up Toby's old online storage locker, a site established at the infancy of the World Wide Web and continuously upgraded and enhanced over the years—presumably beyond his own stewardship of the royal curator mantel.

"What are those other details he sent?" Charlie asked.

"Colin's log-on details." Toby input the username and password into the boxes that popped up. and the details of Colin's project in Lish were laid bare. "Let's get this downloaded. I need to be out there."

"You're in no shape," Dan said.

"Nor are you." Toby pulled a can of disgusting energy drink from the fridge, something full of sugar and caffeine, and popped the top, swigging the too-sweet gunk. "Please watch Ms. Sibal. Charlie can't keep us going and watch her."

"Sibal," Charlie said. "Where do I know that name from?"

Toby faced Prihya as he replied to Charlie. "I was thinking of attempting to recruit her a few years ago. Quite fascinating how she came to be hunting us now. Unfortunately, that question will have to wait."

Prihya pulled her line of sight away from the helicopter now almost upon them, and focused on Toby, her lips parting minutely.

"She has similar interests to ourselves," Toby said. "But when we researched her deeper, we found a studious person, extremely intelligent, but—"

"Given to impetuous actions," Charlie said. "Yup, I remember now." She winced as she turned to Prihya. "Likes to confront people who disagree with her. Lots of accusing organizations and governments of cover-ups instead of focusing on proving them wrong."

"And now she has joined the quest for this orb." Toby scanned the files inside the master copy that Colin allowed them to access.

"What is this orb, then?" Jules asked. "Thought you were gonna come clean."

"The message from Colin is government clearance. It explains what this place is—as much as they know. The church is set on a former pagan site. There's a far older structure under the foundations that connects directly to the ancient warren out in the sea. They never knew what it was supposed to hide, only that there was a section they could not access."

The helicopter came in low for a sweep, presumably checking they were all okay.

"Why?" Jules said. "Seems dumb that they couldn't get through an ancient door with modern tech."

"Charlie, can you load this up to a tablet?" Toby called over the roar of engines.

"Yes, of course." Charlie slurred her words now, the act of typing and clicking the mouse proving strenuous. "Why?"

"You need medical treatment. I need to ingest it on the way. Get Phil to commandeer the chopper."

"Why?" Dan said. "What's going on?"

The little information Toby had gathered from the thumbnails and auto-loading files wasn't much to go on—about enough to understand Colin had unearthed more than anyone expected. "This is not a giant cavern. It's a cave, and Colin *will* be forced to reveal its location."

"So, we're sunk?" Jules said.

"I told you Colin Waterston was a slippery guy, but he's also a pragmatist. Oh, my. I'm almost ready to hug that man."

Then Charlie slumped in the chair and fell sideways like a downed tree. Toby caught her and Dan helped lower her to the floor.

"Get that chopper down!" Dan yelled.

Jules waved at the helicopter as it swung past. A loud hailer squawked to life, asking if they needed assistance, and Jules gestured for it to land.

Between shouting for help and maneuvering Charlie into a recovery position, Toby noted Prihya glancing feverishly between the team and the helicopter.

"Ms. Sibal," Toby called, "you are not a prisoner or hostage. You are free to leave at any time. But do not interfere while we see to our friend."

Jules got that Prihya needed to trust them, and stashed the gun on the workstation before heading to the port side to guide the rescue vehicle down. They had more important things to worry about than a competitor getting the drop on them.

Charlie's lips moved.

Toby couldn't hear, so lowered himself. "What? Charlie, are you okay?"

"Stop… them…" Charlie managed.

"As soon as we're done with you, my dear. Then we conclude matters on the mainland."

CHAPTER
FIFTY-EIGHT

5:35 P.M

MONTROSE, EAST COAST OF SCOTLAND

Allowing himself, Jules, and Dan time only to change into dry clothes, Toby found the rescue helicopter medics were superb and whisked their patient away as soon as they'd stabilized her. Suffering dehydration and exhaustion, she needed to be on a drip urgently—which was what they hooked up in under five minutes.

Then they shipped Charlie, Toby, Jules, and Dan to the mainland, ensuring the three drank and ate what they could along the way, where an ambulance was idling. Beachgoers were in for a treat as they scattered so the vehicle could land, and paramedics rushed the stricken woman over the sand to the ambulance.

Most beachgoers enjoyed the spectacle, anyway.

At least one person's day would end on a different note when they realized their Land Rover, circa 1992, had been stolen from the parking lot adjacent to the coast, to transport three men to a point where they might retrieve their friend and teammate.

"With Charlie down, we only have basic comms," Toby said from the passenger seat. "Phil is on his way here and is quite miffed at us, understandably so, but he did re-establish our satellite phones."

"No earbuds?" Jules said, driving.

"No time to sync them to the new frequencies. From what Colin sent us, though, Harpal is ready and waiting on our signal. Do we have an approach?"

In the back seat with his foot encased in a plastic sleeve and elevated, Dan put down the computer tablet on which he'd been analyzing *Google Earth* for the lay of the land and comparing it to Colin's data. "Yeah, but we only got one gun."

"Harpal will bring more with him," Jules said.

"Let's hope."

"So, what's the approach?"

Dan draped himself over the passenger seat and showed them.

"Great," Jules said. "Haven't done that in a while."

CLIFFSIDE TUNNEL, NEAR THE CHURCH OF LISH

Still in his wetsuit, Harpal had banked on the two guards either retiring together or separating to escort Colin and Garrett to the boss lady. Sure, the mercenaries could have killed the pair on sight, but Colin was of use to Yanovna, and he made it immediately clear that his cooperation rested upon no more death. Colin proved surprisingly adept at lying, although Harpal's surprise waned when he remembered that Colin and Toby were cut from the same cloth, trained in the same affairs of state and security.

One thing he'd learned about the man today, which Toby had explained in the past, but no one believed, was that the most effective operatives were those underestimated by their opposition—and everyone underestimated Colin.

A ground-trembling *thu-whump* from deep inside the hill confirmed they were on the right track.

Colin was cooperating.

It left Harpal to sneak from his hiding place in the dark—behind oil drums covered in tarps—and advance on the guard with a submachine gun braced against his shoulder. The guard was not defending a position, but posted as a lookout, retracing his steps to defend two approaches: the first from outside by the door which cast daylight onto the four seamen's bodies, and then the tunnels leading inside to the cavern where others had died.

Only one man.

This should be easy.

Harpal stalked to the right, waited for the mercenary to reverse his route, then advanced. He settled into a shooting crouch as he would on a range, then drew a bead. Fifteen meters meant he had to account for a slight dip in the bullet's trajectory.

No problem.

Bam—one shot.

In a spray of red, the merc's head snapped back, and the man folded into a heap.

With the explosion up the hill ringing in the ears of those in the vicinity, it'd be unlikely anyone would have heard this.

Unfortunately, not everyone was still absent.

Evidently ordered to return to his post after delivering Colin and Garrett, the second gunman popped into the passage, gun leading, and spotted Harpal. A trained military professional, the mercenary closed himself immediately into cover and opened fire.

The booming clatter deafened Harpal as he dove for a pile of wooden crates, which he hoped were full of something solid.

No bullets penetrated, just chewing up and splintering the containers. But his hands still felt too big for the gun's handle, his heart yammered, and his brain continued to fight him, demanding he make himself as small as possible and either run or hide. He had to push back hard against the latter instinct.

In a pause, Harpal took a breath, steadied his grip and popped up, brought the gun around, and managed three shots before the barrage resumed.

Harpal dropped back down. His instincts poked him from his subconscious: *told you to run, you idiot.*

This wasn't his key skill set. Sure, he trained hard with Dan, but there was no substitute for experience. While Harpal had gone up against gunmen before, they were usually armed thugs or quickly cobbled-together militia, not fully fledged, battle-hardened soldiers.

His next peek up revealed the man had advanced a couple of meters.

Harpal fired, the recoil hard on his shoulder, single shots to save ammo, and getting close. The reply was a full-bore machine gun barrage, sparking off walls, shattering wood and forcing Harpal down again.

The guard clicked empty and commenced reloading, allowing Harpal a rush of blood to the head. Excitement swamped him, opportunity knocking hard and loud.

He rushed out to the next pile of equipment, firing off bursts of three to keep his opponent pinned.

"Wait!" shouted the Ukrainian in a heavy accent. He held up a hand from his hiding spot.

Had he run out of ammo? Was his gun jammed?

"What?" Harpal called back.

"Nothing." The mercenary poked his head up, meeting Harpal's eye from eight or ten meters away. "Just I need to know where you are."

In the man's other hand, a grenade appeared. He pulled the pin, its lever still held in place.

Harpal's throat almost popped with the surge from within. His adrenaline raced, his heart rate spiking. His flight response took control.

Grenades weren't simply a loud bang followed by someone fleeing and leaping through the air to cover; they fragmented, and blew other things apart, which created more shrapnel. In an enclosed space like this, Harpal knew he wouldn't be able to outrun it.

"Hey, what's all this?" came a man's voice.

American.

Specifically, Brooklyn.

It was enough to catch the merc's attention and make him hesitate in throwing the grenade as Jules was already halfway to the guy. In a split second, he covered the final meter and smothered the man's fist, trapping the explosive in a double grip. The lever remained in place, the fuse not live.

The mercenary swung his gun around but struggled to point it in the tight space.

Jules slapped it away and rammed his knee into the man's groin, but he must have been wearing a cup since he used the gun straightaway as a club. He found it blocked at the wrist and Jules twisted the joint to disarm him.

Harpal tried to aim but couldn't get a clear shot.

The mercenary slammed his fist into Jules's arm, over and over in the same spot, then went for his head.

Mistake.

Jules ducked it, still holding the grenade hand tight, and popped up the other side of the swing, closed down the arm, and somehow lifted the soldier off the ground, spinning him in midair. A snap sounded and the man screamed, and Jules came away with the explosive.

Harpal ran over, his gun braced to his shoulder, and pointed it at the man on the floor with the floppy hand, wrist broken. He was about to shoot and take the guy out when Jules knocked the gun to one side.

"Let's not," Jules said.

"Fine." Harpal turned the gun around and smashed it into the mercenary's head. Then a second blow rendered him unconscious. "Happy?"

"Let's go."

CHAPTER
FIFTY-NINE

After Jules replaced the grenade's pin, he stripped the guard of his trousers and outer clothes for Harpal to change into, then tied up the unconscious half-naked man in his underwear, and pulled the body of the dead one to rest by the naval personnel.

While Harpal dressed, Jules filled him in on the situation so far, explaining they'd parked nearby and Jules had run up the beach and climbed the cliff to rendezvous with Harpal, while Toby and Dan had followed behind at a slower pace due to their lack of athleticism and injury, respectively.

They'd originally built the path for civilians, so it was a winding staircase past new signs warning of the risk of death from unexploded ordnance; this was all thanks to Department of Defense testing and exercises. They'd only had to wait ten minutes for Toby and Dan to catch up and then had continued ascending the route to the hill where the Church of Lish stood. There, National Trust signage had taken over from the DoD's.

"Approach is blind," Dan said. "Any idea of numbers up there?"

"Can't be many," Harpal replied. "They figured we were all trapped under the seabed. Can't believe they blew the hatch just to slow us down."

"No, they wanted us cornered," Jules said. "But Yanovna ain't stupid. There'll be someone on guard."

They talked it out some more before Toby and Dan moved up to the front door, hands raised, while Jules and Harpal skirted the outer contour of the hill. The slick grass made it difficult but not impossible, and the notion of a guard with a bird's-eye view remained. Without the subvocal units, they were relying on line of sight, and the assumption that Yanovna believed them dead or trapped.

Would they have heard the gunfight?

Muscles burning with the effort, Jules reached the peak and pressed against the church wall, while Harpal kept his path covered with the rifle, now fully loaded. They waited for Toby and Dan to crest more winding stairs and for the sole guard to order them to halt.

Dan limped ahead of Toby, visibly sweating. "Hey, I just need to offer an exchange."

"No." The mercenary crunched over the gravel path, emerging from the church's entrance, gun aimed at Dan's chest. A grin. "No exchange. We find cave already. General wins."

But he *crunched* over the gravel.

No silent approach.

Jules signaled to Toby. Dan was unable to look away from the guard without giving away the deception. Two fingers waggled, then pointed to the ground. Toby appeared to get it.

He shuffled forward, kicking as much gravel up as he progressed, saying, "Tell the general I survived and wish to bargain for the hostages."

The Ukrainian mercenary crossed sideways, out of Dan's reach but within Toby's.

Jules nodded to Toby, who sighed.

"I don't normally do this kind of thing," Toby said.

"What you don't normally do?" the guard asked.

Toby fell to his knees, pretending to choke. The guard stepped back, surprised, loosening his grip for under a second—enough time for Dan to close the distance, jam his finger behind the man's trigger, and slap one hand over his mouth and nose. It was nowhere near secure, but Jules hurtled over the gravel while Harpal cleared the entryway. Jules initiated a chokehold, pressing until the sentry went limp.

Using the man's own zip ties, Dan cuffed him, took his gun, and Jules joined Harpal by the door.

They poked their heads inside.

Empty.

The nave—the main part of the church—was a wide space, just like a million other old buildings Jules had visited: open plan, stinking of age, with plaques denoting areas of interest. Several sections were cordoned off, with modern doors designed to look ancient, all except the gift shop to one side, which seemed an odd choice given the absence of tourists and the apparent lack of appeal for such a place.

Hiding the church would be suspicious.

Disguising it as a boring National Trust property kept people away.

Those who did show wouldn't question anything.

Clever.

The old building was drafty and cold, and Jules would have guessed deserted too if not for the sounds of crunching, banging, and clumps of dirt being moved in a place that muffled the noises but couldn't hide them—a room out back somewhere.

While Dan watched his rear, Harpal covered the corners—or *transepts*—and the apse at the far side, then finally the gift shop, or "visitor center" as the sign had it. This section, near the exit, appeared to have been a little shot up. The lock on its roll shutter was blackened and mangled, with the shutter itself stalled halfway up the entry door.

Jules had offered to act as cover, but Dan was nervous about Jules's alleged phobia of killing, instead handing him the Russian pistol liberated from Prihya Sibal, whom they'd left on the *Ny Bakke To*.

Once cleared, Harpal and Dan huddled with Jules and Toby to figure out what to do next.

"Digging," Jules said. "You heard it?"

They followed the noises through where the central aisle would have stood, around the altar position, and down the south transept. They passed a door with a plaque explaining what the priest's quarters were for, the room apparently still containing "authentic" furnishings. Along a narrow passage off the transept, an additional rear hall opened out and, much like the main feature of the building, it felt airy, the walls well preserved, if marked by age.

The big difference was a seven-foot-wide hole in the floor. Bricks and mortar were strewn all over, and dust hung in the air. Someone had blasted this apart recently.

Jules crouched, signaled everyone to wait, and advanced to the hole. He listened and watched all the way.

Down there, a cave was visible, with a ladder positioned to allow access. A shadow patrolled beneath, and Jules overheard discussions, protests, and a shout. Someone, a male, was saying it was "useless" to keep digging. Accented agreement could be heard.

The Ny Bakke To crew.

Press-ganged into digging and searching. Not dead and tossed overboard as he feared.

Yanovna said, "Keep looking. It must be here."

Then the *chuff* and *clunk* of spades in dirt recommenced.

Jules retreated, having confirmed they were down there and all hands to the task, but he hadn't heard Bridget.

Toby, though, was smiling.

"What?" Jules asked in a whisper.

"Colin lied," Toby said. "He isn't cooperating after all. Not really."

Dan glanced toward the hole, then back to Toby, his brow low. "What do you mean?"

"Remember when Colin said the items *might not be located*

somewhere you can just drop in and find them? Well, look at that. They've dropped in and found nothing so far."

"And they won't," Jules said, starting back the way they came. When they followed, tiptoeing silently, he said, "If he knows where they are but ain't telling the general, he's decided Yanovna can't have them. Means they're somewhere here, but you said they can't be accessed."

"Correct, Jules," Toby said, moving faster and more freely than Dan for a change. "Meaning, what?"

"Meaning you gotta stop asking questions you already know the answers to."

Toby chuckled.

Dan said, "Look, you brainboxes might be running at the same speed, but how about you let us in on it?"

"What's this place been from the beginning?" Jules asked.

"And now *you're* doing it," Harpal said. "Asking questions you know the answers to."

Jules thought about that and gave Toby a pat on the shoulder. "Oh, yeah, that's kinda fun. I see why you do it." Back to Harpal. "So, how'd this place stay secret so long?"

"They hid its real purpose," Dan said. "A church when it's really an… I don't know."

"In other words…?" Toby said.

"Hiding in plain sight," Harpal answered.

"And what's a useless part of this structure?" Jules said. "Which part can hide something but also be made safe?"

They arrived back at the nave and saw what Jules meant. Everyone reached his and Toby's conclusion together.

"The visitor center," Harpal said. "They hid it in there."

"Come." Toby led the way. "We have some work to do."

CHAPTER
SIXTY

The gift shop was standard fare for the UK. Jules had been in plenty and recognized a lot of the same items manufactured in sweatshops around the world. A cash register and an old PC lay in one corner, with aisles of cheap crap alongside for people to browse. Lunchboxes, tea towels, bath towels, and underpants were on offer for every occasion, together with Union- and Scottish-flag key fobs, teddy bears dressed in various ways, and a stash of dolls and action figures sporting blue faces like Mel Gibson in the movie *Braveheart*. There were knickknacks such as coasters, tee-shirts, hoodies, plus Big Ben models and red bus toys despite being 509 miles north of London; and every bit of kitsch rubbish they could cram into the tiny cavity just off the nave. All of it bore a fine layer of dust, the result of three and a half months of inactivity.

"What are we looking for?" Harpal asked.

"Anything that doesn't belong," Toby said. "A feature in the building, not a… whatever this is." Toby held a blob of squidgy plastic painted in the Scottish flag's colors, which regained its shape no matter how much he squeezed it. He tossed it away. "This gift shop was not here ten years ago. So, let's move quickly."

Dan hobbled to where the cash register sat and unearthed the humming PC, but discarded it to check the floor and paneling, then shifted a folded wheelchair beside a first aid kit on the wall. Harpal heaved a shelving unit away from the wall and started pressing bricks.

Jules pointed to Toby's jacket, and Toby took out the tablet on which he'd stored the files Colin sent over. There wasn't much more than what he'd told Jules already: the Doggerland flood, the hill that once stood on the Mesolithic land, the discovery of a vault and the imagery of a full circle with a zigzag, or energy, power, something interrupting the cycle...

The lifecycle of man.

The circuit.

There were so many photos of the pictograph, but not of any artifact they'd found to date. No photographs of agricultural seals, nothing of the Reaper Seal, nor the outer hatch that granted access to the Doggerland tunnels. The photos in Colin's files were predominantly carved into walls or stones of some sort, a couple smooth, but mostly rough. Some were in daylight, others illuminated artificially, clearly from different locations.

The filenames gave some clues, strings of numbers Jules recognized as coordinates, but beyond an approximate land mass he couldn't work out the locations, except for three; these, he isolated as being parts of the British Isles. He tapped on each of these and swiped back and forth between them.

He held still on the middle one that opened, then moved the tablet screen away from him.

While Dan and Harpal carried a case between them, Jules zoned in on a plastic box high in the corner where one wall met the one running to the nave.

"Toby, what kinda sense of humor does Colin have?" Jules asked.

Toby considered for a moment. "Dry."

"Ironic?"

"He prefers a joke one has to think about. Isn't very quick in terms of comebacks or—"

"Does he like to show off how clever he is?"

Toby chuckled. "Have you met him?"

Jules had indeed spent time with the man. "There."

Everyone stopped and looked at the plastic box in the corner.

"What is it?" Harpal asked.

Jules hopped up onto the counter and braced his hands on the twelve-inch by nine-inch box with the translucent frontage. "No wires going into this fuse box."

"Or a circuit breaker," Dan said.

"A Brit using an American term." Jules fiddled with the box.

"Because much of this dates back to Columbus." Toby brightened. "Clever boy."

Jules wasn't sure if Toby meant him or Colin, but he found the right level to lift the box and it came away from the wall, revealing a brick of a darker color than those around it.

Etched into the surface was the pictograph they'd been seeing since the beginning.

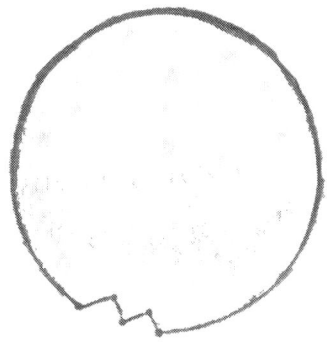

"Think we're gonna see exactly what this is all about now."

UNDER THE CHURCH OF LISH

"I said I would give you until six." Yanovna was growing impatient with Colin Waterston, as the man, filthy and sweaty from the dig, proposed a third section of the floor to try. "If this is another failure, you die. Am I clear?"

"Crystal." The tall, skinny Englishman nodded rapidly, like a child given a final chance to tidy his room before his parents cut off his allowance. "This… this is the spot. I'm sure of it."

Since Colin revealed the location of this chamber and Igoravich blasted through with directional charges, Yanovna sensed something wasn't quite right. Everything so far had indicated only "worthy" people could access the secrets within these places—the Reaper Seal, the scroll, the scythe blade… now they could simply *blast* their way in?

The three crew members had remained silent and obedient—sailor-scientists who'd never experienced a gun pointed at them—while Bridget argued weakly against these actions. The Navy man—Garrett—struggled, his nasal passages blocked, eyes watery. Yanovna allowed Bridget to tend to him, but there was no more than a basic first aid kit around, so it was left to the wonders of splashing water on his face every so often to keep him lucid.

The final Ukrainian kept watch by the hole while the group dug in the places Colin suggested.

They'd buried the items, he told them. They'd hidden them there a decade ago, burying them in this, a nondescript basement with no markers, no X-marks-the-spot, then resealing the room. Originally, he had pleaded for an extra fifteen minutes to locate the access point, but Igoravich manufactured his own entrance in less than three. Afterward, he paced under the glare of the spotlights and chose a spot in which to dig.

With two areas now dug up, the cellar resembled a serial killer's home, searched by the police for bodies, and now with a third grave commenced.

"General," Igoravich said. "How can you be sure he is honest with you? The frigate is near now, and police could come at any time."

"No police," Yanovna said. "In this country, police are civilians. The curator will wait for military backup. They take orders. Keep secrets. And Mr. Waterston has less than five minutes before I kill him."

A new sound clanked through the basement—metal on stone.

"I think we have it," Colin said.

"Watch him." Yanovna holstered her weapon, pulled the clip over it, and crossed to where Colin had struck the hard surface. "The rest of you against the wall."

Colin dug around the object, found the edges, the two corners, the curve of the top end. A stone tablet became clear, shaped like a gravestone, a blue-gray color.

"What is it?" Yanovna asked.

"We honestly do not know." Colin wiped sweat from his brow, leaving a dirty smear. "They were left by people we cannot understand. Toby and his silly friends believe this sort of thing is from prehistory, but we have little evidence of this beyond faulty dating processes—"

"Pass it here."

Colin bent at his knees, wiggled his fingers into the sides, and dislodged the tablet. He strained but managed to present it to the general, wiping off the dry soil as he did so.

Bridget was the only one who dared come forward, both hands clasped by her chest, eyes scanning back and forth. "What is it? What have we found?"

"Back up, girl." Igoravich hefted his gun in her direction.

She obeyed, retreating to beside the four men.

Peering into the ditch, Yanovna spotted another identical stone beneath where the first had lain. "How many?"

"There are six in total," Colin said. "Each buried under the other."

Yanovna turned the tablet over in her bare hands. Alien script had been etched into the surface, similar to the writing she'd seen in the Canadian mine. No glow. Not even a flicker. "And I assume the excavation of these other items will require more time."

Colin's shoulder rose and then fell with what looked like a great effort. "Sadly, yes. If you want the whole story, we'll have to get them all free—"

Yanovna lifted the stone tablet over her head and lobbed it at the foundation wall behind Colin. It split in two and crashed to the floor, lumps cracking away.

Colin's boggling eyes followed the action. When he returned his gaze to Yanovna, her arm was already moving. Her flat hand became a blade and jabbed into Colin's throat, blowing the air out of him. She kneed him in the groin, drawing a pained *ooh* from the other men in the room, including Igoravich. Finally, she booted him in the ribs.

Her blow dropped him to the floor beside the shattered tablet, a gun pointed at him. "It is a nice effort, Mr. Waterston. But I am the foremost authority on antiquities in my country. I can spot fakes at one hundred paces. Fake artifacts, and fake people. Goodbye."

And General Yanovna pulled the trigger.

CHAPTER
SIXTY-ONE

CHURCH OF LISH GIFT SHOP

Jules ignored the gunshot, placed his hand on the pictograph, and pressed. No light emanated from behind the dirt and grime on the brick, nothing to reveal its origin as harking back to the Witnesses. It was impossible that they'd built the church, but not inconceivable that whatever lay beneath, whatever this was built upon, belonged to them. Unlike the bangle carvings, this "circuit" pictograph appeared only to require the intelligence to recognize it rather than a specific *worthy* touch.

As the block slid smoothly inward, several more bricks on the adjacent wall clicked away from one another in a jagged line following the build of mortar. Hampering access was the cash register's counter and a stand full of pamphlets and flyers for other local attractions, mostly National Trust properties.

Jules jumped down, and he and Harpal shifted the stand aside, then opened the crack wider.

A breeze blew from within, then died, the release of air trapped for a long time.

Hesitation came from both.

Then, with a solid nod from Toby, and Dan raising his submachine gun, Jules swung open what proved to be a door, and stepped out of Dan's line of fire. Dan glided aside, so he wasn't a target.

Inside, the light from where they stood gave them a view of a short passageway, but not much beyond ten yards.

"How many flashlights have we got?" Dan asked.

"One apiece from the boat." Toby fished his small flashlight from his pocket.

"Won't need it." Jules walked across Dan's aim, drawing an annoyed "Hey."

One step inside, Jules checked around and found the switch, throwing it. Lights came on, hanging in loops along the passage. The sound of electricity crackling to life followed, echoing deep into the structure. Like the tunnel below, much of this place had been explored before their arrival, leading Jules to wonder what, exactly, was left to uncover.

"Time to hit another mysterious corridor," Jules said. "Everyone agree there ain't any reason to think there's folk down here waiting?"

Toby came up behind Jules. "Given that they'd have been sitting in darkness for several years already, it's unlikely. Let's tidy up, then get moving."

Once they replaced the fuse box and found a space for the brochure stand, they ventured inside. Dan suggested posting a guard, but Toby said it would be futile.

"Yanovna will overwhelm any of us," he explained, and Jules agreed.

Superior firepower, explosives, desperation. Deadly combination.

"We get what we came for," Jules said. "Plan's never changed since I threw back in with you guys. 'Cept now we're grabbing something to trade for Bridget instead of Toby. More important, we control *it*, so we control *them*. Yeah?"

"Whatever 'it' is," Dan said.

They pulled the door closed and followed the corridor, a

smoothly hewn circle as if extracted by a drill. It curved to the left, as the others had, and brackets sat on the walls with poles sticking out of them—when lit, they would have served as torches.

"A spiral again," Harpal said.

"And steeper." Jules's calf and thigh muscles ached more than they should, a residue of the enormous stresses of the day. A high-protein diet beckoned over the coming weeks.

They plodded on for several minutes, Harpal sweeping ahead, Dan at the rear. With all the features stripped, presumably by Colin and his people, there was little to comment on.

"You never got this far?" Jules asked Toby.

"No. We knew there was more to Habib Masouli's church, and geological surveys suggested more waited beneath, but never something like this. Colin's progress has been remarkable."

The march ended in a hexagonal room, lit from the same supply as the route down. The floor was an even fifty-three-feet wide with each wall appearing flush to the next, the angles as close to uniform as Jules could make out with the naked eye. Polished flagstones, the walls displaying the same smooth, black marble-like finish as the maze. Except for one.

This single expanse was a different shade, a different texture, one that shifted in the light, like a two-tone paint job on an automobile.

Darker than the surrounding surfaces, there were two holes in the walls either side, rectangular gaps which appeared chiseled out and squared off braces made of a metal that wasn't steel, yet hadn't corroded, embedded in the doors' surface. The only other item of note was a circle the size of a manhole cover, its design a relief of a Fibonacci Spiral, linking the two doors, sealing them together like a blob of wax on an envelope.

Jules and Toby examined the seal and the doors, while Harpal and Dan watched the entrance.

There was no second way out.

"A buttress." Toby indicated the rectangular brackets and the corresponding slots in the walls.

"That's what I'm thinking." Jules ran his fingers over the smooth surface, ending at the right side where the end of a bar would have been inserted. "There's damage here. Like it was smashed open. Colin's folk?"

Toby was at the other end. "This was inflicted by non-mechanical instruments. Colin would have used small charges or industrial equipment. They have no problem snaking cables down here."

"True." Jules accessed the parts of his memory associated with medieval battlements, of castles and keeps the world over. "Lairds of Dun. King James the Fourth. That's the late 1400s. They'd have had enough tools to do this. But what about that?"

He approached the seal, the only rough section of the glass-smooth doors. At least, Jules assumed they were doors.

"Yanovna's scroll could only be accessed by someone worthy," Toby said. "Meaning someone genetically attuned to the seal in which it was contained. Back in Masouli's day, it may have been interpreted as commanding objects with God's will."

"And they became priests or whatever," Jules said.

"So, this Habib Masouli was like you?" Dan asked.

"More likely Father Goswelt." Jules traced his finger over the door and around the seal without touching it. "They'd have sent him away instead of keeping him where he could open this."

"But why?" Harpal said. "To open the scroll case when he got to Rome?"

"Nah, I think that was just an excuse. They needed him out of the way. Because whatever's in here was scary to folk back then. Commanding the power of God. That's heavy."

"With the Lairds ransacking the region, King James the Fourth ordered it be secured," Toby said. "Habib Masouli was sent here for that purpose. A respected scholar who had traveled the world before becoming an advisor to the ruling royal family." Toby nodded as if he'd worked out a puzzle. "If an enemy of the Crown could have gained access..."

"So, what do we do now?" Jules said. "We get in, then what?

Risk Yanovna taking it? We already seen she's willing to kill for it. What'll she do when she gets her hands on *the power of God*?"

"Better us than her," Dan said. "I say we ambush them, get Bridget clear, and take down the general and her pit bull captain. Then we let Colin clean this up."

"He'll let us go," Harpal said. "With Charlie and Phil still out there, he knows he can't hold us. Can't charge us without going into what this place is. Dan's right. We turn off these lights, take the bad guys out, walk away."

Jules placed his hands on either side of the spiral seal. "You know I ain't killing her."

"You don't have to," Dan said.

Jules considered his role in this group. They sought non-violent solutions first, but were not averse to it, allowing the deaths of enemies who were trying to murder them, as if they held some sway over the universal scales of right and wrong. Good vs. evil. The needs of the many over the needs of the few.

No one had that right.

Or was that Jules retconning his own phobia into a philosophy? An excuse to avoid confronting fears hardwired into him?

"There's another way," Jules said. "*If* we got all the pieces right, me and Toby understand what all this talk of power and circuits and worthiness means. Right, Toby?"

"A very big 'if' indeed." Toby inhaled, craned his neck back, and stared at the ceiling as he released the breath. "I do not think we have much of a choice." Toby returned his gaze to the three men in the room. "This will be a huge risk, Jules, especially for you."

"I know." Jules prepared to place his hand on the spiral seal. "But I'll trust you this final time."

CHAPTER
SIXTY-TWO

UNDER THE CHURCH OF LISH

Colin's left ear was numb and his right stung with pain from the gun's report. The left side of his neck was damp, so he was fairly sure he'd burst an eardrum on that side. Pain many times that of his right would follow in time.

The general stood over him as he cowered. He'd actually screamed and covered his head, wrapping it in his arms and drawing his legs up to his chest where he screwed himself into a tight ball, assessing whether he'd died.

After he ascertained he was not dead, his muscles relaxed and even a guff of nervous laughter escaped him. But the woman was not done yet.

"The next bullet goes in your knee." Her voice warbled as if filtered through a fish tank. "These are decoys. Meant to buy you time. Your frigate is less than thirty minutes away. I will play no more."

The only time Colin had been shot was with a .22 round during a firearms familiarization exercise on Bodmin Moor with a group from the SAS. He'd been one of a party of civil servants who might have expected—in rare, completely unlikely circumstances—to face a gun. That session had ended when a young upstart ignored the instructions on the safety aspects of checking the chamber before attempting to put the firearm into a holster, and the gun had gone off. The bullet had ricocheted and burrowed through the fleshy part of Colin's thigh, leaving a scar that intensified when he tanned.

While the youngster was relegated to desk analyst duty, Colin now faced the prospect of repeating the single most painful moment of his life, although he suspected the kneecap would be far worse than either the thigh or a ruptured eardrum.

"Madam." Colin propped himself on his elbow. "I do not know what you are talking about. We keep these here safely. You have destroyed something none of us fully comprehends—"

Yanovna pressed the barrel of her pistol onto Colin's knee. It was hot, burning through the wool-cotton blend to his skin. He yelped and lay back, trying to calculate how much time it would take Toby to work out where Colin had hidden the circular symbol, to get to the vault, and to retrieve what it contained. If Toby had half a brain, he would run with it. But there was one wildcard: Toby's Alabama princess.

Colin must have been looking at Bridget Carson because Yanovna turned to the girl and signaled her forward from the group of men gathered by the far wall.

"No, wait," Colin said. "There's no need for this sort of tactic. I can show you a way in. Another chamber. Something we haven't been able to excavate. But this place had more of interest. The tablets. The other has nothing. Yes, I can show you, just… let's not be rash with our… persuasion techniques, hmm?"

"Bridget." Yanovna removed the barrel from Colin's knee and transferred her aim to the girl. "You have a pretty face and an impressive brain. A fine catch for many men." To Colin, she said, "In the old country, the Soviets used many *persuasion techniques* to coerce men into cooperation. Including the threat of violence against women. For some reason, the prettier the woman, the more worthy she was of a man saving her through capitulation. I never understood that. As if an ugly woman has less value." She shook her head. "We still have a very male society in my country, though, no matter my own accomplishments... no matter I was once considered as fetching as Bridget. I swore I would not do that. Ever. To use a woman to make a man compliant is cowardly and does *nothing*... except break that woman or make her far stronger than her torturer. More likely to survive the future."

Colin sensed she was speaking from experience but held his tongue. He could not predict where this was heading. At least with the increasing pain from his left ear, his right could hear properly again as Yanovna continued.

"I also believe you value your Crown's sovereignty and reputation ahead of the wellbeing of such a lovely thing, so perhaps today, I reverse the scenario and appeal to the tender heart of this young woman."

Yanovna pressed the gun into Colin's knee, harder this time, forcing it, and him, flat to the floor. He found himself in an oddly stressful position, the pressure on his hip and knee causing him to whimper.

"I don't think he knows anymore," Bridget said. "If this isn't the right place, I can help work out the supposedly blank one. Please, just give me a chance."

"This is exactly what I am thinking. Denis." Yanovna twitched her head to the captain.

Igoravich directed the Ukrainian mercenary toward the trio which Colin understood to be the crew who'd brought Toby from Norway, and Garrett, who seemed to direct a seething anger at Colin as much as their captors. The mercenary took out plastic snap ties to bind the men. The crew and Garrett complied silently.

Yanovna grabbed Colin by one lapel and forced him to his feet. "Show us the real entrance. You could not figure out how to retrieve the true contents of this place, but *she* might. If she does not, I will pull you apart one piece at a time."

Igoravich accompanied Bridget to the ladder and climbed up first, then covered her with the gun while she followed.

As Colin placed one foot on the first rung and both hands on the sides, Yanovna pressed herself against his back, pulling him tightly to her. He gripped the ladder as if it would save him.

In his ear, she whispered, "There are many things I wish I did not have to do. But I grow angry at you. I feel you are endangering me, and my country's freedom with your stalling. I will enjoy seeing you punished if you lie again."

She released him, and Colin made the decision right there and then. As he ascended, he concluded this level of valor was not for him. He would show her the fuse box, the entry to the hexagonal cavern below, and pray that Toby and his ragamuffin outfit worked things out in time. If not, Colin had no idea what the consequences would be, but he suspected losing his job—or a bullet to the kneecap—would pale in comparison.

CHAPTER
SIXTY-THREE

Bridget grew dizzy as the gift shop's wall cracked open and the corridor lay bare before them. She found her steps slow, jerking faintly as she set off at Yanovna's command, and she tensed to ease the hammering in her chest as the modern spotlights burst on in quick succession. Colin really had cooperated.

Since leaving the hole, which Bridget had guessed was a decoy, she'd been hoping Colin might pull another trick from up his sleeve. A room full of Marines waiting for them, perhaps. But no—this had to be the real destination.

With the mercenary guarding the other site and the hostages, it was just the four of them now.

"What is it?" Yanovna asked as they coiled through the passage. "Down there? What is it?"

"We thought it was a vault," Colin said. "Looks like a door but can't be shifted. Nothing touches the surface—it's like power tools skim off it, and the small explosive charges we have attempted, just... *poof*." He splayed his fingers to demonstrate. "It easily repels anything we try. We were going to dig from the other side, but it's difficult to get permission and funds. The National Trust has a surprisingly long reach when it comes to excavations around its properties."

"You scanned it, I assume?"

"Radar, sonic pulses, yes. But it appears solid. Like there's nothing behind that part of the vault."

Bridget tensed. She wanted to beat Colin, slap him, yell at him to shut up, just shut up! It seemed he had resigned himself to this defeat.

She hoped Jules had been there already and done what he does—liberated something from a person who shouldn't have it. And if Colin couldn't look after it, surely it was better off in the hands of LORI.

That brought a faint smile. "We still didn't know what 'it' is, do we?"

"We will find out soon," Yanovna said.

"Aren't you going to be disappointed if it turns out to be just a book?"

Yanovna stared ahead, the end of the passageway upon them. "Why are you so certain it is not a weapon?"

"A book. A weapon. Is that the breadth of our imagination?" Bridget wracked her brain for words of discouragement. "Probably another ceremonial scythe."

They arrived at an entrance that opened out into a wider room. Before entering, Igoravich checked it out.

"Empty," the captain reported on his return.

They entered. The hexagonal cavern was deserted, shaped like something from a low budget sci-fi film's interior, offering nowhere for that room full of marines or SAS to hide.

"How can you be so certain?" Yanovna asked.

Bridget shrugged. "How can *you*?" She turned a full circle, giddy inside, aching to explore, despite the walls being blank. "The texts all talk about cycles, completing circles. Why can't this simply be about farming? Instructions on how to get through the winters? It's all on high ground, places they'd have to live if the world flooded. The circle of life. But you only want death."

"For my enemies," Yanovna said. "Is that so wrong?"

They crossed to the only feature of interest, what appeared to be two closed doors with a spiral pattern inlaid on the join.

Yanovna pointed at the design. "What is this? Have you seen it before?"

"It's like a shell," Colin said. "A Fibonacci Spiral. But beyond that—"

"I was talking to your savior, not you." Yanovna beckoned Bridget forward. "And she can only be your savior if she helps me open this."

Colin shook his head. "It doesn't open, I told you—"

"*Igoravich.*"

The captain threw a fist into Colin's solar plexus, doubling him over and dropping him to the flagstone floor.

"Do I just touch it?" The general pressed her bare hand flat to the pattern that Bridget assumed to be a seal of sorts. Nothing happened.

Bridget just stared at her.

"I will kill him. Slowly." Yanovna again pointed her gun at Colin.

Bridget switched her gaze to the seal, tracing the pattern with her own finger from the outside in. "My expertise is in language. I don't know if—"

"It is the only item here," Yanovna said. "You call these people Witnesses. They speak to us from the distant past. This might not look like writing. But it must *say* something."

Back in Striovia, Bridget hurt Jules's feelings by playing the same game Toby did, believing Jules would do the thing she expected him to without question. He'd been a thief in his former life, after all. She hadn't banked on him holding such strong ethics, such robust feelings about origins and who had the right to own objects from antiquity. He told them he got a kick out of stealing from assholes, but Bridget never stopped to think if there was more to his actions than that.

This lifecycle symbol, this circuit, this instruction... whatever it was... it did not belong to Yanovna. She shouldn't possess it.

"Trace the line." Bridget demonstrated from the outer line. "It's the path we've followed so many times to get here."

Yanovna put her finger on the groove, starting on the outside, then her hand, the design big enough to accommodate her palm at the beginning. She swiped inward, following the path, her hand narrowing to fingers, leaving behind a dull green glow. It reminded Bridget of running a hand through water full of bioluminescent algae.

In the center, Yanovna reduced her contact to a single finger, the light following her until she stopped.

"Press it," Bridget said. "Just a guess, but..."

Yanovna pressed with her finger and the double doors cracked down the middle like an elevator, bright light spilling forth.

They didn't slide apart, but opened in on themselves, lighting the inside through a series of mirrors angled upward. The mirror in the center was a convex ball, a shaft from above evidently the light source, like a laser fired at the glass.

That was all it appeared to contain. Spectacular, but no weapon.

"There's your orb," Bridget said.

Yanovna's mouth fell open, as did Igoravich's and Colin's.

Hunched and suffering from the punch, Colin was somehow the first to step inside and check the shaft.

"Sunlight," he said, wheezing. "Down a mirrored tube. It's... genius." He stroked his hand over the ball in the middle of the hexagonal funhouse room—the orb Bridget mentioned. His voice came out as a gasp. "It isn't glass. Some sort of... metal."

As the dazzling effect wore off and Bridget acclimatized to the sight, she saw the mirror ball sat on top of a wide plinth carved into two hands, which cupped the whole object. Below that, on a miniature altar-type frame, sat a miniature sculpture of the hands, large enough for a basketball.

Empty.

"There is something missing." Yanovna's jaw clenched as she

approached the smaller hands, nostrils flaring. "They have taken it!"

"Too late," Bridget said.

Colin was smiling, too. "This vault may have been designed to keep grubby hands like Toby's off the contents, but I suppose he must have beaten us to it."

"He was trapped underground." Yanovna turned to the pair, teeth bare, fury burning. In one hand, she gripped the gun, the other balled into a fist. "How would he…?"

Her shoulders were high, and she breathed quickly, attempting to calm, seemingly unable to think clearly through her anger.

"Then you are both useless to me." She glanced at Igoravich. "Kill them."

CHAPTER
SIXTY-FOUR

"Wait, wait, wait, wait!" Colin pleaded, making Yanovna hate the worm even more. "I can help you get it back, I swear."

Igoravich leveled his gun at the man's head an appropriate distance away. "Is lying."

"You have killed my country." Yanovna held her own weapon on Bridget. "We are defenseless. Russia will descend, and… it is the end."

Igoravich waited for the final order. "General?"

Yanovna's whole body felt as if someone had reached in and removed every organ, every bone, every ounce of blood, all she'd worked for… everything she'd sat back on and enjoyed, assuming the government above her would protect them all while she pursued her passions. She deserved to retire. She deserved to die a free woman, not forced under the boot of a foreign power.

"I will use the girl to vacate these waters," Yanovna said. "We have failed. But I have no more use for the Englishman."

Colin screwed his eyes closed, hands out before him, leaning away as if that fraction of a second of additional life would mean something. He said, "Anytime now would be excellent."

Yanovna asked, "What did you say?"

The clunk sounded.

Yanovna and Igoravich whirled to the vault. No way should anything be free in there. No person. All she saw was her own reflection.

Her own reflection… with the surrounding area expanding—

No.

The mirror—the highly polished metallic sheet—rushed closer!

It rammed into her and she tumbled backward. A man leaped out from behind. *Two* men—those from Toby's group, Harpal Singh and the blond killer with the beard, Dan Vincent.

Bridget tipped her head back and let out a half-*whoop* sound. "Dan, you're here!"

Harpal was holding the reflective panel while Dan trained a submachine gun on Igoravich. Yanovna squeezed out from under the sheet, which was lighter than it looked, but had lost her weapon in the attack.

"Good timing, my man." Colin exhaled in relief.

Igoravich kept his gun on Colin.

"Rules of engagement?" Dan asked.

Colin frowned, aiming an element of steel into his glare. "They were going to murder us in cold blood. Kill them, and I promise I'll take care of any resulting red tape."

"No!" Another member of the group—Jules, the one who was like Yanovna—sprang from the depths of the vault. "Please don't."

Yanovna now understood how it worked. The reflective panels were not secure, and the three men had hidden behind them. They'd been down there the whole time, waiting.

Jules stepped toward Dan. "They're beaten. No need for killing."

"Jules, they really were going to kill us," Bridget said.

"I know. But this ain't right. Look, I already been a part of death in the past. I figured it was like vegans in a burger bar, y'know? 'You go ahead, but it ain't for me.' But I wanna be better than that. If you gotta kill, Dan, like *really* gotta, I can't stop it. I'll look for another way, but… I always thought it was 'cause killing leaves people to grieve. Makes the law come after you."

Yanovna spotted her fallen weapon. Too far to dive for it. Yet.

"Bridget, I… that job I wanna apply for, I can't be a part of an international incident. I need to be clean."

"What is this job?" Bridget asked.

"A cop. I was applying to be a *cop*, okay? After the crap they put me through, slacking off on my mom's bangle after they caught the killers… I figured I got the skills and brains for it. Juvie record aside, I'm okay so far as I know. But here we are, with this… unbelievable substance." He touched the door's exterior. "Nothing gets through this. Imagine making a vest out of it. It's like… it's like it absorbs kinetic energy and repels it. Some other branch of science, like the rocks repelling seawater. And we're here pointing guns at each other."

The young man's speech came from somewhere other than the real world, but it was working for Yanovna. Everyone's attention held on him.

"I don't know if it makes any sense logically—heck, I know it don't." Jules's shoulders sagged. "But I'm tired. I saw those sailors die. I saw Striovian soldiers die. I saw these Ukrainians go the same way. All for what?" He swept his arm to the vault. "For an empty room that we don't know what to do with."

Now everyone was holding on Jules, and Yanovna's almost imperceptibly small movements had brought her within lunging distance of her gun.

"I can't stop you killing anyone," Jules said, addressing Dan directly. "But I'm asking you. Man to man. Let's just try and send this through the right channels."

Dan firmed his grip and told Igoravich, "Drop the gun. Kick it over here. We'll wait for the cavalry to arrest you."

Igoravich lowered himself at the knees, placed his weapon on the ground, and slid it over.

Dan caught it under his foot.

And Yanovna dove for her gun.

Dan twitched to the side. "What—"

Bridget flung herself at Yanovna. "No!"

The redhead tackled Yanovna at the waist, inches from the gun. The general swung an elbow, connecting, rolling with her, while Harpal approached.

But Igoravich took advantage of the moment, and leaped from his crouch, flinging himself into Dan Vincent. The gun went off, firing into the ceiling, then fell from his grip as Igoravich laid into him.

The fight was on.

Jules moved to intervene, but Dan yelled it was all right. He'd got this. Perhaps it was the injury that made him feel less macho, incapacitated, or somehow not a complete man. Whatever crap motivated the hand-to-hand matchup, at least guns were out of the way.

"I fight for those you murdered," Igoravich said.

Dan jabbed a fist in the man's mouth and jigged like a boxer, the plastic boot seemingly no hindrance. "Quit yapping."

On the ground, Bridget had subdued Yanovna with help from Harpal, pinning her arms behind her, with none of them able to reach her gun.

Igoravich carried a lot of bulk for an older man, in great shape, but in his own peak form, Dan should have taken him. Except this wasn't peak form. His boxer jig resulted from his sprained ankle rather than any fighting technique, which would soon be obvious to his opponent. Since Jules was exhausted from the physical strain of the dive, and the oxygen deprivation, Dan must've been operating on fumes.

Igoravich attempted a jab, then a haymaker, which Dan easily ducked, except... the haymaker was a feint, and the captain lashed out with his foot at Dan's standing leg, making him drop his weight to his bad ankle.

Dan shouted something indecipherable and hopped back to the first leg.

Igoravich grinned. "Lame horse against a bull. Easy."

The Striovian then concentrated on keeping Dan off balance—a brute force flurry of punches and kicks, one after the other, some of which Dan took in muscles more than capable of it, while others he blocked. A few bloodied his head. He replied with some slugs of his own, but the foot really hampered him, so much that it was over in under a minute.

Igoravich went in low, a snap kick at Dan's groin, which missed, but made him defend that region before a forearm smashed him in the cheekbone. An open hand to the throat sent him reeling, and—unable to focus or balance—an almighty kick to the jaw from Igoravich dropped Dan hard.

Bridget left Yanovna to Harpal, running to Dan's side. Jules could see he was conscious, but only just.

"Mind if I try now?" Jules said.

Igoravich stretched his neck from side to side—a tough guy gesture. Then he took up a loose fighting stance as he had with Dan. "You the scaredy cat, huh? Not kill."

"I prefer not to. It's impractical." Jules strolled the space, keeping Igoravich in front of him. "Keeps people from trying to put me in jail. Plus, there's always a brother or son, father or mother, wanting revenge. Like you and your friends who got buried or shot. And I bet you each of them Navy guys got pals on the boat coming our way who'll drop you on sight."

Igoravich came in with a flurry of feint punches, then went in for a real one. Jules sidestepped, pivoted, and nudged the man's hip. Igoravich flew onward instead of connecting. Jules had barely shifted position.

Igoravich composed himself and rolled his shoulders, ready for another round.

"Even if you got asylum here," Jules said, "these folks' families will finish you on sight. Ain't no coming back from that."

Igoravich remained calm but was still using his aggression, his strength to throw those punches, which Jules evaded with ease, hands behind his back all the way. When one blow came close, Jules ceased dancing and caught the swing; he continued the man's kinetic force, and dropped his weight, turning the arm back on itself. It lifted the captain as if he was as light as air. Releasing him left the soldier in a heap.

Jules scurried back to prevent a sweep. "I don't kill 'cause of many reasons. Call it philosophy, call it self-preservation, call it fear. But ultimately, it comes down to one simple thing."

Igoravich flipped to his feet and charged, pulling up short of a full-on bull-rage assault. He was trained well enough to resist that. But he swung harder. Faster. With more options, more variations, different combos.

Where he could, Jules stayed out of the way. Where he couldn't, he eased himself into the right position, then shoved Igoravich in the direction of his attack.

"When you understand an opponent," Jules said, "you can use their own strength against them. No one is unbeatable. No one is infallible. But if you work at it and put in the effort..."

Igoravich's uppercut came close, and it was now Jules stepped back into his arcing swing, caught it at the shoulder, and trapped him in position.

"If I had more energy," Jules said, his face inches from Igoravich, "I'd explain it better. But basically, you put in the effort, there ain't no enemy you can't stop without resorting to killing 'em."

He twisted Igoravich's arm, yanked down hard with his whole body weight, and a *pop* sounded. Igoravich yelled in agony as his shoulder wrenched from its socket. Jules let go, and the man fell to the floor, kicking out at Jules as he scrabbled around, his free arm thrashing.

"You might even make a full recovery." Jules glanced between Igoravich and the groggy-but-conscious Dan. "But right now, you're incapacitated, and I'm happy you're alive."

"But you will not be," Yanovna said.

Harpal lay at her feet, her knee in his back and her gun pointed at Jules.

"You send Toby away with my prize," she continued, finger tightening. "Condemn me to failure. If you'd killed me earlier, I would not be able to shoot you now."

Igoravich spat blood. "Still think there is always other way?"

"Yes." Jules nodded slowly. "When we can bargain."

Yanovna had him cold, but hesitated.

"You ain't a bad person," Jules said. "Just freaked out about losing something more valuable than life. More valuable than the lives you've taken. 'Least, the way you see it. I got another perspective."

"What is that?"

"That you ain't killed me yet. So there's hope. You don't like cold-blooded killing."

"Does not mean I refuse to do it."

"No. But I can buy your soul." Jules snapped his fingers. "Toby ain't gone."

Toby exited the room from his nook behind the nearest mirror. He was holding a ball in both hands. The same color as the door at first, but swirling, changing to a pearl, then graying to black.

"Give it to me," Yanovna said. "Or your friend—"

"That's actually the plan," Jules said. "We *want* you to have it."

CHAPTER
SIXTY-FIVE

Jules's plan to cold-cock the pair went south when Yanovna decided to off Colin. That, and the fact Colin's angle allowed him to spot Toby in his hiding place and announce it to the room. The group had to improvise and was ready to surrender when Dan and Harpal made their play, leading to that testosterone fest in the chamber.

They'd opened the door by tracing the Fibonacci Spiral from the outside in, then found the sphere. An *orb* to match the scythe located in Canada. When they waited instead of running, they turned off the lights and listened until they heard people approaching, then hid inside the sunlit room to wait, knowing they'd get the door open eventually.

"It does nothing, unfortunately." Toby extended his arm, offering the orb to Jules.

About two-thirds the size of a basketball, it weighed less too. As with the mirrors, it felt like metal, but looked like glass. The big difference was the colors, which swirled and changed when the sphere shifted, adding to Jules's theory about kinetic energy.

Jules held out his hands.

"No." Yanovna moved off Harpal and everyone froze as she

advanced on Toby, taking a long route to keep away from anyone who might rush her.

"You can have it," Jules said. "You win. I'd rather you have it than anyone else dies."

Dan had regained his senses, battered as he was, shifting his weight off Bridget, who kept her arm around him.

Igoravich lay still, having found a position where his shoulder hurt the least.

Jules simply watched.

He watched Yanovna stand close to Toby.

Watched Toby gaze up at her.

Then, he watched Bridget's mouth moving as if speaking with someone unseen, and followed Yanovna reaching her bare hand to the orb.

"The circuit reveals it," Bridget said.

Yanovna halted, gun on Jules, eyes on Bridget. "What is that?"

"*United,* the circuits—*plural*—reveal the power of the god. *That* was the nuance I couldn't see before." Bridget stared at nothing, as she was seeing some language, some words no one else could, embedded in her mind the way images did for Jules. "That ball is not *the* circuit. It's *part* of a circuit. But it contains power." She looked at Yanovna, her words reaching deep into Jules, stirring a series of synapses, of links, of conclusions. "You were right all along, General. Not intended as a weapon, though. It was there as part of something bigger. The map in Canada, it pointed to more than just there. It went east, west, south. *That's* the circuit. Their god was linked to harvest, to survival, to *life.*"

"No," Jules said. "Their god was the cycle. *To* god. Not a name or a being, but more like a verb. Change 'god' to a verb. To cycle, to *enact* a cycle, to *act* as a god… the sun, the rain, the crops. If *the* united *power of the* circuits *reveals the* cycle..." Jules's head spun. To Yanovna, he said, "Touch it. Seriously. It don't do squat."

Yanovna landed her hand on the orb and pulled it back. Nothing. She placed her palm flat on the surface while Toby kept hold of it.

"How?" she said.

"Like Bridget said," Jules replied, "it's part of something bigger. A cog in a wheel. *United.* Meaning they had a bigger plan."

"Like what?" The general sounded angry now.

"Like bringing farming to the other humans who weren't quite as smart as the Witnesses. The power of God. Of *a* god. The power of the *cycle.* What would you need to bring farming to the masses?"

Yanovna scooped the orb from Toby's arms.

Dan heaved himself to his feet—well, his foot, leaning on the wall.

Bridget rose beside him.

Harpal stood, too.

Colin moved behind Toby.

Finally, Igoravich pushed up off the floor, a lopsided gait in which he was clearly in pain.

"It was intended to bring an end to the Ice Age." Toby had cottoned on to what Jules was getting at. "They worked out how to reflect the sun's rays more intensely, to generate some warming event. Like a greenhouse effect."

"Nonsense..." But Yanovna's mind worked as quickly as Toby's. She glanced at Bridget. "You... you said *this* was the circuit."

"One of many," Bridget said. "United. I haven't worked out the language fully. Uniting one circuit or uniting the circuits—plural. Maybe more than one has to be united. Linked. And no one person can activate one orb."

"We gotta work it together," Jules said. "Like this."

His arm shot out and the sphere vibrated, as his mom's bangle had done, only more intense.

The colors spun within, floating, finding the points of contact, coalescing near the hands.

Yanovna pointed her gun at Jules, the orb in one hand. "What are you doing?"

"You wanna activate this properly?" Jules felt pressure

building in his head, like diving deep. "Wanna see if you can use it as a weapon?"

"Yes, of course!" She emphasized the gun.

"Then let go of the weapon in that hand and concentrate on what you got in the other."

Yanovna's creased face suggested she felt the pressure build-up too.

"Let go of the gun," Jules said. "Two hands on the orb."

"Why?"

"It's a damn *circuit*."

Yanovna flipped on the safety and tossed the gun to Igoravich, then touched the orb with her other hand too.

Instantly, both sets of her fingers sank into the surface. Jules's one hand remained free, but the vibration strengthened, a buzzing now audible while the sheer pounding in his head rolled like thunder.

"We should leave," Colin said.

"Not without Jules." Toby staggered back, meeting Dan and Bridget.

"*Everyone move!*" Jules shouted.

Yanovna screamed, her hands almost absorbed by the ball, the colors spreading to her skin. "*I can't let go.*"

The glow brightened.

"In the vault," Jules said. "Go!"

All gathered together.

All except Igoravich, who watched aghast. "I stay."

"In the *vault*," Jules repeated.

"What are you doing?" Bridget cried over the louder buzzing, deepening to a growl.

Jules focused on her. "Trust me, okay?"

She nodded and helped Dan move alongside Harpal.

The orb's vibration spread up Jules's arm and along his shoulder, painful now.

"We can't seal it," Toby said.

"Don't matter, just go," Jules said. "I need to do it."

Yanovna couldn't speak now, her forearm the color of pearl. Fear, pain, Jules couldn't tell. But he had to do one simple thing.

The team made it inside the mirrored vault, the door closing.

Yanovna screamed, blood coughing forth.

She can't handle it. She's dying.

Jules eyed the two doors meeting, a line of light down the middle. He'd hoped to seal it with his touch, but there was no time. General Yanovna was about to die because of him, and he could not allow that.

He brought his free hand down onto the frenzied orb.

Closing the circuit.

It shut off, fell dark, and ceased vibrating.

The relief in Yanovna's face was unmistakable, and her hands slowly disengaged from the absorption of the sphere. Maintaining contact, she panted desperately.

Igoravich laughed. "Why you lock friends in vault?"

"Honestly?" Jules's hands remained on the orb. "I kinda thought something else was gonna happ—"

WHAM.

As soon as the orb returned to normal, with Yanovna's hands touching it the same as Jules's, a concussive wave exploded outward. The sheer force knocked Jules off his feet, blasted through his head, and dropped him on his back.

He remained conscious enough to see Yanovna and Igoravich suffered the same. He saw the orb hang in the air for a second longer than gravity would normally allow. Then it clanked to the ground.

And darkness slid over Jules, carrying him away from the chamber under the Church of Lish.

CHAPTER
SIXTY-SIX

AN INDETERMINATE TIME LATER...

Jules awoke in daylight. His last memory was of the almighty thump in his chest and the pressure released from his head, and the blinding flash from the orb.

Had the explosion blown away the church?

No, a blast that powerful would've torn his body apart, too.

And anyway, it was early evening in late summer in northern Britain. For him to have been rescued, carried outside, and revived would have taken the day darker, not brighter.

And his back was wet.

His limbs creaked stiffly as he attempted to move.

"He's awake." Dan's voice.

Hands upon him, easing him upright.

A bottle reached his lips, and he drank the water.

Two gulps… three.

Jules's head pounded, the light exacerbating the roll and pitch of his brain inside his skull. "Man, what the—"

A surge from his gut cut him off, racing up his throat. He waved off the helping hands and lunged aside, vomiting first the water, then a thick bile. His stomach must have been all but empty.

Knocked unconscious.

Agonizing headache.

Triggered by vomit reflux.

Jules had a concussion. Hopefully not a serious one.

He took the water again and sipped—dainty, tiny drops that didn't trigger a gag reflex. When he was satisfied it wouldn't go anywhere, he lay back down on the dewy grass, the hill elevating his shoulders. He twisted to the side, his eyes slits.

Toby, Bridget, Harpal, and Dan surrounded him.

Bridget shook his arm. "Are you with us? Can you hear me?"

"Yeah..." The vibration of his voice box reverberated around his head. "What... happened?"

"We're not entirely sure." Toby came and kneeled beside him. "We woke up a few hours ago. It was still dark."

Jules forced his eyes to open and blinked away the fug. The fug regrouped and descended quickly, but not before he established two things: first, they were on a grassy bank at the base of the hill on which the church stood, intact; second, the sun sat low in the sky over the ocean.

The ocean is east.

Sunrise.

That's around six-thirty a.m. in this part of the world. At this time of year.

"I was out all night?"

"We all were," Harpal said. "Woke up here. I checked the church. It's empty. No bad guys, no good guys, no... semi-bad guys."

Jules understood who he meant. "Colin's gone too?"

"I was left with this. Unlocked." Toby held up a large-screened Android smartphone with no brand name. He activated it and Jules could tell it was a high-end screen. "There was a message from an anonymous number telling us to stay put."

A helicopter approached from the south.

Jules lay on his back, unable to focus. "Anyone tell if that's a friendly or we gotta run again? If it's running, someone's gotta carry me."

"Isn't military," Dan said.

Jules checked on Dan; he'd taken a beating, but other than bruises and cuts, he appeared to be sitting up fine.

"That don't make it friendly," Jules said.

"So… what was that thing?" Harpal asked.

"The orb? Hell if I know."

"You figured out how to activate it," Bridget said. "But couldn't be sure it wouldn't kill you?"

"Or the bad guys," Dan said, pointedly.

At the time, Jules only had seconds to reflect on that possibility. "I had no idea what it'd do. I just reworked our priorities in my head. Then it… got complicated."

"Complicated, how?" Toby asked.

"I didn't know how two people would affect it. Bridget worked out it's part of a wider network, but you also need to activate the individual component. Power. Energy. Playing God. I couldn't take the chance on them getting it home and starting some huge war, some scramble for more items. If I died, if they did, it wasn't intentional. It'd have been an accident. And I'd have had to live with that."

The helicopter could be heard now. Waves still crashed on the shore, and a breeze picked up.

"Y'know," Dan said, "you wanna be a cop, you might have to kill someone. With a gun."

"Yeah." Jules managed to sit upright. To keep himself from wobbling, he hugged his knees. "I might shelve that idea for a while."

The four shuffled forward and surrounded him. They knew he wasn't a big hugger, and he appreciated them keeping their affection to themselves. Instead, they shared the view.

"Charlie," Jules said.

Bridget faced him. "Sorry?"

"Ten bucks, that's Charlie in the helicopter."

No one responded, just watched the transport grow larger, less than half a mile away.

Dan patted his pockets as if about to accept the bet, when the phone rang. Everyone stared at it in Toby's hand.

"Gonna answer that?" Jules asked.

Toby's thumb hovered over the on-screen slider. "I'm not sure I should."

"If was a bomb, they could've triggered it anytime. Tracker too."

"Okay." Toby slid the icon to answer mode and tapped the speaker so all could hear. "Hello?"

A digitized voice said, "Toby, great to see you up and about."

"Hello, Colin."

"I can neither confirm nor deny my identity, but suffice it to say things are back to business as usual at this end. I understand you and your third-rate treasure hunters are still alive?"

Toby smiled. "I cannot confirm or deny that."

A brief digital laugh replied. "Very well. I suppose you are wondering about your status?"

"Are you going to tell me?"

"It's the least I can do, old chap. I mean, I can't go into anything too deeply, but let's just say the captain of the frigate charged with investigating my disappearance prioritized a foreign incursion, seeking a weapon of mass destruction over some ragamuffin amateur archaeologists. That's *prioritized*. Not *forgotten about* if you get my meaning."

"I think I do."

"Then you'll be pleased to know everyone in the second chamber has recovered nicely and returned to their vessels. And we have arrested the foreign nationals discovered with them. General Yanovna and her friend woke up several hours later—just now, in fact."

"Which is what prompted this call, I assume," Toby said. "Are they well?"

"Something of a giant hangover, but their vitals are fine. I trust your boy is conscious again?"

"Boy?" Jules said.

Colin had also used the term when they'd first met and appeared ignorant of its pejorative use in the States, making no apologies. "Good, good. We'll be swinging back around once we secure the two spies, and we will arrest anyone without a valid visa, then turn them over to immigration. Hopefully, your papers will all be in order, and we can avoid an uncomfortable scene."

"Yeah, we'll be cool." Jules knew they should hang up. The helicopter was almost with them, an extraction run between Charlie and Phil, ignored by Colin, who could easily have stopped or intercepted it. "What was it? The orb?"

The line was open, but no one spoke.

The chopper circled, likely seeking even ground, the hill being too steep.

"We do not know," digital Colin replied. "As far as I can tell, it was an EMP-type assault that left buildings intact but short-circuited anything with an electrical signal. Including a few synapses. Anyone locked inside the shielded room would have been fine, but those in the vicinity were rendered unconscious."

"But the doors didn't close properly," Jules said.

"Meaning we got zapped," Bridget said. "Just not as bad as everybody stood next to it."

"That appears correct." The digital voice was harder to hear as the helicopter landed a hundred yards away. "I assume you have a lift waiting?"

"What happens to the orb now?" Jules asked.

Toby bowed his head. "You have it, Colin, don't you? What are you planning?"

"Hmm, well, that's the thing. It's a powerful object that we have scant hope of understanding. I think it might be better if it remains lost a short while longer. At least, until we can gather more information on it. Then, when we need assistance in the form of a… person with the right *touch*… perhaps we'll call on you again."

All looked at Jules.

"You want me to wait by the phone?" Jules said. "And leave you to pick up where we left it?"

"You'll be involved, young man. But Toby, you and your friends should stay away. If you can be of service, we will call. If not, we are in a much better position to handle this."

Jules couldn't be sure if the tightening in his stomach stemmed from the concussion or the orders coming out of the phone. He wanted to throw the handset over the cliff and call Colin several unkind names. "Sure," he said. "We'll hang back. Course we will."

The helicopter door opened and Charlie Locke climbed out of the back, a night in the hospital evidently allowing her to move under her own steam. She strode toward them, hair tousled by the rotors, not running, slightly bent where her injury was still troubling her.

"We didn't shake on it," Dan said.

"Goodbye, Toby," the digitized Colin said. "And please, don't let that be sarcasm I heard from your... rather talented young colleague." He hung up.

Charlie made it up the rise, pale but healthier than the last time they'd seen her. "I hope you had a good nap."

"I've had better nights," Jules said.

All but Jules stood and hugged Charlie in turn.

"Let's get out of here." Dan hobbled toward the landing zone.

"Not on your nelly," Charlie said. When the rest of them turned to look at her, she elaborated. "I'm not going anywhere until I see what you found."

And she tramped on up the hill. "We've got about half an hour. Come on."

Jules offered his hand to Harpal, who heaved him upright.

"I saw a wheelchair in the gift shop," Bridget said.

Jules could barely lift his eyes, but after what Colin said, his orders to keep their distance, Jules's fourteen-year-old rebellious self who took no crap and listened to no one reared his head.

No way was he standing back. No way was he going to let

Colin beat him to the places the Witnesses touched and designed. They made these items for people like him, for those who could understand and reveal the secrets.

Not *secrets*.

Secrets were meant to be kept. These were teachings, things people were supposed to discover, supposed to find out. Maybe even use. The only question was whether he went it alone or stuck around Toby and Bridget and the others.

He stared at his hands as he leaned on Harpal for support. "Definitely putting that cop thing on hold a while."

CHÂTEAU CACHÉ, BRITTANY, FRANCE

Jules remained in the care of a private physician for three days, provided courtesy of Bridget's EU citizenship and her parents' money. He came by twice a day to monitor Jules's vitals and ordered someone to wake him in the middle of the night to be sure he could be roused. The concussion wasn't as severe as feared, so Jules was able to function normally with frequent rests, although the near-continuous worrying from Bridget and the butch-but-concerned check-ins from Dan grated on him after the first day.

Dan... who had his own injuries to nurse. To his credit, Jules only curled his toes in annoyance when wearing slippers or shoes and set a series of different smiles on rotation so they didn't appear false.

Objectively, he should be grateful, understanding he needed people on hand if he suffered a greater injury. He hadn't been for an MRI after all. Plus, they were being nice, and hurting their feelings served no purpose beyond venting his own frustration.

Tact. He was learning tact.

Upon their initial return, the housekeeper, Margarete, spoke at length with Bridget, who came clean with the group about how she'd let Prihya in due to her worry over Bridget's safety. Margarete offered to quit, but Bridget had none of it. The older lady often railed against them bringing home pagan items and heretical texts to examine, but ultimately, her concern was for the welfare of the young woman who lived under her care. Jules learned that Margarete had once served as a part-time nanny to Bridget during long summers there, so it was understandable she'd grasp at anything that provided hope when Bridget disappeared for days on end.

Bridget agreed to keep her better informed as to her welfare in the future.

Luther's death had reminded them all of the dangers they faced in ancient and unstable places, and in competing for those discoveries. Shortly after returning to Brittany, the whole team had gathered to place a video call to his children and ex-wife, regaling them with the man's bravery, and how it had saved many lives. The kids cried. The ex-wife cried. Toby and Bridget shed a few, too.

It was as much as they could do for the family.

In the days that followed, Toby and Harpal mostly kept their distance from Jules, working out new security measures, while Bridget—when not tending to Jules—pored over the books they had retrieved earlier that year, and compared the new writings she remembered and which Jules had sketched out for her. There wasn't much in terms of a Rosetta Stone to help decode it, but she made a little progress. She was waiting for Charlie to return before discussing it fully.

With Charlie on bedrest for the first 48 hours herself, she had remained in Greenwich, London, where her husband and kids could feed her soup, bring her magazines, and basically lock her away from the outside world. There was plenty she could do from there, though.

Over an internet connection, and with Jules's memory combining with her own examination of the mirrored room, they produced a working 3-D model. On the third day, she was released from captivity and able to travel to Brittany.

Except she was not alone.

Two girls and a boy galloped into the château ahead of their mother, seemingly familiar with the surroundings and the people, hugging "Uncle" Dan, "Uncle" Harpal, "Auntie Bridget" and "Poppa Toby." Jules hung back, leaning out from a lounge, watching. A model-good-looking man pushed himself in, seated in a customized wheelchair, his handsome stubble and floppy hair reminding Jules of the character of Sawyer from the show *Lost*, in which his interest had waned severely over the past couple of days. Finally, Charlie came in and asked where Jules was hiding.

Jules stepped out into the entrance hall and waved meekly. "Hey."

The man in the chair rolled toward him. The cardigan could not disguise his muscular arms and shoulders. "I'm Phil. Good to meet you in person at last." He extended a hand. "Heard you brought Charlie up when she was ready to die on the seabed."

"Phil..." Charlie's tone held an echo of some argument they must have run through once already.

Jules shook the man's hand. "Jules. And she'd have done the same for me."

"Yeah. She would. Shame she put herself there to begin with." Phil took back the hand. "You met the brood?" He gathered the three kids. "Joan, Alexander, and Boadie. Meet Jules. One of Mommy's friends."

The kids returned little waves and a "hi" each.

Jules didn't associate with children much, so he mimicked the gesture. "Hi, nice to meet you. Joan of Ark. Alexander the Great. And Boadie. I'm guessing your folks named you after Boudica, yeah?"

"Boudica's my full name," Boadie said.

Charlie placed a hand on Boadie's head. "But she isn't keen on the full pronunciation. Are you, honey?"

"You saved my mum?" Alexander asked.

"She saved me first," Jules said. "Shot down a helicopter, actually—"

"Juice, I think," Phil said, interrupting.

But it was too late. The two youngest kids gazed at their mom. Alexander said, "A *helicopter*? Seriously?"

"Wow." Joan's face lit up, a huge smile. "Did it blow up?"

"*Juice*," Phil said again, ushering the brood down the hall with a faintly amused frown aimed at Jules.

Jules sensed he perhaps crossed some social boundary but wasn't quite sure what it was. Perhaps detailing a parent's violent anecdotes wasn't acceptable when directed at children under a certain age. He'd have to ask about that later.

"Ready to do a little work?" Charlie asked.

Jules stood aside. "Lead the way."

Phil left the kids in the study playing on a games console hooked up to Bridget's massive Ultra HD TV and decided to join the group he'd quit several years earlier, all gathered in the control room which looked like the bridge of a spaceship.

He hadn't ventured into this business since being crippled through his own gung-ho stupidity. The last time he'd been there, the most advanced tech had been a projector through which Charlie presented her analysis, and on which Phil demonstrated all the ways in and out of a place, and the dangers involved.

Now there was a freestanding slab of glass that made the images appear three dimensional, as well as several screens down each side—a workstation apiece—and a touchscreen desk that worked like an enormous iPad. He'd also seen how the servers had expanded, how Charlie's savant-like mind focused on the computing power and the functionality of her comms equipment like relay pods and tiny subvocal earpieces which would make her a fortune on the open market.

But she stuck with Toby, with the Lost Origins Recovery Institute.

While Phil stuck around on the periphery, arranging transport, equipment transfers, and light secretarial duties, he wanted no serious involvement. He participated only to be sure the woman he loved stayed as safe as possible. In fact, he had always assumed Charlie would drift away as the years went on, perhaps gravitating toward a university post or working as a private contractor for some professional institution. But seeing this place, how her heart and soul shone from every flat screen, every diode and button, Phil knew that wouldn't be happening anytime soon.

She promised to be careful.

She promised to stay safe.

She promised she was the backup, the person in the chair offering direction.

Phil didn't believe she'd lied intentionally, but he wished she would keep those promises more often. He'd screwed up once, proving they were not indestructible, even finding a list of candidates to replace him as Toby's security specialist (or "man-at-arms" as Toby liked to name the position).

Now Charlie had been shot, escaped an avalanche, almost drowned, and strained the first injury all over again. And she couldn't wait to get back to work.

Phil agreed to a long weekend, a quick debrief with the group, then two days of just hanging out with their friends and the kids.

He hadn't intended to be there. But as he rolled in, saw Charlie at what she named her "Demon Hub"—the guts of the free-standing glass screen at the center of the sci-fi room—he understood what drove her.

"The room is a funnel," Charlie announced. The rendering on the screen was a result of hers and Jules's recreation of what they called "the mirror room" where they found some orb that knocked out a bunch of people. "Although most of you were closed in the room to help avoid injury, I think people were meant to stay *outside*."

"Shielding works both ways," Jules said. "I built up a picture of the setup. Remembering the chamber with the light funneled in, the mirrored walls, the globe above the smaller orb… we were supposed to activate the orb *inside* the locked mirror room. The sealed room."

"The angle of the mirrored plates worked by redirecting sunlight from outside," Charlie went on, manipulating the graphic to highlight a tube leading to the side of a cliff, also rendered in architect-like clarity. "We think it dates to much more than thousands of years ago, but got wiped away with the land's erosion, or the moving of tectonic plates."

"Doesn't light's energy fade when reflected through mirrors?" Harpal said. "I mean, you can't just bounce it off a ton of them forever."

"Yeah, that's right," Jules said. "But look what we stole from the site."

Charlie held up a panel of the reflective metal that she'd told Phil about. "Most mirrors are silver foil, backed up against the glass. Normally, light enters this and loses some of its potency. This isn't glass. I think it's metal. An alloy I haven't quite identified."

"New element?" Dan asked.

"There's no such thing as new elements," Toby said. "There are only a finite number of ways molecules can exist, and we have mapped them all. Hence, 'the elements.' Even if an alien landed in a spacecraft tomorrow, its materials would contain the elements we know of."

"But," Charlie went on pointedly, "not necessarily bonded in a way we've understood. That's what I think this is. A new alloy. Almost perfectly reflective. Loses hardly any of the energy it redirects. Which brings me to the big point."

Phil advanced, jealous suddenly of his wife.

In his time with LORI, they'd sought out items that didn't belong, or figures who'd appeared as footnotes in historical accounts but might have played bigger roles than academics currently believed. Essentially, they set out to return stolen artifacts to their rightful place, which in turn led to discovering historical inaccuracies, and that meant they started seeking out proof that would flip received wisdom on its head.

But this was far more than that, bigger than they'd imagined back then.

Charlie hadn't kept anything from him, but now he had to wonder: when exactly did this escalate? And what did it mean for them? For him and Charlie?

"So, what's it for, exactly?" Dan asked.

Charlie highlighted the diagram as she spoke. "The orb would either sit in its cradle or be handled by two Sensitives, like Jules and Zimina Yanovna, and that would send an energy pulse out. The mirrors would bounce that pulse around and expel it through the funnel."

"Light coming in was a consequence of the design," Jules said, "not the intent."

The graphic showed light flashing out through the tube they mentioned.

"To what end, though?" Toby asked. "We still haven't got a definitive answer."

"I had some ideas," Bridget said. "Remember when we talked about the circuit being part of a bigger network? *United, the circuit reveals the power of the god.* The map connected to the stone scythe pointed east, west, and south. It was a project generations in the making."

"Intended to...?" Harpal waved his hand in a circle.

"Their god was linked to life giving," Jules said. "But who were they?"

"You're doing that thing that Toby does again," Dan said. "The thing you find so annoying."

"And I'm enjoying life on this side of it." Jules looked straight at Toby. "Well?"

Phil remembered these sessions. Questions, prompts, making everyone think, so they landed on the same page together.

"The Witnesses were super intelligent," Toby said, going along with it. "Evolved pre-Toba but cut off and isolated before venturing out into the wider world. So, they wanted to share."

"We *think*," Jules said. "And if they had access to these compounds that react with certain genes, they probably developed a lotta social structure. People at the top able to use it, people under them... not."

"Their god *was* the cycle," Bridget said. "The united power of the circuit reveals the cycle... the thing they valued most."

"Life," Charlie said.

"They knew farming, and they knew seasons, and they knew the other humans were dying out. They were small in number and needed to interbreed to survive, so they had to save the other humans first. From everything I can see, they were trying to pass on their knowledge to that end."

"I agree," Toby said. "But what about this room? This energy pulse?"

"We dismissed the idea of them ending the Ice Age," Charlie said.

"Correct. The times don't add up. This is all far older than the Younger Dryas. Their buildings, their mines, the Striovian Mummy. If they ended the Ice Age, it would've happened much sooner."

"Suppose they failed," Phil spoke up at last.

All looked at him.

He rolled closer. "It might have been their *intent*, but they failed. Or they succeeded, and it took longer, but was much worse than they planned."

"Tsunamis across Doggerland," Jules said. "The mass destruction that created New York and Long Island."

"The waters rising meant they built the tomb in India to repel seawater," Charlie said.

"They screwed up." Dan laughed without much humor. "These hyper-intelligent people screwed up."

Toby was pacing now, finger to his chin. He folded his arms but kept walking back and forth. "This is all theoretical, but… it makes sense. They do something that accelerates the meltwater, understand it will take generations for the full consequences to be felt, and set about gathering their knowledge, and hiding the dangers, only allowing those with sufficient intelligence to access it."

"And the right genes," Jules said.

"When their tasks were done, they disappeared." Toby stood before Charlie. "There's no record of them because they hid intentionally."

"Then what?" Harpal said. "Died out?"

"Went the way of the Neanderthal," Jules replied.

"Killed by other tribes?" Dan said.

"Neanderthals weren't wiped out," Toby said. "They didn't starve to death. They were supplanted by superior people. Homo sapiens. Us. We absorbed them."

"Can't prove it outright, but yeah, makes sense." Jules waggled his fingers. "They buried their genes through interbreeding. That's why my mom had the bangle. Because she knew she lit it up."

"The big question is," Bridget said, "did she know about the Witnesses?"

"Love to ask her," Jules said. "For now, we gotta speculate. And if there's something out there more powerful than the orb, something that can be linked up with other stuff… do we want that in the hands of politicians?"

"You're suggesting you investigate even more." Phil moved among them now, watching Charlie, a combination of worry and joy radiating from her. "You're all into this?"

Charlie remained still, staring at the graphic.

"I need to know," Bridget said.

"I don't trust Colin," Toby said. "Or who he answers to. And I don't mean the Queen."

Dan shrugged. "Someone's gotta keep you all safe."

Harpal stood, peering at the static graphic of the room with the orb at its center. "We can speculate all day about ice ages, big bangs, whatever. The only way to know for sure is to get out there."

Charlie faced Phil, hands clasped before her. "I'll keep as far back as I can. I promise, Phil, I'll—"

Phil held up a hand to cut her off. "I know. And I'll be there for you too. Just need to know one thing. Where's this guy going to be?"

Jules was the only one who hadn't spoken. He kept his gaze on the floor. "I dunno. Dunno if I can keep playing well here. I like being alone. Working alone."

"It's more than knowledge for the sake of knowledge, Jules," Bridget said. "It's more than that. It's bigger than your bangles, bigger than your mom's death, bigger than you. We need you if we're going to go on."

Phil had guessed as much. Without his touch, without this "Sensitive" as they'd termed him, their expedition was at an end before it began. It was the only hope Phil now had of settling down, of living a small life with his big family, and going to bed without the stress of wondering where his wife was. She could put her talents to good use, and make a little money, and forget all about mysteries that had little bearing on the past.

"Really," Phil said, "if everyone just forgets about this. Lets it stay buried. What's the difference?"

Jules looked up and met his eye. "Difference is, we're not the only people looking. But we're the only people I trust right now. So yeah. I'm in."

For some reason, Phil smiled.

It was almost as if he didn't *want* the quiet life now. As if he knew deep down that his wife needed this, needed to know, to be a part of something bigger. And the smile spread to his chest as he felt a warmth spread there. That, he realized, was where his smile had come from.

This was where he'd met his wife.

It was where he felt most alive.

It was where he—and Charlie—needed to be.

"Okay," Phil said. "I'm in too. All the way."

EPILOGUE
AUGUST 27, 1:00 P.M. (GMT)

WINDSOR CASTLE, UNITED KINGDOM

In Colin Waterston's office, Simon Pickard was enjoying his time deputizing as the curator took a little well-deserved leave. Not that it was voluntary leave, mind you.

Simon was well aware the older man had not been looking forward to his meeting with the home secretary last night and envisaged something of a chewing out for allowing the freelance archaeologists a pass with an item removed from the church in Lish, but Colin remained unrepentant. The priority was securing the psychopathic woman who was able to activate certain compounds in rocks and other materials, and who ordered the killing of up to ten naval personnel on British soil.

Simon was not privy to the full details.

Colin did make a point of calling him to emphasize the forced leave of absence was not a euphemism for being fired or suspended and would definitely be back at his desk the next week. He would appreciate it if Simon spread the word. "You know how gossipy the royal household can be," he said.

Simon's role was one of assistant curator of the House of Windsor, but unlike Colin's position, it did not come with clandestine duties that he wasn't allowed to talk about. He actually *was* an assistant to the curator—setting travel plans, meetings, accommodating guests, sourcing freelancers.

However, to some, the focus of his job title was on the *assistant* rather than the assistant *to* part, meaning they saw him less as a glorified secretary, or bat-man as Colin sometimes called him—an obscure military officer reference dating back to the days of the Empire—and more as Colin's deputy, his stand-in when the man was unavailable.

And Simon rarely corrected that assumption. Hence, he was deputizing now. And he deserved to, damn it.

Having graduated with a double-first in art history and archaeology and a master's in political science, he assumed this would be an ambassadorial role, acting more like a diplomatic mission than a simple housekeeper or personal assistant. Not that there was anything wrong with those jobs; Simon's parents were very much working class, and he never forgot that, no matter his academic achievements.

Simon just believed he'd be traveling to more places than Perth on a frigate while Colin ran off to deal with trespassers in a remote church—trespassers who turned out to be murderous rogue operatives from a small Eastern European nation that disavowed their people in a heartbeat.

It was this tense situation in Scotland combined with Colin's absence and another civil servant assuming Simon was a genuine deputy, that he came into possession of Colin's custom-made mobile phone, relinquished to ensure Colin rested thoroughly.

Although it required a thumbprint or eight-digit passcode to access the contacts and other confidential information, some alerts were deemed too urgent and could be swiped to view without such precautions.

So, when the phone charging beside Colin's desk lit up to show activity in Lish, Simon could not help but be curious.

After the other archaeologists removed a mirrored panel from the site, Colin ordered the installation of several covert CCTV cameras that activated with significant movement. It fed back to the phone and to Colin's personal computer, allowing them to view the stream in real time.

Simon opened the app.

He did not recognize the woman accessing the main part of the church, and she did not try to hide her face. In her late twenties or early thirties, the Indian-looking woman moved with the confidence of someone who knew exactly where she was going.

She must have staked out the property for some time.

Whenever she changed location, the cameras followed, switching the view on Colin's phone. Eventually, she came to a hole in the floor of one of the back rooms and descended. There was even a camera down there.

Using the desk phone, he called Colin Waterston. When his boss picked up, he explained how he "accidentally" stumbled across the footage and Colin told him to hold.

When he returned to the phone, it was clear he was now watching the same pictures as Simon.

"Facial recognition on my computer has her as Prihya Sibal," Colin said. "Hmm. I recognize that name."

"Who is she?"

"Oh, just a crank. We've encountered her before, hassling some of our finer professors with crackpot theories—much like some of Toby Smith's more outlandish ones. I heard a rumor she was in France at the same time as General Yanovna. Looking for the same thing, but not having a clue what it was."

Simon watched her a while longer, as she pulled something out of the ground about the size of a laptop. "She's taking things."

"It's nothing," Colin said. "We found those slates among Habib Masouli's possessions. Just knickknacks. Blank tablets on which they must have jotted notices to parishioners. We buried them to serve as a decoy to would-be treasure hunters."

"Should I alert the police?"

Colin remained quiet for a moment, thinking. "No. If we do, we reveal there are cameras watching the place, which will draw more questions. I'd rather leave it for a true thief, or to catch Toby in the act if he's stupid enough to return. Let her have the pieces of stone. They're worthless."

SRI SATHYA SAI HEART HOSPITAL - HIRUSH, INDIA

As Prihya rolled the trolley onto the ward, Valerio Conchin looked stronger than he had for some time. She trundled right up to him and waited for his bed to prop him up.

He was still far from *well*, but his withered arm appeared to have more meat to it, and his face was fuller. His eyes stayed on the trolley as he rose.

Although she flew business class with a layover in Dubai, the tablets were shipped directly from Glasgow. She would have liked some help to unearth them, but she managed on her own, transporting all six of them two at a time to a car hired in the name of Michaela Watson.

They were far lighter than they looked. Altogether, including the broken one, they weighed a lot, hence a trolley of the sort that she normally saw hauling boxes between offices. Someone had cleaned the tablets too, the scratched lettering much clearer than before, but still indecipherable to her.

Valerio appraised them for a moment, then looked at Prihya. "Well done."

"Are you sure this is valuable?" she asked.

Valerio cast a glance to his friend in the bed opposite, the one called Horse. The curtains were closed, just a gap revealing the man lying on his back.

"Absolutely," Valerio said. "I heard the British found them the same time they realized Habib Masouli was a keeper of way more secrets than first thought. When that stash of seals was unearthed in the Striovian salt mine and Goswelt's scroll showed up... ah, the hubris." Valerio sniffed the air. "Can you feel it? While they were all running around looking for a shiny orb, they didn't know what they had under their noses the whole time."

"What *do* they have?" Prihya asked.

"More than they could imagine."

"And what about the Lost Origins people? They… didn't seem so bad."

"They are officially our competitors, Ms. Sibal. And with these supposedly useless objects, we've taken the lead. Are you ready to participate? Or would you prefer to return to your keyboard and try to persuade everyone you were right with a snappily edited video about ancient civilizations and a bit of ominous music?"

Prihya wondered about this man, wondered about his motives, and what he hoped to gain. She hadn't seen anything of the magic he promised, nor the evidence of civilizations far older than people believed possible. And other than the electrics on the *Ny Bakke To* blowing out temporarily, there was no proof anything odd happened in Montrose or the small church from which she stole the tablets.

"Well?" Valerio asked.

"For now," Prihya said. "But I want to see something big next. Something that will amaze me."

"Oh yes, Ms. Sibal." Valerio hit the button on his bed, commencing the slow whirr that returned him to a sleeping position. "That is a promise I can most assuredly keep. Things are about to get very interesting indeed."

Curse of The Eagle Plague

The Lost Origins team returns to prevent a geneticist from releasing an ancient plague upon the world.

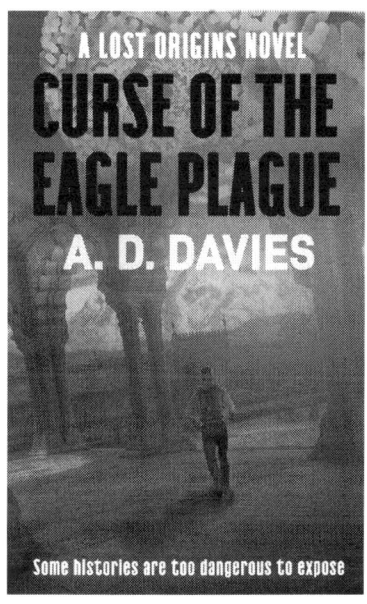

For news, cover reveals, and exclusive subscriber-only previews, sign up for the newsletter:

addavies.com/lori-news

You can also follow A. D. Davies on Amazon or Bookbub.

ACKNOWLEDGMENTS

I get so much support from so many people, and it's worth acknowledging those key players.

The map of Canada was rendered by "Schwabenblitz" and licenced via Canstock Photos.

Licensing Maps of Doggerland proved surprisingly difficult so I was fortunate to find one on Wiki's Creative Commons, produced by Wiki user **Juschki** based on the Generic Mapping Tools and ETOPO2, also on the Wiki Creative Commons. This map was cropped and relabelled by myself, but all other work is by those mentioned above.

The "circuit" symbol was created by me, using a cup, a ruler, a rough pencil, and rudimentary photoshop. I don't normally have sketches in my books, but including one here was suggested by more than one of my early readers.

I have too many sources of research to credit full, skipping through the internet and the library like a roadrunner consuming facts and dates. In particular, though, I will highlight:
    - ancient-origins.net/ - a great source of inspiration for ideas, and the starting point for several aspects of pre-historical people.
    - The Encyclopaedia Britannica - which explained spirals to me, including the Fibonacci Spiral, and a whole host of mathematics which were cut from the story in the name of progress.
    - A paper by Joshua J. Mark which helped me map out the

Sumerians' history, something important in anchoring me in the right time.

- The BBC Radio 4 series "Around the World in 100 Objects" was the first to bring my attention to the Sumerian seals featured in this book. They are real artifacts and their history as told here is absolutely true. Other than them turning up in a fictional Eastern European country, of course.

- The history of the Younger Dryas, the creation of New York harbor, etc, was all gleaned from multiple sources, not least articles from the New York Times, history.com, and newyorknature.net ... plus my friend who told me about the boulders in central park, which fascinated me enough to start researching this part of the novel.

In picking through all these sources, I often come across far too much to include all in one book, so I will save much of this for future work. Such is the richness of human evolution - and the gaps and inconsistencies admitted by all historians - that I could spend the next 20 years writing books like this and never run short on inspiration.

I won't do that, though, and while the story of the Witnesses will continue to percolate, the Lost Origins guys have more stories to tell and adventures to enjoy. They will follow soon.

Do sign up to be kept informed of new releases and exclusive previews:

addavies.com/lori-news/

And check out Antony's straight up crime novels written as A. D. Davies.

NOVELS BY A. D. DAVIES

Lost Origins Novels:

Tomb of the First Priest

Secret of the Reaper Seal

Curse of the Eagle Plague

Co-Authored:

Project Return Fire – with Joe Dinicola

Adam Park Thrillers:

The Dead and the Missing

A Desperate Paradise

The Shadows of Empty men

Night at the George Washington Diner

Master the Flame

Under the Long White Cloud

Alicia Friend Investigations:

His First His Second

In Black In White

With Courage With Fear

A Friend in Spirit

To Hide To Seek

A Flood of Bones

To Begin The End

Moses and Rock Novels:

Fractured Shadows

Made in the USA
Coppell, TX
26 August 2022

82121149R00282